NAKED AS A JAYBIRD

AT THE MOON-YOUR-MAMA BAR & GRILL

PRAISE FOR

NAKED AS A JAYBIRD

AT THE MOON-YOUR-MAMA BAR & GRILL

"*NAKED AS A JAYBIRD* has a plot as crazy and twisted as a ride on a Tilt-A-Whirl™ (but with less nausea). Three people trying to get to a 25th Woodstock reunion to claim a fortune are up against others selfishly determined to stop them. But first, the fortune seekers must find a mysterious nudist named Jaybird who disappeared twenty-five years ago. Which would seem to give their adversaries the upper hand ... if they weren't so inept. *NAKED AS A JAYBIRD* is hilarious, irreverent, and yet, in the end, a heartwarming tale. Bob Chenoweth is a genius!"

— Tony Perona, author of the Nick Bertetto mystery series and
co-author of the Murder on the Bucket List series

"Hilarious journey! A wild, entertaining ride that reminds me of Carl Hiaasen, Hunter S. Thompson, Douglas Adams, and even the Coen and Farrelly Brothers. Enjoyed the hell out of it!"

— Jeff Stanger, humorist and author of The Fungo Society and
other Quick Baseball Mysteries

"Absurd. Ridiculous. Funny as hell. And utterly charming. Bob Chenoweth is at the top of his writing game in this irreverent, laugh-out-loud caper."

— Teri Barnett, Amazon bestselling author (The Oracle Trilogy,
Romance is Murder, and more) and award-winning artist

"Epic insanity! It takes balls to write a book like this, and, well, Bob Chenoweth's nuts! I couldn't love this book any more even if all the characters were fully clothed!"

— Mark A. Lee, Writer, Historian, and Activist

"Such a hoot! Well-crafted. Beautifully woven. Excellent comedic suspense with one twist after another from a truly twisted writer."
— *Sylvia J. Hyde, Writer and Poet (Living at the Speed of Dark)*

"Most writers don't 'get' nudism. Bob Chenoweth gets it – and gets it very right – in this nakedly funny page-turner."
— *Carolyn Hawkins, American Association for Nude Recreation*

"Rollicking narrative drive! What a wild ride of creative artistry! It's sure to be a cult classic."
— *John Clair, Playwright and Writer*

"I've hooted and laughed at the predicaments these characters find themselves in. What a story! So clever, so twisted, and soooo funny! I've never read anything like it."
— *June McCarty Clair, Playwright and Writer*

"So cinematic! Quirky characters. Witty dialogue. The laughs come a mile a minute!"
— *C. L. Shore, Author of Cherry Blossom Temple,*
Maiden Murders, and more

"The twists and turns will keep you guessing as you laugh your way through the madcap mayhem."
— *Ramona Henderson, Writer*

"Brilliant! I love it! Reminiscent of Tom Robbins, whom I absolutely love."
— *Annie Sever-Dimitri, Animal Communicator*

NAKED AS A JAYBIRD

AT THE MOON-YOUR-MAMA BAR & GRILL

BOB CHENOWETH

NAKED PUBLISHING

NAKED PUBLISHING

NAKED AS A JAYBIRD AT THE MOON-YOUR-MAMA BAR & GRILL

First Printing: July 2020.

Cover design by the author, © 2020 by Bob Chenoweth

Naked Publishing LLC

www.NakedNovel.com

ISBN: 978-1-7352209-0-1

DEDICATION

This book is for my husband, Dan. Thanks for your ever-present love, generous spirit, and support – and for keeping your eye rolls to a minimum all these years.

And for our daughters, Nikky and Courtney. Thanks for making the world a better and brighter place. Proud of you always – and glad you're proud of me despite, well, ya know, this book.

And for the grandkids. Fast-growing, remarkable, and always lovable critters, one and all. (Yes, Grandpa's weird. Get used to it.)

And for the rest of our family and friends who still invite me to join them on occasion – even if they're not coming apart.

And for my clients who, over the years, have entrusted (and paid) me to bring written voice to their wisdom.

And for the writers and artists in all media who've made me think, laugh, and cry, but always inspired me to excellence in the craft.

And for the readers whose human experience makes each story uniquely theirs.

And finally, for nudists and free spirits everywhere. Thanks for the shameless inspiration.

Love you all!

Peace | Love | Equality | Unity

NAKED AS A JAYBIRD

AT THE MOON-YOUR-MAMA BAR & GRILL

"The nude alone is well dressed."

– Auguste Rodin

Friday, August 12, 1994

PROLOGUE
(In Which We Sneak a Peek at What's to Come)

Tranquility, Florida
The Moon-Your-Mama Bar & Grill (on the Grounds of the Grin and Bare It Family Nudist Campground)

Early evening

THE BLIND MAN WALKED INTO THE BAR, HIS WHITE CANE ARCING AND tapping before him.

Sonny was an attorney, 45 years-old, slightly graying, slightly balding, and more than slightly gaunt. He shouldered a tropical beach towel and wore amber-tinted wraparound sunglasses. Otherwise, he was naked except for cheap flip flops and a ribbon of toilet paper trailing the left one.

His niece and nephew – fraternal twins Janis and Jimi – followed him inside. Two decades younger and also nude, they appeared to be polar opposites: the young man dark-haired and self-conscious as he clutched a strategically positioned towel; his sister prematurely gray and animated, gesturing and nudging and marveling. "My first nudie bar!" she cried. "Well, for today, at least."

"Sit anywhere," a voice called out from shadows behind the bar. "I'll be right with ya."

The twins stepped around their uncle and led him to a table with four chairs near the center of the room. Jimi draped his towel over an ice-cream parlor-style chair and sat. Sonny and Janis did the same.

"I don't really like being, um, exposed like this," Jimi said, eyeing the bright light over their table.

"For cripes' sake, Jiminy, you should be getting used to this whole 'naked thing' by now," Janis said. "How many nudist colonies have we visited so far this trip?"

Jimi shushed her. "First off," he whispered, "stop calling me *Jiminy*. Sheesh! Most important, don't call this place a 'colony' or you'll get us kicked out of here. Have you learned nothing this trip? Don't you at least remember the sign?"

"What sign?" asked Sonny.

"By the door of the restroom building," Jimi said. "It read something like, 'We're nudists. We're not ants. We're not lepers. Please DO NOT call this a colony!'"

"Okay, okay," Janis said. "We're in another freakin' resort, then. Family-friendly with an on-site nudie bar. I guess already being naked eliminates a lot of the mystery when coupling up at last call."

Jimi shushed her again. "Just behave yourself for once. We've come too far to get kicked out now."

Sonny cleared his throat. "I know we're all nervous being this close to our goal, but please stop bickering. Be my eyes. Tell me what you see."

Jimi leaned closer to Sonny. "Nothing fancy. Looks pretty spartan actually—"

"Wow, looka that moon shot!" Janis shouted, pointing to a giant framed black-and-white poster hanging behind the bar. It featured a retro lunar image, complete with a man-in-the-moon face whose right eye has been penetrated by a giant rocket. "That's gotta hurt," she said.

"I believe that's the iconic image from the classic silent film, *Le Voyage Dans La Lune*," Jimi informed her. "That means 'A Trip to the Moon'."

"Hey, I wasn't born yesterday, mister know-it-all," Janis said. "If I can talk to cats, I can figure out your fuzzy Italian."

"French."

"Whatever."

Again, Sonny cleared his throat.

"Yes, so, as I was saying," Jimi continued, "aside from the Méliès poster and these tabletop framed pictures of a motherly type – presumably the mama we're supposed to moon – it's pretty basic décor in here. Mostly ashtrays and fly strips. Lighting's pretty good, maybe a little too good. Tropical-style white ceiling fans here and there, on low. About ten tables with two or four chairs. The bar has eight stools. Seating is empty so far except for us," he said, "probably because that fried turkey Testicle Festival is going on."

"Everyone but us is out there having a ball," Janis said. "Or two." She crossed her arms over her chest, a smug gesture of triumph for landing the definitive Testicle Festival pun.

Sonny leaned forward, unbunched his towel, and then leaned back again. "So, no sign of our target, then?"

Before either twin could answer, the bartender approached their table. He, too, was naked, except for the de rigueur flip flops and an apron tied at his waist. He had ponytailed white hair, wore round glasses, and bore a scar extending from the corner of his mouth halfway down his chin.

"Welcome, gents," he said, not quite discerning that Janis was no gentleman. His voice was soft and carried an accent – vaguely of New York but perhaps diluted by many years in the south. "Must be visitors," he said. "Glad you could join us tonight. Grill side is closed this evening, but I'll be glad to bring you some drinks."

"That voice," said Sonny.

"That scar," said Jimi.

"That moon shot," said Janis, pointing not to the framed poster but to the bartender's butt and the bird tattoo just visible beyond his apron.

In unison, they whispered, "Jaybird."

Now, their true mission could begin. But time was running out.

Four Days Earlier:
Monday, August 8, 1994

CHAPTER 1
(In Which We Learn of a Matter of Extreme Urgency and Importance)

The Near Northside of Indianapolis, Indiana
Late Afternoon

JIMI JOHANSEN REMOVED HIS SUNGLASSES AND SLOWED HIS WHITE 1993 Volvo 850 wagon to a crawl, pissing off drivers behind him on North Academy Avenue. Through his open window, he counted the rising address numbers on tidy two-story homes that had mostly been converted to office buildings. The numbers rose in increments of four: 6140, 6144, 6148… He was looking for *6146*.

Confused (numbers frequently confounded the former financial advisor), Jimi inched the Volvo past 6160 North Academy Avenue and then mashed the brake pedal. His worldly possessions, stuffed into the back of the wagon, clinked and clattered and clanked, but mostly stayed put. As an overdue courtesy to the honking tailgaters, Jimi clicked on his left turn signal.

When the clotted oncoming traffic finally thinned, he made a U-turn into a narrow gap just after a bus full of nuns. Once upon a teenage time, Jimi had imagined himself dropping trou and merrily mooning just such a transport. Why? The urge still mystified him. He had never exhibited any tendencies toward, well, *exhibitionism*; nor did he harbor ill will toward celibate women of any persuasion. Or sisters, for that matter. Yet in that freeze-frame moment, the compulsion….

Alas, the nuns pulled away. Spared. Today would not be the day. *But where in blazes was 6146?*

Jimi drove a few houses south and parked against the curb in front of 6144, officially the home of the Kurls for Gurls salon. He raised the driver's side window and then exited and locked the Volvo. Within a few steps, he could tell that Kurls for Gurls specialized in perms, the ammonia-like odor assailing him as he approached the brick-wrapped portico. He was about to step onto the porch to ask directions when he saw an embossed and rusting white metal sign shaped like an arrow. It pointed right and bore lettering that declared: *6146 Around Corner.*

Indeed, it was. Mostly hidden by the salon, 6146 was a two-story but otherwise compact cottage, with mellow-yellow wood siding and a pair of 8-foot-tall white columns flanking the entry. An ornate sign hung slightly askew on the column to the right. It read "J. Buckingham Muckle II, Esq. Attorney at Law."

Jimi opened the door.

* * *

Twelve cars back in the impromptu parade line that had assembled behind the Volvo, a pink-over-white 1959 AMC Metropolitan hardtop crept forward. The car bore giant fiberglass cat ears on the roof. A rainbow was painted on the center hub of its continental kit spare tire. And magnetized door signs revealed the driver to be *Janis Grack, Cat Psychic.*

Janis also searched for 6146 North Academy Avenue. And while scoping out addresses and waiting for traffic to advance, she, too, spied the bus full of nuns. Janis flipped them off. *Take that, you evil Sisters of Our Eternal Suffering Salvation,* she thought, even though she knew these nuns were almost certainly not the knuckle-rapping tormenters of her youth. Nonetheless, she sang the memory away: "The nuns on the bus go round and round, round and round, round and —"

Where the holy hell was 6146?

It occurred to her that the call from the office of J. Buckingham Muckle II, Esquire, might be a scam and she was a pathetic patsy. "It's a matter of extreme urgency and importance that must be discussed in person," the attorney's representative, a Ms. Pepper Duckenfield, had said. "But it will absolutely be to your financial advantage now and in the future." *Too good to be true,* Janis had thought after hanging up. And caveat emptor and a sucker born every minute and no such thing as a free lunch or a free cat... Probably a damn pyramid scheme like when she had signed on to sell "highly collectible" hand-painted glass thimbles. "Don't miss this ground floor opportunity to build your network AND get the original classic delicate designs no-longer available to the general public – all by simply enlisting five of your closest friends and blah blah blah…" With hopes high and don't-be-a-dumbass defenses low, she had signed on to represent these "tiny-but-treasured modern artifacts." Three-point-seven seconds after her check for the initial investment cleared, she remembered that she hated pretty, delicate things of any type and didn't have five close friends to enlist. And if she *had* had five close friends, they sure as hell wouldn't be the types to sell fucking hand-painted thimbles. God, she was a sucker.

"…*it will absolutely be to your financial advantage…*" Yeah, right.

Then again, what did she have to lose? Her professional animal communication practice – counseling emotionally disturbed felines – wasn't exactly thriving. Plus, she had spent well over a grand on the giant cat ears and was saving up for a set of whiskers for the grille of the "Catropolitan."

So, what the hell, right?

Janis made a U-turn and doubled back, heading south on North Academy. Still no 6146. She'd have to investigate on foot. Parking behind a white Volvo in front of Kurls for Gurls, she followed the same ritual as the Volvo man: approach, sniff, and follow the arrow around the corner into the unknown.

* * *

Both visitors to the Muckle office felt the hackles on the backs of their necks rise as Janis entered through the cowbelled door. Jimi, standing at Pepper Duckenfield's desk, turned to assess the source of his sudden unease. Janis smiled as she approached but felt light-headed and wobbly. *Creepy, knee-buckling shit,* she thought. *Keep your feet beneath you. Keep your wits about you. Keep your money in your pocket.*

Standing together at Pepper's desk, their faces grew flush and their heart rates spiked. Neither knew why. Not yet.

Pepper dog-eared her place in the year-old *Glamour* magazine she had swiped from Kurls for Gurls during a pre-wig-era perm gone wrong. She forced a smile. *Johansen and Grack. Yes, the ones she had spoken with on the phone. Yes, Ms. Grack, this is a legit law office. No, Ms. Grack, this is not a scam. Restroom to the right, Mr. Johansen. Have a seat, please, both of you. Mr. Muckle will be with you shortly.*

The strangers sat on opposite sides of the room, each occasionally stealing a look at the other, each wondering what business they might have with Mr. Muckle, separately or together.

From inside the attorney's office came a thud and the sound of breaking glass. "Sonofabitch! Did it again!" Pepper sighed and rolled her eyes. She leaned down beside her desk, retrieved a small broom and dustpan, and said, "Mr. Muckle will be needing these."

The intercom buzzed. Pepper pushed a button and the box spoke: "Send in our guests, would you, Ducks? Oh, and could you bring the broom and dustpan, too, please?" Pepper motioned the visitors toward the door.

Inside the office, its overbearing knotty pine walls channeling a miniature hunting lodge, attorney Muckle, thin, gray-suited and wearing amber sunglasses, motioned in the general direction of two chairs in front of his desk. A moment later, he extended his hand toward the chair to his left. "Mr. Johansen," he said, but Jimi was already standing before the chair to the attorney's right. He reached across to shake Muckle's hand. The process of adjusting for the misdirection repeated with Janis.

The young visitors took their seats.

Muckle, still standing, said, "Please, both of you, have a seat." Jimi and Janis looked at one another. They stood again and then sat once more, scooting the chairs slightly so Muckle could hear.

Behind them, Pepper swept up remnants of glass that had once protected the lawyer's yellowed Indiana University School of Law diploma. She rehung the credential, dropped the glass into a wastebasket, and leaned the broom and dustpan against the wall. "I'll just leave these here from now on," she said, and left the room.

"Mr. Johansen, I suppose you've noticed that I am visually impaired," Muckle said, facing Janis. "Blind as a stone, you might say." Jimi cleared his throat and said, "Yes, I can see that."

"Oh, there you are," Muckle said, turning toward Jimi. "Please don't change seats; it makes it hard for me to stay oriented."

"Of course."

Janis spoke up: "Mr. Muckle, this is starting to weird me out." As she said it, she strung the latter words together – "me out" sounding like "meow" – and it occurred to her she really needed to start having more human conversations.

"I understand your apprehension, Ms. Grack. Believe me, this is an unusual situation that may come as a bit of a shock as we proceed. Are you both still sitting down?"

Pepper buzzed the attorney to let him know she was leaving for the evening. "Turn the lights out when your visitors leave," she said. "Or leave them on all night – like it matters, right?"

"Thank you, Ducks. Have a good evening."

Janis tried again: "Mr. Muckle, I'm on pins and needles here, and I imagine Mr. Johansen—"

"Call me Jimi."

"I'm reasonably certain that Jiminy here feels the same. Can you please tell us what this is all about?"

"Jimi, not Jiminy."

"Of course," Muckle said. "Forgive me." He swung his arm in the general direction of a pitcher. "Water?"

"No!" Jimi yelled, pulling the pitcher and two glasses out of harm's way. "Just, please, as Ms. Crack—"

"Grack, not Crack!"

"As Ms. Grack... Janis, was it? As Janis said, please just tell us why we're here."

Muckle sat tall in his high-backed chair. Then he took a deep breath and leaned forward again, the motion causing a farting noise that can only emanate from faux leather or actual farts – or, most impressively, from actual farts on faux leather. Aiming his attention at the space between his guests, J. Buckingham Muckle II said, "Consider this little meeting a family reunion of sorts. Janis, meet your brother Jimi. Jimi, your sister Janis. You're twins, by the way. Fraternal. I'm guessing there's not much resemblance."

The twins stared at one another in silence, mouths open, breathing suspended.

"And I'm your uncle, as it turns out," Muckle said. "Your uncle Sonny. And in a moment, I'll introduce you to someone you might not have known existed. My sister. Your birth mother."

Janis began chittering like a cat eyeing a squirrel through a window. Jimi, eyes glazing, reached to get a glass of water after all. The pitcher spilled across Muckle's desk and wetted the attorney's lap. Without flinching, Muckle began rummaging through desk drawers. "Now, where did I put my spare pants?"

* * *

Three blocks from the attorney's office, Pepper Duckenfield entered the courtyard of her apartment complex and could already hear the little beast yapping; a few steps later, she saw a note taped to her door. *Final Notice #3*, it declared, detailing noise complaints against her Shih Tzu ("Tuffy" to the AKC, but "Effyu" to those who knew and loathed him.) There was an envelope taped to the door, as well. "Bone Appeteet, Evil Bastard Dog!" someone had scrawled on it. Inside, a gift: a double-thick, triple-rich chocolate bar.

"Dog poison?" Pepper said aloud. "Thanks, neighbors, but maybe I'd better not share this little gift." She stashed the chocolate bar in her purse and opened the door. The dog snarled and barked at her from the couch, but barely raised his head.

Pepper kicked off her shoes and also removed the blonde bouffant wig she had started wearing after the bad perm episode. Collapsing onto the couch, she stroked Effyu until his barking subsided. Effyu then stood and launched into avaricious licks that methodically removed troweled-thick layers of Pepper's makeup. A few minutes later, when the dog started choking, she set him aside to hack, swoon, lick his chops and fall into a barkless semi-comatose state.

In the sudden solitude, Pepper stared at the answering machine next to the desk phone. The red light was blinking three times. *Someone's getting antsy,* she thought. She picked up the handset and pecked at arrows and digits until she reached speed dial number 9.

The call was answered on the first ring. "Well?"

"They're in his office even as we speak," Pepper said. "He's giving them the lowdown, probably going over background details before he plays the videotape."

"Do you think they'll go along? Will they believe him?"

Pepper sighed. "They won't *want* to believe him at first, I suppose. Quite a shock, after all. But he's ultimately a very trustworthy person, the bastard. My luck, I hook up with the only honest lawyer in the Circle City, eh?"

"Get over it, Peps. You know it'll be worth it very soon. What was it you had in your script? 'It will absolutely be to your financial advantage now and in the future?' Something like that, right? Same is true for you, Peps, and very soon. The clock is ticking. And besides, revenge is gonna be the bitchinest reward – for both of us."

Pepper nodded, her face growing flush.

"You still there?"

"Yes, sorry," Pepper said.

"So, tell me, has he given them the deposit yet?"

"He's got the cash to give them, as instructed, but I'm sure he's holding that for the end of the meeting."

"And... What's your best guess here?" the man on the other end of the line asked. "Will they take the money and run, or will they go for the big payoff?"

Pepper blew smoke at Effyu. The dog sniffed but did not otherwise stir. "I think just about anyone would go for the big prize, don't you?" Pepper said. "I mean, what's the downside? A few days of searching, and if they succeed, they'll turn ten grand each into another ten plus all those millions. They'd be fools to not take on the challenge."

"So, are they fools or not?"

"Of course, they are. A lesbian cat psychic and a disgraced financial advisor? Fools to be sure. But desperate and curious fools, too, so my guess is they accept the mission."

"It's on, then. We know what we have to do."

"Yes, LB, it's on."

CHAPTER 2

(In Which We Learn About Birth, Death, and Bunnies at Woodstock)

SONNY MUCKLE HAD EXPLAINED THE SITUATION FROM VIRTUALLY EVERY angle. He had answered their questions, deflected their doubt, and talked them through the shock of learning that not only had they been adopted out at birth, but had been living within a few miles of one another in the same city all their lives.

There had been clues they were adopted, of course: pragmatic Jimi of the jet black hair and solid physique being raised by wispy, free-spirited blond Swedes, Ingemar and Ilsa Johansen. Good people, *Volvo* people, but very unlike their son. And Janis, raised by a single father, Gary Grack, after the death of his wife when the future cat psychic was still learning to walk. Her daddy was a good man, as well, but a bit too rock-solid, which caused friction at times, given her unquenchable affection for both sarcasm and other girls.

Over time, each twin had simply accepted what they were told: they were who they were, and sometimes recessive genes step to the head of the line after skipping a generation or two. End of story. Except it wasn't the end of the story at all.

As they tried to process the attorney's revelations, Jimi and Janis took turns in the restroom, heads spinning and stomachs reeling. Jimi cried. Janis got the shits.

When they returned to the lawyer's office, Muckle was fiddling with a VCR on the lower shelf of a tall cart topped by a 19-inch Zenith TV. "Should have already had this loaded, I suppose," he said. "Didn't think to have Pepper do this in advance. Generally speaking, I like to do things for myself when I can." Behind the twins, the glassless framed diploma fell off the wall again.

"Perhaps I can help," Jimi said, stepping up to assist "Uncle Sonny." He tuned the TV to channel 3, powered up the VCR, and pushed the eject button. Taking the VHS tape from his uncle, he inserted it in the machine.

"What are we about to watch, anyway?" Janis asked. "Please tell me it's not adoptee porn."

Sonny remained silent but nodded in the general direction of Jimi, who pushed the play button.

The screen came to life, a hospital room coming in and out of autofocus as the camera shook and panned without apparent aim. A raspy voice arose from somewhere in the scene. "F'chrissakes, Sonny, I'm over here!" The woman went into a coughing jag as the cameraman, apparently their blind uncle, got his bearings. "Hold that fucker steady," the woman demanded.

Finally, there she was. Their mother, Winnie Muckle DePew. Gowned, bedridden, oxygen-tubed. Black hair like Jimi's. Skin that appeared to be the color and consistency of a crumpled brown paper bag. And cat-eye glasses Janis found playful and appealing.

Finally semi-centered in the camera shot, Winnie pulled the oxygen tube from her nose, hooked it over a pointy corner on her glasses, and then took a puff from a cigarette. She coughed again. The tube fell around her neck. "Sicker'n hell," she said. "Whaddaya gonna do, right?"

"You could put out the cigarette," the cameraman said. "For starters."

"A little late for that, brother dear. Just keep your trap shut. Am I in focus?" The woman exhaled, forcing the camera lens to auto-adjust in and out. "What am I saying? How the hell would you know?"

A nurse walked into the room. "Goddammit, I said no interruptions! Give me 15 minutes before you take my last ounce of blood f'chrissakes." The nurse shrugged and started to leave. "But before you go," Winnie said, "make sure that damn camera's in focus." She pushed the bedside cart over toward Sonny. "Here, mount that fucker on the table so Mr. NBC over there can keep it steady."

After several moments of fidgeting, the camera was set up on the steady surface. As soon as the nurse left, Sonny bumped the table, changing the camera angle and bringing an empty juice bottle into the lower-left corner of the frame. The jostling forced Winnie into the far-right side of the shot, but the woman did not notice – and of course, neither did Sonny.

She continued:

"Let's get started," she said. "First off, I'm dead. Not at the moment I'm recording this, of course, but I'll surely be dead by the time you see it. Second, I'm your mother. Surprise!" She laughed and hacked and then started crying, but only for a moment. "No time for this shit," she said, regaining control and stubbing out the quickly consumed Camel.

"I don't know if Sonny has told you much yet. I've asked him to let me tell you this part of the story. He can handle the rest, provide the details, and coordinate things as you carry out my wishes. If you choose to, that is."

The twins looked at one another, frowning, skeptical, intrigued.

"As I said, I'm your mother. Your birth mother anyway. A week or so after you were born, I gave you up for adoption. It was the hardest thing I ever had to do. This dying thing is a piece of cake in comparison. Whatever. What's done is done.

"The fact that you're watching this now means I'm dead, and Sonny finally brought you together to learn the truth. I don't expect you to mourn for me or even forgive me. I haven't exactly earned that privilege, have I? But I did what I had to do. And here's why..."

Their mother lit another cigarette, but inhaled slowly this time, keeping the coughing subdued.

"You see, I was at Woodstock. Sonny was there, too. Along with a half-million other clueless twerps like us. What the hell, right? It was *a happening* and it happened. And it was there that I – well, Sonny and me, that is – met your father. Quite a fella, unlike anyone I'd ever met in my life. Definitely nothing like *our* dad, your grandpa. Our dad, you see, was very successful but very regimented. High expectations for each of us. Mama went along – a real society bitch, God rest her soul. And dear ol' Dad – he made us call him 'Father,' capital 'F' by the way – was very demanding. His brand of love, I suppose. Basically, he was scared shitless we'd fuck up. I got off easy. He was harder on Sonny than on me. But I digress..."

An ash fell in her lap. When she lifted the top of her hospital gown to blow off the ash, the twins could see more burn holes in the thin fabric. "They keep trying to give me a new gown," Winnie said, "but I say why ruin more? Besides, they probably charge me $500 for each one, so no thanks... I'll just keep this one.

"Anyway, when Father and Mama went off on some African boondoggle for a month in August of '69 – I mean, who the hell goes to the goddammed Sahara in August, right? – I'd already been plotting to go to Woodstock and drag Sonny with me. Believe it or not, we made the trip in Father's Mercedes. A fucking limo, that thing was. God, it got trashed. Ever notice how the Mercedes hood ornament looks a lot like a peace sign? Go figure.

"So, Sonny and me, we meet this guy at Woodstock. He had some really good weed and was a really generous and sweet guy, this kid. I call him a kid, but at first, we thought he was older. He had this long whitish-gray hair. Completely natural but so young. Prematurely gray, I guess. Quite the wild look at Woodstock, let me tell ya."

Janis unconsciously touched her right temple, smoothing her own prematurely whitish-gray strands.

"Well, long story short, I fuckin' fell for the guy. Peace, love, and music were what Woodstock was all about, right? So, Sonny and me spend a night with this dude in his VW van – very cliché, I suppose, but the fucker sure-as-shit had a goddamned VW bus. Anyway, while Sonny was sleeping off a good buzz, me and your dad go at it like bunnies. Nine months and one trashed Mercedes later, there you were, much to Father's dismay."

Winnie stubbed out the cigarette and leaned toward the camera.

"Giving you both up was the right thing to do, even though it hurt like hell. Still does. But as I said, what's done is done, right? Anyway, Father pulled some strings and moved things along. But I was pretty stubborn, too, and I threatened to tell everyone at the country club about the jack mags in his office if he didn't let me have a say. So, at the very least, I got to choose your new parents from four overall sets of candidates, two of which turned out to be convicts. After some consideration, I rejected those. I sure hope the parents you got turned out to be good ones.

"Another thing: I had one condition before finalizing the adoptions," she explained. "Your names. In honor of Woodstock, you were to be called Jimi and Janis."

Sonny spoke up. "Can you tell them what you want them to do, Win?"

"Gettin' to it, goddammit. Okay, so, here's the thing. I want you to find your dad. And I want all of us to be together at Woodstock for the 25th anniversary that's coming up. Oh, I know it's coming up soon, and I also know I won't live long enough to see it. But I want you to find your dad and bring him to Woodstock, figure out the right special place, and then spread my ashes there, crowd or no crowd. We'll all be together, ashes to ashes and circle of life and all that shit. Seems to me it will be just about perfect that way."

Their mother started coughing again, moving in and out of the viewfinder. The camera lost and found its focus, over and over, until she regained her composure. Now she was barely visible at all, mostly in profile, ears forward.

"Enough from me," their mother said. "I'll come up with a letter or something telling you what we know, and Sonny can fill in the blanks about your dad. Hell, we don't even know the guy's real name or have that much to go on. But Sonny can explain what I want you to do. Now, I don't expect you to do this just for me. But I sure as hell hope you'll do it for yourselves, not only to find your father, but because it'll earn you enough money to make your dreams come true.

"Oh, yeah, I guess I forgot to mention that little nugget. I'm rich. In the end, I didn't get much from Father and mama but ended up rich anyway and haven't been able to quite gamble it all away. Sonny can give you a sample of the product that made me wealthy. He'll also give you each ten grand just because you took the time to hear what I had to say. Not a bad hourly rate for these few minutes, but my fortune is sizeable, and a good chunk of what's left can be yours if you do as I ask. Just find your needle-in-a-haystack dad, reunite us all by, oh, say, 3:00 on Saturday, August 13th, and then live happily ever after. Sure wish I could be there in the flesh. But I will definitely be along for the ride. Sonny can tell you about that, too.

"Oh, and one last – even if it's technically my first – bit of motherly advice. Don't blow the money like your half-brother has all his life. Shit! Forgot to mention that you've got a younger half-brother. Actually, more like a *half-wit* brother. But that's another story. So, don't blow your money. Always remember that a fortune saved is a fortune earned. And that, my children, is the sum total of my wisdom."

She blew a kiss toward the camera. "Now shut that fucker off and get the nurse back in here."

CHAPTER 3

(In Which We Learn About Holes in the Wall, Anatomically Correct Potato Chips, and What's at Stake for the Twins)

Early Evening

"I NEED A DRINK," JANIS HAD SAID, BREAKING THE AWKWARD SILENCE AFTER the video introduction to her mother.

"I don't drink," said Jimi, "but this sure seems like the perfect time to start."

"I know just the place," said Sonny.

So, the three of them walked in the steady warm breeze three blocks north to the Wide Waters Village area. They would have driven, but the Catropolitan could only comfortably seat two, and Jimi's Volvo was filled with everything he could haul, having been unceremoniously evicted from both his place of employment and his apartment.

Sonny had offered to drive, too, but then confessed that a judge had strongly recommended he forever refrain from that privilege as it tended to alarm other motorists to see a driver with a red-tipped white cane extending from the driver's side window.

Nonetheless, in short order, they arrived at the Hole In The Wall Pub.

"The sign says, '*Holes* In The Wall," Jimi observed. "Plural, as in multiple holes."

"No, no," said Sonny, "As I understand it, the place was originally a gay bar, and the holes in question were a strategically placed popular feature, but now it's just a regular old hole-in-the-wall type of establishment. No need to change the sign as long as the 'S' isn't lit up after dark."

Jimi shrugged, and they entered. The lighting inside was so muted it stopped Janis and Jimi in their tracks until their eyes could adjust. Sonny forged ahead, tapping with his cane.

After a minute, the twins got their bearings and moved further into the central space. It was early, so the pub was sparsely populated, just four men on stools at the bar, presumably having gone directly to the tavern after work, and a few other patrons at small tables dotting the room. The twins found their uncle in the darkest corner booth in the place. They sat on the bench opposite Sonny, but Janis rose again and swiped a lit candle in a jar from a nearby table. Using it as a lantern, she scanned the graffitied beadboard walls of the booth.

"How long ago did this place change from a gay bar?" Jimi asked.

"A week ago, Tuesday," said Janis, "judging by the messages on the wall and the positioning of the holes beside us."

"Oh, my," Jimi said, "what a day this is turning out to be."

The bartender appeared at the table. "Boilermaker, as you like it, Sonny," he said, placing a mug of beer and shot of whiskey in front of the attorney and directing Sonny's hands to them.

"Thank you, Ticker. And bring some bags of our favorite snack while my guests decide what they want to drink." The bartender nodded, said, "Sure thing," and stepped away.

"Boilermaker?" Jimi asked. "As in Purdue? Didn't I see that you were an IU grad?"

Sonny laughed. "Very observant. Call me unpredictable. So, what's your poison of choice?"

Jimi sighed. "No idea. I'm a lightweight when it comes to this."

"He'll have a Long Island," Janis said to the bartender who had quickly returned to the table. "And I'll have the same, but with an extra shot of tequila on the side."

"Got it," Ticker said. He placed three bags of chips on the table and walked away.

"So," Janis asked Sonny, "why is this your favorite snack?" She picked up a bag and shook it in front of him so he would know they'd been delivered. Then she held the bag near the candle for a closer look. "Seriously? *Tat'r Nips?*"

"What are *Tat'r Nips?*" Jimi asked.

Janis laughed. "Only the best chips ever, from a lesbian perspective, that is." She opened a bag and pulled forth a single chip. It was bowl-shaped, roughly 2 inches in diameter. She flipped the chip so Jimi could see the convex side. In the center was a dark pink circle, perhaps a half-inch in diameter, with a slightly darker small circle centered in that. Very clearly, the chip looked like a female breast, complete with nipplage.

"Wow-w-wa..." Jimi mouthed, and then said, "How have I not discovered these before? I really need to get out more often."

Sonny spoke up. "*Tat'r Nips*, Jimi and Janis, are the source of the fortune up for grabs. You see, your mother was frying up some potatoes in the deep fryer one day while I was visiting her, and one of the slices inexplicably, well, it just 'cupped up.' The potato slice in question was dark in the center. Immediately, she thought it bore a striking resemblance to that portion of the female anatomy."

"A tit," declared Janis.

"Yes, that," Sonny said. "She let out such a hoot that I immediately rushed to her side. She said, 'Here, look at this,' and forced my fingers onto the chip as if I could read it in Braille. The burn healed soon enough, but your mother was inspired. She marshaled her financial resources into testing, branding, production, and distribution. Before long, she had a bonafide hit on her hands – *Tat'r Nips*. After a few years of scraping and clawing together a small, single-product empire, she sold out for roughly $10 million. She's gambled and given away more than $4 million, leaving just over $5.5 million to be divvied up."

"Incredible," Jimi said. "And tasty, too." He crunched chip after chip, nip after nip.

"I may have contributed a few hundred dollars into that empire since I discovered these little delights," Janis admitted. "And not surprisingly, they are extra delicious with milk. But back to the business at hand. You said $5.5 million up for grabs. Assuming we find our bio-dad, what's the split? How will all this get divvied up?"

Ticker delivered their drinks, nodded, and stepped away.

"Fastest bartender in the Midwest," Sonny said. Then he reached into his trouser pockets. "Back to the money... For starters, you each get the $10 thousand Winnie mentioned." He placed two banded stacks in the center of the table. Each stack of bills included hundreds and fifties. Janis began counting hers.

"From there, if you find your father, with me, working as a team, he gets ten grand, and we each get ten thousand more. And then, if we complete the mission at Woodstock, the remainder of her financial assets gets evenly divided between each of you, me, your 'bio-dad' as you called him, and your half-brother."

Jimi sipped on his drink, raising his eyebrows as if surprised at its tastiness. "And if we don't find our father?"

Sonny shifted in his seat and cleared his throat. "Then I get twenty-five thousand, the Moroccan Poodle Rescue charity gets $1 million, and your half-brother gets the rest. You each get only the money already on the table before you."

"What!? How is that fair – or legal?" Janis shouted. "If we're her biological offspring, why aren't we entitled to equal shares regardless of this so-called 'mission'?"

Sonny downed the shot of whiskey and chased it with a slug of beer. "Simply put, there's no proof you are her biological offspring. The adoptions were privately arranged and subject to gag orders in perpetuity all around. DNA matching isn't possible now that she's been cremated."

"But the videotape—" Jimi began.

"What videotape?" Sonny asked. "The one I secretly lobbed into the rushing waters of the canal as we walked here? Sorry about that, of course. Dutifully carrying out my sister's orders, you know?"

"We could DNA match against you, couldn't we, Janis asked? After all, she's your sister."

"Sorry, but like you, I was adopted, so matching against me won't do you any good."

Janis chugged her Long Island. Jimi followed suit.

"But surely there's a will, right?" Jimi reasoned.

"Of course, and it spells everything out, except for the genetic relationship between the two of you and my sister. You are simply named as individuals asked to carry out a task in exchange for a sizeable reward."

Janis chugged the shot of tequila next. "And you would lie under oath if we sued your ass, wouldn't you?"

"Let's just say I would be inclined to turn a blind eye."

"Another round!" Jimi shouted to the bartender.

They sat in silence for a few moments, Janis alternately eyeing the ten grand and the suspicious hole next to her, and Jimi's mind racing as it welcomed a virgin buzz.

"It might all seem hopelessly unfair," Sonny said, finally, "but the bright side is that you have a choice to make, and it's a choice that can indeed prove highly rewarding. Find your father, with my help, and we all come into a lot of money. Otherwise, your half-brother and a handful of African poodles get nearly all of it."

"To hell with the poodles," Jimi said. "Tell us about this half-brother of ours."

CHAPTER 4

*(In Which We Meet LilBuckaroo and Junior Agent Junior,
and Learn of the Pipe Organ Incident)*

Evening

THE BACKSTORY BALLAD OF LILBUCKAROO: SHORTLY AFTER FORCING Winnie to give up the twins, her father, J. Buckingham Muckle (the first), brought his iron will to bear again, hoping to stifle any lingering Woodstockian tendencies in his children. Hence, the marriage he arranged between Winnie and one Dennis Leland DePew.

Denny was the pockmarked, socially awkward heir to the DePew church fixtures conglomerate. Winnie protested at first, but eventually went along with the hook-up because, despite her free-spirited fling at Woodstock, she was quickly learning that money speaks louder than pot and daisies. So, after a six-month courtship, she married Denny DePew. Ten months later, their son was born.

Because Winnie's brother, Sonny Muckle, had been adopted, only Winnie's child would be able to advance the true Muckle bloodline. Ever the arm-twister, however, J. Buckingham Muckle – "Buck" as he preferred to be known – once again exerted his will. Literally. Winnie's inheritance, along with that of her son, would have one contingency: name the child after him.

Well, sort of.

Buck Muckle, it seemed, was enamored of calling the child, still in the womb, Little Buck. This quickly morphed into Little Buckaroo. And as the pregnancy wore on, the fetus became Lil Buckaroo and finally, LilBuckaroo. And that was what the birth certificate read: LilBuckaroo Muckle DePew. A heavy load for a cone-headed six-pounder.

By age 8, LilBuckaroo was plotting revenge against all parties to his naming. The exact form of said revenge would change from time to time as the youngster became more worldly and upwardly nefarious. His ultimate revenge fantasy involved him rear-ending an explosion-prone Ford Pinto in which his mother, father, and grandfather rode.

Kaboom, fuckers! LilBuckaroo Muckle DePew, indeed. Ha!

Alas, the vehicular annihilation was not to be. LilBuckaroo was still some eight years away from getting his driver's license when the two men – his father and grandfather – rudely died on their own, within weeks of one another, denying the boy his vengeance.

First went Big Buck Muckle, gored lifeless on a return trip to the African plain by an elephant who, possessing a particularly good memory even by elephant standards, had ID'd Buck as the white warrior who had killed and de-tusked his mama.

Denny, meanwhile, met his demise in a pipe organ installation gone tragically wrong.

It happened at the 3rd Church of the Infinitely Superior Grace and Ever Righteous Holiness. Denny was assisting with the install, having not yet risen to executive authority in the family firm. Still an underling, he was tasked with damage aversion. Specifically, on that particular day, he was to make sure the upper echelons of the organ's pipe ranks did not scrape low-lying ceiling structures in the back of the chancel. Being a skinny, wiry sort, Denny decided the best way to monitor clearances was to monkey up and straddle the upper pipes. Having steeled his nerves with a joint and shot of vodka after lunch, he clambered up and rode the delicate musical instrument as if it were a bucking bronc. Clinging to the pipes as the organ was transported through the narthex, he began whooping and hollering like a bull rider for Jesus. And indeed, each ill-advised gyration caused the organ to buck and roll. Predictably (to observers but not to Denny), young Mr. DePew flew with sudden religious fervor and previously untapped gymnastic flair into the choir loft.

Somehow, Denny (being a skinny, wiry sort) emerged mostly unscathed. A miracle, many said. What was not immediately known, however, was that in that moment of premature ejection from the massive organ, one of the sharp-edged pipes upon which he had been perched sliced into his trousers and nicked the not-nearly-so-massive organ of his personal attachment. Painful, yes, but only a small amount of blood, Denny had figured. So, he decided not to report this minor injury as news of it could only add to his mounting embarrassment. So to speak.

Denny, it turned out, in addition to being dumb as a post, was somewhat lax in his hygiene. And since the appendage in question was out of commission for self-enjoyment purposes (though God knows he tried), he ignored the little bugger for self-care as well.

Even as the infection took root, Denny said nothing. And wife Winnie, not being amorous with her husband beyond the moment of LilBuckaroo's conception, noticed nothing out of the ordinary. Except this: her husband was becoming quieter than normal. She took this as a blessing. Until, that is, one morning, Denny was *much* quieter than normal. As in dead quiet. As in dead.

The autopsy revealed the cause, which Winnie had already surmised when identifying the denuded body. The culprit was ballooned and yet somehow also shriveled. Hued with reds, purples, greens, and a shade of black that did not correlate with Winnie's most secret interracial fantasies. Denny's dingus was quite the sight. Something she couldn't unsee...

...And this was the story Sonny told the twins at the Hole In The Wall Pub. He told them, too, about the subsequent lawsuits and appeals the DePew group had filed against the church and the insurance company. And how the failed litigation had left no substantive inheritance from the DePew side for LilBuckaroo.

"So, no one had to pay the piper, then," said Janis.

* * *

Among other things Sonny also mentioned as the story unfolded and drinks were consumed:

First, LilBuckaroo did get some money eventually, in the form of a trust fund payout from Big Buck when LilBuckaroo turned 21; the money became his because he had resisted all urges to legally change his name. LilBuckaroo also got a car: a 1971 white Cadillac Eldorado convertible Big Buck purchased the day the boy was born – also held in trust until LilBuckaroo turned 21 (at which point LilBuckaroo added steer horns to the grille).

Next, LilBuckaroo had already squandered most of the trust fund money in an attempt to replicate his mother's success as a potato chip mogul, vis a vis the "*lickTat'r* fiasco" (otherwise called the dick*Tat'r* debacle).

And finally, LilBuckaroo knew about the will and the mission to find the twins' father – and was none too happy about the prospect of losing out on yet another substantial windfall.

"So, will he interfere with us trying to find our – it's still hard to say this – our father?" Jimi asked, feeling a full-on buzz for the first time in his life.

Sonny nodded slowly. "I'd say it's likely. But I'd also say there are two things in our favor. First, LilBuckaroo's a fuck-up of the highest magnitude, so it should be easy for us to stay a step or two ahead of him."

"And the second thing in our favor?" Janis prompted.

"The second thing, the most *important* thing, is that there's no way he could possibly know what I'm about to tell you..."

* * *

Except that in a booth on the opposite side of the wall from Sonny and the twins sat LilBuckaroo Muckle DePew. Now going by the name "LB," he wore a construction worker disguise complete with fake mustache. Despite an urgent need to pee, LB listened intently, his left ear inches from the hole nearest his uncle's voice.

LB had come to the Hole In The Wall Pub after his phone call with Pepper Duckenfield. He knew this was Sonny's favorite neighborhood haunt, and it occurred to him that no matter the reaction of the twins – disbelief, shock, jubilation, *whatever* – drinks would be called for.

Now, as he listened, at times seething, LB was sorely tempted to knock down the wall and exact his revenge right then and there. For once, however, he held his impulsiveness in check. Dollar signs danced before his eyes and kept them fixed on the bigger prize. So, he sat and listened and squirmed.

And then...

"…there's no way he could possibly know what I'm about to tell you," he heard Sonny say.

Finally, what I've been waiting for, LB thought, but *Goddammit-I-gotta-peeee!*

"I totally have to take a piss," LB heard the woman say on the other side, as if reading his mind. "Really want to hear what comes next, but I'm talkin' racehorse-filling-a-trough level of pissing here. Be right back."

At that moment, LB loved his urinary kindred spirit, this twin named Janis. He vacated his booth and headed for the men's room. Inside, he rushed to the closest of three urinals and was midstream, barely into his voiding, when the door opened again. He turned slightly but did not make eye contact. Still, he knew it was Sonny and Jimi; and could tell from the tapping of the cane that Sonny had entered first.

"Jimi, could you direct me to an unoccupied urinal?" Sonny said. "It's better that way. Avoids mishaps. Don't want to make *that* mistake again."

"Sure thing," Jimi said, guiding his uncle to the middle receptacle. "I'll take the one to your right."

After a moment, Jimi belched, drunkenly giggled, but then gathered himself and quietly said, "I didn't want to ask this in front of Janis, but this LilBuckaroo character, how much of a problem is he likely to be? I mean, can someone named LilBuckaroo actually be considered dangerous?" He giggled again and hiccupped once. "How far will this guy go to, ya know, keep us from getting what's coming to us?"

The man at the first urinal emitted a guttural noise that registered somewhere between a cough and a growl. *Oh, you'll get what's coming to you all right!*

"If being stupid is dangerous," Sonny replied, "then he's an atomic bomb."

Another cough-growl. *Kaboom, fuckers!*

"Maybe we should keep that concern to ourselves, though," Sonny said. "No need to trouble Janis with it. At least for the time being."

"Okay," Jimi agreed. "So, I guess we just need to keep an eye out for this guy."

"I'll leave that to you," Sonny said. "Perhaps Pepper can provide a picture of him." He flushed, turned, and walked into the closed door of a stall. "Sonofabitch! Did it again!"

* * *

Meanwhile, as Sonny, the twins, and LB were emptying bladders in Indianapolis, hook-handed Special Agent Pete Peebles was downing another shot of vodka in a DC-area bar called Quantico North. Actually, Peebles was no longer a federal agent; his decades-long stint had ended with his retirement the previous Friday, and now his unofficial going-away party was in full swing. If you could call it a party. Eight attendees, including Peebles and his wife, Penny. And all more glum than festive.

Junior agent Carducci (Junior Agent *Junior* Carducci, Jr., to be exact) was among the rather subdued revelers. He didn't really like Pete Peebles – no one did, for that matter – but was obligated to *pretend* to like him because of "the incident." It had happened ten months earlier in this very bar when a long-sought extortionist who had stolen millions from a famous acrobat troupe was spotted here. Phillipe Souplesse, once a performer himself, had been buying rounds for the house and entertaining the barflies by twisting himself into a human pretzel and pretending to be silently trapped inside an invisible box. Peebles and Carducci watched the antics from the shadows for a while, awaiting the opportunity to make a mime-worthy quiet collar. When Souplesse took a deep bow and headed for the restroom, Carducci had waited a few moments and then followed while Peebles stood guard outside the door.

But the contortionist extortionist had already spotted the agents. Thwarted in his hopes to escape through an exterior restroom window (there was none) or a ceiling vent (it was too small) or a drainpipe (too yucky), Souplesse did the next best thing. He perched atop the thin wall of a stall and got the jump on Carducci when the agent entered the room. This he did quietly, as mimes do.

A minute later, Peebles entered the restroom and found the fugitive unceremoniously waterboarding Carducci via a rather aggressive toilet swirlie. Agent Peebles intervened. And Junior Agent

Junior Carducci, Jr. was not only grateful for the intervention, but also for the fact that Peebles never revealed the embarrassing manner of the near-fatal attack. In fact, Peebles credited the collar to Carducci, thus elevating the younger man's status at the agency.

So, yes, Carducci owed Pete Peebles. Big-time. Owed him enough, in fact, that the Junior Agent took pity on Peebles's wife Penny, who sat alone in a corner booth in the bar, reading a drink coaster.

Like the others in attendance, Penny didn't really want to be there. Like the others, she didn't really like Pete. But *unlike* the others, she did love the man. So, here she was. And when Carducci spotted this seemingly meek wallflower, he took a deep breath and approached.

"May I join you?"

The woman smiled rather joyously. "Of course," she said in a voice that had apparently stopped maturing at age 5 despite the rest of her body having advanced to its late fifties. She stole a look toward her husband and the men who were dutifully gathered around him. "Oh, my," Penny Peebles cooed, twisting her blonde and silver hair. "I don't think I've been picked up in a bar in years. Decades, probably. Not that I'm all that old, of course."

"Of course."

As Junior Carducci, Jr. slid onto the seat opposite her, Penny Peebles whispered, "What shall I call you, young man?"

"Um, it's me, Junior."

"Junior, eh? Well, we can work on that."

"I've worked with your husband off and on the last couple of years," Carducci said. "Maybe he's mentioned me? I'm here for his retirement party. May I call you Petunia, Mrs. Peebles?"

Penny slumped. Deflated. *Defeated.* "Insult to injury, Mr. Junior." She sighed and then managed a smile. "Petunia is our dog. Our miniature Poodle. Actually, her name is Princess Petunia."

"Oh, forgive me," Carducci said, his ashen face visibly flushing even in the shadows. "Why did I think the dog's name was Pixie?"

"That's our other daughter. The human one. Mostly."

"Oh," Carducci said, still a bit confused. "I guess I just recalled hearing your husband mention Petunia's name and assumed it was *your* first name."

"Oh, that's all right. Petunia *is* his pride and singular joy these days. Have to admit she's a lovable little bitch." At that, the soft-spoken woman unleashed a cackling guffaw that brought the room to dead silence. She covered her mouth, surveyed the room, and finally waved her hand to insist the patrons resume their conversations. "No, Agent Junior, my name is Penny. Penny Peebles, married to Pete Peebles and co-existing with our pretty Poodle, Princess Petunia Peebles. I know, it's pathetic." She winked at Carducci. "Buy me a drink?"

"Sure, what'll it be?"

"Patron Pineapple – to keep it alliteratively in the family, as it were."

"Absolutely."

"Oh, God, don't use the 'A' word. 'Absolutely' this and 'absolutely' that. It's Pete's favorite expression. Hell, *Absolut* is even all he'll drink, and he drinks a lot of it."

Carducci smiled. "I've noticed that's the only alcohol he drinks but never asked why," he said.

"Oh, come now, Agent Junior, surely you can figure this one out."

"Actually, it's Junior Agent…Junior."

"Well, of course it is."

"Never gave his drink of choice much thought," Carducci replied. "So, tell me, *Penny*, why is Absolut his favorite?"

"Oh, very well." Penny Peebles leaned in and started to reveal the answer but stopped short. "No, actually, I want to see if you have the makings of a Senior Agent, Junior Agent Junior. Tell me what you think of my husband, and I'm sure you'll have the clues you need to figure this one out."

Carducci sighed and started to speak but was rescued for a moment when the server stopped at the table to take the drink order. "Patron Pineapple for the lady here," Carducci said, "and I'll have a Bourbon on the rocks. Top shelf. Oh, and a couple more shots of Absolut for the gentleman over there."

"Of course," the server said. "Which gentleman?"

Penny perked up and pointed. "The love of my life, that withered old goat with an angry *left hook* in the center of the pallbearer convention."

The server laughed uneasily and stepped away. Penny, in her deceptively sweet child-voice, badgered Carducci again. "Back to the assignment. Describe my husband and see if you can figure out why he will only drink Absolut."

The Junior Agent took a deep breath, gathered his thoughts, and exhaled slowly. "Okay, here goes: Your husband, former Special Agent Peter Peebles, is a good man, a determined man, relentless even, but also very straightforward."

"Blunt, you mean. Rude at times," Penny said, "but continue."

"Despite his world-famous hunches, he generally sees everything as right or wrong, black and white…"

"And yet his drink of choice is *not* the Black & White brand of Scotch Whisky," Penny interjected. "Do you know why?"

Carducci shook his head.

"Because James Bond drank Black & White in the Moonraker novel and my husband thinks James Bond is a pussy, that's why. But I digress. Continue, Junior Agent Junior. You may be on the right track."

"Well, let's see. In the end, there are always clear-cut good guys and bad guys, rights and wrongs… Aha, I have it!" Carducci shouted, also bringing the small crowd to silence for a moment. He lowered his voice. "Everything ends up as an absolute, right? So, there it is. *That's* why he drinks Absolut!"

Penny smiled but said nothing.

"So, am I right?"

"Not quite," Penny said. "He drinks it because he likes the taste: 'rich, full-bodied but smooth, with a distinctive character of grain and an ever-so-subtle hint of fruit.' Or something like that." She smiled smugly. "Sometimes, the easiest answer is the right answer, young man. Kind of like Ockham's Razor and all that shit."

Carducci laughed. "Touche'! Nonetheless, you tricked me into revealing what I think of your husband, didn't you, Mrs. Peebles? Penny, I mean."

"Not really. You were ever the soul of tact. My husband is all you said about him. But he's also a jerk. A curmudgeon. A *dick*. And a foul-mouthed pain in the ass who farts in church, but only during silent-but-deadly prayers."

"And yet, I'm guessing you still love him, don't you, Penny?"

Mrs. Peebles sighed. Her shoulders slouched. "What can I say? When he gets home, he kisses me first before he lets Petunia have her way with him."

The server returned with the drinks. Penny picked up her Patron Pineapple, tilted it toward Carducci with a nod, and took a sip. Carducci did the same with his Bourbon and then said, "Penny, there's a couple of things I should also tell you about your husband. First, he saved my life."

"He's done that for several people over the years," Penny said. "Nonetheless, I'm grateful he did that for you. Otherwise, I'd be talking to thin air."

"And second, I admire his tenacity. He's a bulldog. Always gets his man."

"Well, almost," Penny said. "There was that *one* who got away, the solitary blemish on his otherwise perfect record. The one he still obsesses over."

"Woodstock man," Carducci said.

"Yes, Woodstock man."

CHAPTER 5

(In Which Our Principals Learn of Woodstock – Then and Now)

Evening

"WHEN WE RETURN, A ROCK AND ROLL EVENT UPDATE."
Pepper Duckenfield had turned on the TV, indulging her crush on nightly news anchor Jennings Prokoff while she awaited another call from LilBuckaroo. To Pepper, Prokoff was the perfect mix of stone-cold studmuffin and trustworthy teller of truth. She found his voice intoxicating: its folksy authoritative slur (or *shlur*, in Prokoffian delivery) told her he was firmly in charge but also likely a drinker.

Pepper was also fond of drinking during the nightly newscast; it helped her tolerate the days' events. So, while Prokoff was in a commercial break, she went into the kitchen and poured a shot of Jack. Her dog, Effyu, was on the couch, drifting into doggy dreamland after his own nightly cocktail of chewy dog treats laced with cannabis. Pepper had begun using marijuana herself during her brief and frustratingly *un*romantic romance with her boss, Sonny Muckle. Although weed had helped her cope with her sexual frustrations, the lawyer had disapproved of both the herb and her persistent physical advances. Finally unable to turn a blind eye (or two) to her offenses, he ended the relationship.

Pepper had never really been attracted to Sonny. In fact, she had begun the relationship only because she anticipated him coming into money. Someday. Somehow. But then, after three years of laying the groundwork for a potential life of financial comfort, it was over. In addition to the weed and the unspoken lack of sexual chemistry, Sonny said he had become increasingly uneasy about the professional conflict of interest – ergo, dating his subordinate. Still, he wanted her to remain with the practice, given that she knew how the files were arranged and could rehang a fallen diploma in record time.

The breakup happened shortly before Winnie kicked the bucket, at last putting the *Tat'r Nips* millions in play but leaving Pepper on the outside looking in. Her wound had been salted, leaving her with one remaining channel to the Muckle-DePew money: LilBuckaroo.

So, Pepper had reached out to Winnie's primary heir. Told him she could be his "insider," an informant who could make it easier for him to keep most of his mother's money. Told him she could help ensure that Sonny and the twins wouldn't find the man from Woodstock. Told him that even if they *did* find him, she could help LB thwart their efforts to reach ground zero (Woodstock) in time. Hell, she might even figure out a way to shut out those Moroccan poodles.

LilBuckaroo, dumb as he was, saw the brilliance of the scheme and bought into it. Bought into it for a hundred grand; that's what he promised Pepper for her services – *if* the plan worked, that is. And all LB had to do was let her take the lead. Be patient. Be cool. Sit tight. Naturally, she had grave concerns.

Pepper downed the shot of Jack and replayed in her mind the end of her phone conversation with LB:

"So, are they fools or not?"

"Of course, they are. A lesbian cat psychic and a disgraced financial advisor? Fools to be sure. But desperate and curious fools, too, so my guess is they accept the mission."

"It's on, then. We know what we have to do."

"Yes, LB, it's on."

But after a moment, LilBuckaroo, with a proverbial burr up his butt, had added, "Okay, but I can't just sit here and wait around. As I see it, fools or not, Sonny will need a drink. My guess is he'll ask them to escort him to his local haunt and his favorite booth."

"Probably right, LB," Pepper had said, stroking his ego.

"Then maybe I should get there ahead of them," LilBuckaroo had continued. Sonny won't see me, of course, and the twins won't recognize me yet, but still, I think a disguise is in order."

"You do love a good disguise, don't you, LB?" *God, he's gonna "muckle" this up, too.*

"I'll call you when I can. I have a feeling I might just pick up a tip or two from our rivals."

LB had hung up on her then. *Shit!* Pepper thought. *This is the jackass I've hitched my wagon to.* While it troubled her that LB might think he could go this alone, he had at least called them "*our* rivals." So, for now, anyway, the nitwit still saw them as a team.

Downing another shot, she watched as her darling Jennings Prokoff came back on screen after a series of commercials, delightfully slurring *(shlurring)* his report:

"*Twenty-five yearsh ago thish coming weekend, the Woodshtock rock mushic feshtival in upshtate New York brought nearly half a million young people together for an Aquarian Expozhition, three daysh of peash and mushic.*"

Over Prokoff's shoulder, familiar images and video B-rolls played. Hippies, bare feet, concert footage of Hendrix, Joplin, Guthrie, Country Joe McDonald, and more.

"*Now, a quarter shenshury later, one of the two eventsh planned to commemorate the original feshtival has been canshelled while the other ish being condemned for itsh corporate shponshorship by a shoft drink giant. That remaining event, to be held at Shaugertiesh, New York thish weekend, hopesh it can reshonate with the Pepshi generation the way the original event at Bethel, New York did with young people a generation ago.*"

As Prokoff offered details about the "official" celebration in Saugerties, the telecast ran familiar images from the 1969 gathering at Yasgur's farm in Bethel: a nun flashing the peace sign, the man called Wavy Gravy doling out food, distant skinny dippers in a pond. And the final lingering frame: a woman and two men, unclothed but covered in mud, having indulged in mudslide frivolity after torrential downpours had turned Woodstock into a swamp.

"I'll be damned," Pepper said, studying the mud-laden trio on the screen. "I'll be a double-dog-damned sonofabitch." From the couch, Effyu snarled.

* * *

Prokoff's Woodstock report on the television above the bar caught Janis's eye.

"Story about Woodstock on TV," she said, interrupting Sonny just as he was starting to share details about the twins' father and how they might track him down.

"Really?" he replied. "Is it closed-captioned? Be my eyes. Tell me what the report is saying."

So, Janis did, with Jimi chiming in to provide play-by-play of the images on screen.

When the final image lingered on-screen, Jimi said, "Three people covered with mud, and I mean *covered!* Except that they seem to be naked otherwise." Janis read the slur-less captioning: *"While the original Woodstock turned into a financial disaster that took years to resolve, organizers of the anniversary event in Saugerties, New York hope to clean up. Judging by the hygiene of original Woodstockers, good luck with that."*

Silence lingered for a few moments before Jimi said, "Isn't there a drink called the Mudslide? Suddenly, I wanna try one of those."

Sonny ignored him. "Tell me about that last image. The one of the three people covered with mud. Was it a woman and two men?"

"Yes, it was," Janis answered.

"And were the two men side-by-side with the woman on one end?"

"Yes."

"And was the man on the other end staring at the man in the middle?"

"Yes, I think so," Jimi said. "How could you know all that?"

Sonny removed his sunglasses. He dabbed at a suddenly teary eye and then replaced his shades. Voice faltering, he said, "That photo, to my knowledge, was the only one ever taken of your mother and your father and me. Your mom saw it once in a book and told me about it. We had been, what's the word, um, *frolicking*, I suppose, on the mudslide hill at Woodstock. So much rain, everything so damn wet. We ditched our clothes so they didn't get totally ruined for the rest of the weekend, and —"

"But how did you know a picture was being taken?" Janis asked.

Sonny took a deep breath. "Because I could see then. I was blinded soon after." He sipped his beer and continued: "But that's a story for another day. Suffice to say that shortly after that photo was taken, we encountered one very angry hook-handed lawman. That angry man was the reason your father took off when he did. And that angry man was also the reason I've spent a quarter-century in darkness."

* * *

In DC, Pete Peebles tilted up a shot of Absolut. In doing so, he caught a glimpse of the muted TV in the corner of the bar. There he saw Jennings Prokoff (God, he hated that man's voice) silently mouthing the closed-captioned words that appeared at the bottom of the screen:

"...the Woodstock rock music festival in upstate New York brought nearly half a million young people together for an Aquarian Exposition, three days of peace and music.

"Now, a quarter-century later, one of the two events planned to commemorate the original festival has been canceled while the other is being condemned for its corporate sponsorship...."

Peebles removed himself from the center of his small gathering of retirement well-wishers and ambled closer to the screen. Hippies. Nuns. Rock musicians. Skinny dippers. And finally, the all-too-familiar mud people: the brother and sister flanking the object of Pete's twenty-five years of frustration and obsession: the fugitive named Jay Finch, Jr.

Peebles pointed his hook at the on-screen image, and then, with his good right hand, hurled his shot glass at the TV. It missed the screen but hit the power button. The display went dark.

* * *

And at the Moon-Your-Mama Bar & Grill, Jay Finch, Jr., the naked bartender now going by an alias but known to most as Jaybird, watched from behind the bar as the mud people on television faded into a commercial. He sighed, turned off the TV, and reached into the full assortment of supplies beneath the counter. Locating his hidden bottle of US-banned Absinthe, he poured a half shot, hoisted the glass toward the darkened screen, and toasted his younger self: "Here's mud in your eye, kid."

CHAPTER 6

*(In Which We Learn of Pepper's Dilemma, LB's Agony,
and Former Agent Pete's Retirement Plans)*

Evening

SOMEONE WAS KNOCKING ON PEPPER'S DOOR. POUNDING, ACTUALLY. SHE pulled back the edge of her front-window curtains and spied the agitated man. For once, it was not an angry neighbor. "Christamighty!" she said, and then, "Just a minute!"

Pepper pulled her wig from beneath the sleeping dog and wrestled the hair onto her head. It perched there somewhat askew. She opened the door but blocked the opening, one hand on the door frame, the other on her flared hip. "I've never been a fan of the pop-in visit, LB. Why didn't you call first?"

"I did call. Your line was busy. May I come in?"

Pepper exhaled heavily and stepped aside. "Why not? You're here, aren't you?"

LilBuckaroo took impressive strides into the center of the rather small living room. He liked making a grand entrance, but this particular ingress bore a flourish of irritation. He landed in the brighter area of light where the glow of three lamps converged, and when he turned to face her, Pepper erupted in laughter. LB was wearing a fake mustache and a blue-collar construction worker shirt, complete with a crushed cigarette pack rolled up in the left-side short sleeve. "This is what you wear to a former gay bar?" she asked. "What happened, did you lose your cop and cowboy sidekicks at the YMCA?"

"All right, knock it off, will ya?" LB said. He surveyed the apartment. "What's wrong with your dog? And for that matter, your hair?"

Pepper adjusted her wig but ignored the question about Effyu. "Okay, so, tell me… What happened at the bar?"

"That's just it," LB said, throwing his hands into the air. "Nothing happened. Nothing!" He spat at a rogue mustache hair that had worked its way into the corner of his mouth.

"What do you mean, nothing happened? Sonny and the twins were there, weren't they?"

"Oh, yeah, they were there, all right. And they drank and talked about me and about mud people at Woodstock and they drank some more and Sonny started crying and Jimi hurled into his Mudslide mug and it all went to crap from there."

LilBuckaroo plopped on the sofa next to the sedated dog. Effyu tried to snarl but only farted.

"And this you had to tell me in person," Pepper said, only half-heartedly trying to hide her annoyance. *Hundred grand*, she reminded herself. *Hundred grand.*

"Look, I said I tried to call, all right? As it is, I was lucky to get out of that bar alive."

"Okay," Pepper said, genuinely curious now. "Fill me in."

LB snorted. "Well, for starters, apparently someone lit up the 'S' on the sign, so the bar became '*Holes* in the Wall' again. A whole different set of customers showed up out of some sense of nostalgia, I guess. And because of the way I was dressed, they assumed I was there to perform – one way or another." He dug into his pocket and pulled out a wad of ones and fives and tossed them on the table. "They were pretty insistent."

"What on earth did you have to do to earn those?" Pepper said, chuckling and sorting the money. "And why are these bills sticky?"

"Don't ask … and don't ask," LilBuckaroo said.

"Yeah, I guess I don't really wanna know," Pepper admitted. "So, again, why are you here?"

"I'm here, dear Peps, because I think you might be holding out on me."

She glared at him. Folded her arms but did not dignify his remark with a verbal response. Effyu grunted and passed wind again.

LB waved at the air. "What *do* you feed this dog!"

Pepper sat in the side chair, still glaring. "Pancakes and weed. Forget the dog," she said. "What the hell are you talking about, LB? I'm not holding out on you. Haven't I told you everything I know, little as that is at this point?"

"Ha! So, you don't know anything about a sheet of paper with important information on it? Information about my dear mother's long-lost lover, this Woodstock guy? About his possible whereabouts? About the mission to find him?"

"Are you sure about that?" Pepper asked. "Did you see this paper? This 'alleged' sheet of information?"

"Don't go speaking lawyer-like with me, Peps—"

"I'll stop if you'll quit calling me Peps!"

"Fine. And yes, I saw the paper. One copy for each of them, the twins and Sonny – lotta good it does Sonny to have a copy, right? I saw it all through the hole between our booths."

"Okay, so you saw it. What did this paper say?"

"I don't know! I saw the paper but couldn't read it. They were finally getting down to brass tacks when the nostalgia boys showed up. But what I want to know, Peps, um, Pepper, my dear, is how your blind employer could have an info sheet to discuss with Jimi and Janis. You had to have been the one to type it, right? So, come clean – what do you know that you're not telling me?"

LilBuckaroo began spitting again, trying to expel another invasive hair. And this made Pepper laugh, which made LB madder – spitting mad, as it were.

"For God's sake, LB, take that damn mustache off!"

"I can't. It seems to have grown rather attached to my upper lip. I think the glue I used was the wrong kind."

Pepper stood and stepped beside him. She clawed at a corner of the 'stache, managed to get a good hold, and jerked it toward the opposite corner. It came off. But so did significant acreage of LB's skin. His upper lip instantly turned beet red and spouted dozens of little blood puddles. His scream was chilling. Effyu snarled and farted but kept dozing.

"What the fuck ya do that for! I told ya it was stuck!"

"And now it's not stuck anymore, you twit. You're welcome!"

LilBuckaroo moaned and writhed and grabbed the lip toupee for examination.

Pepper continued: "I didn't care for your accusation that I'm holding out on you, that's all. Look, Sonny is completely inept and inadequate in many areas. Surprisingly, however, he's an excellent typist. Better than me, in fact, except he sometimes forgets to load the paper."

"So, he secretly types up several copies—"

"No need," Pepper said. "He knows how to type, but he also knows how to run the copier. Most of the time, he even remembers to keep his necktie away from the auto-feeder." She shook her head. "Three cut-and-dried cases of near-strangulation by copier and the stupid sonofabitch is too honest to sue!"

Pepper wanted to vent further, but she noticed that LB was in agony. "Let me get you something for that lip. It's looking awful."

She returned with cotton balls but failed to mention she had doused them with rubbing alcohol.

This time LilBuckaroo's screams woke the dog.

* * *

Okay, maybe Pepper *was* holding out on LilBuckaroo. The way she saw it, though, she hadn't really lied to him; she was merely being careful to share information strategically – only when it became relevant and necessary. Too much information too soon, she reasoned, would only fog up LB's already clouded brain.

She did not find it necessary, for example, to tell LB about her earlier phone conversation with Sonny. He had called from the bar a half hour before LilBuckaroo came knocking:

"Hey, Ducks, sorry to bother you in the evening," Sonny had said.

"It's okay, boss. What's up?" (She called him "boss" ever since the breakup.)

"Well, I just wanted to bring you up to speed," Sonny said. "It's been kinda hard to talk business with Jimi and Janis tonight. For some reason, there's been an influx of the bar's former clientele, and things are a bit rowdy with some guy named Elby. He's still surrounded by admirers even now."

Pepper heard a cheer go up in the background.

"They really need to close up those holes," she said, "or this kind of thing might happen from time to time. Or maybe it's always like that in the evening."

"Um, I wouldn't know anything about that," Sonny said. "Nothing at all. Really. Anyway, I shared with the twins what little I know about their father. I typed up an info sheet last night and ran copies – without incident, I might add."

"Good; you're learning. So, how did they take it? How are they handling everything coming at them?"

"Very calmly for the most part. Extra trips to the bathroom, maybe, plus a few tears and some occasional vomit. Otherwise, they're handling it well. I'm sure they'll continue to process everything as best they can."

"Do they understand the stakes and the timeline?" Pepper asked.

"Yes, I believe they do. We're supposed to get back together tomorrow late morning or early afternoon."

"So, are they onboard, then? What's next?"

"That's why I'm calling, Ducks. I need a favor. I need you to head over to Before You Go-Go in the morning."

"The car rental place?"

"Yes," Sonny continued. "I need you to arrange for a car for the rest of the week. Will probably need it as soon as tomorrow afternoon. And I also need you to contact the office of that nudist organization down in Florida again. We need to make one last attempt to get some information from them. Do that first thing if you can. Time is of the essence, as you know."

Pepper stroked Effyu, the drugged dog quite mellow. "Yes, I know. The clock is ticking louder and louder for this needle-in-a-haystack expedition. I also know what I transcribed in Winnie's letter describing the twins' father, but—"

"But what, Ducks?"

"Well, I'm just curious about that info sheet and what else you may have shared with Jimi and Janis."

"You really know most everything there is to know for now," Sonny said. "The sheet I typed up just kind of summarized it all."

Hooping and hollering had arisen again in the background noise from the bar. Pepper had pulled the phone away from her ear until it died down, and then said, "Okay, but look, boss, about that rental car... I'm not sure that the people at Before You Go-Go—"

"I know what you're gonna say, Ducks. Just reassure them that I will *not* be driving this time."

"Okay, I'll try. You want the car in my name, then?"

"For now, yes. I'm sure Jimi or Janis will have to sign for it or provide their licenses at some point. Just make sure it's a good-sized vehicle, something comfortable but ordinary. We could be logging a lot of miles. A minivan, perhaps. Nothing flashy."

"I'll see what I can do," Pepper agreed. She was already making mental notes to arrange for a bright pink clown car if one was available. "But isn't there a better alternative? Is this road trip really necessary?"

"Unfortunately, I can't think of any other way," Sonny had replied. "We don't have a name to go on yet or a location. Because time is short, we have no choice but to play the odds and start the journey. Maybe we'll get lucky and find our guy early on, but we might have to visit dozens of places before we find him."

"If he's even still out there," Pepper said.

"Yes, there's certainly the possibility this is all for nothing. But we have to try. There's too much at stake to give up before we start."

"Okay, but you'll keep me posted at every stop, right?" Pepper had asked. "I'll do what I can do on my end to come up with something about our missing person, but I'll need to know where you are and what's going on."

"Of course," Sonny assured her. "Ducks, you're the best. Maybe I was wrong about us. Regardless, you can be certain I won't forget all you're doing," he said just before hanging up.

Goddammit, Pepper thought. *What the hell was that supposed to mean? Is he thinking of reconciling? Is he going to give me a bonus? A reward? What kind? How much?*

She was still deep into pondering Sonny's choice of words when LB had shown up, fake mustache and all. And after LB left to nurse his wounded upper lip, she was certain of only two things: she was in a precarious position between these two, and she needed some weed herself.

* * *

Meanwhile, at Quantico North, the DC bar, the hurling of the shot glass at the TV had effectively ended Pete Peebles's official retirement party. The group dispersed. Pete was permitted to stay because he had spent thousands on Absolut there over the years. Nonetheless, having been asked to step away from the bar and the TV, Pete gathered up his retirement plaque and went into the restroom.

He looked up as he entered the room, in case the acrobat Souplesse was again perched overhead. Satisfied he was alone, Peebles went about his business on the former waterboarding vessel and tried to put Jay Finch, Jr. out of his mind. To no avail.

In the twenty-five years since Finch, Jr. had eluded him at Woodstock, Peebles had often attempted to console himself with these facts:

First, Finch Junior had never really been his prey. That had been the kid's father, the embezzler Finch Senior. Second, Peebles successfully nabbed the elder Finch only to watch him die in the hospital. Thus, he *had* brought *that* man to justice. Success by any measure, he reasoned. And finally, even though the case had been officially closed years ago, his retirement would now permit him to revisit everything from a fresh perspective. To finally track down the younger Finch. But first, to retrieve the missing money and remove the single stain from his long and storied career.

Peebles stared at the plaque clasped in his hook. Beneath a gold-plated gavel, it bore this inscription:

"Presented to Special Agent Peter Peebles
in recognition of his unflinching patriotism,
his tireless dedication to The Agency,
and his nearly perfect record
of bringing fugitives to justice."

Nearly perfect record.
Fucking *nearly* perfect!

Peebles flushed the toilet, immediately brought to mind a drenched and gasping Junior Agent Junior Carducci, Jr.

Upon leaving the restroom, with the image of the Woodstock mud people still fresh in his mind, Peebles tossed the plaque on the bar and joined Carducci and Penny in the booth. To Penny, he said, "Start packing your things. We're going back to East Kibosh."

"East Ki? South Carolina again?" Penny protested.

"Yes, dammit. I want one more crack at finding that money Finch Sr. embezzled." And to Carducci: "Junior, I need a favor. My gut tells me this Woodstock reunion coming up might just bring our muddy threesome back together. One of my famous hunches, I guess. Regardless, if that happens, I want to be there. But I'll need to know where they're coming from, where they'll be once they get there, and when they're likely to arrive!"

Carducci looked puzzled. "Whoa! Hold on, Pete... How do you recommend I get that information?"

"Yeah, about that... I know I can't really request manpower on a hunch, especially now that I'm retired, but if you could – off the clock and off the record – set up a wiretap on that attorney in Indy."

"The one you blinded," Penny said, nudging her husband's elbow.

"That was an accident, dammit!"

"I know, honey," she said. "Just keeping the details clear in my mind." She smiled. Subtly.

Carducci seemed to struggle as he gathered his thoughts: "Okay, well, um, supposing we actually get wind of a reunion for these three – and assuming they're all still alive—"

"Muckle and his sister were alive and well the last time I checked, a few months ago," the retired Senior Agent offered. "Obviously, I can't be certain about our fugitive."

"Okay, so if we *do* hear from this Finch guy after all these years, why does the collar have to be at Woodstock? Why not nab him before he gets there?"

Pete's eyes grew glassy and his lips twisted into a sneer. "Because I *need* this, Junior. And I need it on my terms. I need to make the collar at Woodstock because that's where the bastard slipped through my fingers."

"Slipped through your hook," Penny corrected him.

* * *

None of the three noticed the man standing at the bar in DC – the man on the phone who was studying Pete Peebles's retirement plaque.

"Prokoff," the man said into the phone, "Max here."

He listened for a few seconds.

"Cut the crap, Prokoff; you know 'Max who.' Thibodeaux, for fucks' sake. 'Black Max,' if that helps. Anyway, shut up and listen. I found your report interesting tonight. The one about Woodstock."

Max looked over his shoulder at Pete and his two booth companions. They were engrossed in their own conversation. Jennings Prokoff, meanwhile, blathered on.

"All right, all right," Max said, interrupting the anchor. "I said the report was interesting, not Pulitzer-worthy. Anyway, I'm in our favorite watering hole in DC, and there's a guy here who had quite a remarkable reaction to your Woodstock story."

Prokoff responded at length. Max rolled his eyes. *God, the people I deal with,* he thought.

"No, the guy here wasn't applauding or singing your praises, Prokoff. Damn, you are full of yourself these days, aren't you? Let me clue you in," Max continued. "The guy had the opposite reaction, in fact. He chucked a shot glass at the screen."

Max watched the bartender head into the kitchen.

"No, Mr. TV star, I'm sure he's not another disgruntled fan. The bartender says he's a former Special Agent and he's got a twisted nut over some dude that got away a long time ago, got away at Woodstock. Anyway, look, Prokoff, I don't have a lot of time, so it's like this; I'm still checking out the details, but here's what I know: the Agent's name is Peter Peebles according to his retirement plaque which I'm looking at right now. The barkeep says he's a regular here and always whining about this Woodstock guy who ruined his perfect record.

"Anyway, here's the angle: I think this Agent guy is gonna pull out all the stops now that he's retired. I overheard conversations he was having earlier. I think he wants to settle this score once and for all. And judging by the shot glass incident, I'm pretty sure your Woodstock report sent him over the edge. You want that Pulitzer,

Prokoff? Put on your pants and step out from behind that anchor desk. Do a human-interest piece on this Agent dude, this protector of the people recognized for his, um, here it is, his 'unflinching patriotism … tireless dedication to The Agency … and nearly perfect record of bringing fugitives to justice.' Imagine the ratings if you're there when Agent Peebles finally gets his man. And correct me if I'm wrong, but aren't you currently embroiled in contract renewal negotiations?"

Max stepped away from the plaque, stretching the phone cord to its limits. "Yeah, I thought you might see it that way," he said. "As always, I'll do the legwork. For a price, of course. Start by putting five grand in my account, and I'll see what I can come up with."

For once, the anchor's response was brief. Max nodded.

"Yeah, yeah, you're welcome," Max said. "If this lead pans out, you can swoop in at the last minute for a live report. Just make sure you have the network helicopter ready to go from NYC to Woodstock. Till then, keep this whole thing quiet. Oh, and Prokoff, I'll expect a significant bonus for this little assignment. I can already tell I'll be putting in a lot of hours and will have some unusual expenses."

* * *

After leaving the Holes in the Wall Pub and escorting Sonny back to his office-slash-home, Jimi stayed with Janis, thus doubling the unauthorized occupancy of her former girlfriend's condo. The twins had that in common: both had been unceremoniously dumped by women who had sent them packing. Jimi's version of *sent packing* meant stuffing all his possessions into the Volvo's voluminous vault of a back end. Janis, on the other hand, had simply used her previously undisclosed spare key and moved back in when her ex left for a three-month sabbatical to Paris.

"She owed me three days on my share of the last mortgage payment," Janis had explained.

"And how long have you been here since moving back in without her knowledge?" Jimi asked.

"Three days," Janis said, "give or take a month and a half. But hey, it's a good thing I was here because, well…"

"Yes?"

"Well, because the chain on that toilet-tank-ball-thingy broke the first week, and I fixed it good as new."

"In other words, you fixed something that wasn't broken until you moved back in and broke it."

"Missing the point," Janis said. "Someone had to do it. That toilet was filling up pretty fast."

So went the rest of their evening, bantering and bickering as brothers and sisters do (even long-lost siblings, given enough booze). They talked about Sonny and their biological mom and this Jaybird guy. They talked about their adoptive parents and their upbringing, too. And Janis was still talking, about the money and the journey to come, long after Jimi had passed out for the night.

Tuesday, August 9, 1994

CHAPTER 7

(In Which We Encounter a Barefoot Spy, Learn More from Winnie, and Meet Anthony Purrkins)

Early Morning

AT 2:37 A.M., THE LAW OFFICE OF J. BUCKINGHAM MUCKLE, II HAD A VISITOR.

Mike Smyth (not his real name), phone technician for Ameritech (not really) parked his generic white van in the alley and placed orange cones around a telephone pole (this was true). After observing the consistently dark law office for ten minutes, Smyth then abandoned the van and the pole and the cones and approached the two-story cottage office.

Being a sneak-of-all-trades, master of some, Smyth quickly gained entry to the office via the carelessly unlocked front door. He entered delicately, easing his way inside to keep the cowbell from cowbelling. (Having worked in central Indiana for six months, Smyth had discovered that Hoosier city-folk loved attaching cowbells to their business doors, perhaps a nod to bygone days when the bells would warn of covert bovine attacks.)

Once inside, Smyth was ready to ply his trade: wiretapping.

In simplest terms, wiretapping's a two-step process: first, plant a listening device in each telephone receiver to be bugged, and then tap into exterior wires to create a listening and/or recording feed. Because Smyth wasn't being paid adequately to sit in the van 24/7 and listen to any and all phone conversations as they happened, this tap would be a record-and-review-later job. Thus, the listening devices would be sound-activated, set to begin recording with each incoming ring or outgoing dial tone. Smyth would listen after-hours and report anything of importance to the Agency – specifically to Junior Agent Junior Carducci, Jr.

That was the plan.

So, with a small penlight held in his mouth to add focused light to the faintly streetlit interior space, the wiretapper worked his magic in Muckle's personal office. Done in less than three minutes, he then returned to the reception area to bug the phone of the receptionist – Pepper, according to the copper nameplate. Again, a quick task, but perhaps not quick enough. The wiretapper was reattaching the receiver unit cover on Pepper's phone when he heard a different kind of tapping. It was faint but methodical, almost metronomic. Next came the creaking of stairs under feet and then the tapping again, closer now. Smyth froze at first, but then stealthily ducked into the corner knee space beneath Pepper's desk. He clicked off his penlight and stuffed it into his shirt pocket; and then pulled his legs up into a fetal position, ankles crossed, making himself as small as possible.

The tap-tap-tapper came very close and set a heavy object on the desktop. It clanked against something glass which toppled and began rolling. Instinctively, Smyth reached out from beneath the desk and caught the glass bud vase in mid-air. But he immediately rethought the reflex; after all, the clumsy intruder would expect the vase to land. So, Smyth dropped it the last few inches to the floor. After defying gravity for that extra second, the pear-shaped vase landed intact, rolled away and then circled back toward Smyth. He pushed the vase away again, and once more it orbited back. Finally, he grabbed it and set it upright on the floor.

"Sonofabitch! Did it again!" a male voice said from above the desk. At that point, a single rose tumbled from the desktop and a stream of water began dripping off the edge, splashing and pooling near Smyth's crossed ankles. "Well," the voice above said, "I know she keeps a rag around here somewhere."

Tap-tap-tap around the desk until a white cane, barely visible in the dim light, appeared and hit the upright vase. It rolled again under Smyth's upraised right knee. *Give me a goddamned break*, Smyth thought. The man at the other end of the stick stopped in front of him and leaned his cane into the crux of the L-shaped desk's inside corner. The man's bare feet inched forward, toes finding the puddle. "Rag, rag,

rag, I need that rag," he said, proceeding to open and rummage through desk drawers.

Coming up empty, the man said, "Maybe she keeps it under the desk."

Smyth needed a distraction. He rolled the vase back out into the open. "Aha!" the barefoot man said. He knelt, picked up the vase, and then stood to place it again on the desktop. While he did this, Mike Smyth eased off his own right shoe, pulled off his sock, and tossed it to the floor. He grimaced when it landed on the man's left foot. "Ah, there you are, Mr. Rag," the blind man said. Picking up the sock, he wiped up the water from the floor, and then apparently did the same for the desktop. "Whew, Pepper really should wash this thing," he said before finally stepping away from the wiretapper, sock in hand.

Fifteen minutes later, safely ensconced in his white van with his middle-of-the-night mission complete, Mike Smyth screamed into his mobile phone at a groggy Junior Agent Junior Carducci, Jr. "Fuck the rush job, Carducci! You could at least have mentioned this attorney guy was blind! You could've mentioned that *lights out* is the same as *lights on* to this guy! You could've mentioned that he lived upstairs over the office, for fuck's sake!"

Carducci let his field tech vent. "Sorry about that," he said finally. "I guess that little detail got lost in the shuffle. At any rate, is the tap in place?"

"Yeah, it's there," Smyth said, calming down. "It'll activate whenever a call is placed or received and then shut off at the next dial tone. I'll go over any recordings each evening and let you know if there's anything out of the ordinary."

"Thank you. I appreciate your trouble," Carducci said, "and I appreciate you keeping this on the QT. Just you and me. Could turn out to be a wild goose chase, but you never know."

Smyth sighed. "So, how long will this could-be-a-wild-goose-chase go on? I've got a full slate of assignments, and my kid's got a summer theater program next week."

"Should be all done before then. D-Day for this operation, for all intents and purposes, is this coming weekend. If nothing has happened by then, it's not likely to happen at all."

"Good," Smyth said. "This kind of work is *not* why I went to spy school, ya know."

"You went to spy school?"

"Correspondence course, but yeah, I'm a trained professional. And yes, I keep things quiet. That's why you brought me into this little operation, isn't it?"

"Absolutely," Carducci said, and he thought of Pete Peebles when he said that word. "All right, Smyth, anything else I need to know?"

"Just one thing," Smyth said. "You owe me a sock. Might as well make it a pair."

* * *

The night before had been restless. For Janis and Jimi. For everyone else, too:

Sonny had packed his personal effects anticipating a quick trip into the unknown – practically a metaphor for his entire life, he figured.

Pepper continued to feel off-balance and stuck in the middle between Sonny and LilBuckaroo. Her mind had raced with all that could go wrong.

Pete had spent about two minutes feeling grateful for his going-away party, ten minutes reflecting on the many triumphs of his long and storied career, and hour after hour gnashing his teeth over the Finch men – Jay, Sr. and Jay, Jr. – who had rendered that career to be nothing more than "nearly perfect." The looming trip to East Kibosh, South Carolina, was fraught with uncertainty as he continued to search for a veritable needle in a haystack. At least he had Penny to handle the trip logistics.

Penny, meanwhile, had spent the night dreading not just the trip but the future itself – a future that would include having Pete always underfoot. She hoped he would get a hobby – maybe bird watching – other than Jay Finch, Jr., of course.

Max Thibodeaux, Jennings Prokoff's news chasing field operative, had done additional intel late into the night, learning what he could about Pete Peebles, wife Penny, their grown and married daughter Pixie, and their other daughter: Princess Petunia, the petite Poodle.

Above all, Max knew he must avoid detection while shadowing an agent who had made a career of shadowing others. No easy feat for a 6-foot 3-inch thirty-something black man tailing white people into God-knows-where. Max also figured he might need his best surveillance gadgetry, his keenest instincts, and a little luck to make it all work between now and the looming Woodstock anniversary event. He would also need Jennings Prokoff to keep his mouth shut. *Too much room for error*, Max thought, but money was money, and Prokoff paid well for scoops.

As for LilBuckaroo, he masturbated. Three times. Twice successfully.

* * *

But morning came, as it tends to do...

In Indianapolis, in his living quarters above the law office, Sonny stood at the bathroom sink, shaving. Occasionally, he would lean toward the mirror, a relic of habit.

This particular morning, he was a little constipated and slightly more than a little hungover. Absent-mindedly taking one last stroke with the razor, Sonny nicked his chin. He immediately dropped the razor into the water-filled sink and placed his right thumb over the cut to quell the bleeding. More questions as he waited for the nick to clot: *Where in the world was Jaybird? Could they really find him? And if they did, would they find him in time?* So many uncertainties. And all he could do was stand there in darkness. Clotting.

After the bleeding stopped, Sonny sniffed his underarms and then uncapped his can of Right Guard. He lifted his left arm and misdirected the spray onto the mirror before correcting his aim and spraying in the general vicinity of his armpit. He repeated this for the other side, again deodorizing the mirror first.

As he inhaled the musky mist, more questions: *What on earth were Janis and Jimi doing and thinking about this morning? Would they join him on the quest? Both of them? Today? Tomorrow?*

* * *

Janis told Jimi he needed something in his stomach. She suggested Zuzu's, a little cottage-style diner a few blocks from Sonny's office. "Best coffee this side of Columbia," she said. Jimi merely groaned and held his throbbing head.

Approaching Zuzu's and squinting behind blue-tinted mirrored Aviators, he spoke delicately and deliberately: "This," he said, "is the brightest daylight ever." As they entered the diner, Jimi covered his ears to soften the tinkling of the bells atop the entry door. Then he slumped onto the vinyl booth bench across from Janis and slid gently across the seat to brace himself against the wall. The vinyl squeaked loudly. He grimaced.

"First day after getting your new drinking license is always the toughest, kiddo," Janis said, catching her reflection in his glasses. She kind of liked the blue tint the Aviators added to her short, prematurely white hair.

Turning toward the counter, Janis yelled, "Zuzu! Coffee, black, and plenty of it!" When she turned back to face Jimi, his fingernails were clawing the laminated tabletop. "Oops, sorry," she said. "I'll try to be quiet. No guarantees, though. Being quiet really isn't my strong suit." She watched him for a moment. "Forgot to ask... Sleep well?"

"Very funny," Jimi whispered. "My head was spinning all night, and now it hurts to move. Hurts to move *ev-e-ry-thing*. It also hurts to see and it hurts to breathe and it hurts to talk. So, remind me, why am I doing those things?"

"Because if you weren't doing those things, you'd be dead, and I'd be chatting with a corpse," Janis said. "I'm guessing that would be bad for Zuzu's business."

At that, Zuzu came to the table, coffee in hand. Janis held up a shushing finger, beseeching quiet. "First hangover," Janis whispered, pointing at Jimi. "Thanks for the coffee. Leave the pot."

"It also hurts to think," Jimi said, "so please do the thinking for both of us."

"My pleasure," Janis said, a bit too loud, but then more softly as she continued. "Actually, I've already done a lot of thinking about this situation. Now, as I see it, no matter how scammy this all seems, I think Sonny is on the up-and-up."

Jimi removed his sunglasses and dropped his head into his hands. "Go on, I'm listening."

"Well, first off, there's the money. I worked at a bank for half a day once, so I'm pretty sure it's real. So, the next question I asked myself was if there would be some *reason* to scam us. I mean, *us*, of all people. I sure don't have any money – or at least I didn't until yesterday – and I gather you don't either."

"Broke. Living in car," Jimi reminded her.

"Yeah, sorry about that," Janis said. "Love to hear more about what happened, but I think that's a story for when your tongue works better."

Jimi turned slightly, his back to the window now, the sunlight behind him. He still held his hands over his eyes. "Still listening," he said.

"Right, but while I talk, you need to drink coffee. It'll help."

"Don't like coffee." His brain rattled with each syllable. Succinctness helped.

"Learn quick," Janis said. She pushed the cup in front of him but then altered its chemistry with cream and sugar. She waited until he took a wincing sip before continuing. "Anyway, there's no sense scamming us. And we're not worth much for ransom either, right? I mean, my dad is no millionaire. Your folks have any real dough?"

"No dough. Some. Not mush."

"Mush?"

"Whatever."

"Okay, so if we don't have any money and Sonny can't get any money by kidnapping us – a *blind* guy kidnapping us, I might add – and he's *giving* us money to take a trip for a few days, well..."

"No scam. Agree."

"Okay, so far so good. So that suggests what he says is true. Or at least worth pursuing. Drink your coffee, brother. Big day ahead, it would seem."

Zuzu returned to the table. "I'll seat others as far away as possible," she whispered. "Ya know, to keep the noise down. I also taped the clapper down in the bell on the door."

"You're the best, Zuzie Q," Janis said softly. "Jimi here will leave you a big tip."

"Thanks," Zuzu said, "Leave bills; they don't make as much noise as coins." At this, Janis cackled, but her laugh made Jimi claw the table again.

"What can I bring you to eat?" Zuzu asked, order pad in hand.

"Toast," Jimi said.

"What kinda toast, darlin'?"

"Yes. Toast."

"Just bring him some lightly buttered wheat," Janis said. "That okay, brother?"

"K."

"Great," Janis said. "And I'll have a ham and cheese omelet – swiss, please. No potatoes unless… Ooh, do you have any *Tat'r Nips?*"

"Got some in yesterday. They're yours, honey."

Zuzu stepped away, and Janis continued: "So, Jiminy Cricket, any concerns from your perspective?"

Jimi leaned forward. Sort of. He opened his eyes to the size of piggy bank slots. "How to find him…"

"Our father – assuming he *is* our father? I mean, I guess we can have a paternity test when the time comes, but… Are you asking how we'll find him in the first place?"

"Uh-huh."

"Good question," Janis said. "I think we have to trust Sonny on this. I know he's got Pepper working some angles, right? Other than that, all we have is the letter from Winnie, from our *birth mother*, that is." Janis reached into the sizeable cat-shaped bag at her side and pulled out a folded sheet of paper. She smoothed it on the table and began softly reading aloud the letter Pepper had typed, apparently from Winnie's recorded dictation:

Hello, kids. It's me, your new-old mom again. I guess before I ask you to take on the mission I mentioned in the video, I should tell you more about the man I need you to find. Your father. We called him Jaybird at Woodstock, but we might have been the only ones who called him that back then. More about that in a bit.

First, keep in mind [coughing] … keep in mind that everything I'm about to tell you about him is from damn near 25 years ago. People change. Some people change a lot, but I have a feeling Jaybird is the kind of guy who doesn't change much at all because he doesn't need to change. I'm pretty sure he's always known who he was meant to be, so I doubt he's ... [inaudible word or words] from that over the years. He'd be older now, of course ... [inaudible 3 seconds followed by more coughing] somewhere, and maybe even dead. Who knows? I hope not. I surely do want to be reunited with him, even if it's just my ashes at this point. [Crying, words inaudible for approximately 35 seconds]

... Anyway, in August of '69, Jaybird had this long gray hair, nearly white, even at his age. I think he was maybe in his mid-twenties then. He was slender and tall enough, maybe five-ten, give or take. [Coughing] He liked ... [inaudible 4 seconds] wore round glasses, too. Granny glasses, we called 'em. He said that by looking through those focused circles, it was like looking through a connection between past, present, and future. He said circles were eternal – no beginning and no end. He said circles are the stuff of life itself. He talked like that, your father did. Maybe it was the weed, but I think it was some genuine, truthful, amazing shit. Sounds a bit crazy now, perhaps, but sure never sounded crazy when he said it. Just kinda beautiful.

Speaking of beautiful, behind those glasses were the most beautiful, sensitive, blue-gray eyes. Soulful as shit, those eyes were. Sure wish ... [inaudible 5 seconds] and not much to go on so far, I guess. Unfortunately, I don't have much more to tell you. But here are the best clues you'll need, I think [extended coughing]:

...First, he has a tattoo on his hip – left butt cheek as I recall. A few months after we got separated from Jaybird at Woodstock, Sonny got a tattoo to match. Sonny's is on his right side, but same basic spot. I sketched it out for the tattoo guy. Sonny was blind by then, so he couldn't verify, but I'm pretty sure it's a close match. Find the man with that tattoo and you've found your father. He said the tattoo was of a Jaybird, so that's why we called him that. He liked it. Maybe the name stuck, maybe not.

So, where could he be? That's the $64,000 question, isn't it? Actually, the several million-dollar question, I guess. [Extended coughing] Sonofabitch I hate being sick! Anyway, all I can tell you is this: At Woodstock, lots of people were going around naked, but Jaybird, your father, was that way practically all the time. Naked wasn't just a Woodstock thing for him, but a way of life. He said he was born naked *and hoped to live that way as much as possible for as long as possible. [Coughing] So, unless he's changed his ways – and believe me when I say that nudity seemed to be almost a religion for him – well, I suspect your best bet is to search for him among the nudists, wherever they are.*

One other thing: When we got separated at Woodstock, he had just been attacked by some nutjob with a hook for a hand. The guy was a cop or undercover agent of some sort, and he was trying to … [word inaudible] your father for some reason I don't think we ever understood. [Coughing] Anyway, the guy's hook caught Jaybird by the corner of his mouth and ripped it open. Badass gash, had to hurt like hell, so he's probably got some kind of a scar.

Now, because this cop or agent guy was after him, it's possible Jaybird ended up in jail, but maybe Sonny can rule that out before he gets you involved. If you're reading this now, though, I guess you are on the hunt after all. Thank you for that. [Coughing]

Good luck. I … [inaudible words] Jaybird back to Woodstock by 3:00 on Saturday the 13th. "Back to the garden," as they say. Full circle. Past, present, and future, and all that shit.

That's it. Thanks again. Love, Mom.

After several moments of silence, Jimi leaned forward and sipped his coffee. His eyes were half-open now. "Among the nudists," he said. "Wherever they are."

* * *

Meanwhile, in his trailer at the Grin and Bare It Family Nudist Campground, Jaybird woke to a scream. It was brief but loud and followed by cursing. He could guess what happened.

He grabbed his glasses from the nightstand, lowered his feet to the trailer floor, and padded the ten steps to the open doorway of the bathroom. His cat was there, pawing violently at the shower curtain. Jaybird cleared his throat. The cat suspended his attack. The visitor in the shower turned off the water and threw back the curtain.

"That cat is, is, is, well, he's a *psycho*! Scared the bejesus outta me!"

"Sweet little Anthony Purrkins?" Jaybird said coyly. He picked up the cat and stroked its silky sable brown fur. "Why would you call him a psycho?"

"Little shit probably has a knife around here someplace. He's a full-on Norman Bates!"

"And yet you survived the attack, Robin dear," Jaybird said, smiling.

"No thanks to you," Robin said. "At least hand me a towel."

Jaybird grinned. "Give me a minute. I kinda like the view."

"You're as twisted as your cat."

Jaybird sighed, ushered Anthony Purrkins out of the small steamy space, and pulled the bath towel from the rack over the toilet. "Here you go," he said. "You're up early."

"And you were very late to bed," Robin said in a muffled voice beneath the towel. "Watching that video ... what was it, *Woodstock*? Remind me how old you are again."

"Old enough to know better but young enough to not give a damn," Jaybird said. "Coffee?"

"No thanks," Robin said, drying off lower parts. "Gotta go to town and get some provisions for the Grill before lunch. Might stop by the church on the way to, ya know, confess my sins. Especially after last night."

Jaybird stroked the scar at the corner of his mouth. "Did we fool around last night?"

Robin handed over the damp towel and stepped past him, their naked bodies touching briefly. "I didn't say *we* fooled around. But horny and alone in bed inevitably lead to, well, ya know…"

"Got it," Jaybird said. "Next time, perhaps?" He folded the towel and placed it over the rack, and then joined Anthony Purrkins, who was in the bedroom watching Robin dress.

"Your cat is a psycho *and* a voyeur. Big-time Norman Bates."

Jaybird shrugged. "What can I say – I guess I just like bringing in strays of questionable moral fiber."

"Funny stuff. I'd love to stay and laugh, but I'm running late."

Quickly dressed, but with hair still damp and unruly, Robin planted a kiss on Jaybird's forehead and stepped out the exterior bedroom door. A tall hedge hid the door from the view of nearby trailer dwellers.

"Speak kindly of me at confession," Jaybird said, "and don't trip over the gnomes!" He closed the door, picked up the cat, and looked him in the eye. "Well played, Anthony Purrkins. Well played."

CHAPTER 8

(In Which We "Read" a Cat with Janis, Discover dickTat'rs, and Get Ready to Roll in Rather Distinctive Vehicles)

Mid-morning

AFTER BREAKFAST, JANIS HAD A CLIENT APPOINTMENT SHE COULDN'T cancel: a troubled cat needed to chat. Jimi went with her.

Inside a small and thin-walled apartment painted the color of grapefruit juice, they met the cat's human. Gretchen was a gruff forty-something bone-thin woman whose streaked hair, wide eyes, and splotchy black eye shadow made her look like a lemur. Between drags on her Virginia Slims cigarette, she said it was okay for Jimi to stay and observe as long as it was all right with Horace (her rather tubby tabby cat). Horace gave a thumbless thumbs up, telepathically, through Janis.

And so it began, in silence at first, with Janis and Horace sizing one another up. Much meowing and trilling and purring then ensued (from both Horace and Janis). This was followed by Janis offering periodic affirmations in English: "I hear you," and "I can see why that would make you question your place in the household," and "Just remember that love can manifest itself in many ways, even ones that might seem like anger," and "Remember that overeating doesn't make the problems go away." Jimi wanted to laugh a few times, but as the session wore on, he found himself touched and even a little amazed at the earnestness of it all for everyone – Janis, Horace and especially Gretchen, whose lemur eyes were streaking.

The session wound down with Janis saying to the cat, "I thank you, young sir, for sharing your concerns. Thank you for your honesty and your willingness to work through this problem. I respect you. I affirm you."

Then, after respectful nods and a nuzzling of foreheads, Janis smiled, and the tabby lumbered into the bathroom to take a shit.

"Well?" Gretchen finally asked, stubbing out a Slim. "What's his problem?"

"You want me to cut to the chase? Reveal the big furry issue at the root of all others?"

"Yes, yes, what is it?"

"He hates his name," Janis said.

"He hates his name?"

"Hates his name."

"Why does he hate his name?"

"Well, to be frank—"

"No, no," Gretchen interrupted, "his name is Horace, not Frank."

Janis cleared her throat. "To be perfectly *blunt*," she continued, "*Horace* says there's an awful lot of yelling in this household, and that his name – 'Horace' – sounds too much like when your husband yells at you to 'Get your *whore ass* outta here!'"

Silence.

Janis smiled. "Or something to that effect."

"Hmmm…" Gretchen mused. "I guess I could call him something else." She turned to face Jimi. Made flirty eyes at him, he thought, although it was hard to tell. "What's your name again?" Gretchen asked him.

"Jimi," said Jimi. "J-i-m-i."

"J-i-m-i, Jimi…" the lemur repeated.

"Yes, Jimi," said Jimi.

"Interesting. Well, maybe I can just call the cat Elmer or something. I'll give it some thought."

From the bathroom, they could hear scratching in the litter box. A covering of poop, perhaps a symbolic burial of a shunned identity.

Janis continued: "Actually, your cat already has a new name in mind."

"A new name?"

"A new name."

"What kind of new name?"

"Well," Janis began, "he wants to be called…" She paused. "He wants to be called 'Oh, God, Oh, God'."

"*Oh, God, Oh, God?*" Jimi and Gretchen said together.

"Yes," Janis said. "Oh, God, Oh, God."

"Oh, God, Oh God," Gretchen repeated. "Why on Earth...?"

Janis sat up straight. "He wants to be called Oh, God, Oh God because, well, out of all the words that get thrown about in this house, those words have the most loving vibe."

"You can't be serious," Gretchen said.

"Very much so," Janis assured her. "Straight from the source's meowth. Of course, he might not mind being called Horace if the hateful yelling simply stops around here."

At that, Gretchen chuffed and shook her head. She then wiped her eye stains, took as deep a breath as a heavy smoker could take and loudly called out, "Oh, God, oh, God!"

A neighbor banged angrily on the wall. Nonetheless, the former Horace gallumped back into the room. Heeding the call of his new name. Affirming his affirmation.

Janis accepted payment in cash, sixty dollars, including tip. She smiled and nodded at Oh, God, Oh, God and Gretchen, and pulled from her pocket a small stack of business cards. "Tell your friends," she said.

On the way out, Jimi picked up one of the cards:

Janis Grack, Cat Psychic

Anyone Can Understand a Dog, But It Takes a Lesbian to "Get" Your Pussy!

* * *

LilBuckaroo often heard voices from inside his head. Well, only one voice that was not his own.

His late father, Denny Muckle DePew, spoke to him frequently in quiet times, often urging his son to act in ways that seemed, even to LB at times, foolhardy. Still, fathers knew best, didn't they? Especially dead ones?

That very morning, for example, Denny DePew's voice had told LilBuckaroo to quit staring at those cases of unsold *lickTat'r* chips lining his bedroom walls and do something about them. Denny did not, however, share any fatherly advice about what, precisely, his son should do. For that, LB would be on his own. So, he lay in bed that morning, pondering the situation.

The problems with *lickTat'rs*, LB had come to realize, were several. First, product quality was flawed. The processed chips were supposed to be a sturdy and consistent saddle shape, something his food engineer called a "hyperbolic paraboloid." Consistent in shape they were; sturdy, they were not. Hence, too much breakage inside the round canisters. This was a problem to be fixed in future production runs by marking cases of chips as "fragile" and by slightly thickening each chip.

The packaging was problematic, as well. A smiley face placed too close to the lower-case letter "l" in 'lick' made it appear instead to be a lower-case letter 'd'. Consumers mistook the brand name, therefore, to be *dickTat'rs*. Further fueling this misconception was the appearance of the product inside. To wit, per a syndicated newspaper article that appeared nationwide on a slow news day:

> "LickTat'r™ chips were intended to be pink in color, according to product creator LilBuckaroo Muckle DePew (Editor's note: yes, this is his real name). 'They are supposed to be deep pink and look like a tongue,' DePew said, 'in keeping with our marketing tagline, 'The Chip That Licks You Back'.' However, production problems led to variations in the spray-applied Red Dye #2.1 coloration. Some consumers reported the chips appeared to have faces. One buyer recognized Hitler-like mustaches on chips in his canister; another saw not a tongue but a face resembling Mao Tse Tung.
>
> "This has led consumers nationwide to angrily return their purchases, commonly calling the product 'dickTat'rs,' a misnomer further bolstered by still more buyers who said the chip designs resembled male genitals. While prized in certain urban bars, the genitalia-like chips have, nonetheless, been removed from all food and retail outlets, including grocery stores and all Woodchuck Chucky's children's party restaurants.
>
> "Sources confirm that lickTat'r chips are not affiliated with the hugely popular Tat'r Nips™ brand even though DePew is the son

of Tat'r Nips creator Winnie Muckle DePew. The elder Ms. DePew declined to comment for this story, pending possible legal action."

And there it was.

As LilBuckaroo had revisited the details at the urging of his dead and chatty father, he experienced a couple of epiphanies. First, his mother's death may have invalidated the injunction she'd filed to keep him from selling the product (he would check with an attorney about this later – maybe – but not his uncle Sonny). And second, one line from the news report had suddenly jumped out at him: *"...prized in certain urban bars..."*

After his recent popular appearance at the Hole(s) in the Wall Pub, it occurred to LB that he may have a market for his product after all. And since he was soon to embark on a road trip anyway, why not take *dickTat'rs* – yes, he would proudly embrace that name – along for the ride. What could it hurt? And if one type of tavern could be a viable market for the chips, maybe others would, too. Plenty of bars in the world, right? Suddenly, his prospects for specialty chip moguldom brightened.

So, that morning he had packed the white Caddy with his luggage, a cache of *dicktatr's*, and his construction worker outfit, complete with hardhat, mustache (just in case), and the correct glue (he hoped).

He then called Pepper and learned that Sonny and the twins were likely to embark on their quest that afternoon after she returned with a rental car from Before You Go Go, which, she said, rather abruptly before hanging up, she needed to do right away.

* * *

At half-past 11 a.m. at Before You Go-Go Car Rental, a lanky rental agent sat long-legs-across-desk, heels out of his loafers, in front of a concrete block wall painted with their rather uninspired tagline: "Call Before You Go-Go *Before You Go-Go!*" Indeed, someone had phoned in just as Pepper entered through the cowbelled glass door. Fielding a relentless stream of questions from the caller, the agent gave Pepper the just-a-minute gesture of an upraised index finger.

This he did every 33 seconds, on average, for more than eight minutes. Yes, Pepper was counting.

After several minutes, however, to keep her sanity, Pepper started playing a small mental game of subtle intimidation. It went like this: Every time the agent lifted that damn finger, she stepped halfway closer to his well-worn soles. From six feet to three feet, from three feet to 18 inches, from 18 to 9. At the 9-inch mark, his shoes twitched nervously, and at four and a half inches, the agent retracted his legs from the desktop. But since his feet were already halfway out of his loafers, both shoes dropped over the front edge of the desk. Sweat beaded on the agent's forehead. He smiled. Raised that finger again. And Pepper inched forward once more.

The agent practically screamed into the phone, "Gotta go!" and in one fluid motion, slammed down the receiver and rolled his chair backward until it crashed into the concrete wall behind him. Pepper kicked his shoes beneath the desk.

Releasing a soft, nervous laugh, the agent – Todd Z. according to his badge – leaned down, corralled the shoes, and put them back on. "Thank you, ma'am," he managed. "Sorry about that. How can I help you today?"

Pepper smiled and took two steps back to give him some relief. "Need to rent a car, of course."

Todd Z. stood. "Super. Super-duper. Plenty of cars, plenty of cars," he said, making a broad, sweeping motion toward the lot. "How long will you be needing a rental?"

"The rest of this week," she said. "Probably."

"Excellent!" agent Todd said, a bit too eager. But suddenly, he seemed to recognize Pepper – and his demeanor changed. He smiled. "Um, we've rented to you before, haven't we?"

"I've been in here before, yes."

"And you're the one with the blind boss or boyfriend or—"

"Both actually, at least once upon a time," she said. "But don't worry, he won't be driving the car this time. It will be his niece or nephew at the wheel. Probably both at various times."

"So, you said once upon a time... Does that mean he's no longer your boyfriend?"

"Yes, that's correct, if it matters. Can we focus on the business at hand?"

The agent exhaled. "Certainly. Thank you for clarifying your present status. Anyway, I'll need to see licenses for the primary drivers as soon as possible, of course. Perhaps they can stop by later." He then directed Pepper toward the lot. Passing through the door, she saw her reflection in the glass and adjusted her wig.

"So, one driver, two passengers, plenty of cars at your disposal."

"Could be a third passenger, too, in a few days, so four people total," Pepper said. "We'll want something big and roomy, plenty of comfort for a long trip." She desperately wanted to add, "*If you have a hearse with a giant chicken on top, that would be perfect,*" but held back. Instead, she said, "A minivan perhaps or something like that."

Todd Z. said, "Got you covered. Right this way."

Three minivans sat in a corner of the lot, all looking drab and thoroughly, unsatisfyingly perfect for the mission. "Each of these beauties is very well appointed," the agent said, staring not at the rentals, but at Pepper. When she noticed his attention, he looked away and added, "all automatics, air, power everything. Just comes down to color, make, and model, really."

"And the price, of course," Pepper said.

"Well, if your boss isn't driving, we can make you a pretty good deal."

"I'd rather have your *best* deal?" Pepper said, with a subtle wink.

Again, Todd Z. laughed nervously. "Well, frankly, our best deal is on a vehicle I doubt you'd want at this time even though they do seem popular in certain places."

"Try me."

"Um, the vehicle we're having trouble renting lately is this one over here." The agent directed her to a large white vehicle that looked quite familiar.

Pepper stared, her mouth open. After a moment, she said, "Tell me this is *not* the O.J. Simpson Bronco."

Another nervous laugh. Agent Todd seemed to sense he was on the brink of losing the rental. "No, ma'am, of course not. I can state unequivocally this is *not* the Bronco from that recent low-speed chase in California. Nor is that one over there," he added, pointing to a virtual twin Bronco at the end of the row.

"Sure looks like it," Pepper said.

"Well, yes, these are Bronco XLTs, and they are white—"

"And if I rented one, it *would* stick out like a sore thumb on the highway these days, wouldn't it?"

"Well, I suppose it might." The agent's eyes twitched. "But keep in mind that any of these other vehicles – these minivans, for instance – would make an excellent—"

"I'll take the Bronco," Pepper said.

* * *

Across the street from Before You Go-Go, in the parking lot of a local burger joint, sat another large white vehicle, this one a 1971 two-door Cadillac convertible with Cotillion White exterior and Dark Carmine interior with leather seats. The car was fully optioned as purchased new by Buck Muckle the day his grandson was born. In fact, except for a few parking lot dings and the massive set of steer horns permanently affixed to the grille, the Caddy was like new. It was LilBuckaroo's pride and joy.

Through the windshield, he watched Pepper discuss the Bronco with the rental agent. *That's my girl*, he thought. *It'll be easy to keep my eyes on that one.* The notion made LilBuckaroo grin so broadly it cracked open the skin above his upper lip again. Groaning in pain, he reached into the glove box and pulled out a small jar of petroleum jelly. He popped the cap and slathered the goo beneath his nose.

Behind him, the smell of burgers greasily perfumed the air. His stomach growled. So, when Pepper followed the rental agent back inside his concrete hovel, LilBuckaroo drove the massive Caddy to the drive-thru lane. The speaker was broken, so LB pulled around the building for a face-to-face order at the first window. A spiky-haired teen boy – suspiciously skinny for a fast-food worker – took LB's order and payment without making eye contact. But when handing LilBuckaroo his change, the boy looked up and said, "What happened to your face? Flash fire?"

"Not exactly," LB grumbled, "but keep it up and I'll make sure *you* get fired in a flash!"

The boy said, "Dude," and turned away. As the Caddy began rolling toward the food pickup window, the boy yelled to the grill cook, "Cheeseburger Deluxe combo, SOTO." (SOTO, of course, being code for Spit On This One.)

LilBuckaroo enjoyed his extra-juicy burger on the way to Sonny's office. There, he pulled into a strategic shadowy parking spot behind the Kurls for Gurls beauty salon, slouched behind the Eldorado's steering wheel, and hid behind the most recent Sunday newspaper. Minutes later, Pepper pulled the Bronco up the alley and parked beside the office. LB lowered the paper a tad so he could watch her walk in, hips swiveling and bouffant bouncing. He licked his greased-up lips.

The twins arrived a few minutes later in a car with cat ears on the roof. *People are crazy*, LB thought, as he watched them through the Caddy's steer horns.

When the door closed behind them, LB started to fold up the paper. A small headline stopped him:

NOSTALGIA TRIP TO WOODSTOCK RUNS OUT OF GAS.

Quickly scanning the report, a reprint from the August 2nd Washington Post, LilBuckaroo caught several key phrases:

"... Reunion at Yasgur's Farm ...   re-creation of the 1969 Woodstock concert at the original site ... scratched."

LB lowered the paper and stared at the sky, processing what this meant. If he was interpreting this correctly, even if Sonny and the twins succeeded in finding Janis and Jimi's father, they couldn't bring him to an event that doesn't exist. Thus, their mission would fail, and he, LilBuckaroo Muckle DePew, rightful heir to the *Tat'r Nips* fortune, would retain his full inheritance. (Notwithstanding those crummy rescued Poodles.)

A good day just turned great, he thought. Except that he then saw another article, same paper, same page:

OFFICIAL WOODSTOCK 25TH ANNIVERSARY FESTIVAL EXPECTS 200,000+.

Another Woodstock? The *Official* Woodstock?

LB fidgeted. Desperate for answers, he needed to *do* something. So, he exited the Caddy and took up a surveillance position behind a butterfly bush at Kurls for Gurls, hoping to see what was going on inside the law office. But as he stood there, the blooms and perm chemicals assaulted his nose. He sneezed hard. The chapped skin above his lip tore open again.

* * *

"Did you hear that awful yowl?" Jimi asked from inside the law office.

"Pretty sure that was *not* a cat," Janis said. "Isn't there a psych hospital near here?" Not expecting an answer, she took Jimi by the arm and they approached the desk.

Pepper and Sonny leaned forward and said, in unison: "Well?"

"Actually, no, I'm not well at all," Jimi said. "I have a hangup."

"Hangover," Janis corrected.

"That, too," Jimi said. "Other than that, I'm fine. Thanks for asking."

Sonny cleared his throat. "Actually, we meant, 'Welllll … have you *decided?* Are you on board to go find your father?'"

Janis pursed her lips, caught her blue reflection in Jimi's Aviators again, and then spoke for the two of them: "We thought about it and talked it over. Yes, we're in. Crazy as that sounds." Jimi nodded, and Janis continued: "I just have one question. You mentioned the will. Can we get a look at that? Just seems like something we should ask about."

"Certainly," Sonny said. "It's a fairly lengthy document, of course. Is there anything in particular you were curious about?"

"Well, yes," Janis said. "Curious about the money as it relates to the mission and our part in it. Just want to make sure the ducks are in a row."

"Okay, speaking of ducks," Sonny said, turning toward Pepper Duckenfield, "Ducks, do you have the will handy?"

"Sure, it's right here, a copy of it with the papers you wanted to take with you."

"Then please read the section pertaining to the mission, if you would."

Janis and Jimi pulled reception-area chairs forward and sat while Pepper scanned the document for the relevant section. "Here it is," she said. "Something, something, something, and then… *do hereby magnanimously bequeath to twin siblings Jimi Johansen and Janis*

Grack (hereafter referred to as 'The Twins'), both believed to be residing in Indianapolis, Indiana as of the date of this instrument, individually, the sum of ten thousand dollars plus one-fifth of the remaining financial assets of my estate —"

Outside, another yowl, more mournful than the first.

"Mental hospital is six blocks from here," Pepper said. "But sometimes the patients get loose. Now, where was I? Oh yes ... *individually, the sum of ten thousand dollars plus one-fifth of the remaining financial assets of my estate provided they accompany my adopted brother, J. Buckingham Muckle II (hereafter, 'Sonny') and collectively collaborate to complete the following mission as herein described: Locate The Twins' biological father (hereafter 'Father'), whose name and place of residence are, as of the date of this instrument, unknown, per the description of Father provided in Exhibit A —"*

Pepper looked up at Janis and Jimi. "I believe Exhibit A was the letter you've already reviewed," she said.

"And the ten thousand mentioned in the will is in addition to the money you've already received," Sonny clarified.

Pepper resumed scanning the will: "...Locate your father blah blah blah per the description yada yada yada..."

"Gotta love legal jargon," Janis said.

"And, together, The Twins and Sonny and Father, must return for a reunion at Woodstock during the weekend in which the 25th anniversary of the original 1969 festival is to be observed, and reach the destination by the date and time specified in Exhibit A. During said reunion, the parties are to spread my ashes at the site and say whatever is in their hearts."

"As you can tell from the wording of the will," Sonny added, "per our earlier discussion, neither of you are specifically identified as Winnie's biological children, so there would be no legal standing to any claim that you are entitled – by birthright – to any portion of her estate. Your only option is to complete the assignment as directed."

"I just have one more question, then," Jimi said. He was staring at a large object on Pepper's desk. "Is mom here with us right now?"

"Was wondering about that myself," Pepper said. "Hoping that's not just a new paperweight."

"Ah," Sonny said. "Guess I overlooked that little detail." He stepped forward to the desk, felt for the urn, and cradled it between his hands. "Children, your mother will be joining us on our mission."

CHAPTER 9
(In Which We Meet Max's Experts and Anthony Purrkins's
Flat People While LilBuckaroo Gets Shunned)

Midday

MAX THIBODEAUX WAS ON A MISSION OF HIS OWN.

Parked in his black Pontiac Bonneville near the T-intersection which faced the Peebles's Westover Village two-story brick home in Arlington, Virginia, he watched for comings and goings. Although he couldn't tell what was going on inside the house, that would soon change, as Max's operatives were ready to install listening devices at strategic locations inside. But for the time being, Max could only watch in silence, wait for the subjects to leave their house, and hope to remain unnoticed when they did.

All so Jennings Prokoff might – *might* – get a scoop. And maybe – *maybe* – a ratings boost. And perhaps – *perhaps* – a new contract with a healthy salary increase. All so Prokoff could continue to exercise his rather keen abilities to sit, wear a tie without appearing stiff, and stare into a camera while half-smirking and half-slurring words written by someone else. A *team* of someone elses, actually; writers tasked with making sure, per network edict, that "no more than two slurrable words ever appear in tandem, and with no more than fifteen total slurrable words in any single report, unless said report is delivered in two or more segments separated by field reporter engagement, remote news delivery, and/or commercial break(s)." This edict resulted from focus group feedback about Prokoff that concluded "one or two slurred words here and there" were endearing. Three or more slurs grouped together in a single sentence, on the other hand, tended to "make him look drunk." Which, of course, he often was. But endearingly so. Two slurrable words at a time.

Despite the writers' best efforts, however, Prokoff tended to go "off script" with *psheudo folkshy ashides* that frequently became easy fodder for late-night comics. Ironically, his bumbling impediment contributed to high ratings. So did human interest stories and newsworthy scoops. And those were Max Thibodeaux's specialty.

"Why do you have to shpy on him at all?" Prokoff had wondered during a late-night follow-up phone call with Max. "Why can't you jusht go up and tell him you want him to be a human interesht feashure on the evening newsh? A goddamn feashure with Jenningsh Prokoff, no lessh!"

Max had sighed and explained that no one as stubbornly proud as Pete Peebles would want his one great *failing* exposed unless and until it could be cast in the light of a grand triumph – justice deferred, but justice finally served. Further, Max had continued, federal agents – even retired ones – didn't always have the best relationships with the media. That would make the story even harder to get, and Max's gut told him this could be a gripping story, an award-winning and ratings-boosting story: good versus evil, hero against villain, cat pursuing mouse.

"That is *if* we don't blow our cover and spook Peebles before the game is afoot," Max had contended.

"Award-winning, eh?" Prokoff mused.

"Very possibly, yes."

"A real patriotic human interesht shtory, eh?"

Max took a deep breath. "Most likely a watershed moment in American media," he riffed. "This could very well be a defining journalistic allegory of the, um, well, of the power and invincibility of the American spirit. They'll teach this case study in journalism schools for decades, centuries perhaps. Might even name a school after you."

"Of coursh," Prokoff had readily concurred. "And good for ratingsh, too, you say?"

"Certainly," Max said. "With the right promos, why the hell not?"

"Promosh, awardsh, and ratingsh…" Prokoff had repeated, trailing off into extended silence, before finally adding, "Jusht keep me poshted."

Which brought Max to watch the Westover Village home, car windows down, sweating and waiting and counting on the fact that even though Pete Peebles had spent decades in the business of surveillance, he probably had few worries of *being* the one surveilled. A few minutes later, at quarter past noon, Pete and Penny and Princess Petunia stepped out into the warm breeze and began a leisurely walk. Max figured they might be heading out to grab lunch at J. Edgar's, a venerable greasy spoon three blocks from their home. It was a dive that Pete – according to Max's quickly gathered intel – frequented whenever he could, not unlike the Quantico North Bar in DC. As they headed up the street, Pete carried Petunia in the crook of his good arm, his hook dangling. Penny followed a few paces behind.

Even if they were just out for a walk, Max figured they'd be gone a good ten to fifteen minutes. So, when his subjects vanished in the distance, Max looked to his right just past the street corner. He nodded to the driver of a *Summer Breeze AC Repair* van and then sent a simple alphanumeric pager message to the electronics crew inside: GO. Three rubber-gloved and coveralled "electro-boys" exited the van, walked quickly but casually up the embankment and disappeared around the side of the Peebles home, toward the back yard where they could practice their craft away from street view.

From previous engagements, Max knew that each man had a role even before they gained access to the home: Chubbo Chuck was the security scout, looking for cameras, electric eyes, or signs of wired security systems; Ernie Joe was the neighborhood scout, scanning nearby homes and paying special attention to windows with direct sightlines; and the third man, Hez, was the team lead and "entry technician," a veteran B and E guy skilled in unlawful entry, picking locks and opening safes if necessary. First, however, Hez would test the door to see if it was unlocked. Chuck and Ernie would do the same for ground-floor windows. Max remained out front, stationed in his Pontiac on the street, serving as lookout in case the homeowners returned prematurely, and ready to intercept if necessary.

Several minutes passed; clearly, Hez had found it necessary to pick the door lock. Finally, Max received a pager message that read simply: IN. Soon after, Max's listening device receivers came to life with voices: "Living Room test," Ernie said. "Kitchen test," followed

Chuck; and then Hez came through with "Bedroom test" and "Den test." The sound was clear on all four units – the boys were good at their jobs.

Max responded by pager: "ALL OK VACATE." Within a minute, the men had reappeared at the corner of the house, scouted street activity, entered their vehicle and pulled away, with Hez driving. The van turned at the T and stopped beside Max's Bonneville. Through his open driver's side window, Max tossed an envelope filled with cash. Hez caught it and winked.

The electro-boys drove away, and Max settled in more comfortably behind the steering wheel. He yawned. Having gotten virtually no sleep, he was close to dozing off. *Five minutes,* he thought. *A five-minute catnap would help.* So, he reached into the glovebox and extracted the kitchen timer he kept on hand for such occasions, turned the dial five ticks, and settled in again. The ratchety spring-loaded dial provided drowsy white noise as it wound its way slowly back toward zero.

A set of knuckles rapped suddenly on his passenger's side door.

"What the fuck!"

"Relax, Max. So jumpy today!" It was Harry Lucas, Max's printing guy and occasional forger. He held a card and envelope in his hand. "Here you go," he said through the open car window. "You said this was urgent."

"Jesus, Harry. How'd ya know where to find me?"

Harry pointed to the address on the envelope. "Figured you'd be here on watch and thought you might need this sooner than later. Again, rush job and all. Worked through the night to have it ready for ya."

Max sat up straighter in the driver's seat. He half-smiled. "Just wasn't expecting any visitors on my, um, stakeout." He took the card and envelope and examined each detail, even the faked cancellation of the stamp. "Looks like you've outdone yourself, Harry," he said.

Harry knelt beside the car door. "Ya know, I looked it up. This 'Special Agent's Benevolent Fund' is a real thing. Got their logo and even matched their typography."

Max read the card in detail:

Confirmation:
A generous donation in the amount of $10,000 has been made to the
Special Agent's Benevolent Fund, in the name of:
Special Agent Peter Peebles, Ret.

This donation will help fund special programs and
provide assistance to Agents, their spouses and families,
as well as innocent victims of Agency actions.*
Donor: Jay Finch, Jr.
* In some cases, a portion of donated funds may be applied toward damages
and/or legal fees
in defense of alleged illegal Agency crimes and/or misdemeanors.

"Looks totally legit," Max said. "Even the bullshit disclaimer."

Harry surveyed the neighborhood and lowered his voice to a whisper. "So, Maxy, who's this Peebles guy, anyway? And the donor, this Finch dude? I'm guessing this is a scam and that no donation was actually made, right?"

"The less you know about these two, the better, Harry," Max said. "Let's just say your little work of artful deception here should help light a fire that might bring a fugitive to justice." He admired Harry's handiwork again. "In any event, it should make a helluva story for Jennings Prokoff."

"The drunk anchor guy?"

Max smiled again. "I've said too much already." He reached into his wallet, counted out five fifty-dollar bills, and handed them to Harry. "Payment for services well-rendered," he said. Then he inserted the card into the envelope, sealed it, and gave it back to Harry. "Do me a favor and put this in the mailbox over there, will ya?"

Harry stood and backed away from the car. "Isn't it a Federal crime for a regular schmo to put something in a mailbox?"

"Could be, Harry, but I doubt you'll attract as much attention as I would approaching a door in this neighborhood. In case you hadn't noticed, you're decidedly less black than me." He pulled another fifty from his wallet and handed it to the forger. "Does this help?"

As Harry pocketed the cash and stepped away, Max made sure the Peebles bunch were still nowhere in sight. And after watching

Harry drop the envelope into the box and skulk away, Max slumped in the car seat again and closed his eyes. The timer went off immediately.

Less than an hour later, Max spied the trio returning home, Pete's hook glinting in the sun as he walked. When they unlocked their front door and went inside, Max closed his eyes so he could focus on the listening devices. Small talk and then extended silence until 1:30 when the regular postal carrier – not Harry Lucas – dropped mail into the box without noticing the envelope already there. Moments later, Penny opened the front door and retrieved the haul.

"Bills mostly," Max heard her say over the front room listening device. "Also, something here from the Special Agent's Benevolent Fund," she called out. Through another device, Max heard Pete say, "Go ahead and open it. Probably the bastards wanting a donation. Not even retired one complete lousy fucking week and they're already hitting me up."

An audible sigh from Penny was followed by a few moments of silence. And then, "Honey, you may want to look at this … but I don't think you're gonna like it much."

Soon the tirade began. It continued unabated for ten full minutes before Pete's anger pivoted to directing the mission at hand. Twenty-five minutes after that, Max had the details he needed: Pete, Penny, and the dog would leave first thing in the morning (driving because Princess Petunia feared flying). Destination: East Kibosh, South Carolina. Penny – having demanded a nice place to stay – made reservations by phone. Unfortunately, she never mentioned the name of the lodging as Max could hear only her side of the conversation. As soon as she hung up the phone, Pete said. "Don't count on me to be a white-socks-and-sandals tourist. I'm gonna be busy. Once and for all, I'm gonna find that money, and then, by God, I'm gonna get that goddamned sonofabitch Jay Finch, Jr., wherever the fuck he is!"

* * *

In his trailer at the Grin and Bare It, Jay Finch, Jr., now going by the alias Jayson B. Stockwood, was getting ready to head out to the Moon-Your-Mama Bar to prep for the evening. His cat, Anthony Purrkins – a three-year-old silky sable-brown Burmese, compact and solid with surprising athleticism and a predilection for sneak attacks – was happily dozing after watching TV. Being a Burmese, Anthony Purrkins could, unlike most cats, see images on television as actual moving pictures rather than mere flashes of modestly colored light. Purrkins thought of television as the box where the tiny *flat people* lived. Inside this box, they went about their days, some in color, some not. Mostly the flat people in the box wore clothes. *This was strange*, the cat thought.

Anthony Purrkins even had his favorite programs. Despite being a three-year-old, he didn't care much for the cartoon flat people; they were loud (like the commercial people), and they moved stiffly and threw solid black shadow puddles in their attempts to look less flat. But he *did* like the people in the land without color that Daddy Jayson would soon switch the box to. Those people wore gray hats. They drove gray cars with gray tires protected by gray metal balloons (was *fenders* the word?). Sometimes they said funny words like *flivver* and *flim-flam* and *grifter* and *shyster* and *patsy*. Sometimes they used today-words but in different ways than his human – words like *finger, big sleep*, and *canary*. And *private dick*. (That meant something very different in the land without color.)

For now, though, Anthony Purrkins was content to nap. He had just finished watching his most favorite TV people of all, the ones with color who were very – what was the word – *dramatical?* They lived in a place a hidden talker called *"Like Dust in a Whirlwind, So Are the Days of Our Bold and Restless Lives."* Purrkins was addicted to the show and would plan his catnaps to make sure he didn't miss the goings-on of the Talbotts and Mortons and Hopewells. Weekends were frustrating because *Like Dust in a Whirlwind, So Are the Days of Our Bold and Restless Lives* did not come into the TV box then. Fridays were frustrating, too, because there was always something important that was just about to happen, but then the program would end, and the important something wouldn't really happen until Monday. But sometimes the Monday thing would still be happening and keeping him guessing for *several days*. Here it was, Tuesday, for example, and he was still waiting to find out what would happen when Eliza finds Felicity naked in bed with James. Naked was a good thing in the bigger box world where

Anthony Purrkins and Daddy Jayson lived. Inside the small box called TV, however, it sometimes caused fights.

From the shallow places of his nap, Purrkins could hear his human in the shower washing his mostly furless skin. There was little sense for the cat to rally for a surprise attack; Daddy was seldom surprised anymore, even though he sometimes pretended to be. Scaring that *Robin* person earlier, on the other hand, had been most satisfying, and the cat dreamily relived the episode until...

"*Good afternoon, I'm Radiance Reynolds! Coming up on News Watch Tonight at eleven: the latest in the quest to identify a mysterious Good Samaritan who has apparently, for many years in this area, financially assisted people in need.*"

Anthony Purrkins opened his eyes.

"*We have new information about this mystery man, including an eyewitness description from a child who believes he saw the benefactor in action. Don't miss this feel-good story update. That's tonight at eleven, on WTFU.*"

Daddy Jayson, toweling off, stepped into the living room. He threw the towel over his shoulder, opened the newspaper to the TV listings, and then aimed the stick he called the "remote control" at the TV to change the channel. "Bette Davis marathon, Anthony Purrkins. Let's see, it starts soon with *Dangerous,* and then *Dark Victory,* and *Now Voyager* and then *All About Eve*. I'll be home soon after that."

He leaned down to Anthony Purrkins on the sofa, kissed him on the head, and said, in a hopelessly bad Bette Davis voice, "Heaven help me. I love a psychotic!"

* * *

And in Indianapolis, having grown confident his inheritance was assured because of a loophole (thanks to the cancellation of the Woodstock reunion at its original site), LilBuckaroo went to Lafayette Square mall. He normally hated shopping, but this day was different; he wouldn't be spending his money, but his mothers'. A pair of boat shoes and two knit pullovers later, he returned home.

It was getting late, a little past 4:30. LB figured he'd better catch Pepper at the office and tell her he wouldn't be needing her services after all. Generous soul that he was, however, he would offer to take her to dinner. Maybe Popcorn Shrimp at Red Lobster. He'd been wanting to ask Peps out for some time anyway; that blonde bouffant was mesmerizing, and her callous nature reminded him of his mother. (He wondered if such a maternal attraction was a creepy thing or not. He made a mental note to ask his ghost-dad about it later.)

LB called from his bedroom phone. Pepper answered on the third ring.

He waved the newspaper in the air as if she could see it. "Did you see this? The Woodstock reunion is canceled!" he yelled. "There's no way for Sonny and the twins to fulfill the mission now. Woohoo!" He began dancing awkwardly around his bed. "Gonna be rich, gonna be rich, gonna be rich, rich, rich!"

Pepper lowered her right foot from the edge of her desk and capped the bottle of plum-colored nail polish. "Not so fast, *LilBuckaroo*." She only called him that when she wanted to put him in his place.

He stopped dancing. "What? Whaddaya mean, 'not so fast'? It's right here in the paper. Reunion canceled!"

"Yeah, yeah, Prokoff mentioned that last night on the news. You must've missed it – probably too busy earning dollar bills from admirers right then. Anyway, the story's actually few days old, I guess. I won't bore you with the details about why the cancellation doesn't necessarily change anything – you wouldn't understand anyway—"

"Hey, I ain't as dumb as I look, ya know."

Pepper pictured his flaming red upper lip. "Yeah. Right. Anyway, the bottom line is that there's another Woodstock anniversary event happening, so they're still gonna try to find their guy, and if they do, you're still screwed."

LB practically melted onto his bed. He groaned sorrowfully.

"Oh, don't crash and burn like that, LB. It's still a longshot they'll actually find him, let alone get everyone where they need to be in time. Meanwhile, I'm still your best friend because I can keep you informed if – and that's a big if – you need to get involved. In that case, I'll know it and you'll know it. For now, probably best to sit tight and wait for news."

LB rolled off the bed and started pacing. He was silent, but Pepper could imagine the gears grinding, always a sign of trouble. "Don't tell me you're hearing the voice of your daddy again," she said.

"Shhh!" LB covered his free ear but continued pacing. A minute later, he stopped. "I'm going after them," he said.

Pepper shook her head. "Fuck's sake, LB, you don't even know where they're going. Neither do I. Hell, they don't even know where they'll end up yet!"

"You must know something, though, right? Don't you at least know a direction?"

Pepper sighed heavily. "This is what I know," she said. "I know they're headed south, toward Florida. We haven't been able to get any information over the phone from the ASA – that's the American Sunbathing Association – because they strictly protect the privacy of their members. They won't give up any member names or even provide any clues on where to look. All they'll do is share a list of clubs with locations and phone numbers.

Nonetheless, Sonny and the twins want to try to appeal to them in person at their headquarters in Kissimmee. But even if that fails, they're gonna visit nudist clubs near there and coming back north, club-by-club as long as there's time. There's a heavy concentration of nudist places in Florida, so they're playing the odds and starting there. Again, it's a long shot, but it's their last, best, and only real hope."

"Then I should head to Florida, too. I need to peddle my chips anyway."

"You need to what your what?" She could only imagine what that meant. Rather than dwell on images that might spoil her dinner, Pepper forged ahead. "Anyway, LB, in case you didn't know, Florida's a pretty big state. No telling where they'll be at any given time. And besides, you're already way behind."

LB started pacing again but stopped short halfway across the room. "Look," he said. "Even if I don't know where they are right now, I can still go to this ASS place myself and get the same info."

"It's ASA, and I'd advise against it."

"I'll bribe the ASA people."

"Think again."

"Okay, Plan Z, then. Wherever they're headed, they're gonna keep you in the loop, right?"

"Yes, Sonny is supposed to call whenever he has news."

"Then I'll do the same. I'll head south, so I'm at least closer to where they end up, and I'll call you whenever I can for updates. I might be a step or two behind, but I can at least be in the neighborhood."

Pepper slouched. "Look, LB, I'm not gonna stay here in the office 24/7, waiting for you to call."

"I can call you at home."

"Again, not gonna be a hermit waiting to hear from you."

"But you'll be waiting to hear from Sonny."

"Sonny will leave a message at both places."

"Well…" LB was momentarily stumped. "I'll just have to keep trying till I reach you. Or we could set a specific time for me to call each day and night. All I know is I can't just sit around. I need to be moving in the same general direction as our rivals so I can crash the party quickly if I need to."

"I still think it's a mistake," Pepper said.

"My daddy thinks it's the right thing to do," LilBuckaroo said. Over the phone, he heard the law office cowbell jangle.

"Look, LB, call me here between ten and noon each day, and call me at home between five-thirty and six-thirty. Miss your call window and you'll probably be outta luck. Gotta go. My date's here."

Just before Pepper hung up, LilBuckaroo heard her say, "Hi, Todd. Give me just a minute to close up shop before we, um, before we go-go."

CHAPTER 10
*(In Which Winnie and Sonny Pull a Fast One to Reach Woodstock,
and Sonny Explains How They Met Jaybird)*

Late Afternoon

"WINNIE'S PLAN FOR GETTING US TO THE WOODSTOCK FESTIVAL HAD BEEN perfect – if also perfectly devious," Sonny said during the first leg of their trip together. And then he told the twins the story of how it happened:

"Winnie had concocted several plans for getting us out of Indianapolis and to New York without our parents being any the wiser. Without *me* being any the wiser either because she knew I'd blow our cover if she told me too soon. You see, I was the practical one, the cautious one, the I'm-adopted-so-I-can't-make-too-many-mistakes-or-I'll-be-disowned one. It was rubbish, of course, but Winnie decided it was best to keep me in the dark for a while.

"She considered several plans for getting the tickets. It was too risky, she thought, to simply order them and have them mailed to the house where our mother might intercept them. And she didn't really trust anyone else to order them for us. She thought about asking Esperanza, our family housekeeper, but didn't want to put her in a bad position with our parents. And finally, she thought she might be able to get the tickets at a local 'head shop.' But again, it seemed too risky. She figured she'd be seen by an associate of our father and presumed to be a druggie. This, in turn, would *somehow* damage Father's reputation, squelch a crucial business deal and leave the family in financial ruin. And all because she smoked pot. Which she didn't. At least not yet. And besides, she soon learned the only authorized ticket outlets were record stores in the New York City area. Any shop in Indy would only be selling counterfeits.

"The big problem with going to Woodstock – if we could even get there – was that we still lived at home. Sort of. I was 20 and studying law at IU in Bloomington. I lived on-campus but came home during the summer. Winnie was 18 but hadn't yet joined me at IU for her freshman year. So, with classes set to begin at the end of August, she wanted Woodstock to be her grand rebellious farewell-to-youth adventure. Still, it was going to be next to impossible to put anything past our parents with everyone under the same roof.

"But then a stroke of luck came her way – came *our* way, I guess. The 'parental units' announced they'd return to Africa. In August. For nearly the entire month! To Winnie, who was still plotting all this in secret, it seemed like a gift from God.

"And then, even more good fortune: Just a few hours after learning of the African expedition, Winnie heard our mother on the phone with Great Aunt Geneva, age 96, still alive and still living *alone* in a small bungalow in Jessup, Pennsylvania, a town just outside of Scranton which happened to lie squarely on the route from Indianapolis to Woodstock!

"It was all coming together. Winnie reasoned there would be time to mail-order tickets, have them delivered care of Auntie Gen, stop by her house for a quick visit, retrieve the tickets, and then disappear for a few days at the festival.

"Finally, she put the wheels in motion with our parents. At dinner one night, she casually said, 'I think it'd be nice while you both are away in Africa if me and Sonny took a quick trip to visit Auntie Gen. She probably gets so few visitors, and it must be tough on her being alone all the time.

"Naturally, our parents eyed her suspiciously. So did I, because, you'll recall, at this point, I knew nothing of her plan. I glared at her, burning holes in her brainpan. I didn't want to drive all the way to freaking Pennsylvania and visit a 96-year-old woman who wore too much perfume because she liked the decorative decanters from Avon. But I held my tongue because I knew Winnie probably had something up her sleeve.

"Father was more gullible. He said, 'I think that's a grand idea. We can give Esperanza a few days off – hell, I'll even *pay* her this time – and you two can have an adventure of your own while we're off bagging elephants. Very mature suggestion you've made there, Winnie, my girl. In fact, I think it's only right you take the Mercedes, too. Treat Auntie Gen to a ride in a *real* car before she croaks.'

"That was too much, and I finally chimed in that I thought the car was a tank. Of course, Father was having none of that. The car was his pride and joy. 'The 600 is an ultra-luxury sedan,' he said. 'A very sensible and practical limousine. Just the kind of car that will make Aunt Geneva feel like a goddamned queen. Best car she'll ever ride in – not counting the hearse that's soon to come calling, that is.'

"So, there it was. Everyone but me agreed it must be a surprise visit, too, so Auntie Gen wouldn't tire herself out making the place presentable for guests.

"Still, Winnie kept me in the dark until weeks later, when we were on the road alone. Auntie Gen's was not our destination, she admitted; the Woodstock Aquarian Exposition was. I was relieved to be dodging several days of boredom with Auntie Gen, but I still freaked. I had things to do, and I hadn't packed anything appropriate for a rock festival. Of course, Winnie had the bases covered. She had secretly taken care of everything, even packing a week's worth of clothes for all likely weather conditions. She also had a backpack for each of us to hold what we might need each day. She'd packed cigarettes, too, a whole carton, as well as sleeping bags and enough non-perishable food for a couple days – not that we'd need it; after all, there would be food available for purchase at the festival. How could there not be, right? And we had plenty of money, too. Father had given each of us two hundred to have on hand while they were in Africa.

"Mile after mile, objection after objection, Winnie beat me down. She was certain she'd planned for everything. Until I protested that 'I'm not even a hippie!'

"She stopped the car alongside the road and stared at me. 'Good point,' she conceded. 'You're not a hippie, and neither am I. We should buy something appropriate to at least look the part.'

"So, we stopped at a mall in Scranton and bought faded bell-bottoms and tie-dyed tees. We hit a head shop for fringe vests and huaraches. Bought beads, too. And a roach clip with a peace symbol on it. While there, we listened to the 'lingo' of regular customers and tried to act hip.

"'Hopeless,' I complained after we walked out. 'Gotta start somewhere,' Winnie said.

"Anyway, when we reached Aunt Geneva's place, we rang the bell. Knocked on the door. Rang and knocked again. Nothing. We went around the side yard and found the back door. Knocked there, too. Again nothing.

"'Deaf as a post,' Winnie said. And a chill ran up my spine as I asked, 'You don't suppose she's *dead* as a post, do you?'

"'Well, the odds get better every day.' Winnie said. Around back, we forced our way into the back door. Inside, the house smelled like the house of a 96-year-old woman, but not, thank God, like the house of a 96-year-old *dead* woman. She simply wasn't home.

"Well, it took a while, but we found the tickets buried in a pile of crossword puzzles and then headed out again for Woodstock. Never did see Auntie Gen, and that caused a bit of a problem because there was one thing Winnie had neglected to arrange: a backup place to stay that Thursday night. Naturally, area hotels were booked up, even as far out as Scranton; so, we drove to within ten miles of the festival site and overnighted in the Mercedes in a supermarket parking lot. It sat next to a gas station with a dirty but well-stocked restroom.

"Well, let me tell ya, that damn Mercedes limo stuck out like a finely manicured sore thumb, and we couldn't wait to get out of there and make it to the festival. So, come Friday morning, we freshened up at the gas station and started out again, on the road by 6:30. Within ten minutes, we were stuck in traffic, still a couple miles from Max Yasgur's farm, the festival site near Bethel. It looked like we'd have no choice but to do what others were doing: abandon the car and walk the rest of the way, carrying what we could.

"But here's where we got lucky, thanks to that big-ass limo. It commanded attention. And attention it got. What a ride it turned out to be from that point on…"

August 15, 1969:

A uniformed cop on a motor scooter pulled up alongside the limo and motioned for Winnie to lower the driver's window.

"Good morning, Officer," Winnie said. "Bit of a jam here, huh?"

"You might say that."

"Man, I'm sure you've got your hands full."

"Yep, you might say that, too," the cop agreed. He was eyeing the Mercedes. "Haven't seen any cars as nice as this one today. You trying to get into the festival?"

"Yes, sir," Winnie said. "'Trying' is the right word."

"You know," the officer continued, "the performer's VIP entrance is on the back side near West Shore and Hurd. So, who do you have in the car with you there? Rock star? Anyone I've heard of?"

Winnie turned and looked at Sonny. He was wearing sunglasses and his vest and some beads.

"Um, yeah, actually," Winnie improvised. "Some confusion at his manager's office about where to enter, I guess. The supporting musicians probably know where to go, and we don't. Typical, right?"

"I'm sorry," the officer said, "but who did you say you're transporting?" He removed his sunglasses to get a better look at Sonny.

Winnie leaned forward to block his view and whispered, "Sorry, sir; we just don't want to create a frenzy out here by being too obvious -- other than the car, of course. You've got enough on your hands keeping things peaceful-like, I imagine. Donny-boy here doesn't like to be a brother, I mean a *bother*."

"Donny-boy?"

"Oh, sorry," Winnie said, "Please keep it hush-hush, but I'm sure you probably know him better as Donovan."

Sonny leaned forward and lowered his sunglasses just a tad, stealing a glance at the officer. "They call me Mellow Yellow," he deadpanned.

"Quite rightly," Winnie added. "Can ya dig it? He's not on the bill this weekend. Kind of a surprise performance." She smiled at her brother. "A very *surprising* performance, I might add."

Suddenly, they were being escorted, slowly, not to jail but toward the rear of the venue and the performer's entrance. When they got close, Winnie honked to get the officer's attention. He stopped, turned his scooter around, and came back to the Mercedes.

"Right here will be just fine," Winnie said. "Thank you so much, Officer, um, what's your name?"

"Sergeant Moon. Sergeant Franklin Delano Moon. Off-duty volunteer. Just doing what I can."

"Ah, Sergeant Moon. Thank you so much. No relation to the drummer, Keith Moon, I suppose."

"Who?"

"That's right."

"What's right?"

"The Who."

"Huh?"

"The Who."

"The what?"

"No, the Who," Winnie explained. "Keith Moon, drummer for The Who? Oh, well, no matter. Thank you again."

Officer Moon started away but then stepped back to the car. He leaned in and smiled. "You don't suppose I could have an autograph, do you? It's for my daughter. She's a big fan of anyone I can't stand."

"Certainly, Officer Moon, Donny-boy will be happy to." Even with her brother's eyes hidden by the sunglasses, Winnie could tell Sonny was glaring at her.

Officer Moon handed her a ticket and a pen, which she passed over to her brother, the rock star. "Just make it out to Olivia, O-L-I-V-I-A," the officer requested. "Maybe call her your biggest fan. She's a rather big girl, my Livi."

Sonny exhaled forcefully, expelling his rising fear in a way that feigned prima donna exasperation. He scribbled on the ticket, double-folded it, and handed it and the pen to Winnie, who passed them back to Officer Moon. She allowed the car to roll forward.

"Much obliged, Mr. Mellow Yellow," said Franklin Delano Moon. "Thank you, young lady. You all have a safe time here now."

"Keep going," Sonny said.

"What?"

"Just find a place to hide the damn car."

Winnie stared at her brother. "Why? We're in! We fooled him."

"For now."

"What do you mean, *for now*?"

"Let's just say Olivia might not like the autograph much."

"Oh, God, Sonny, you didn't sign your real name, did you?"

Sonny removed his sunglasses. "Maybe you should call me Tricky Dick now instead of Donny-boy."

* * *

"Just like that, we were in," Sonny continued. "Winnie stood in the middle of the madness and yelled, 'I've never felt so alive!' The days that followed reinforced that feeling for both of us. With the crowd swelling to nearly ten times the anticipated fifty thousand concertgoers, we found ourselves in a different world. Sure, there were delays in getting the concert started. Sure, the place was plagued with rain and mud and overflowing porta-potties. Sure, there was too little water and too little food and too little sleep. But there was an abundance of harmony, on stage and in the crowd. And as the festival posters had promised, there *was* peace and music.

"There was also … love. What else could it be called, with everyone sharing and getting along? With everyone simply letting others *be*.

"The love at Woodstock wasn't the only revelation. Freedom was epidemic. Freedom to experiment, to smoke weed, to drop acid, to drink from communal bottles of wine. To have sex with strangers.

"Freedom to kick off your shoes and abandon your clothes. Nudity was common. It was accepted. It was natural and normal and more sensible than wearing heavy garments made even heavier by the downpours. I went barefoot and shirtless the first day. Winnie waited till evening to lose her top. By Saturday, however, she could care less. It felt good to be free.

"And then came Sunday…"

* * *

As the Bronco moved deeper into Kentucky on I-65 with Jimi at the wheel, Sonny told the twins about their father:

"It was on Sunday during Joe Cocker's set that we saw your dad for the first time. The skies were starting to get pretty ugly, but Cocker was killing it on stage. No one wanted to leave even though we were sure to get seriously wet or struck by lightning real soon. During his final song, a blistering cover of the Beatles hit, *With a Little Help from My Friends*, your mom looked up at one of the lighting towers, and there he was. Your dad.

"You know, they called a hippie's long hair the 'freak flag' back then, and your dad's white freak flag was waving proudly. At first, I thought maybe it was Johnny Winter up there because Johnny hadn't performed yet, and he had this long white hair, too.

"Anyway, your mom pointed him out, not so much because of that hair or because she thought it was Johnny Winter, but because there he was, this man, maybe fifteen or twenty feet up, standing on these big tube-steel cross members and hanging onto crossbars as naked as the day he was born. Just groovin' to ol' Joe, free as a bird with not an ounce of self-consciousness. I mean, think about it: he was naked on that tower right by the stage in front of hundreds of thousands of people, and he couldn't have cared less. He was in the moment; he was *at one* with the moment. Your mom was instantly smitten. I was mesmerized. Jealous, I suppose. I wanted to be like him. I wanted to be that kind of person who could easily not give a damn about anything. To be the kind of person who could just lose myself in the experience."

Sonny became quiet. Jimi looked at him in the rearview mirror, saw him clutching the urn, saw his tears. Janis broke the silence. "So, you both saw him on the tower. But how did you all actually meet? Did you climb the tower, too?"

Sonny sniffed and managed a laugh. "Oh, hell no. First off, I'm afraid of heights. Scared to death then and still am, even though I can't see what I'm afraid of these days. Second, as I said, I envied his lack of inhibitions, but I wasn't carefree or brave enough to be exposed front and center in that amphitheater.

"No, he had to come down before we could meet. And that happened pretty quickly. Right after Cocker finished that song, they started making announcements about the weather and how we were all gonna get pretty wet. You could see it in the sky, of course, the clouds looking angrier by the minute. As peaceful as we all were on the ground, the sky was just the opposite. Hateful looking, threatening, almost boiling. 'Come down offa those towers,' someone kept saying from the stage, and then they told people in the crowd to move back away from the framework. I think they honestly thought the lighting equipment or even the structures themselves might come down and kill people.

"But even with the danger and the warnings, your dad took his time coming down. He was watching the sky, like he was committing the moment to memory. And then, just before he finally started down, he turned and saw us in the crowd. Out of all those people, he locked eyes with *us*. Your mom started to pull up our blanket and move back, but I said, 'No, just wait a minute.'"

"And then?" Jimi asked.

"And then he was there. Next to us. With us. *Part* of us. The connection was undeniable that quickly. The rain started then, and it came down hard. We held the blanket and our sleeping bags overhead, and your mom gathered up our backpacks and we headed away from the amphitheater. Your dad led the way, so we didn't really know where we were going at that point. We just followed. Not a word had been spoken, but we followed this naked, down-to-earth man. Wherever he was going, we were going there, too, no questions asked. We were that trusting. Maybe that *naïve*. But in that moment, I think we would have followed him to the ends of the Earth."

Sonny, Janis, and Jimi were silent for a while, the road rolling out before them, until Jimi said, "To the ends of the Earth... I wonder if we're on that kind of journey now."

CHAPTER 11

(In Which We Learn About the Jaybird Tattoo and an Oversized Pixie; and Meet a Reporter Named Radiance and a 4-Year-Old Armed with a Crayon)

Early Evening

THE TRAVELERS STOPPED THEN, ON THE OUTSKIRTS OF CHATTANOOGA, Tennessee, at a diner so well-lit it was a suicidal mecca for June Bugs. After Janis read menu highlights to Sonny, an elderly server, a Granny Clampett type named Bertie, approached the table. She made small talk, filled water glasses, and boasted the burgers were the best around. They all took the bait: cheeseburgers and fries all around, Janis's with bacon. Bertie jotted it on her order pad, smiled, and turned to leave, stopping long enough to hug a customer on his way out the door.

"Can you tell us more about what happened with our dad?" Janis asked. "You went off with him during the rainstorm after Joe Cocker's set. What then?"

Sonny sipped his water and then carefully lowered the glass to the table. "Well, after we left the concert area, just being pounded by that downpour, we followed him to his VW van. It was a delivery van, a '59, I think he said. But unlike most of the hippie buses there, his was a 'plain Jane,' a dull grayish-blue, lots of rust, the kind of vehicle that wouldn't get a second glance anywhere. At the festival, it sat at the crest of a slope near Filippini Pond. As we approached it from below in the rainstorm, it kinda blended into that drenching sky. But at least the van offered shelter, so we ducked inside.

"Your dad was already naked, of course, but your mom and me stripped off and just left our clothes and sleeping bags in a heap outside the bus. No use getting the inside of the vehicle any wetter than it needed to be."

Bertie-the-server returned. "Sorry, but I forgot to ask… Should we hate your buns?"

They stared at her.

"Your buns. Ya want 'em hated?" she repeated, louder this time. Jimi and Sonny sat with their mouths open, unsure how to respond.

"Oh," Janis chimed in, "you mean *'heated,'* right?"

"Yes'm, you can have your buns room temp, hated or toasted. Waddle-it-bay?"

"Um, just regular," Jimi said. "Room temperature is fine." Sonny and Janis nodded in agreement.

After the bun situation was sorted and they were alone at the table again, Janis asked, "So, you're all together in the VW bus. Is that when it happened? When we, I mean, when Jimi and I were, well…"

"Conceived?" Sonny said. "No, not then. Inside, we huddled for a few moments under a big dry blanket your dad had. Then we smoked a couple joints. Your dad wasn't into the acid scene, and your mom and me were way too green to trip out on anything stronger than weed. So, we sat in the van, talked and smoked. It's like we were the only people in the world then, even though there were nearly a half-million more just like us right outside the van."

He paused and sipped his water again, then continued: "It seemed like … well, I'm not quite sure how to put this, but even though there were hundreds of thousands of us there, it seemed like we were all just part of a collective *'one'*. That might not make any sense, but it felt like – to me, anyway – that we were individual cells in a larger being. Each of us a tiny but essential piece of a huge harmonious soul. Sounds like a load of bullshit, I know."

"Actually," Jimi said, "it sounds kind of amazing. To have that sense of belonging to something bigger than you, and yet it's a part of you at the same time."

"Well, maybe it's just more magical and mythical to me because it's the last thing I ever truly saw," Sonny said.

Janis sighed. "Head trip just trying to imagine it. Do you remember what you talked about inside the van?"

"Not much," Sonny replied. "It was a bit of a blur, and the weed didn't help. I remember one thing very vividly, though. Your dad lit a candle inside the van – those delivery van models can be awfully dark inside, especially on a rainy day. When he set the candle between us, I noticed his tattoo."

"The bird on his butt," Janis said.

"That's right. I asked him about it, and he said it was a Jaybird because his mama always said he loved being 'naked as a Jaybird.' He had gotten the tattoo only a year or so before Woodstock. He had been away in Canada for a while, but he made a surprise visit to his parents shortly after getting it. When his mom asked to see it, he dropped his pants and showed her." Sonny laughed at the memory. "At that point, his dad yelled something like, 'Goddammit, son, you're a grown man. Pull your pants up!'"

Jimi laughed, too. "I can understand that."

"Well, anyway, I guess his mom said, 'it's all right, honey, you've always been a free spirit. You go right ahead and moon your mama!'"

"That's kinda awesome, isn't it?" Janis said quietly, wistfully. "To be that free and open. To have such an easy relationship with a parent."

Jimi and Sonny both nodded.

"So, when did the mudslide happen?" Jimi asked. "The one where you all ended up in that photo?"

"Right after we left the van," Sonny said. "You see, the downpour was a monster, but didn't last all that long. After an hour and a half or so, the sun started breaking through the clouds. We tumbled out of the van and went back to the amphitheater. The mudslide was in its full glory. We just stayed naked after the rain. No use putting wet clothes back on, so we took our turns on that slide." Sonny grew silent. He was smiling. Remembering. "It was gross," he said softly. "And it was awful. And … it was heaven."

"The stuff of legend," Jimi said.

"A legend captured in that photo," Janis added.

"And it was all practically perfect," Sonny said. "Until the lawman showed up."

* * *

When Pete Peebles arrived at Quantico North, the DC tavern, Junior Agent Junior Carducci, Jr. was already there, standing at the bar, with two shots of Absolut waiting for the former Senior Agent. "You know me well," Pete said. He downed the shots and exhaled with gusto. "Let's grab a seat where we can talk." To the bartender, he said, "couple more of these, plus an Absolut and Tonic and whatever my friend here is having."

Pete led Junior to a well-lit booth. Another patron hurried past and took the next table. Once seated, Junior said, "Well, Pete, you've been officially retired for several days now... Got any new hobbies?"

"What I've got," Pete said, "as of this very afternoon, is a colossal pain-in-the-ass freeloader in my house."

Carducci squinted and tilted his head.

"Did I ever tell you about my daughter, Junior?"

"You have a daughter named Junior?"

"Wiseass! No, *Carducci*, I have a 250-pound crybaby named Pixie who, in her usual train-wreck style, picked *today* to leave her husband and move back home."

"Wow, that's tough, Pete. For her *and* for you and Petunia – or was it Penny?"

"Penny," said Pete. "Petunia's my other daughter, the adorable little furry four-legged one. Tough for all of us, actually."

"So, is this a permanent move back home? What caused the breakup, if you don't mind me asking?"

"The breakup," Pete explained, "happened because her namby-pamby weasel of a husband – who's too good for her even if he is a weasel – finally grew a pair and spoke the truth. It seems Pixie was acting like herself, ragging the poor boy all day long. They go out to lunch and run into an old high school pal of Pay's."

"Pay's?"

Pete laughed. "The weasel's name is Paydro. P-A-Y-D-R-O. Like Pedro, only it's Pay-fuckin-dro. Paydro Abercrombie, fer Chrissake."

"Paydro Abercrombie," Junior repeated. His forehead wrinkled. "Abercrombie? Like the—"

"Same spelling. But no relation to anyone of means, I'm reasonably certain. However, there is a connection to the retailer if you'll bear with me," Pete said. "So, they run into the old high school buddy, and the buddy starts to introduce his wife to Paydro and Pixie. 'Honey,' he says, 'this is Paydro Abercrombie and, and, and...' The guy's struggling, see, 'cause he doesn't know Pixie's name yet. Well, ol' Paydro, having found his balls after having them knocked around by Pixie all morning, says, 'Just call us Abercrombie and Bitch.'"

Junior exploded with a laugh and instantly covered his mouth.

"Oh, it's okay to laugh," Pete said. "She's my daughter, and I do love her, but I think I'da hugged ol' Paydro right then. Anyway, as you can imagine, the shit hit the fan, so now Paydro is livin' easy in a quiet house while I'm stuck with a blubbering hormonal whale ruining my fuckin' retirement."

"Sorry, Pete. I know that probably puts a kink in your post-retirement agenda."

"Hell, it puts a kink in my *colon*, if you must know. But not for much longer, Junior. If Penny wants to stay and mollycoddle Pix, that's her choice. But I'm at my wit's end and ready to try one last time to find that Finch money in East Kibosh and then, finally, get my hands around the neck of Finch, Jr. ... Junior."

The bartender delivered two more shots of Absolut plus an Absolut and Tonic, all for Pete. "And a diet soda for the gentleman," the server said, setting a glass in front of Carducci before stepping away to serve the man at the table behind them.

"A damn diet drink, Carducci? Maybe it's time you grew a pair, too."

Junior lifted his glass and nodded toward Pete. "Have to maintain my girlish figure," he said.

"Ha!" Pete laughed. "You'd be a good influence on my Pixie then. You dating anyone these days, Junior? I know a sweet little gal who just became a free agent."

"Um, thanks, Pete. Very tempting. I'll think about it. So, does Pixie have any more endearing qualities?"

"Well, let's see... She farts a lot. Real ladylike, huh? I don't think she even knows when one's about to launch. It's like her behemoth butt cheeks smother any brain signals of imminent olfactory doom."

Carducci smiled and stared into his glass. "She sounds so alluring, Pete. Let me know if she and Paydro don't patch things up." He lowered the glass to the tabletop and leaned in closer to his old partner. "In the meantime, I have good news for you."

"What could be better than you taking Pixie off my hands?"

"The tap is in place."

"The wiretap? At Muckle's firm in Indy? Outstanding, Junior! You work fast. I trained you well."

"I owed you for the Souplesse incident. Besides, I know you won't rest until you resolve this Finch situation – the money and the man."

"You got that right," Pete said, and then chugged the last of the shots for emphasis.

"Don't get too excited," Carducci continued. "So, here's how it'll work: my operative in Indy can't be on this 24/7. He's got it set up to record incoming and outgoing calls. He'll check the audio each evening and report back with anything unusual."

"Sounds good. I appreciate the hustle on this, Junior."

"Wasn't easy on the op's end. He nearly got caught by the target. Didn't know this Muckle attorney guy was blind, and so he figured lights out meant it was safe to do the taps."

"But he got in and out without being detected, right? I can't afford to be linked to anything not authorized by the Agency, Junior."

"We're good for now. I'll keep you posted. The tap was just put in place overnight, so I don't have any calls to report yet. If you're on the road, I'll need you to check in with me each day in case I learn something."

Pete downed the Absolut and Tonic, released a belch for emphasis, and said, "Absolutely." He pulled out his wallet, left some bills on the table, and stood to leave. "By the way, I'll be at a place called the Ol Swimmin Hole in East Kibosh. That's Old without the 'd' and Swimming without the 'g'. They left the 'e' on Hole for some reason. If you come up with anything urgent, I'm sure you can call them and leave a message for me at the desk. Or they can ring you through to the room. I probably won't be in the room very much, especially during the day, but you can try."

* * *

Max Thibodeau had slipped in unnoticed and sat in the booth behind Pete and Junior. He had been listening and jotting down notes:

> *Pete meeting with man named Junior Carducci*
> *Ready to bail for Kibosh – will go alone if he must*

Wiretap
Indianapolis Muckle firm
Blind attorney
Recording phone convos
Connection to Finch money and Woodstock man?
Ol Swimmin Hole

And when Pete left the bar, Max followed. Discreetly. He decided he might need to make a reservation at the Ol Swimmin Hole in East Kibosh, South Carolina.

* * *

"We're going to East Kibosh first thing in the morning," Pete announced to Penny when he made it home from the bar. "No if, ands or … buts," he said. The house smelled of bonbon farts.

"Oh, that's fine, dear," Penny Peebles said in her stuck-in-time little girl voice. "But we're going to have to be extra sensitive with Princess Petunia. I took her to the vet this morning, and Doctor Sund says she's in heat. Nearing the end of her *Proestrus* phase, I think he called it. Peeing a lot. Licking herself. Maybe more aggressive. We'll just have to be careful she doesn't get knocked up down south, or the puppies might bark with drawls."

"Holy hell, if it's not one bitch, it's another," Pete mumbled.

"What's that, dear?"

"Nothing," Pete said. "Just glad we're finally getting out of town."

"Oh, I'm excited, too, honey," Penny continued, "and I have even more great news for you!"

"Yeah, what's that?"

Just then, Pixie clomped down the stairs, encased like a sausage in a too-tight nightgown. "Daddy," she said, "as soon as we get to East Kibosh, can we please-pretty-please stop at the Go Get Fudged factory? They have the world's best bonbons, and I seem to have run out."

* * *

In Florida, at 11:11 p.m., the Radiance Reynolds report began on WTFU's *Weekend Watch News*. Robin Paloma, manager and server at the Moon-Your-Mama Bar & Grill (grill side only), and sometime lover of Jayson B. Stockwood, was tuned in.

"...*Authorities admit they only recently came to realize there could be a connection between recent anonymous monetary donations and similar acts dating back several years. A local law enforcement official, who declined to be interviewed on camera, said, and I quote: 'We have enough trouble finding people who steal from others; so why would we look for someone who's actually giving money away?'*"

The raven-haired reporter continued: "*Indeed, it's only because of the seemingly random nature of these gifts, along with the lack of any apparent connection between the beneficiaries, that this Good Samaritan has gone undetected for so long. In fact, at WTFU, preliminary research indicates our mystery man may have been operating anonymously for as long as a decade or more in this area.*"

The camera pulled back for a full-body standing shot of Radiance Reynolds. She went on: "*So, why do we believe our kind-hearted hero is a man? Well, we base that belief on the eyewitness account of four-year-old Vinny Vedere, who, while playing hide-and-seek with an imaginary friend, recently saw a man leave a trinket-sized garden gnome and nearly $500 cash in an envelope on the doorstep at the home of the boy's grandmother, Agnes Schwartz. Mrs. Schwartz had recently been robbed of more than $400 she had earmarked for her rent. Her story appeared in the* Weekly Sun *newspaper last week, and within days, our Good Samaritan had quietly come to her aid. But this time, little Vinny Vedere saw our man in action.*"

In a pre-recorded segment, the reporter, microphone in hand, knelt before a big-eyed boy whose coal-black hair had been pasted into submission for his moment in the spotlight. "*Vinny, can you describe the man you saw leave the envelope with the money in it?*"

Vinny fidgeted and then leaned not toward the reporter's microphone but toward the camera. Loudly, he said, "*He was a grown-up, and he had long white hair stuck together in a rubber band at the back of his head.*"

"*Do you remember anything else about him?*"

"*Yes.*" The boy stared into the camera.

"*Could you tell us what else you remember?*"

"Yes." Still staring.

"And what is it you also remember about the man, Vinny? Please tell us. Please tell us now."

"Um, he had long white hair stuck together in a rubber band at the back of his head ... and he wore glasses."

"What kind of glasses?"

"Clear ones."

"The frames were clear?"

"No."

Radiance Reynolds was struggling. *"I'm not sure I—"*

"The lookinta part was clear."

"I see," the reporter said.

"So could the man," Vinny added, *"'cause he had glasses."*

Reynolds stood and stretched her back and then leaned down again to the small witness. *"What shape were the glasses, Vinny?"*

"Round."

"Good, we're getting somewhere. So, the frames were round —"

Vinny formed circles with his fingers to demonstrate.

"Very good, Vinny. Now, I believe you drew a picture of this man; is that right?"

The camera panned to a drawing lying at the child's feet next to the tiny gnome. A man depicted in red-crayon on the paper was little more than a stick figure with a circular smiley-face head, long hair (stuck together in a rubber band at the back of his head), and round glasses. Protruding from his stick-fingered hand was a rectangular object, presumably the cash-filled envelope.

The camera held the shot for a few seconds and then found the reporter again. *"There you have it,"* Radiance Reynolds said. *"Possibly the only eyewitness – so far – and the only clues to the identity of our Samaritan. We'll keep you—"*

"Wait!" Vinny yelled, tugging on the reporter's microphone cable. The camera found the boy again as he pulled the red crayon from his pocket and knelt beside the picture. He added a comma-shaped crayon mark at the corner of the man's smiling mouth. *"He had one of these, too,"* Vinny said, gesturing a gash on his own mouth. *"A big boo-boo. And that's all."*

With that, Robin Paloma, manager and server at the Moon-Your-Mama Bar & Grill (grill side only), and sometime lover of Jayson B. Stockwood, switched off the TV. The child had drawn a man with long ponytailed hair. The child had drawn the man with round glasses. The child had given that man a scar at the corner of his mouth. And a small garden gnome lay at the child's feet.

"So, he's giving money away, huh?" Robin said. "Maybe I should be nicer to his damn cat." He laughed then, took a swig from his can of beer, and continued to drink away the suddenly surprising and complicated night.

Wednesday, August 10, 1994

CHAPTER 12
*(In Which We Learn About East Kibosh, the Aliens,
and LilBuckaroo's Lament)*

EAST KIBOSH LIES PRECISELY 3.14 MILES WEST OF THE TOWN OF NORTH IN THE state of South Carolina. This would be insignificant if not for the fact that East Ki was established on March 14, 1816. As in 3/14/16. As in 3.1416. As in the approximate value of *pi*. Coincidence?

It didn't take long (in cosmic time) for alien life forms to unearth this geospatial mathematical confluence. Legend has it they arrived a century later, at precisely 3:14 (and 16 seconds) on the morning on March 14, 1916. (Yes, advanced life forms appear to be a bit anal on such matters.)

Legend further has it that 22 humans and 17 animals then accompanied the visitors on an interstellar road trip of infinite duration. That is, they were abducted by the aliens. The population of East Ki at that time was 23 humans. The one person left behind? Mordecai Flagg, age 17. Mordecai, it is said, passed out behind a grain bin upon seeing the visitors, thus unwittingly sparing himself from the otherworldly adventure (or, perhaps, cosmic dissection). When Mordecai awoke, he was alone. His parents were gone, his friends were gone, sheep he had flirted with were gone. "Even my doggone dog was gone," he later said.

Mordecai then did what any 17-year old male might do: he wiped away a single tear for each of his parents, three tears for the dog, and then went on an extended bender, having unlimited access to all the liquor in the village. Again, Mordecai passed out, this time in the privy.

Soon, the young man found himself in custody – not in the clutches of aliens but rather of authorities in Orangeburg County's castle-style jailhouse. He was accused of murdering and hiding the other Kiboshians. Nearly three years later, however, after extended incarceration, endless questioning, a couple of trials, and a sabbatical in the South Carolina State Hospital for the Insane, Mordecai Flagg was finally set free. After all, there were no bodies, no damning evidence, only conjecture.

By the time he returned home, East Kibosh was a ghost town. Looted. Dilapidated. Not a drop of liquor to be found. Mordecai cut his losses and moved on.

Enter Brody Tully Chance, a Columbia-based construction mogul who sought – and was granted – claim to the land in exchange for demolition, waste removal, and infrastructure improvement services. By 1922, East Kibosh had been rebuilt from the ground up. It was once again alive and growing and newly settled by seven reputable families, six of whom proved adequately fertile for repopulation purposes. Only one homesteading couple proved not terribly prolific: The Finches.

James Lee Finch and wife Mary Louise produced but a single child – Jay Finch (later to be known as Jay Finch, *Sr.*). James Lee, being good with his hands, opened *Finch's T and A Shoppe*. The Finch shop(pe) provided car maintenance and repair for Ford Model Ts and Model As. In short order, James Lee Finch became so well respected for his craft that customers came to East Ki from as far away as Charlotte, Savannah, and other cities with girl names.

The Finch boy helped his father with the *T and A* for a while but eventually left to pursue dreams in the "big city" of Lackawanna, New York. There he won management roles in small companies, which he helped grow into medium-sized companies. From there, it was on to Schenectady and then to Poughkeepsie. In New York state, Jay Finch made his livelihood, married and – like his father before him – sired a single child: Jay Finch, Jr. – or *Jaybird*.

When Jaybird was 21, his father ran afoul of business partners and federal agents – Pete Peebles chief among them. The strain of this afoulness took its toll and led Finch, Sr. to suffer a debilitating heart attack and two subsequent strokes. In late June of 1969, at age 46, he died in Grasslands Hospital in Valhalla, New York. His body was transported back to his boyhood home of East Kibosh for burial, to lie for eternity in a town that soon after fully embraced its heritage – as a destination for aliens.

Kibosh's revitalization began innocently enough. Its first East Kibosh Founders Day festival was held March 14, 1951, with a few dozen in attendance. Within a decade, however, this low-key event had transformed into the week-long *East Ki Pi-in-the-Sky Festival,* which again attracted visitors from beyond: human tourists getting their cosmic jollies in space garb. It was great fun and contagious. Soon, festival vendors began opening permanent shops. And by the mid-1970s, an out-of-this-world cottage industry had been born. East Ki had become a mecca for seekers of space-age hillbilly kitsch – part year-round flea market and part Roswell-of-the-southeast.

It was the kind of place Pete Peebles would typically avoid like The Plague. Except he believed the embezzled Finch money – all $207,000 of it – might still be there. After all, it practically said so on the note Finch had tried to pass to his son from his deathbed. Pete carried a copy of that note in his wallet.

The case was closed, decreed the Agency. Pete disagreed. He had the note. He had a burning need to find the money. And now he had the time.

If only he could get the hell out of Westover Village.

* * *

Wednesday morning in Westover Village, Max Thibodeaux was going stir crazy. He had already spent long hours in his black Bonneville sitting, reclining, dozing, snacking, reading, and occasionally using his pee bottle. He was listening, too, of course, courtesy of the planted devices in the Peebles house. Listening and hoping to gain additional morsels of information that would either validate or refute his hunch that this Peebles guy was worth the trouble. Mostly what he got, however, were the routine sounds and chatter of an ordinary couple doing ordinary things. From that ordinariness, Max had learned this much: Pete Peebles was an asshole, Penny was a long-suffering saint, Pixie Peebles Abercrombie was an emotional train wreck, and Princess Petunia was simply a dog. Max hated dogs.

But there *had* been that glimmer of hope Tuesday evening when Max had learned the foursome planned to leave first thing Wednesday morning for East Kibosh. With that understanding then, Max had readied himself overnight to follow them on their journey. He had gone to his apartment and packed what he might need for a trip of several days. Clothes. Food and drink. Toiletries. Books and magazines.

On the front passenger-side floorboard, he also had that box of gadgets: a high-powered zoom camera and film; an instant camera with film packs and flash bars; and the extra listening and tracking devices Hez had provided (minus the one he had placed in the Peebles's Plymouth – strong signal at first but now much weaker, probably a dud). Max also had his newfangled cellular phone, big as a brick of processed cheese. It was the best on the market, Hez had said, but Max had since learned it worked in very few locations and would be practically useless on the road.

But for the time being, Max continued listening via the planted devices in the house: Pixie had locked herself in the bathroom again, bawling, still distraught over the "Abercrombie and bitch" comment, not to mention the fact that Paydro still had not called. Pete had cursed and threatened, as was his habit. And Penny, on the other hand, had played "good cop" and coaxed their daughter out by sliding half a Hershey bar under the door, with the promise of the other half if she emerged. Pete blamed PMS for the whole nightmare. Penny claimed it was merely "bonbon withdrawal."

Minutes later, they all finally emerged from the house and began packing the Plymouth. This was not easy. Two of the three large suitcases Pixie had brought with her in exile were going with her to East Kibosh. (She argued her clothes were larger and took up more space.) Penny had a large suitcase and a smaller one. Pete carried what appeared to Max to be an accordion-style file folder. While Pete arranged everything in the car, Penny went back inside and fetched Princess Petunia. The dog now wore a diaper.

It appeared the trip would finally begin, so Max took hold of the ignition key. But then, through the listening device planted under the dashboard of Pete's Plymouth, Max heard a rapid-fire "Fuck, fuck, fuck, fuck, fuck...!" He watched as Pete bolted from the car, opened the hood, disappeared behind it for two full minutes, and then reappeared upon slamming it shut. The car shook.

Max heard Penny say, "Oh, dear." Petunia whined. So did Pixie. A minute later, the Peebles crew was out of the car; and Pete began to transfer everything and everyone into Pixie's pink Pontiac Parisienne, circa 1985, parked in front of the house.

It was then Max noticed Pete wasn't just packing their luggage; he was also packing "heat," the gun dangling from a shoulder holster. "What *am* I getting myself into?" Max whispered.

* * *

At the same moment the pink Parisienne pulled away, Junior Agent Carducci's phone rang – his private line. He picked up the receiver, said "Carducci," and closed his office door.

"Got something for ya." It was his Indianapolis freelance field operative, Mike Smyth. The wiretapper.

"Go on."

"Call came in yesterday from someone called Little Buckaroo. At least that's what the secretary, this Pepper chick, called him."

"Actually, that was probably *Lil*Buckaroo, I believe," Carducci said. He opened and sorted through Sonny Muckle's file. "Yes, I know about him. That's the attorney's nephew. Continue."

"Yeah, *Lil*Buckaroo. Whatever. I think Pepper also called him 'LB.' Anyway, he calls, and they have this conversation where she brings him up to speed on where the Attorney guy is off to."

"Good," Carducci said. "Tell me everything. Play by play."

"Yeah, yeah, here's what they said, practically verbatim." Carducci could hear Smyth sorting papers. "Okay, so it went like this: First, this LB character calls, and he's all excited and says the Woodstock reunion has been canceled. Says there's no way for Sonny and the twins – whoever they are – to complete the mission. Then he starts singin' that he's gonna be rich."

"Interesting," Carducci said, taking his own notes. "What then?"

"Then this Pepper person squashes his excitement like it was a bug. She says there's another Woodstock reunion still taking place and that – and I'm quoting here – 'the mission is still on. They're still going to try to find their guy.' She says that if Sonny and the twins succeed, this LilBuckaroo fella is screwed."

Carducci scrambled to take it all down. He wanted to be able to call Pete right away. After a moment, he said, "Okay, I've got it so far. What else?"

"So, this LB guy is super-bummed, but Pepper tells him the mission's a longshot anyway, that even if they find who they're looking for, they still have to get him 'where they need to be in time.' She then tells LB she'll keep him informed and let him know if he needs to get involved. Said he should sit tight, but I could tell he's not the sit-tight kinda guy."

"Okay, good," Carducci said, "but did Pepper say where Sonny and these twins you mentioned are actually headed?"

"Just this," Smyth said. "She said they're headed south, toward Florida. Gonna stop in at this organization in Kissimmee called – are you ready for this? – the American Sunbathing Association. It's like this big organization for nudists. Who knew there was such a thing, right? Sounds like Sonny and the twins are gonna try to find the person they're looking for by getting info from the ASA. Pepper said that's unlikely, so if they can't find out what they need to know, they're gonna visit as many nudist clubs as they can while there's still time."

"Great, this could be helpful. Anything else I should know?"

"Two things, I think," Smyth said. "First, this LB dude is gonna call from time to time and get more info from Pepper at her home. It looks like I'll need to tap her place of residence. That okay with you?"

"Sure, why not? Just be discreet."

"Always."

"Okay, what was the other thing?"

Smyth lowered his voice to a whisper. "Well, LB says while he's going after Sonny and the twins, he's gonna 'peddle his chips'."

"What the hell does that mean?"

"Who knows? Maybe it's some kinda drug lord or hit-man lingo. Ya think this LilBuckaroo is dangerous?"

* * *

For LB, the call to Pepper had been a one-two gut punch: first and foremost, learning that his inheritance was still at risk, and then, hearing that Pepper had a date with some *Todd* fellow. "Before we go-

go..." she had said just before hanging up. It had taken LB till well past midnight to put it together: Todd must be the guy from that car rental place. Maybe it was time to resurrect the Pinto fantasy, with Todd squarely in the back seat. *Kaboom, Fucker!*

But his daddy had come to him in the night and said to wait. There'd be time to settle scores after he had his millions. The critical task at hand was to head toward Florida and hawk his chips along the way. He was ready to do just that; the *dickTat'rs* were in the car, uncovered. And when morning came, they were still there and it hadn't rained. It was a promising start to the day.

LB should have left it at that. Should have simply headed south. But instead, he found himself at 8:25 a.m. in the parking lot at Pepper's apartment building. Her car was there. But so was a Teal-and-faux-woodgrain Dodge Caravan with a *Before You Go-Go Car Rental* bumper sticker.

Yes, LB should have left it at that. Should have quieted his impulses and headed south. But instead, he found himself exiting the Caddy, keying some extra grain into the Caravan's fake wood, and proceeding to Pepper's front window. The curtain was closed, except for a slim opening just big enough to steal a glimpse inside.

Again, LB should have left it at that. Should have quieted his impulses, respected her privacy, and headed south. But instead, he peeked through the opening in the curtains. And there they were, his sweet little Peps and this *Tahhhhddd* asshole! It looked like they never even made it to the bedroom, just collapsed in a heap of steaming hormones right there on the living room floor. They were either in a stuporous state of post-coital bliss (he'd read about those) or had been murdered. Bloodlessly. Either way, there they lay, head to foot. *Kinky positioning*, LB thought (he'd read about that, too, and studied pictures – at length).

Both angry and sad, LB was going to leave it at that. Except that Effyu popped his little Shih Tzu head up from under the curtain. LB smiled tentatively at the dog. "Good boy," he whispered. "Go get Todd. Go bite his balls off. Go on, they're right there. You can do it..." But Effyu was having none of it. LB could hear the dog's low growl building into a full snarl and then suddenly into a belligerent barking fit.

"No, no, no, no, no," LB said, and then placed his finger to his mouth as if the dog would respect the universal shushing symbol. The door opened. Pepper appeared. Wrapped in a blanket.

"LB? What the fuck are you doing here?"

LilBuckaroo smiled unconvincingly. "Um, just on my way out of town and figured I'd check in one last time before I go-go, er, I mean, before I head out. So, hey there… anything new?"

Todd appeared in the shadows ten feet behind Pepper. He was *not* wrapped in a blanket.

"No, LB, nothing new. You know everything there is to know."

Indeed, he did. Without another word, LB slouched and walked away. The time had come. He was definitely going south.

* * *

Junior Carducci phoned the Peebles home. No answer. Most likely on their way to East Kibosh. He'd have to wait for Pete to check in. Meanwhile, maybe he could find out who these "twins" were; and what it might mean that LilBuckaroo Muckle DePew was planning to "peddle his chips." *Sounded sinister*, Junior thought.

* * *

At Motel 247 on I-75 near Forsyth, Georgia, Sonny and the twins were late getting started. Determined to avoid Atlanta rush-hour traffic, they had driven so deep into Tuesday night that it became Wednesday morning. Jimi and Janis had taken turns at the wheel, driving almost to Macon (and virtually to exhaustion) before stopping.

Sonny and Jimi had shared a room at the 247 while Janis got the adjoining space. They had hoped to be on the road again by 8 a.m., giving them plenty of time to reach the American Sunbathing Association office in Kissimmee by mid-afternoon. But it was almost 9 when Jimi and Janis made it to the parking lot. There, Jimi stopped in his tracks. He stared at the Bronco.

"What is it?" Janis asked.

"Look at him," Jimi said. He pointed toward Sonny, who sat in the driver's seat, his hands on the steering wheel.

"Crazy fucker," Janis said. "If he really thinks we're gonna let him drive—"

"Not that," Jimi interrupted.

"What, then? What's wrong?"

Jimi looked away, his eyes watery. "It's just that… Well, it's just that we're on this mission for the money…"

"Yeah, and to find our dad," Janis said.

"Of course," Jimi agreed. "But Sonny… Well, I just get the feeling this journey is more than that for him. Sure, he'll get more money if we succeed. And yeah, he'll reconnect with Jaybird after all these years…"

"So, what else is there?"

Jimi turned to face his sister. "I think Sonny is trying to find something else, something more. I think he's trying to find *himself*, maybe. Or at least to find a way back to when his life had … I don't know, *possibility*, I guess. I think he was full of hope up till that last day at Woodstock, but since then, well, I don't know. He just seems empty. Lost, maybe. Like the life he's been living is not the life he thought he was supposed to live."

"I guess so," Janis said. "What are you trying to say here, Jiminy?"

Jimi inhaled and exhaled sharply. He dabbed at the corner of his left eye. "I'm saying we should get going. But I'll drive. And stop calling me Jiminy."

CHAPTER 13

(In Which LB Confronts a Convict, Max Pursues the Pink Parisienne, and the Wiretapper Goes into Hazardous Territory)

Late Morning

THE CADDY WAS A GAS HOG – 8.5 MILES PER GALLON ON A GOOD DAY. SO FAR, this was *not* a good day. LB figured he'd spend a fortune making it to Florida, not to mention the *time* he'd spend making frequent gas stops.

The first refueling stop came just south of Indianapolis off I-65. He had devoted much of the morning to spying on Pepper, circling the Before You Go-Go lot, and plotting revenge against Todd. Perhaps, someday, he could put sugar in the gas tanks of all the rental cars. In the meantime, he was on a mission: make it to Florida to be closer to Sonny and the twins in case he needed to intervene. That meant first traversing Indiana and Kentucky and Tennessee and Georgia. But here it was past eleven, and he was still just on the outskirts of Indy. And low on gas.

Deep in thought, LilBuckaroo missed the exit where reputable gasoline brands were clustered. Instead, he dived off the highway at the Fongusburg exit and pulled into the Quickee Fill Gas 'n Go. Ramshackle to the verge of ruin but with two modern pumps and a missed-the-good-exit-Sucka price of $1.19^{9} per gallon, the Quickee sat surrounded by what looked like millions of uninterrupted acres of corn. Strangely, though, another building, surrounded by stalks, stood across the road like an oasis: it was an old Burger In The First Degree that looked as if it still operated. It was early for lunch, but it had been years since LB had stopped at a Burger In The First. Maybe a KillerGriller with cheese would help take his mind off Pepper and Todd.

When the car's gas tank was full, LB's wallet was $31 lighter. He figured he'd have to stop for gas again by Lexington. But first things first: *Burger In The First!* Excited, he crossed the road, aimed the steer horns at the front door, parked, and stepped past the window decal that read, "We proudly give second chances to first offenders. Apply within."

Inside, true to its brand, police-style radio chatter provided low-level background noise, a red light flashed over the order counter, and vintage crime scene murals adorned the walls. Caution tape embellished the bathroom corridor; the slippery-floor warning cone read "GRIME SCENE." And the extended hand of a chalk outline on the floor pointed toward the order station. LB approached the counter.

A tall, acne-scarred man in his early thirties stared at him. He wore prison stripes and his name badge ID'd him as Billy Wayne Bundy – three names, serial killer-style. He spoke without inflection: "Welcome to Burger In The First Degree™. Our lawyer says we have to say the 'TM' part from now on when greeting a customer. I'm also supposed to say this: Where were you on the night of the 17th, and what can I get for you today?"

LB grinned. "Play nice with the lawyers," he said. "I'm guessing you might need one from time to time. Nice outfit, by the way. Prison stripes are always a good look. From your personal wardrobe?" He laughed. Billy Wayne Bundy did not. "What can I get for you today?" the counterman repeated.

"Um, well, let's see. I used to love the KillerGriller, but I'm thinking maybe I should try the Double Hamicide."

"That's one KillerGriller and one Double Hamicide."

"No, no," LB said, waving his hand for emphasis. "I don't want the KillerGriller. Just the Double Hamicide. With cheese, please."

"That's one Double Hamicide and one KillerGriller with cheese. Anything to drink?"

For a moment, LB was speechless. He shook his head. "No, you don't understand. Forget the KillerGriller; I don't want one of those. All I want is the Double Hamicide."

"Want to make it a Triple Hamicide for an extra fifty cents?"

"Sure. Whatever."

Billy Wayne Bundy punched an improbable number of buttons on the cash register. "That'll be six dollars and eighty-seven cents."

"What? Wait a minute." LB tilted his head. "Six eighty-seven for just a Double Hamicide?"

"Triple. With cheese."

"Right."

"And the KillerGriller."

LB exploded. "Forget the fucking KillerGriller, you muscle-bound goon! All I want is the goddamned Triple Hamicide with a fucking slice of cheese! Swiss, if you have it."

An older man stepped from the kitchen area. He wore a badge that read, "*Chef* of Police." He smiled artificially. "Hello there, sir. Is there something I can help you with?"

LB gritted his teeth. "Just trying – repeatedly – to place my order."

"That shouldn't be a problem," the Chef of Police said.

"No, it shouldn't."

Billy Wayne Bundy stepped aside and allowed the C.O.P to take over the register. His name tag read "J.D. Purvis." He smiled and said, "Billy, why don't you take over grill duty for now?" *Oh, boy*, LB thought.

"All right, then," J.D. said, "where were you on the night of the 17th, and what can I get for you today?"

After a deep breath, LB said, "Triple damn Hamicide with swiss cheese. Ple-e-ease!"

"Very good, sir. That's one Triple Hammy with Swiss. Care to make that a combo?"

"Sure."

"Small, medium, or large?"

"Medium."

"You can make it large for just a quarter more."

"Fine."

"Okay, that's one Triple Hamicide with Swiss, large fries and a large drink."

"Right."

"On white, wheat, or rye?"

"White."

"Any condiments?"

"Pardon me?"

"Oh, we don't pardon people here, sir. We only arrest and incarcerate." J.D. laughed heartily. "Sorry, sir. Favorite joke of us franchise owners. I was asking about condiments. Ketchup, mustard, Dijon mustard, salt, seasoned salt, pepper, mayonnaise, relish, barbecue sauce, horseradish sauce, Worcestershire sauce, soy sauce, marinara sauce? Salsa? Guacamole?"

"You have guacamole here?" LB asked.

"Now that you mention it, no," said the Chef of Police.

LB sighed. "Mustard. Please. Regular mustard. And that's all, for the love of—"

"Very well," said J.D. "So, let's recap. That's one Triple Hamicide with Swiss on white, side of fries, and a drink. Upsized to large. And with a couple packets of mustard. Regular style."

"Right."

"And what to drink?"

"A fucking diet whatever!"

"Really, sir," J.D. said, "I'm just trying to make sure we get your order correct. In any event, I think I have it. That'll be four dollars and two cents."

"Fine," LB said. He handed J.D. a five-dollar bill. "Just keep the change."

"Oh, sir, thank you, but I'm afraid that would be like stealing. However, we *can* place your spare change in the donation cup for the employee legal defense fund."

"Yes, yes, yes, fine, what-the-fuck-ever!"

J.D. smiled. He was well-trained. He took a deep breath and yelled toward the kitchen, "Billy, that's one Triple Hammy with Swiss and a large fry, please. Oh, and SOTO!"

* * *

As the Peebles clan pulled into the parking lot of a full-window-fronted restaurant near Lynchburg, Virginia, Max Thibodeaux turned into a Mickey D's across the street. For a little more than three and a half hours, he had maintained a prudent pursuit of Pixie Peebles's pink Pontiac Parisienne. Keeping tabs on the car in traffic from a safe distance had been easy enough; after all, the Parisienne was a vehicular eyesore – a rolling case of pinkeye. But Pete Peebles was erratic at the wheel. Weaving left. Weaving right. Speeding up, slowing down. Shaking his hook at other drivers. Nonetheless, Max was up to the challenge, quite skilled at furtive pursuit.

The gas station stop two hours earlier had been dicey, however. As Pete gassed up the Parisienne, Max did the same for his Bonneville, careful to stay on the opposite side of the same set of pumps to use them as a visual barrier. As he filled his car, Max watched Penny take the leashed Petunia beside the station. Needing a potty break himself, Max stopped the pump and hurried into the station. As he left the restroom, Pete caught the opening door, grumbled, "Excuse me," and entered without making eye contact. Max figured he could get by with one or two such fleeting encounters, but he was beginning to think it might be best to simply pull ahead and go on to the Ol Swimmin Hole at East Kibosh before his targets arrived. For the time being, however, he would continue the pursuit.

Near Lynchburg, Max surveilled from across the street as Pete walked the dog. When Petunia had finished watering car stops at the restaurant, Pete locked her in the car, with windows cracked for ventilation, and then joined Penny and Pixie inside at a window booth. Max watched as a young male server approached their table and greeted them. He watched as the server soon returned with drinks and took their order. Watched as Pete got up from the table and approached the checkout stand. Watched as he appeared to flash a badge. Watched the cashier hand Pete a desk-style telephone. And watched as Pete made a call. A brief one. Max could tell by the former agent's body language that he'd only been able to leave a message. *Probably a message for the agent named Junior,* Max thought.

When Pete returned to the table to await lunch, Max ducked into Mickey D's, used the restroom, grabbed a burger and fries to-go, and returned to his vehicle. As he ate, he noticed two dogs barking and jumping against the Parisienne, desperate to get at Princess Petunia, that poor, petite, potentially pregnable Poodle.

* * *

"You good with dogs?" asked the landlord as he sorted through keys on his impressive key ring. At the door to Pepper's apartment, Indy operative Mike Smyth could hear worrisome barking and snarling from inside.

"Depends on the dog, I guess," Smyth said.

"Actually, I'm not sure this one *is* a dog," the landlord said as he found the correct master key and unlocked the door. "She calls him Effyu, but he's more like a Tasmanian devil. I wouldn't turn my back on the little fucker if I were you." He stepped aside. "You sure you won't need access to any of our other apartments today?"

"No, just this one. Need to test an inside phone line and replace it if necessary. Ms. Duckenfield reported it as having a kind of interference that affects call quality in the evenings. No one else around here has reported anything like that. Have you heard any similar complaints?"

"Nope, nary a one. And believe me, I'd hear about it if it was a widespread thing. Our renters are the whiniest sonsabitches ya ever saw."

Smyth nodded. "I'm sure that's a constant headache for you."

"Got that right. So, anything else I can do for you, Mr., um…"

"Bell."

"Ha! I like that," the landlord chuckled. "Phone man named Bell."

"Yeah, ironic, huh? Actually, there is one thing you can do for me. I'd be happy to have you stay here while I work, but what would be even more helpful is if you could go back to your office and call Ms. Duckenfield's number. That way, I can check the quality from an independent equipment source. I'll test on my end, of course, but it always helps if we can do a dual test. If you get a dial tone or I don't answer right away, just stay there and keep trying. I might be changing out the line or performing a ring test."

"Ring test, huh?"

"In layman's terms, yes."

"Okay, I can do that. But hey, if you finish up before I can get back over here, just lock up when you go. I'll check in on the premises later this afternoon."

"Appreciate that," Smyth said, with a reassuring grin.

"On second thought, it wouldn't break my heart if you forget and leave the door open for that damn dog to get loose and run away."

"Sorry," Smyth said. "Really can't do that. Too much liability."

"Yeah, I figured that was a longshot." Effyu's barking ratcheted up. "Speaking of liability," the landlord continued, "you got good insurance?" With that, he shook his head and left Smyth to open the door and step inside.

Fifteen minutes later, finished with the inside and outside work, the wiretap man called Junior Agent Junior Carducci and left a message. "Completed the Duckenfield installation," Smyth said. "And you owe me a new pair of pants."

* * *

Shortly after noon, sitting in a jail cell-style booth at the Burger In The First Degree, LilBuckaroo was feeling better. His car was full and so was his belly. The Triple Hamicide had been so delicious that savoring it had even brought clarity about Pepper and Todd. So what if they had a date? So what if they had sex? So what if Todd had spent the night? Once Pepper knew of LB's interest, she would undoubtedly drop Todd's skinny ass like a hot potato. After all, he and Pepper made a good team, working together to secure LB's rightful millions – with Pepper to get her cut, or at least some popcorn shrimp.

It was settled then. He could deal with Pepper and Todd later. For now, he reminded himself he was on a mission – actually a two-part mission: 1) put himself in position to stop Sonny and the twins if necessary, and 2) peddle his chips.

J.D. Purvis, Chef of Police, approached his cell table. "And how was your food today, sir? Did we get everything correct to your satisfaction? Did you get what you deserved?"

LB swallowed the last delectable bite of his sandwich. He nodded and swallowed. "I must say," he began, "that this was the best sandwich I've had in a while. So flavorful and moist. Nice thick juice. Just excellent."

"Very happy to hear that, sir." The Chef of Police started to step away. His smile was more of a smirk.

"Excuse me," LB said. He smiled as J.D. Purvis stepped back to the table. "I just wanted to apologize for being frustrated earlier, with you and your employee. I'm just under a lot of pressure, and I guess I let it get to me."

"Well, thank you, sir," J.D. said. "I'm sorry if we gave you cause to become frustrated."

"Water under the dam," LB said. "Or is it 'water over the bridge'? No matter. I'd like to make it up to you. Wait here."

In seconds, he was back inside, carrying a couple of canisters of his chips. "Here," he said, "one for you and one for … Billy, I believe his name was?"

J.D. Purvis smiled and studied the canister. "*DickTat'rs.* Interesting. Kind of reminds me of *Tat'r Nips*, for some reason."

"Yes, well… Go ahead and try one."

J.D. popped the top and retrieved a chip. "Is that a—?""

"Some people think so," LB admitted.

"Very tasty, though," J.D. said, and he pulled out another chip. "And this one looks like a—"

"Yes, I know."

"Where did you get these?"

"I manufacture them. They're my creation," LB said, beaming. He reached into his pocket and produced a business card.

The Chef of Police studied the card: "J. Buckingham Muckle, the second, Esquire, attorney at law," he read. "Never woulda figured you as the lawyer type. Guess we shoulda been nicer, eh?"

"Sorry," LB said. "Wrong card." He reached into another pocket and made the exchange.

"LilBuckaroo (LB) Muckle DePew, Renowned Specialty Chip Entrepreneur," Purvis read. "Yes, this one I believe." He tasted another chip. "Ya know, if you have more of these available for distribution, I know someone who'd probably love to have them in her establishment."

"Really?"

"Oh, yes, I think these would fit in right nicely at Miss T's Place."

"Miss T's?"

J.D. Purvis chomped still another chip. "'Bout a mile up the road in the center of town. Right-hand side. Can't miss it. The owner –

everyone calls her Miss T, naturally – should be there. She sure is some-kinda-lady, that one. Just tell her J.D. sent ya and that you deserve one on the house."

"One what?" LB asked, but J.D. Purvis was already walking away.

CHAPTER 14

(In Which LilBuckaroo Meets Some-Kinda-Lady, Sonny and the Twins Arrive at Nudist Central, and Junior Comes Through for Pete)

Early Afternoon

MISS T'S PLACE WAS INDEED IN THE HEART OF FONGUSBURG. IT WAS A SMALL heart – a cluster of six buildings on either side of the street – but a heart, nonetheless. LilBuckaroo pulled the Caddy up to a parking meter in front of the building's two-story brick colonial façade. In its most recent updating, the building had been painted pastel pink. But beneath that peeling layer of paint, former dressings of green and white showed through in places.

The day was cloudy but pleasant, and LB drove with the Caddy's convertible top down. Exiting the car, he discovered the meter still had six minutes left. He needed coins but figured he could get change inside – from his solid lead, an actual referral, a practically guaranteed *dickTat'rs* customer! What a good day this was shaping up to be after all.

Stepping inside and holding a case of chips, he found Miss T's Place to be impenetrably dark, even more so than the Holes in the Wall Pub in Indy. When the door closed behind him, he stopped to allow his eyes to adjust.

"Step right in, Sweetie," came a beckoning call from a sultry but feminine voice deep into the room. LB obeyed the sexy command, stepping carefully, but still stumbling off a single step to a lower floor level. In the slowly yielding darkness, he navigated through a minefield of unseen but rather substantial tables and chairs.

"Oh, honey, let me help you with that box until you get your bearings," said The Voice. And so, the case of chips was taken from him, and a moment later, a delicate hand led him to a table twenty feet away and gently pushed him onto a chair. As LB began to distinguish furniture and fixtures in silhouette, he discovered he was in a corner.

"You must be the chip fella," said The Voice. "J.D. said you'd be stopping by."

"Yes, ma'am. Name's LB. I have a card here somewhere," he said, pulling one out in the darkness.

"And what does LB stand for, Sweetie?"

"Well, it's kind of a family thing, but it stands for LilBuckaroo."

"Little Buckaroo?"

"Actually, it's *Lil*Buckaroo. Long story."

"So, *Lil*Buckaroo has a long story, eh? Anything else long about you, Mr. LilBuckaroo?" The Voice took a chair next to him at the corner table. She lit a candle, which brought to light a glimmering face, heavily made-up, theatrical even. A blonde Pepper-like bouffant took shape. Sequins began to sparkle on her dress. She was old-time movie star glamorous, LB thought. Like Marilyn Monroe but with a Lauren Bacall voice. He was turned on.

Giggling nervously, he finally managed, "J.D. said you were some kinda lady. Guess he was right about that."

"He would certainly know," the bar owner said. "Can I get you a drink, doll?"

"Um, maybe. A bit early in the day, I suppose. I don't have a lot of time. Speaking of which, I'll need some change for the parking meter."

"Always time for a drink between new friends," Miss T decreed.

"Well, maybe just coffee, then, if you have it. Black."

His hostess turned and called out toward a bar still barely visible. "Billy, a hot cuppa black Joe for our guest."

"Lotsa guys named Billy in these parts," LB said, making awkward small talk. "So... I told you what LB means; what does 'Miss T' stand for?"

"Oh, darlin', Miss T stands for many things. Timeless taste, tender touches, tantalizing thrills." She sighed. "But I suppose you want my actual name, don't you?"

Another nervous giggle. "Yeah, that's what I meant."

"Tinkle's the name," she said, extending her hand, with its long, polished, red-sexy nails appearing in the candlelight. "Twaletta Tinkle, at your service." She squeezed LB's hand in an unrelenting clasp, releasing it only when barman Billy came to the table, offering hot coffee in a tall mug.

"Thanks," LB said, grateful for both the coffee and the release of his sweaty hand. As Billy turned to walk away, LB noticed he appeared to be wearing what guys at the pub in Indy called *assless chaps*. Before he could process this dark and fleeting image, however, Miss T continued: "Okay, Sweetie, you say you're in a hurry. Let's have a look at these chips of yours." She reached into the box and pulled out a canister.

As Miss T opened the chip can, LB took a sip of coffee. A big sip. A big sip without blowing on the steaming brew.

"Ho-wee Sheezus, whaddafug!" he screamed, spitting the coffee. And as he fumbled the cup, some of the scorching coffee took flight, assailed his still tender upper lip, and seared it anew. LB slammed the cup to the tabletop and pawed at his own face in such a way that, in the dimly lit bar, it seemed he was choking. Twaletta Tinkle sprang into action. She jerked him out of his chair. Leaned him over the table. Started thrusting upward with an awkward Heimlich hug. LB gurgled. Flopped like a rag doll.

Billy-the-bartender rushed to the table, saw the coupling, and backed slowly away. "Never know what Miss T's gonna be into next," he said.

LB struggled free, fell to the chair again, but upset the table. The cup toppled. The remaining coffee rushed over the edge. It found his lap and triggered a new round of unintelligible screams. Billy flipped on some lights.

Woozy, LB discovered then that abundant lighting was not Miss T's friend.

"Oh, Sweetie, that could be a bad burn," she said, considering both his scalded upper lip and his wet lap. "Let me help you." She led him to the men's room.

A few minutes later, LB emerged from Miss T's Place. Chipless, disillusioned, burned. Hosed down by Twaletta Tinkle. And now, blinded by daylight, he squinted at two figures standing near the front of his car. They rushed away, dropping a spray can and leaving a toxic cloud of paint fumes in their wake.

LilBuckaroo stumbled to the Caddy, leaned against the fender, breathed the fumes, and waited for his eyes to accept the daylight. Still squinting, he studied his formerly pristine white car hood. A hastily painted arrow now pointed to the steer horns, along with the words IM SO HORNY.

LB studied the graffiti and flashed back to 4th grade English. "Oughta be an air-comma between the I and the M," he said aloud. Picking up the spray can, he corrected the error. Then he pulled the parking ticket from his windshield, started the car, and yelled, "Keep the chips!" as he peeled away from the delightful Miss Twaletta Tinkle, some kinda lady.

* * *

A few hours later and several hundred miles south of Miss T's Place, Janis needed to pee. So, shortly before reaching Kissimmee, Sonny and the twins stopped for a restroom break and to gas up the Bronco.

"Hey, OJ!" a man yelled as they exited the vehicle. Another man did the same; and before they could make it inside the station, a small chorus was chanting "OJ, OJ, OJ..."

"Florida does like to promote its orange juice," Sonny said. He waved and said, "Thanks, we'll get some inside."

By the time they exited the station, Jimi had filled him in on the real reason for the chants and the frequent honks and shouts from drivers all along their journey.

"What was Pepper thinking?" Sonny asked. "A *white* Bronco?"

"It's a mystery, for sure," Janis said.

Ever the optimist, Jimi added, "Maybe she just got a special deal on the rental."

"No excuse," Sonny replied. "I told her to get something comfortable but ordinary. Nothing flashy. Pretty sure those were my exact words."

"Sure wish we'd had time to switch cars before we left," said Janis.

"Speaking of time," Jimi said, "do we know for certain the ASA office is open past four?" His concern was based on the nightmarish road construction and clotting traffic they'd encountered as they neared Kissimmee. What should have taken six hours, give or take, from the Motel 247, was already pushing beyond seven hours.

"Should be someone still there," Sonny said. "That's what Pepper told me. Then again, I trusted her to... Oh, well."

By half-past four, they'd made their way from the Florida Turnpike to US 441 – the Orange Blossom Trail – and turned due south into the heart of Kissimmee. With roughly three miles to go, heavy traffic and too many stoplights stood between them and the answers they hoped for. But finally, at quarter till five, they turned left into a small parking lot at the intersection of Main and Walnut. There were two spots available in front of the unassuming L-shaped single-story structure. The door to the ASA office was tucked into the bend of the 'L.' They hurried in.

The lobby was compact but featured a tall counter. Janis and Jimi looked around. Because there was no cowbell on the door (was that just an Indiana thing?), Jimi cleared his throat. Loudly.

Seconds later, a lovely woman appeared and stepped behind the counter. "Hello, welcome to the ASA. I'm Carolyn. How can I help you folks?"

During the drive, they had wondered if the ASA staff would be nude in the office. Carolyn, however, was clothed. Her white blouse was loose-fitting, casual but professional. Her smile was genuine.

The trio had also discussed beforehand who should do the talking and what should be said. They'd agreed to play it cool. Smile. Speak slowly. Don't freak out. (Janis admitted she couldn't be trusted to rise to those standards.) And because eye contact would be essential to establishing rapport, Sonny was out. That left Jimi to take the lead.

"Hi, Carolyn," he began. "I'm Jimi, this is my sister Janis and our uncle Sonny. We're sorry to come in so late in the day, but we've been driving a long time, all the way from Indiana, in fact."

"Not non-stop, I hope," the woman said.

"No, no, we overnighted in Georgia. And took turns at the wheel."

Carolyn looked at Sonny, standing there with his white cane and sunglasses. She cocked her head slightly but said nothing.

"The reason we've come all this way," Jimi continued, "is that, well, we're looking for someone we believe is probably a member of the ASA, or at least could have been. We're hoping you can give us a little assist with finding him."

Carolyn looked concerned. "Must be really important for you to find this person."

"Extremely important," Janis said, unable to remain quiet. "Practically a matter of life and death."

"Oh, dear!"

"Let's just say time is of the essence," Sonny added. "Unfortunately, we don't have much information to go on."

"Well, I'm sure you at least have a name, right?"

"Um, actually, no," Jimi said. "But we believe this man was a nudist. We know he had long white hair, and he had a tattoo of a bird on his, well, on his butt. He liked to be called Jaybird way back when."

Carolyn smiled again but shook her head. "That hardly narrows it down," she said. "When did you last see this man?"

"I last saw him twenty-five years ago," Sonny said, adjusting his sunglasses. Again, Carolyn cocked her head.

"Uncle Sonny wasn't always blind," Janis said. "Ironically, he's our only eyewitness."

"Eyewitness? Is this related to a crime?"

Jimi clarified. "Figure of speech on the 'eyewitness' part. The man we're looking for is our father. It's critical we find him. And find him right away."

"So, let me get this straight," Carolyn said. "You don't have a name, and it's been twenty-five years since your only 'eyewitness' has seen him. All you really know is he's a nudist and has a tattoo."

"Pretty much it," Janis said. She forced a smile.

Carolyn cleared her throat. "The American Sunbathing Association has been around since 1931 … but somehow, I'm pretty sure this is a first." She shook her head. "I'd love to be able to help you folks. But even if we had a name to go on, the ASA has tens of thousands of members. Obviously, over the years, our members come and go. They join, most renew, but some don't, they get older, they die. We'd have to search our records going pretty far back."

"And we'd appreciate that very much," Jimi said. He, too, forced a smile.

"Like I said," Carolyn continued. "I'd love to help, but I'm afraid it's impossible."

"Oh, we're more than happy to help look through your records," Janis said. "Just point us to your books, and we can search for anyone who might be a possible match."

"You don't understand," Carolyn said. "I didn't say it was difficult, I said it was *impossible*. We take the privacy and confidentiality of our members very seriously. We certainly can't open our member rolls to just anyone who walks in here, regardless of how important the reason. We've been around all these years because our members trust us. What you're asking is simply not going to happen. Unless, that is, you have a warrant or a court order of some kind. I assume none of you are a law enforcement official, right?"

* * *

In North Carolina, Pete Peebles had barely brought the Parisienne to a stop at the rest area when Pixie tumbled out and scurried toward the restroom. Call it a motivated waddle. Bonbon's revenge.

"Poor thing," Penny squeaked. She turned toward Pete, "You go on ahead, too, dear. I'll walk Petunia and catch up in a few minutes."

Pete grumbled, watched his daughter push a child out of the way as she forced her way into the building lobby, and headed that same direction. He stopped first at a pay phone, one of those open-air types. Out of order. So, he entered the building, took care of bladder business, and exited into the lobby. An elderly attendant was sorting tourist brochures; Pete hooked his arm. "You got a phone around here?"

"Pay phone outside," the man said, shaking free of Pete's mechanical grip.

"Nope. It's out of order," Pete said.

"Oh, yeah, I forgot. Been on the fritz for better part of a month. Ya know, the damnedest thing about that phone is that—"

"You got another phone I can use? Agency business." Pete flashed a badge he wasn't supposed to still have.

"Oh, well, sure… I reckon I can let you use one here in the back. Not supposed to let the public in here, but…"

Pete handed the attendant a $5 bill. "It'll be long-distance, but that should cover it, in case anyone gets their tits in a twist."

He dialed Junior Carducci's private line. The attendant stood there until Pete's glare burned a hole in his forehead. Junior answered on the third ring. "Carducci here."

"It's Pete."

"Pete, what's the good word?"

"Ha! Good word... You ever travel with a wimpy wife, a whiny daughter, and a Poodle in heat?"

"Somehow, I've not had that pleasure yet, Pete. I'll add that to my life goals. Where are you?"

"North Carolina, wise guy. Rest stop somewhere west of Winston-Salem. Which reminds me, I need to start smoking again."

"Ah, retirement," Junior said, "the time to reconnect with loved ones and resume bad habits. So, ya got everyone piled into the old Plymouth?"

"Fuckin' Plymouth wouldn't start," Pete said. "Had to take the Pixie-mobile."

"Let me guess..."

"Don't even bother. Let's just say her choice in car colors is very Pixie-like. Call it Pepto Pink."

"Oh, my, what a picture you're painting, you and the family in a—"

Pete could tell that Junior had muted the phone. "Laugh all you want," he said. "But when your glee subsides, give me a damn update."

Seconds later, Carducci was back. He cleared his throat. "Yes, well, let's see, I've learned quite a bit since we last spoke. Sonny Muckle, the Indy attorney, is on the road with a set of 24-year-old twins – fraternal – named, um, here it is: Jimi Johansen and Janis Grack."

"Interesting. This Grack woman married, then? Was she a Johansen first?"

"No and no. Apparently, the twins were separated at birth and adopted out."

"I'm not seeing the connection here," Pete said. "What do these twins have to do with Muckle?"

"He's their uncle. Their birth mother was one Winnie Muckle DePew. She gave birth to them in May of 1970. Do the math, Pete."

"What the hell are you saying, Junior? Or *not* saying?"

"I'm saying they were very likely conceived around the time of the Woodstock festival in '69."

"And?"

"And it stands to reason their biological father could be – I repeat, *could* be – one Jay Finch, Jr."

"I'll be damned," Pete said. He paused, processing this revelation. "You got eyes on these guys? You said they were on the road together... You know where they are or where they're headed?"

"Don't have visuals yet, Pete. Not sure I can do that without arousing undue attention and jeopardizing my job here, frankly. But my Indy operative did uncover where they were headed. Got my notes right here... Yeah, so this LilBuckaroo character, Winnie's other child – and thus, as it turns out, the half-brother of Jimi and Janis – calls the attorney's assistant, one Pepper Duckenfield..."

"And?"

"And Pepper tells him they're headed to Florida, to Kissimmee, to stop in at this organization called the American Sunbathing Association. It's a group for nudists, of all things. According to the conversation between LilBuckaroo and Pepper, they're searching for someone without much info other than he's *probably* a nudist. Pepper tells him they're gonna try to get info from the ASA, and if they can't, then they'll just have to visit as many nudist clubs as they can while there's still time."

"Still time for what?"

"That part wasn't entirely clear, but my gut tells me that *your* gut was correct. They're trying to get everyone together back at Woodstock. Most likely in time for the 25th anniversary."

"Jackpot!" Pete yelled. "My gut's never wrong!" The attendant peeked around the corner. Pete shooed him away. "So, a reunion, eh? Finch, the attorney, the twins, and their mother..."

"Not quite," Carducci said.

"Why not?"

"I also learned that Winnie recently passed away."

"Hmmm..."

"It appears," Junior continued, "that this might be a memorial trip as much as it is a reunion."

Pete shook his head. He said nothing.

"Pete, you still there?"

"Absolutely."

"What are you thinking, then?"

"I was just wondering if I should put the kibosh on going to Kibosh and instead track the attorney and his cohorts." He paused. "No, Goddammit! I'm gonna trust my gut again. I *know* I'll find that money if I just go back to East Ki this one last time. Hell, even if I don't find it, I can still make it back to the Woodstock reunion in time and, with an ounce of luck, *finally* apprehend this guy."

"Well, Pete, I'd be remiss if I didn't remind you of two things," Carducci said. "First, you're not a federal agent anymore, so you don't really have authority to apprehend him; and second, there aren't even any official charges still pending for your Finch guy."

"I'll make a citizen's arrest if I have to," Pete said. "Call it suspicion of aiding and abetting… whatever. In any event, I can make his life a living hell for a while."

Carducci sighed. "Two more things you should know," he said. "The reunion was canceled at the location where the original Woodstock went down. However, another reunion concert at Saugerties, New York, is still a go. That may be where everyone ends up, although it's likely to be a big-ass place with tons of people. Also, you'll be happy to learn that my Indy guy got the tap planted in Pepper Duckenfield's apartment – again, not an easy feat. And none too cheap, I might add, considering he has to have duplicate recording equipment to cover both locations."

"I'll make it worth your while, Junior. And I gotta say, this is impressive work you're doing. Proud of ya. Keep me posted on whatever additional intel you come up with. I'll check in when I can, but remember, after today, you can reach me at the Ol Swimmin Hole."

Pete looked out the window toward the rest area's dog-walking lawn. Outside, Penny was running and holding Petunia in the air, fending off three dogs who had broken free of their humans and were pining for Poodle poontang. Pixie chased them all.

"Fuck!" Pete yelled. The phone receiver dropped to the floor.

"Pete? Pete? You okay? You still there? Pete?"

* * *

Earlier, Max had fallen asleep in the Mickey D's parking lot near Lynchburg. Sometime while he slept, the Peebles-packed pink Parisienne had pulled out, putting an end to his pursuit. When he'd awakened, Max did a quick calculation; he figured he could be as much as twenty minutes behind his prey. Even so, it occurred to him that losing track of Pete Peebles and his brood was actually a blessing. They were slow as hell, and if he kept going while they stopped overnight, he could get to the Ol Swimmin Hole Bed and Breakfast well ahead of them and be in position to look like any other tourist (rather than a thinly veiled stalker).

So, Max had found a pay phone and called the Ol Swimmin Hole to update the reservation he'd made after leaving the DC bar the night before. He told Gertilda, the owner, he would arrive a day early (albeit in the evening). *If* they had a room available, of course.

One room left, Gertilda said, the same small one he was going to get the next day anyway. Tentatively, she added, "I understand the guests arriving tomorrow for the adjoining room have a small dog. I do hope that won't affect your decision to stay with us."

"Certainly not. I love dogs," he lied.

CHAPTER 15

(In Which Robin Gets Nosy, Sonny and the Twins Get Naked, and Jimi Gets a Lead)

Early Evening

THE MOON-YOUR-MAMA BAR & GRILL HAD A SPLIT PERSONALITY OF SORTS.

The grill side faced a county road, and at first glance, looked to be nothing more than a 1950s stainless-steel-skinned diner. It soon became apparent, however, there was much more to the Moon-Your-Mama. While first-time visitors might not have known the hidden truth, locals knew what lay in that part of the building behind the tall wooden fence that extended 100 feet from either side of the building and into dense thickets of Southern Red Cedars. Locals knew the back side of the structure, the bar side, lay within the confines of the Grin and Bare It Family Nudist Campground. Where all those *nekkid* people hung out. Literally.

From the Grill side, the nudists remained unseen but not unheard. The diner patrons had heard the jukebox when it played. They'd heard the joking around. The laughter. They'd heard the joyful shouts when the bar TV showed a favored sports team win and the groans when the team lost.

They'd heard the rumors, too. About the bar. About the campground. About the mysterious nudists and their antics.

Rumors of wild *sex-u-al* orgies, hundreds of people at a time, an unbroken chain of lusting, thrusting flesh, as far as the eye could see (if one could bear to look). Rumors of a place so debauched that dried-up 100-year-old men walked around with urgent and insatiable erections. Of a place where lubricant flowed from dispensers mounted on posts every 25 feet throughout the campground. Of a place where amputees cavorted, and everyone acted like animals. Of a place where children – yes, children! – were in a virtual training camp to become professional *pre-verts!*

These were the stories told by "people in the know" who, of course, had never set foot inside the camp or seemingly ever been naked except immediately following their birth. Luckily, those people were few. Most of the locals had a firmer grasp on reality: They knew the nudists to be friendly and kind. They knew them to be loyal and dependable tourists who brought welcome revenue to the county. Nudists, as it turned out, had deep pockets.

And besides, the nudists were hidden. Don't want to see naked bodies? Don't go inside the fence; don't go past the Cedars; don't seek out the bar side of the Moon-Your-Mama.

The locals also understood the grill and the bar were a package deal. They knew that protesting the bar and the campground meant risking the "bestest" damn diner in the county – the place with the bestest Southern Fried Chicken, bestest Chicken 'n Dumplin's, bestest Corn Fritters, and bestest Fried Grits Cakes (which, when drizzled with honey, made even people who hate grits swoon with delight). The Moon-Your-Mama Grill was also acclaimed for its Chess Pie, Hummingbird Cake, and, naturally, their homemade Moon Pies!

(And it was the only place locals could grab a bag of *Tat'r Nips*.)

The grill side of the Moon-Your-Mama was open only for breakfast and lunch, but you could get a burger, hot dog, or grilled ham and cheese through the bar side from when the bar opened at 6 up till 7 p.m. At 5:15, Robin Paloma stepped into the kitchen and tapped the bar-side bell. He peered into the pass-thru. Jaybird was there, cleaning cocktail glasses.

"Did you see this, Mr. Stockwood?" He placed the weekend newspaper on the ledge.

"Must be important," Jaybird said. "You don't usually call me by my last name, Mr. Paloma, so what's up?"

Robin pointed to an article. "Woodstock reunion got canceled. No Woodstock, Mr. Stockwood."

Jaybird examined one final bar glass, rubbing away spots with a clean rag, then tossed the rag near the bar sink. He picked up the paper. "What's this got to do with me?"

"Probably nothing, I guess," Robin said. "I just know you have that Woodstock videotape and, well, your name *is* Stockwood, after all. I always assumed it was a coincidence, but then again, I have to assume a lot of things about you. You're a very private man, Jayson. A hard man to get to know."

"I thought you liked hard men," Jaybird said, being coy, but also doing what he could to derail Robin's train of thought. It didn't work. While Jaybird skimmed the article, Robin persisted: "So, were you at Woodstock? Is that where you got your name? Nice alias, if it is one. Just wondering, that's all. As I said, I'd just like to know more about you."

Jaybird smiled but did not respond.

Robin gave up. "All right, then. Ya know, for a nudist, you seem to have a lot to hide. But take it from me," he said, "confession is good for the soul. And I'm here to listen whenever you wanna open up." He stepped away from the pass-thru. "Keep the paper."

"Thanks," Jaybird said. "Gonna run home for a bit and check on Anthony Purrkins. Be back by 6 to open the place."

"Hey!" Robin yelled. Jaybird turned and stepped back toward the opening. A moment later, Robin's hand came through, holding a brown paper bag. "Some leftovers from the fish special at lunch. Give them to that darling little kitty of yours."

* * *

Anthony Purrkins greeted Daddy Jayson at the door – the cat was rather dog-like in that regard – and followed him room to room, more closely than usual, lured by the fish. Jaybird put the bag on the counter. He looked at the cat. The cat looked at the bag.

"Okay, I see how you are, Anthony Purrkins, you fickle feline, you fair-weather friend." Jaybird took a small designated cat plate from the cupboard, opened the bag, and pulled out a filet. Anthony Purrkins sat up, assuming a prairie-dog position as Jaybird mashed the fish into manageable bites. "It's from Robin," Jaybird said, setting the plate on the floor. Anthony Purrkins stopped inches from the plate and turned away.

"Fickle as fuck," Jaybird said.

He went to the couch and sat on that day's towel. The cat sidled up next to him. "Got about a half-hour with ya, little buddy," Jaybird told the cat. "Might have just stayed at the bar till opening, but Robin was chatty and prying. Wanted to know more about me, about my past, about Woodstock." The cat purred and stared.

Jaybird started to talk but then hesitated. He stroked Anthony Purrkins and rubbed his furry neck and chin. Finally, he said, "Robin said he thinks I have something to hide. Guess he's right about that. He said confession's good for the soul. Probably right about that, too." He pulled the cat up into his arms, held him like a baby.

"Anthony Purrkins," he began, "have I ever told you about my one true love – aside from you, of course? You see, back in '69, there was this girl and her brother..."

* * *

According to the 200-page *North American Guide to Nude Recreation* Janis purchased from the American Sunbathing Association, the closest nudist club was not a campground, but a resort: Lakeside Grove Nudist Resort and Community.

Carolyn at the ASA office had given them good directions to Lakeside and even called ahead for them. Though disappointed they'd have to take the Plan B approach of going club by club – and nervous about entering this strange new world – Sonny and the twins arrived at the gated nudist resort by 6:00 p.m.

Jimi pushed the button at the gate and announced that Carolyn had referred them for a visit and overnight accommodations. The voice inside the speaker box told them how to find the office. Magically, the gate opened.

The office, they'd been instructed, was centrally located deep inside the vast property. To get there, Jimi drove past dozens of campers and trailers, motorhomes and vans. And nudists, of course, who walked along the road, played tennis, laid out on sunning lawns. One man even squatted atop his fifth-wheel trailer, adjusting an antenna.

"People really are naked here," Janis said. "I know we've been anticipating this, but it's kinda trippy just seeing these nudists in the flesh ... as it were."

Jimi tapped her on the arm and nodded toward Sonny.

"Oh, sorry, Uncle Sonny. I didn't mean to focus on the visuals. It's just that... Well, ya know."

"Oh, I'm sure it is indeed a *trip*," Sonny said. "I remember thinking the same thing at Woodstock; not just the grounds there or the music or the enormity of it all – but seeing so many people just being naked and free."

"Maybe this is where the nudists at Woodstock came when they got older," Jimi said.

"Well, we certainly hope at least one of them did," Sonny said. "Carolyn said this was a large and popular place, as good a place as any to start. But it would sure be nice if we could end our search where we begin it."

When they stopped in front of the office for guest registration, Jimi took a deep breath. "So, here we are. You know, all this anticipation and yet it occurs to me we haven't discussed how we'll handle things once inside."

"In the office?" Janis asked.

"No, I mean once inside the resort or the club or the campground or whatever this is. Do we stay together? Do we split up to cover more ground? Do we talk to the staff or the guests? Do we just look around and stare at butts looking for tattoos?"

"Good questions," Sonny said. "Probably depends on the nature of the place. First things first – I think we should check-in and find our rooms, and then get something to eat. Carolyn said there was a nice restaurant here. Maybe we can engage some of the locals and the staff. Chances are, someone will know the man we'll describe. If not, we'll just have to keep our eyes open. I'll count on you two to take the lead in that regard."

So, they checked in, were given a map and the details of resort amenities, and learned where they'd be staying. They were able to land an apartment-style two-bedroom for the night, which they located and settled into. When they'd finished unpacking, Sonny said, "I'm ready for dinner. Anyone else?"

"Oh, boy," said Jimi.

"What is it?" Janis asked.

"Let me guess," Sonny said. "This is the moment of truth, right? The moment of 'naked truth' when we actually immerse ourselves into this culture?"

"Yeah, something like that," Jimi confessed.

"Well, speaking as a lesbian, if you've seen one pee-pee, you've seen 'em all. So, whaddaya say, on the count of three?"

"Okay," Sonny said. "One..."

Janis said, "Two..."

"Oh, boy, um ... uh, three, I guess," said Jimi. He closed his eyes, removed his shirt, kicked off his shoes, pulled off his socks, and then, in one swift motion, pulled down his jeans and his underpants. A few seconds later, he eased open his eyelids.

"You're still dressed!" he screamed at Janis and Sonny.

"Just figured you'd be the one to cheat, and I, for one, wasn't going to let you get by with that," Janis said. "But I gotta say, Jiminy, you've got guts, especially considering..."

Jimi covered up. "Hey, you said if you've seen one, you've seen 'em all."

"Turns out I was wrong," Janis said. "Besides, again speaking as a lesbian, I never really cared to look at that many of them. No offense."

"Arrgggh!"

"Oh, settle down," she said. "I'm just teasing you. Very impressive, actually, in an impressively average way, I suppose." With that, she, too, undressed. "There, you happy now?"

"Happier, yes, but not really happy."

"Okay," Sonny said. "Let's go eat."

"No, no, no, no," Janis chided him. "You don't get off that easy, buster. Time for you to put up or shut up. Drop 'em!"

Sonny laughed. "One little detail you might not have overheard regarding dinner," he said. "While you two were purchasing our beach towels, I got the scoop on the restaurant's dress code."

"Don't tell me..." Jimi said.

Janis was furiously studying the resort amenities info sheet. "I'll be damned," she said. "Sonny Muckle, you've got a mean streak. Clothing is optional at the restaurant."

* * *

Meanwhile, a couple hundred miles away, it the diner side of the Moon-Your-Mama Bar & Grill, Robin Paloma had finished his evening routine of cleaning, counting the day's receipts, and planning the next day's lunch special. He leaned into the pass-thru and caught Jaybird's attention when he stepped back behind the bar just before 6:00. "Probably gonna be a slow night over there. How about you get Sammy to cover for you for a couple hours, and we go back to your place for some R and R, if you know what I mean?"

Jaybird looked away. He took a deep breath. "Look, Robin, the thing is... Well, we need to talk. About us."

* * *

To their credit, Jimi and Janis stayed nude. "No use going back into hiding now," Janis said. And to *his* credit, Sonny joined them. "Clothing optional be damned," he said. "From this point forward, it's balls out' and naked as a Jaybird."

The restaurant was linen tablecloth-fancy, the food above average, and the clientele both dressed and undressed. Some of the older women, in particular, seemed to relish the notion of dressing up for dinner. Nearly all the men, regardless of age, opted to remain nude, seated on their towels.

Lighting inside the restaurant was a tad on the dim side. "Gonna be tough to spot a butt tattoo in a place like this," Janis said. "Especially if guys are always sitting on the evidence."

"I think our best chance is to take a look around in the daylight," Jimi said. "Or to come right out and ask people if they have any info we can use."

"My new brother, Mr. Practical," Janis said.

"You got a better idea?"

"Nope. I kinda like to just take things as they come."

"Somehow, I'm not surprised."

"All right, you two, let's just stay focused on the mission," Sonny said. "Do I remember correctly that there's a bar at the resort, too?"

"Two of them," Janis said. "One poolside and one attached to the restaurant, about sixty feet from where we're sitting."

"Then I suggest we make a stop in the bar here, see if we can find anything out, and then get a good night's sleep. Tomorrow we can go to the pool and explore the rest of the resort."

"Sounds like a good plan," Jimi said, making a smug face at Janis. "How long do you think we should stay tomorrow before moving on?"

"Let's just play that by ear," Sonny said, prompting Janis to make a smug face of her own back at Jimi.

But the bar was a bust. Two drinks each and conversations with the bartender and six other naked patrons led nowhere. No one knew of anyone matching Jaybird's description – not at Lakeside Grove nor any of the other places the guests might have frequented over the years.

Janis and Sonny headed back to the guest apartment while Jimi stopped at the bar's restroom. On his way out, he noticed a brochure rack featuring area attractions – mostly of Disney World and other nearby tourist traps. *No time for such frivolity*, Jimi thought, so he left the rack cards in place. But then he noticed something about the display. It bore a faded sticker:

Display courtesy of the TANNUTS Organization
Totally Awesome Nudists Naked Under The Sun

"Excuse me," Jimi said to the bartender. "Can you tell me anything about this TANNUTS group?"

Five minutes later, Jimi announced to Janis and Sonny, "I may have a lead after all."

* * *

At half-past ten in the evening in Indianapolis, wiretapper Mike Smyth sat in the white van outside the Muckle law office. Still nursing his afternoon calf and thigh wounds from Pepper Duckenfield's evil Shih Tsu, he had retrieved the external recording device and was listening to the day's phone recordings. There were only two of interest, both voice mail messages. The first had come in around 5:35 p.m. It was from the blind attorney:

> *"Ducks, its Sonny, calling to give you an update. Tried to leave a message at your place just now but kept getting a busy signal. Anyway, we made it to the ASA office shortly before they closed for the day. No luck there. They wouldn't let us review their membership rolls, current or historical. Seems they're totally on the up-and-up and could not be swayed by our collective charms. Best we could do was buy a rather thick* North American Guide to Nude Recreation *from them. We'll use that as we go club by club and hunt for the Jaybird. First stop is a place near Kissimmee. That's it for now, I guess. Oh, except for one thing: why the hell did you rent a white Bronco?"*

Goddamned dog probably knocked the receiver off the hook, Smyth thought. He'd have to test the line again in the morning – from the outside, he hoped. Grimacing, he touched the bites on his calf and thigh. If he had to go back in and face the devil dog again, he resolved to take a steak laced with knockout drops.

And then the second call, a poor connection that had come in a few minutes after the call from the attorney. A message from an unnamed caller of unclear gender:

> *"I know what you've been doing. We need to talk."*

Click.

* * *

At home, his disheartening we-need-to-talk conversation with Jaybird concluded, Robin Paloma turned on the TV news. His mind wandered, and he had trouble paying attention to the news reports. But just as he was about to shut off the TV and get ready for bed, he noticed a stationary news ticker at the bottom of the screen:

Got a News Tip? Call WTFU Today!

Robin hurriedly jotted down the number provided, then picked up the phone and dialed. He got a recording: "Welcome to the WTFU News Information Tip Line. After the beep, please leave your name, phone number, and a very brief description of the nature of your news lead. Someone will return your call as soon as possible. Thank you for watching WTFU!"

Bee-e-e-p...

"Hello, yes, my name is... Well, I'd rather not leave my name quite yet, but I would like to connect with Radiance Reynolds about her Good Samaritan story. I've got a lead she'll be very interested in."

* * *

In East Kibosh, Max Thibodeaux had settled into his room at the Ol Swimmin Hole. He took the cellular phone from his box of equipment and tried to make a call. No signal. Damn thing was worthless here and most places. So, he picked up the room phone, pushed the requisite digits for long-distance, and waited for the expected machine message:

"Hello, you've reached the voice mailbox of award-winning ratingsh leader Jenningsh Prokoff. If you have thish number, I may be willing to shpeak with you. Here'sh the beep."

Bee-e-e-p...

"Prokoff, it's Max here. I know it's late and you won't get this message till tomorrow – okay, actually it'll be your today when you get it, but anyway... Just wanted to give you an update on that lead I'm following for you.

"I've landed in a very strange place called East Kibosh, South Carolina. Been following our subject, former Agent Pete Peebles, but decided to come on ahead and be in place here when he and his family arrive tomorrow – again, that would be *today* when you get this message.

"Anyway, odd bunch this Peebles gang: Pete, his wife Penny, their dog Princess Petunia and their indescribable – and not in a good way – daughter Pixie. As a reminder, Peebles is following the money trail of the one great failing of his storied career. He's a bulldog, this

Pete guy, but he seems about to lose his shit thanks to traveling with the family.

"No idea where this is gonna end up yet, Prokoff, but I think it's about to get good."

CHAPTER 16
(In Which Penny Gets Hooked on Helping Pete, Pepper Gets Hooked on Todd, and LB Gets Hooked on Candy at the Knaughty Pine)

Late Evening

WHILE JIMI WAS TELLING SONNY AND JANIS ABOUT THE TANNUTS LEAD; and while Max was messaging Prokoff about Pete Peebles; and while Pete and family were stopping for the night at a fleabag in Rock Hill, South Carolina; LilBuckaroo soldiered on.

He had hoped to make it far deeper into the south by evening – hoping to reach Nashville or beyond – but the events of the day had left him wiped out. Pepper and Todd. Burger In The First. Miss T and his scorched upper lip and the I'M SO HORNY graffiti. And in between, his ghost-dad telling him what to do, what not to do, and what to do to undo things he'd done.

Exhausting.

But he kept going. Wearing a pullover jacket, he had driven with the top down, hoping the night air would keep him awake. It had helped, but only to a point. And finally, shortly before 11 p.m., he had reached that point. Still less than a hundred miles into Kentucky, but yawning uncontrollably, LB decided to stop for the night.

A school bus-size red neon sign of mid-century design lured him from the road. Like a moth to a flame, he followed a twisting side road toward its giant glow, somehow missed his turn off, doubled back, and pulled into the motel's parking lot. The Knaughty Pine. *Rooms for rent by the hour, night, or duration of your marital spat.* LB pulled beneath a jutting buttressed roof that heralded the lobby entrance. He turned off the ignition but sat there in the car, still mesmerized by the sign; its center portion, the 'ugh' in Knaughty, pulsed as if ready to expire. He could relate.

LB swung open his oversized driver's door, made his way out of the car and into the lobby. More pulsing lights greeted him. A pink neon-tubed lamp read 'Hot Stuff,' its shade resembling a purple fire fighter's helmet. Freud would be fascinated, but LB was too tired to be turned on.

The teak counter inside the lobby stood chest high. Its lower part included a glass case, brightly fluoresced, and displaying an impressive assortment of ... paraphernalia. Accoutrements. Accessories. Gadgets. Devices. *Toys*. Even a jet-stream water flosser. And all with sale and rental-per-night price tags. LB took a deep breath and tapped the counter bell.

"Got cash and a credit card?" came a shaky, gravelly voice from a back room.

"Um, yeah," LB said. "Got a card. Some cash. Depends on how much it is."

Smoke spurted through the door, and then its human followed. The smoker was skinnier than anyone LB had ever seen. He could wear straw wrappers as shirt sleeves; except that he had no sleeves at all and barely a shirt – just a yellowed cotton 'wife-beater.' His hair was thin, too, with individual black strands looping high and bringing to mind the Gateway Arch in St. Louis.

"I'm Lou," he said. "Welcome to the Knaughty Pine." He belched smoke like a '52 Studebaker. "You alone?"

LB nodded.

"One of those nights," Lou said, fogging the air between them before stubbing out his cigarette.

"How much for a room?" LB asked.

"Depends."

"On what?"

"On what type of room and for how long."

"What types of rooms do you have?"

Lou leaned forward and lowered his voice, but just a little. "We got sleepin' rooms and fuckin' rooms. Mostly the fuckers. Even if you're doin' shit by yourself, if you ain't sleepin', you'll get a fuckin' room." He looked LB up and down. "You plannin' on doin' any ... sleepin'?"

"Oh, Lord, yes," LB said. "I'm worn out. Been driving too long. Just need a good night's—"

"Twenty-two fifty, then. Out by 10. And if I find any stains on the sheets, I'll charge you for an extra hour at the fuckin' room rate, 'cause we'll have to change the sheets."

"Aren't you going to change the... Oh, never mind," LB said. He reached into his wallet and pulled out a twenty and a five.

"Ain't got change this time a'night," Lou said. "All's I can do is put the diff'rence on deposit against the stain charge. From the looks of things, that seems fair."

"Sure," LB said. "Whatever you need to do."

"Credit card, too," Lou demanded. "For incidental charges."

LB produced his card. "What would be 'incidental charges'?"

"Charges for any incidents, of course, regardless of police involvement," Lou said. "You got a limit on this card?"

"Two thousand, maybe?"

"Good to know." Lou studied the card. "Is this your real name? LilBuckaroo DePew? Sounds like a cartoon or a kid's name."

"It was a kid's name, but then I grew up."

"All the same..."

"Don't mean to rush you, but I'm really bushed."

Lou glared at him. "For a guy who's not here for fuckin', you sure got your panties in a wad." He placed a room key with a pine tree air freshener key chain on the counter.

LB yawned.

"Okay, okay," Lou said. "Almost done. That your car out there?"

"Yes, sir. '71 Cadillac Eldo."

"Know the plate number?"

"Not without going back outside."

"No matter. White with ... looks like red interior?"

"Right." Another yawn.

"Any other identifying marks?"

"Um, well, I've got a mole shaped like Michigan. It's on my inner right thigh."

Lou stared at him.

"Lower peninsula only," LB clarified. "Some people say it looks like a mitten."

"Thanks for sharing that," Lou said, expressionless. "Any other identifying marks *on your car*?"

"Oh, well, it's got steer horns on the front."

Lou looked out the window. "Sure does. Is that writing I see on your hood?"

LB released a nervous laugh. "Yeah, darn kids. Vandals, really."

"And it says…?"

"Um, it says… It says, 'I'm so horny,'" LB said, sighing.

Lou pulled back the room key and replaced it with another. "You'll be in *fuckin' room* 22. And I'll keep your credit card for now."

* * *

In Rock Hill, South Carolina, Pete Peebles, his daughter Pixie, and even Princess Petunia were fast asleep, but noisily so – snoring and farting and growling; in the dark, it was unclear who was doing what. But thanks to their nocturnal concerto, Penny Peebles couldn't sleep a wink. She rose from the bed she shared with Pete (where she always slept opposite his hook to avoid any mishaps) and began rummaging through her suitcase.

Penny was a reader of two kinds of novels: romances and cozy mysteries. Though she imagined herself capable of being an amateur sleuth of the Jane Marple or Jessica Fletcher variety, for this trip, Penny had brought along romance novels – the kind of escapist fare suitable for a short vacation. Truth be told, Penny sometimes fantasized about the type of rapture that consumed the airbrushed cover characters. Her favorite romances were the lusty pirate adventures, especially the ones where male leads had hooks. Go figure.

Penny pulled two such books from her suitcase: *Ahoy to Behold* and *From Wench We Came.* And here in the obnoxiously invasive light from the parking lot, she studied the lovers-on-the-covers – they of the long wind-blown hair, ripped bodices and heaving bosoms. (This was also true of the women.)

Alas, Penny wasn't really in the mood for romance. She looked at her husband, his hook a faint glimmer in the reach of the light. She was worried about him. Retirement promised to be a time he could finally enjoy life and take on new pursuits. So far, however, he showed only a renewed mania for an old pursuit: finding the Finch money, and Finch, too. Penny was forever distressed by an inescapable fact: her husband would never really get on with his life until he succeeded in settling this one last score.

She set the romances on the dresser and stared at Pete's accordion file case. Checking behind her to make sure no one was stirring, she then opened the case and sorted through it in the shadows. Pete had the files arranged in reverse chronological order – oldest info in back, newest in front. She pulled out the most recent pages, noticed he had made new scribbles, but then decided to review the entire contents – to finally see what this Finch business was all about. Grabbing motel stationery and a pen, she sequestered herself with the case and its files in the bathroom. A half-hour later, Pete knocked on the door.

Penny hid the case in the shower, flushed the toilet, and emerged, palming the notepad and pen. Later, confident Pete was asleep again, Penny returned to her new private office. Page by page, she made notes, both mental and on the stationery pad. Her husband was missing something, probably something simple. Penny's gut – as strong an asset for her as Pete's gut was for him – told her that much.

Pixie pounded on the door this time. *Her* gut was rebelling against the gas-station bonbons purchased earlier.

It was nearly three in the morning.

* * *

After getting his room key from Lou and driving to a parking space nearby, LilBuckaroo had been unable to shut the convertible top of the Caddy. Bad switch, perhaps, but no time to troubleshoot. He needed sleep. Unfortunately, with the adjoining *fuckin'* rooms a beehive of erotic activity, even on this mid-week evening-into-morning, sleep was hopeless – especially when every grunt and groan and "Oh, Baby" conjured visions of Pepper and Todd going at it.

Finally, during a top-of-the-hour shift rotation in the rooms next door, LB gave up trying to sleep and got out of bed. From his second-floor window, he looked down at the Caddy. A woman leaned against it; she was staring at the boxes in the back seat. Earlier, LB had convinced Lou to try out the chips as a thematically appropriate midnight snack item to offer amorous guests. But even that conversation had been fraught with confusion. "Wanna taste a *dickTat'r* chip?" LB had asked, with a hopeful wink. But because he had hiccupped between the words *dick* and *tat'r*, Lou apparently heard his question as a lewd come-on, albeit one with an endearment: "Wanna taste a dick, tater chip?"

After the minor melee, with a box of the chips forfeited for the cause, LB had made a hasty retreat to his fuckin' room. He'd been too tired, too *defeated*, to carry more boxes up the stairs, but now, there, down below in the parking lot, was this woman, leering at his dwindling inventory.

LB threw on his pullover and a pair of shorts, rushed barefoot from the room, descended the outside stairs, and scurried toward his car.

"This your ride?" the woman asked. She was smoking. And smoking hot, LB had to admit. Her hair was black, her lips fire-engine red, her dress barely there.

"It is, yes," LB said. "Can I help you with something?"

"The real question is if I can help *you* with something." The woman pointed at the horns and the message on the hood. "Never seen a guy advertise his lust quite so … publicly," she said. "Gotta say, it's quite a turn-on."

LB stared, mouth agape.

"Name's Candy," she said, extending a hand, its fingertips matching her lipstick. "And I think you might just find that Miss Candy is dandy, especially when she's sweet on you."

So strong was his need for sleep, however, that LB resisted and went back upstairs alone. Unfortunately, in his earlier haste to leave the room, he had locked himself out. Miss Candy, it turned out, had a master key. With the door unlocked, LB told her to take a can of chips for her trouble. But the door was open, the bed was there, and the product name of his specialty chips turned her on, too. An hour later, when all was said and done, he was out sixty bucks and another full case of *dickTat'rs;* and was no closer to meaningful sleep.

Worse, he had suffered one more indignity: at the conclusion of the act and in the moment of glory, he had called out Pepper's name. Bad enough. But thanks to his burned and bumbling lip, Miss Candy misheard this as an urgent cry for "Pecker!" Moments later, acting in accordance with the "heart of gold" requirements of her unwritten community service contract, the Knaughty Pine concubine offered to arrange a different kind of experience for LB next time he was in town.

* * *

Asleep, Effyu's tail wagged gently and kept hitting Pepper in the mouth. The dog was happy, curled up against Todd in bed, lightly snoring, his paws gently twitching. *Little sonofabitch just needed a father figure all this time,* Pepper thought. She raised up in bed and squinted in the dim bedroom light at her companions. Todd was worth keeping for no other reason than his tranquilizing effect on the dog. He was more effective than weed and a lot cheaper in the long run. Probably.

But there were other reasons to keep Todd around, too. He was a gentleman; he bought her lunches and dinners; he wore deodorant. He brushed his teeth and hair frequently (using different brushes, unlike Sonny, who could get confused after a single Margarita). Todd's feet were precisely 12 inches long and thus useful as a makeshift ruler – and happily, he measured up in other ways as well. He was a reasonably skilled lover, too, adventurous and giving. He said please and thank you and is-that-good-for-you? and didn't even freak out when her wig fell off moments before climax their first time together. Better still, Todd did an uncanny impression of newsman Jennings Prokoff – a talent that made Pepper moist every time.

But best of all, he wasn't LilBuckaroo, and he wasn't Sonny. Neither of whom had called or left a message at the apartment, by the way. *Odd,* she thought.

Rising carefully from the bed, Pepper stepped toward the door. In the faint glow of the night light from the bathroom across the hall, she noticed the desk-style phone on her dresser. The receiver was off the hook. "Fuck," she said, a little too loudly; and then placed the receiver on the cradle

Behind her, Todd rolled onto his back, erecting a tent, as it were.

Time to lose the dog, Pepper thought. She opened her nightstand drawer, put on her bite-resistant oven mitts, and wrestled the awakened and snarling dog into the hallway. She closed the door, shed the mitts, and snuggled against her man. A moment later, in his best sexy slur, Todd whispered, "Good evening, I'm Jenningsh Prokoff with the Nightly Newsh. Thish jusht in…"

And then it was.

Thursday, August 11, 1994

CHAPTER 17
(In Which Janis Checks Out Man-Butts, Jimi Finds TANNUTS,
Sonny Takes a Dive, and a Clue Goes Up in Smoke)

Morning

IN HIS NETWORK'S NEW YORK CITY PRODUCTION OFFICE AFTER A NEWSCAST planning meeting, Jennings Prokoff isolated himself in his upper-level corner office. Surrounded by framed accolades and shelved awards (though no Murrows or Pulitzers among them), he kicked off his wingtips and reclined in his leather high-back with his feet on his desk. Then he hit the master switch turning on the five TVs mounted high on the entry-door wall. Each set was permanently tuned to a different network – the "Big Three" (including his own), CNN, and C-SPAN. The TVs were mainly for effect; Prokoff seldom paid them any attention unless a commercial for the Mamas & the Ta Tas restaurant chain appeared.

With his "Anchors Aweigh" coffee cup in hand, he scanned the latest ratings report. The overnights sucked. His newscast was in third place again, a disturbing position even in summer, but especially during contract negotiation time. He crumpled the report and tossed it in the general vicinity of the corner wastebasket.

Next, he checked his private-line voicemails. One message from his wife asking him to pick up milk, eggs, and Scotch on the way home. *Delete.* One from his mother telling him she was yeasting again, whatever the hell that meant. *Delete.* One from Max Thibodeaux – scoop scout extraordinaire. *Save.* And a terse message from Radiance Reynolds, that Florida reporter chick he'd chatted up at an affiliates' meet-and-greet two months earlier: "Call me, you sack of shit! I'm preg—" *Delete.*

He replayed the message from Max:

"Prokoff, it's Max here ... Just wanted to give you an update on that lead I'm following for you ... strange place called East Kibosh, South Carolina ... following our subject, former Agent Pete Peebles ... odd bunch this Peebles gang ... He's a bulldog, this Pete guy ... about to lose his shit thanks to traveling with the family ... No idea where this is gonna end up yet, Prokoff, but I think it's about to get good."

"About to get good" meant this could be a scoop, a prime-time news exclusive. If properly teased, with extended features and follow-up reports for weeks, well... Well, it could be a ratings bonanza. A contract bonanza, too!

Prokoff's coffee was getting cold and C-SPAN was boring him to tears, as it was designed to do. He pushed a couple of buttons on his multiline, instant-connect, desktop communication thingy.

Three rings. "Good morning, I'm Walter Cronkite." External line. Wrong number. Click.

Two more buttons, two rings. "Hewwo, Babwa he-uh..." Click.

Again, two more buttons. "Mawning, Mista Prokawff." Finally, his secretary.

"Bring me a hot cup of coffee. One that won't go cold sho fasht. And come in and change the channel on shet 5. Who makesh up thish Congressh crap anyway? Oh, and open my blindsh. I'm gonna need shome shunshine."

* * *

Beneath the rising Florida sun, Jimi was alone in the Bronco, making his way to the Old Seminole Heights section of Tampa. He hated leaving Janis and Sonny alone to uncover answers or leads at Lakeside Grove, but Jimi was following his own lead: tracking down the leaders of the TANNUTS organization.

From an old brochure he'd borrowed from Norman, Lakeside's long-time bartender, Jimi had an address, but the phone number, a toll-free line, was no longer valid. Norman told him that TANNUTS was most likely defunct as he hadn't heard much about it for a few years. A quick call to Carolyn at the ASA office confirmed it: TANNUTS had been a short-lived group that apparently ceased operations at least five years earlier. It mostly had a small regional footprint – central Florida to southern Georgia, if Carolyn remembered correctly. But then she added, "I believe it appealed mainly to minorities and people who considered themselves outside the mainstream – like artsy types and aging hippies."

Bingo!

Carolyn had felt comfortable naming the organization's founders, Bert and Estherjean Fernley. But she wasn't willing to share any direct personal information she might have had about them. However, when Jimi mentioned the address he had uncovered for the organization, Carolyn said, "That sounds like it could be about right."

Acting on those leads, tentative leads at best, Jimi had set out at 9:25 Thursday morning, grabbed a quick breakfast on the road, and headed west. At 11:07, he was driving slowly down the street toward the Fernleys' last known address, wondering if one of these small bungalows could really have once headquartered a nudist organization. When he spotted the address, his hopes rose: a garden gnome stood at the base of the porch – the gnome bent over, its bare bottom mooning the street.

Jimi pulled the Bronco onto the cracked concrete driveway. There was no garage, but a small car sat in shadows toward the back of the property. A Subaru perhaps, and Jimi took that as a good sign, too. Nudists would surely like Subarus.

With Norman's brochure in hand, Jimi stepped from the Bronco and sized up the residence as he approached. The house was a single-story shotgun-style cottage with a low-pitched roof and large overhangs to hinder the invasive sun. It featured a brick-columned porch, the bricks painted mint green to match the aging wood siding which, in turn, may have been painted to match the mint-and-white striped awning extending from the main porch beam. Jimi winked at the gnome, crossed his fingers, and stepped up onto the porch.

He knocked on the Craftsman-style front door, waited maybe twenty seconds and knocked again, louder this time. As he was about to knock a third time, the thin lace door curtains parted, and a single eye sized him up. A woman opened the door, but just a sliver. "I don't talk to no solic'tors," she said. "Go on about your way then."

The door started to close, but Jimi instinctively wedged the brochure into the gap. "I'm here about TANNUTS!" he exclaimed. "Not selling anything. Just trying to locate a member. Is this the headquarters? Is this the Fernley residence?"

Seconds later, the door opened again, just a crack. The pinched brochure fell to the porch floor. And then Estherjean Fernley joined Jimi on the porch. She was not what he expected.

* * *

Janis's arm was interlocked with Sonny's as she led him around the grounds of Lakeside Grove, about to enter the pool and lounge area. Sunbathing central. "Can you appreciate the irony," she began, "of a lesbian making the rounds here with the sole intention of checking out mens' butts?"

Sonny snickered. "And what about me? I've been thinking that I'm probably the only blind man in the world touring a nudist resort with his very own seeing-eye lesbian."

"It's good to be one-of-a-kind in this world, I think," Janis added. "And yet, as I look around this place, I'm struck by both the uniqueness and the sameness of us all. A paradox, perhaps. As different as everyone appears to be – different sizes and shapes and ages and shades of skin – we all have pretty much the same bits and pieces, within our genders, of course."

"Of course."

They walked through a metal gate and into the central community space, Sonny tapping his cane ahead of them. A couple dozen sunbathers reclined on towel-covered nylon-strapped lounges. "Fewer people here now than this morning," Janis said. They were making their second round of the facilities for the day. "Cloudy out and a little too warm for the locals, so I'm guessing many of the sunbathers here now are tourists."

"Or sun junkies who just can't get their tans quite dark enough."

"I just wish I could see more boy-butt," Janis said. "Still can't believe I'm saying things like that. But all the older guys are laying on their asses. Wish we had a way to make them get the hell up."

"Next time we should bring a flag and an audiotape of the Star Spangled Banner," Sonny said. "Oh, naked patriots, stand and salute!"

Janis laughed, but then stopped their progress and turned serious. "Can I ask you a question, Uncle Sonny?"

"It worries me when you, of all people, ask permission, but yes, go ahead."

"What's it like being in a visual place like this and not being able to see?"

Sonny tilted his head toward the sky. "Well, you mentioned a while ago that it was cloudy. I already knew that. I can feel it when the hot rays of the sun hide behind the clouds. And you mentioned there were fewer people here now than before. I knew that, too. I could detect the change in the level of conversations; I can hear the quiet in the pool where before children were splashing and squealing. You also mentioned it was warmer than before. Of course, I knew that too; I can feel the sweat rising on my skin just like you can."

Janis was silent.

"Oh, I don't mean to be critical," Sonny said. "I appreciate all the information, all of your observations. But the thing is, I can receive and process and interpret nearly everything you can – everything *except* the truly visual, that is. Oh, I can imagine the color of the clouds and the grass and the palm trees and the parking lots because I have memories of those things. Memories in color, just like my dreams still bring color to me. But I can't quite grasp the design of things, the shapes of things I can't touch, the essence of things I never got to experience with my eyesight intact."

"What do you mean?" Janis asked.

"I'll give you an example," Sonny said. "To my left, I'm guessing maybe twenty feet away or so, I can hear a different set of sounds. I hear people talking but in a sheltered space. Faintly, I hear sounds of ice being scooped and glasses being filled. I hear a cash register. I heard an order bell ring just now. From that, I assume there's an open-air restaurant or café, probably a poolside bar with food. Is that correct?"

"Yes, you're exactly right."

"But what I don't know is the name of the bar. I don't know the shape of the roof or the colors of the structure. I don't know how much glass there is, how large the windows, the color-scheme inside, or if the place has a design theme. I can smell burgers grilling, but I can't read a menu, so I don't know what else they might offer. Do you get what I'm saying, Janis? My other senses are alive and well; I just need help with those things that are purely visual."

"I think I get it. But does that include body parts?" Janis asked. "Do you want me to describe people in detail as we approach or speak to someone?"

Sonny laughed and shook his head. "I think that's where I have an advantage," he said. "I can interact and deal with people based on their voices, their tone, their courtesy, or lack thereof. And I can do all of this without first making a judgment based on appearance. For instance, I care more about a woman's laugh than her breasts. I value a man's kindness more than his penis. Body parts are window dressing, nothing more. Same for clothes. The real person is not the body; the real person is the humanity that oozes out."

"Sometimes," Janis said, "you say some awesomely deep shit."

Sonny grinned and turned a full circle. "Take me over to the water," he said.

"Okay. This way."

Poolside, Sonny eased out of his flip flops and teased a toe into the water. "Warm," he said.

"If you want to take a swim, maybe we should —"

"For the moment," Sonny said, "let's assume I can't swim very well. But you said you wanted to make the men get up off their butts, right? Well, here goes... Just be sure to look for that tattoo." And with that, he pushed off from Janis and fell, cane flying, into the pool. Yelling, splashing, going under and coming back up. Coughing. Gasping.

A man with many tricks up his sleeve, Janis thought. Even though he was sleeveless.

* * *

After a few minutes of introduction and explaining his motives, Jimi had watched Estherjean Fernley excuse herself and disappear back inside her Tampa bungalow. Beyond merely hoping to locate the Fernleys, he hadn't allowed himself to form any expectation about what they might *look like*. But while he liked to think of himself as an open-minded Gen X-er, he hadn't anticipated the woman – Essie, she asked to be called – who had stepped outside the meet him.

"Still trying to come to terms with a black woman running a nudist organization, aren't you?" she asked as she returned to the porch with a tray of cookies and lemonade. "Here's a napkin," she said. "Grab your goodies. Let's have a seat."

Jimi swaddled two homemade chocolate chip cookies in his napkin, took a foam cup of lemonade, and joined Essie on cushioned wrought-iron chairs. The cushions were mint green, naturally. Essie Fernley was not just a woman of color, but also a woman of color coordination.

"Delicious," Jimi said truthfully. "Thank you. And thanks for giving me some of your time today."

"What else have I got to do?" Essie asked. "Not often I get a tall, dark and handsome gentleman caller to share cookies with." She grinned broadly at Jimi. "But you haven't answered my question. I'm not what you expected, am I?"

"Well, I had no expectation, really—"

"But if you had?"

"If I had, I suppose I would have... I would have expected a woman with a dark tan but not one who's naturally dark. I get the impression that nudism is more a Caucasian thing."

Essie laughed. "Oh, honey, you *are* uptight, aren't you? It's okay to say the word 'black.' I know what color I am. But you're right. I am in the minority. Eternally, it seems."

Jimi blushed. He sipped his lemonade to keep himself from saying something else stupid.

Essie threw him a lifeline. "Okay, let me give you the backstory without making you ask. Yes, TANNUTS was the organization my husband Bert founded, and I helped him run. We began it some ten years ago and gave it up going on six years back. It had a promising start but fizzled out when the novelty wore off. I think the main novelty was the name. Calling it TANNUTS was Bert's idea. It was certainly a memorable name but probably doomed us, too. Hard to take a group seriously or talk about it proudly with a name like that." She sat up stiffly and effected a deeper voice: "'Do you belong to any social organizations, Mr. Jones?' 'Why, yes. I'm with TANNUTS. You might say I'm a fine upstanding member!'"

Jimi spewed his lemonade. He liked Estherjean Fernley.

"Oh, my," she laughed. "But on with what I was saying. The group caught fire, fizzled, and went out. Bert and me kept it going at least a year longer than we should've. And then he died on me…"

"Oh, I'm sorry, Essie," Jimi said. "Was it sudden?"

"I'll say it was. When I said he died on me I wasn't using a figure of speech. We were on a blanket at Black's Beach in San Diego – the name's just a coincidence, in case you were wondering – and Bert rolled over and put his arm around me and just expired. It took a while before I realized what had happened, but by the time I figured it out, it was too late."

Jimi stopped chewing his cookie and looked down at his flip-flopped feet.

"Oh, it's okay," she continued. "I can't think of a better way for him to go than lying on a nude beach on a beautiful sunny day with the love of his life in his arms."

"We should all be so lucky," Jimi said. He meant it.

"Yes, we should," Essie agreed. "Now, in case you were wondering, Bert was white. Very tan, of course, but white, nonetheless. We were together for 28 years. Quite a risky thing back then for a white man to marry a black woman. We may have had the world against us, but we had each other, and that was enough."

"Were you both nudists then?" Jimi asked. "Is that how you met?"

"Oh, no, you wouldn'ta caught me dead without my clothes on back then. Bert had to drag me kicking and screaming to my first nudist club. But once I was there, I never wanted to leave. I was hooked."

Jimi smiled at her and nodded. "That's a pretty common experience, isn't it? For the man to be the initiator, I mean."

"More often than not. Men do like to let their bits bask in the sun." Essie winked at Jimi. "But listen to me going on like this. You're here for a reason. Trying to find someone, you said. Someone you think might have belonged to TANNUTS?"

"My father," Jimi said. "I'm in town with my uncle and my sister. We never met our dad. Kind of a long story, but the gist of it is this: we need to find him to fulfill our mother's dying wish. Unfortunately, all we know about him is that he was a nudist, a hippie type or free spirit way back when, and he had a facial scar and a tattoo of a Jaybird on his butt. That's it. Don't even have a name, although he liked to be called Jaybird and we think his first name might have actually been Jay or started with the letter 'J'. Also possible, though not certain, that his last name might have had something to do with a bird. Just a hunch of Uncle Sonny's, but it's all we've got to go on."

"Tall order trying to find him with no more information than that," Essie said. "Let me guess, you struck out at the ASA."

"Yes, unfortunately."

"Did you try The Naturist Society?"

"Didn't know about that one. Are they around here?"

"Wisconsin, if I remember correctly."

"No time to work that angle, I'm afraid," Jimi said. "We're on a tight deadline."

Essie scratched her head. "Facial scar, you say?"

"That's right. And that tattoo. He also had prematurely white hair, even in his twenties."

The woman closed her eyes. Her face tightened, but she began to sing lightly: "I get by with a little help..." Moments later, she stopped singing and opened her eyes. "Young man, I've met many nudists over several decades," she began. "It takes a lot for someone to be truly memorable."

"Are you remembering someone like I described?"

Essie smiled. "Well, perhaps. Seems like I do recall a man that matches your description."

Jimi leaned forward on his chair. "Do you remember where or when? Do you recall his name?"

Essie shook her head. "So many people in so many places over so many years."

"Was this man a member of TANNUTS?"

Still shaking her head. "I'm sorry; I just can't say," Essie said. "So long ago, it must've been."

"How long ago?" Jimi asked. This was the first real confirmation that his father might actually be out there. If only Essie could...

"Had to be at least eight to ten years ago, I imagine. I think it might have been when Bert and I were traveling from club to club for a couple of months each summer. We were both teachers, once upon a time, so we had summers off. We traveled mostly here in the south – Florida, Georgia, the Carolinas."

Jimi slouched. "But you don't remember which club it was, do you?"

Essie shook her head. She looked genuinely troubled. "I'm sorry, Jimi. I wish I could be more help."

Jimi managed a smile. "Well, you've given me hope that he really is out there somewhere. Deadline or no deadline, that's more than I had when I got here."

* * *

Meanwhile, across the state, reporter Radiance Reynolds had a deadline of her own; she was on assignment and on a rampage. Her temper was the stuff of legend at WTFU, made worse when reporting on children, charities, churches, and animals. Lately, she'd had her fill of all three, starting with Vinny Vedere, the four-year-old Good Samaritan witness she'd questioned a few days earlier. Yesterday she'd gamely interviewed Tommy Pajamas, chief fundraiser for the Beach Narcolepsy and Severe Sunburn Association. And on this day, she was on assignment in Jacksonville for a midday report about the Ark Bark March-in-the-Park event wherein participants strut their dogs, two by two, behind an upside-down hollowed-out Volkswagen Beetle painted to look like Noah's Ark.

Radiance was ready to blow. And she did just that, bolting from her interview with Ark Bark organizer Bobbie June Greeley, whose pencil-snouted Afghan Hounds kept nosing beneath the reporter's skirt in a frenzied bid to reach third base.

Into a nearby children's charity wishing fountain, Radiance hurled her early lunch corn chowder. With her black hair hanging limply in the water amongst the coins and the corn, she stared at her wavering reflection.

Kids! she thought, spitting out a stubborn kernel. *Damn you, Jennings Prokoff!*

* * *

Estherjean Fernley wouldn't let Jimi take the TANNUTS member rolls with him, but she did help him search the rolls for possible Jaybird matches. She suggested that Jimi study names beginning with A through M while she took N through Z. For confidentiality, first names had never been used, only first and middle initials. It didn't take long to pore over the grand total of 898 members.

They considered all names on their own merits but, in particular, looked for members with the first initial of J or maybe first and middle initials of J.B, along with a bird kind of last name. From those criteria, three possibilities emerged:

J. C. Crowe
J. J. Hawkins
J. L. Parrotte

But when Essie had dug deeper into the TANNUTS records, she discovered that J. C. Crowe was female, and J.J. Hawkins was male but died at age 72 in 1986, too old to have been Jaybird. Only J. L. Parrotte appeared to be a promising lead. He was 41 when joining the organization in 1985 and remained a member until the group folded. His last known club affiliation was the Pasco No Pants Club, a small cooperative that operated year-round but did not permit day visitors. Essie called her contact there on Jimi's behalf.

Again, a dead end. Jonas Leon Parrotte was an adopted name. J. L. was one-quarter Seminole and had naturally dark skin and black hair, not the prematurely white hair of the man Jimi had described. No one else at Pasco No Pants matched Jaybird's description either; Essie had asked.

Coming up empty, she gave Jimi brochures from other central and north Florida clubs; and also handed him the mooning gnome he had complimented her on during their visit. "It's a gift," she said. "Old friend gave this to Bert and me. Said it might be a good luck charm. I've enjoyed it long enough. Maybe it'll bring you some luck in your search."

After Jimi had gone, Essie took her copier box of records back into the house and paused as she passed the piano, a photo of her husband framed and resting there in front of a dusty urn. Bert Fernley was nude in the picture, laughing and holding a very large but very phony cardboard fish, as if he had caught such a monster at their small private lake property an hour from Tampa.

"Honey, I think it's time to start letting go," she said to Bert's photo. So, she carried the box of records out to her Subaru. Then she returned inside and collected the photo and the urn as well. Leaving Tampa, she drove to their old lake place, then tramped through overgrown thickets, tolerating mosquitos as she ported everything to the shoreline. On the tiny private beach where she and Bert had enjoyed many glorious campfires, Essie built another by crumpling and burning the TANNUTS records, a few pages at a time until only one page remained. She stared at a member entry on that page: J.B. Stockwood – Grin and Bare It Family Nudist Campground, Tranquility, Florida. "Well, Jaybird," Essie said, "I kept my promise. But in my gut, I believe this Jimi kid's story, and I hope he finds you before it's too late. Everyone needs a family to hold onto as long as they can."

She dropped the page into the flames and watched it blacken and curl and metamorphose into embers that floated toward the sky like souls set free. And then, with the fire starting to die down and her husband's photo standing watch, she sprinkled in Bert's ashes. "As long as they can," she whispered.

CHAPTER 18
*(In Which LilBuckaroo Gives Hitchhikers a Slow Ride,
and Max Discovers a New Way to Hide)*

Midday

ON I-65 AND HEADING SOUTH, HALF AN HOUR INSIDE TENNESSEE, LilBuckaroo saw smoke ahead.

He had gotten a late morning start and was still tired as hell but at least had survived the Knaughty Pine Motel and was on the move, convertible top down on a warm, cloudy and breezy day. Finally – for-the-love-of-God, *finally* – he was making good time.

Until the smoke.

Road construction ahead had provoked a fiery accident. The fiery accident provoked a rapidly expanding backup. And the rapidly expanding backup provoked LB's ghost-dad to navigate. *Turn here,* Denny DePew said. *Keep moving.*

So, LB took the county road exit and approached the fork where the road split east and west. Because eastbound traffic was clearly bottlenecking, he headed west. Toward Poes Point, Tennessee, two miles ahead. Predictably, when he reached the edge of town, traffic was stopped again; but here the stoppage had drawn a crowd, the sidewalks clogged by hordes of Bermuda-shorted gawkers. Clenching his teeth as well as the steering wheel, LB inched the Caddy forward.

"Hey, there you are!" a white T-shirted, stained-armpitted rube said to him. "Man, we were worried as hell! 'Bout time you showed up." In seconds, a small group swarmed his car. Magnetic signs were flung onto the doors and a pant-suited sixty-something woman of ample proportions heaved herself over the side. Standing precariously on the back seat, she wedged herself in amongst the three remaining cases of *dickTat'rs*.

LilBuckaroo's head jerked from front to back and side to side, trying to make sense of the fracas. Above occasional hoots and the constant murmur of onlookers, he heard a persistent high-pitched beeping sound along with a hydraulic, ratchety grinding. A forklift. It approached the right side of his Cadillac, adjusted its angle of attack, and then lowered a double-thick piece of white-painted plywood onto the retracted ragtop. Strapped to the plywood was a rocking chair, and strapped *into* that rocking chair was an elderly man. An *exceedingly* elderly man, sporting suspenders and a jet-black toupee.

A pit crew advanced. They leveled the board by wedging in pieces of stiff foam, and then bungeed the plywood and rocker in position as the forklift backed away. LB heard the woman say, "Okay, Dad, you're all set. It's the big day. Hang on!" She sat beside her father on the plywood, holding fast to the rocker. LB stared at her. She stared back. "Well, go!" she finally said. "But keep it to three miles per hour or less; that's the rule."

As he struggled to give voice to the questions pinballing in his head, LilBuckaroo eased off the brake. Half a block forward, he finally mumbled: "What the fuck is all this shit about?"

"Whadeesay?" the old man asked. To which the woman replied, loudly, "He said, 'What's the fuss?' Dad, that's all. Turn up your hearing aids, please." The man's daughter leaned forward and whispered to LilBuckaroo. "Whaddaya mean 'what the fuck is all this shit?' It's the goddamned Tournament of Poes's parade, of course. Biggest one yet, the Diamond fuckin' Jubilee this year."

"But who is...?" LB nodded over his shoulder.

"Fuckin' hell," the daughter said, no longer whispering, "don't these idiot organizers explain anything to you rich convertible dudes? My dad is the goddamned founder of this town, you moron. Edgar Albert Poes, named after the poet. Well, almost."

"But I'm in a hurry! I'm not even supposed to—"

"You're not supposed to talk or take your eyes off the road. Those are the rules. You're just supposed to smile and drive slow and steady, so Dad doesn't rock too fast and get whiplash again."

Struggling to process yet another delay in his journey south, LB did as he was told. The road ahead was blocked, same for the side streets; his only choice was to endure this latest complication. Creeping forward, he watched the street before him, occasionally stealing glances at the sidewalk crowd. Overhead, a banner revealed he had indeed landed in the *Tournament of Poes's Parade and Summer Festival*.

"Stop!" the woman screamed.

LB mashed the brake. The old man pitched forward, his neck snapping and toupee sliding forward as the straps held his body in place in the secured rocker. "What the hell!" LB yelled at the daughter. "Why'd you tell me to stop?"

"It's a red light, you idiot!"

LB looked up. "We're in a parade and we still have to stop at the red lights?"

"Of course," the woman said, rolling her eyes. "In Poes Point, we obey the rules, mister." LB watched in the rearview mirror as the woman repositioned the hair on her father's slippery scalp. "It's okay, Dad. You're still a charmer," she assured him. And then, to LB: "It's green, dipshit. Go!"

"Okay, okay. I'm going." After a moment, he added, "I notice there doesn't seem to be anyone behind us."

"Well, of course not. Dad is always the finale, the Grand Marshal. Folks stick around at least long enough to see if he's still alive."

LilBuckaroo scanned the crowd again. "But why isn't anyone … *moving*? Everyone seems frozen stiff. It's like a plague of rigor mortis."

"God, you really should do your homework before you volunteer to drive the Grand Marshal."

"But I didn't—"

"It's the goddamned Tournament of Poes's parade, you moron. As in *poses*, that is. Since nineteen-fuckin-fifty-nine, we've had a parade, and since that first year, it's been the tradition that— *Stop!*"

Another red light, another sudden stop, another thrill for the old man. "Holy hell, how many stoplights do you have in this town anyway?" LB cried.

"Just three more. Main Street's a half-mile long, and we've got five stoplights. We like things slow here. We want people to 'stop and smell the Poeses' as they say, take in the sights, see what the merchants have in their window displays. It ain't much, but it's all we got. Also makes for some kick-ass revenue from traffic citations. My husband, Joe Jack, he's the town marshal, so I know these things. It's green again, numbnuts. Go!" Admirably, the daughter kept waving to the crowd throughout her explanation.

LilBuckaroo cleared his throat. "Okay, so about this tradition...?"

"Oh, yeah. Ever since that first parade in '59, whenever Old Edgar – that's Dad, of course – whenever Old Edgar appears in the final car, everyone stands at attention, strikes poses, and holds them as he passes. You'll notice that some of the poses are quite clever, even athletic."

LB took note of the stony crowd. Indeed, while most of the human mannequins stood solemnly, some frozen in salute to the old man, others seemed quite original. Many of the onlookers had black birds – ravens, of course, and presumably stuffed – duct-taped to their heads or shoulders. Others assumed positions of varying decorum, including a dog who froze in place while licking his balls.

"Why in hell are you stopping now?" the woman demanded.

"Traffic light," LB said.

"The damn light is green, genius. It's your upper lip that's red. That looks nasty, by the way; you really should get that checked out." She turned to the old man. "He'll get the hang of it, Dad. Maybe."

With the car rolling again, LilBuckaroo's eyes darted from street to sidewalk to wobbling rocker in the rearview. He swallowed hard and said, "So if this is a 'tournament' of ... *whatever*, is there an actual contest involved?"

The woman huffed. "Help me, Jesus!" she said softly, and then sighed and climbed over the seat to join LB in front. She fastened her seatbelt and spoke quietly: "Yes, there's a contest. We have a mystery judge who quickly studies the poses and picks a winner. My money's on the dog to repeat as champ this year. I noticed that he tucked his tail this time for added flair."

"Wow," LB managed. What else was there to say?

The woman inched closer, her demeanor softening. "My name's Annabel, by the way, Annabel Sweet. I'm Dad's trophy daughter." (Trophy daughter? LilBuckaroo decided not to ask.) "Sorry to be so cranky," she said. "As you might imagine, it's a whole production, a real pain in the ass getting Dad ready for this each year. Took forever to find his best 'faux Poe' hair this morning, and I nearly forgot to put new batteries in his hearing aids. This shit stresses me out to no end."

"Thanks for sharing that," LB said. "I guess." The Caddy was gaining on a three-girl baton troupe whose center twirler spied the steer horns with trepidation. Turning and marching backward, another girl appeared to read the graffiti on the hood. She dropped her baton.

"How old is your dad anyway?"

"Hunnerdanthree duhday," Old Edgar said, his hearing aids now at full tilt.

"That's right," Annabel said. "The big *one-oh-three*. They always hold the parade on his birthday. He rides down the street, people turn to stone when they see him, they think he's nodding approvingly, but it's really just the rocking motion of the chair. And when it's all said and done, we forklift him off, change his drawers and call it a day." Annabel then smiled as she leaned in and whispered, "We've got a stuffed version of Dad all set to go when that becomes necessary. Local seamstress modified a former crash dummy. With the 'toup' stapled on, it's a pretty good likeness."

Another red light. LB aced this one. While the car was stopped, a parade reveler screamed "Woohoooo!" and staggered over to hand Edgar an open beer. The old man giggled, said, "Ankyu," and started chugging.

"Ack!" Annabel cried as the light changed and the Caddy started forward again. "We almost forgot to toss out the parade goodies." Flouting the immutable rules of passenger safety, she unbuckled. Then she turned and rummaged behind the back seat. It took a few moments for LilBuckaroo to realize what was happening as objects sailed over his head and spectators took direct hits from his chip canisters. They gamely held pose.

"Hey, you can't throw those out!" LB cried. "That's inventory. Those are samples. Marketing promos! I'm running low!"

"Great!" Annabel cried. "Then I'm marketing your product for you. You're welcome." She turned to face forward and again buckled herself in. Opening a chip canister, she examined one of the specimens. "Hmmm," she said. "It's either Adolph Hitler or a dick."

"Yes," LB admitted.

At last, still moving at three miles per hour, he cruised through the fifth traffic light while it glowed green. And with the crowd thinning and floats and parade cars pulling off onto side streets, the road finally cleared before him. LB mashed the accelerator but slammed the brake pedal when Annabel screamed. The bungees held, but Old Edgar's straps did not.

The trophy daughter shrieked as her father catapulted forward, toupee flying and beer bottle still in hand but raining brew. The old man pitched over the windshield and tumbled down the I'M SO HORNY hood where the steer horns snagged his suspenders. With surprising agility, Annabel profanely exited the car and raced to her father. A small crowd also rushed forward, but Annabel shooed them away. "He's fine," she said. "Shit his pants, of course."

As the old man twitched and Annabel worked to free him, LilBuckaroo activated the wipers to clear the spilled beer. Old Edgar's toupee swayed back and forth atop a wiper blade, a furry metronome cleaning the glass.

* * *

The innocuously named Ol Swimmin Hole in East Kibosh, South Carolina, was a stately manse, a Queen Anne, oddly regal in a village of otherworldly kitsch. Only the fiberglass flying saucer jutting from its steeply pitched roof validated that this particular Bed & Breakfast was precisely where it belonged.

Max Thibodeaux was where *he* belonged, as well, seated at a small corner table in the dining room with a strategic view of the registration desk. Instead of hiding and spying, Max had chosen instead to sit and sip a cup of afternoon coffee. To peruse the East Ki Merchants Directory and Map. To openly wait and watch for the arrival of Pete and family.

His change of tactics had solidified in the evening hours in his room – the Hollywood Room. As was his habit, he'd first opened all the drawers and even unlocked the door to the adjoining room. Professional curiosity. Then he took stock of the décor, nothing more than movie posters for *Invaders from Mars* and *Killer Klowns from Outer*

Space; and surveyed the assortment of VHS tapes, including *The Day the Earth Stood Still*, *Spaced Invaders*, and *Morons from Outer Space*. But it was another tape that had given him pause. When he had opened the case for *The Brother from Another Planet*, Max found another video inside – the James Caan film, *Hide in Plain Sight*.

It was an epiphany for Max. Why hide? And why risk being caught spying? Why risk the wrath of Pete Peebles? *Gun-toting* former agent Pete Peebles! Why not merely be a fellow tourist – a journalist on assignment scoping out feature stories? Why not ingratiate himself? Maybe even become a confidante?

So, Max sat and sipped, perused and waited and watched. Finally, Pete and his Peebles posse arrived.

Gertilda, owner of the place, greeted them, happily at first but then more apprehensively when she tried to pet Princess Petunia and the dog snapped at her. "So sorry about that," Max heard Penny say. "Poor thing just came into her fertile time, and she's a bit irritable. But don't you worry a bit; she won't be a lick of trouble, will she Pixie?" But Pixie Peebles was eyeing the confectionery case in the corner, doing finger math as she appeared to mentally tally an inevitable order.

Once Gertilda checked them in and gave Penny a room key and complimentary town Directory, Pete said he'd unload the car. Max waited a minute and then grabbed a luggage cart and followed him outside.

* * *

Joe Jack Sweet, Annabel's husband and Town Marshal for Poes Point, had witnessed the chaos at the end of the parade route. And when LilBuckaroo dared to roll out of town, Joe Jack followed in his black and white gumball machine, slowly at first, but then rapidly closing the gap. Before LB could pass into another town's jurisdiction, Joe Jack fired up the lights and siren. LB groaned, pulled off the road, and in his side mirror, watched the gray-haired Marshal stride forward.

"My, oh my, what have we wrought?" the officer declared. He tilted up the brim of his peaked hat, shook his head and lowered his sunglasses to reveal baggy, bloodshot eyes. "License, please, and registration, of course," he said. "And while you're diggin' for those items which I have my doubts you can produce, allow me to introduce myself." He backed away from the car and assumed a fists-on-hips man-of-steel pose that LB imagined might once have been a Tournament of Poes's prize winner. "You are in the company of Mr. Joe Jack Sweet, son. Town Marshal Joe Jack Sweet, that is. I believe you know my wife, Annabel and my daddy-in-law, Old Goat, er, I mean, Old Edgar Albert Poes. And since you have been rather careless regarding the safety of my beloved family members, I advise you to do as you are told."

LB smiled wanly and nodded, furiously digging in the glovebox and then offering his license and registration. He really needed to pee.

The Marshal stepped up beside the car again. He snatched the documents from LB and shook his head. "LilBuckaroo DePew. What the hell kinda fool name is that?" Joe Jack Sweet asked.

"Not my fault," LB said, tentatively. "Not at all. Have to blame my parents and—"

"Oh, so you're one of those 'not-my-fault-blame-someone-else' kinda fellas, eh? Well, let me tell you something, and you hear me good, Mr. LilBuckaroo DePew – as I see it, you're all alone in that car with no one else to blame. Chances are you'll be all alone in my jail cell, too. If you're lucky, that is."

"Oh, no," LB said, "I can't go to jail. I mean, I'm headed south and I'm already way behind schedule. And besides, I really haven't done anything wrong—"

"Nothin' wrong, you say?" Sweet pocketed LB's credentials and leaned against the car door. "Ya know, Mr. DePew, I find it just a tad bit amusin' that you believe you can just roll into town, create havoc and discord, and then leave like the ill wind you clearly are. You must be one of them joker types, a real comedical fella."

Joe Jack Sweet stepped back and pulled out a citation book. "Well, as it just so happens, I don't have a real good sense of humor. Maybe that's because I had you under surveillance durin' your little romp through our fair town. 'Nothin' wrong,' you say, huh? Well, let's just see how many *nothin's* we can come up with." He cocked his head and pursed his lips. "Here's one," he said, writing as he spoke. "Traffic violation; attempted runnin' of a red light."

"Oh, no, I stopped at every light," LB said. "Even though it was a parade, I came to a full and complete stop. Every time. I swear it."

The Marshal exhaled heavily. "Don't go swearin' at me, son. It will not help your situation." He smiled unconvincingly. "But I reckon we can let you by with a warnin' on the traffic violation. This time."

LB relaxed and allowed a smile to crease his burned lips.

"Howeva," Sweet continued, "we do have a few other minor matters to consider, don't ya think?"

LB slumped.

"I'll just make a list for now and then write 'em up all separate and pretty in a bit. Let's see… First was the matter of your unauthorized participation in a civic event without a permit."

"No, sir," LB said. "That was not my intent. I was just passing through when—"

"When you started littering our streets and assailing our residents with these cans you're totin'?" Sweet pointed to the three cans of *dickTat'rs* remaining in the last box. He stopped writing long enough to reach into the car and open a can. Again, a heavy exhale. "Better add distribution of obscene materials to my list."

LB was squirming in the car but kept quiet.

Joe Jack Sweet said, "I will go on, of course. I believe I observed the little matter of your threatenin' a minor – three minors, actually – those baton twirler girls. Seems to me you threatened 'em with a deadly weapon." He motioned toward the steer horns. "And speakin' of said deadly weapon, I believe we can make a case that you assaulted dear Old Edgar with those horns as well. Miracle he wasn't gored to death and cut down in the prime of his life."

LilBuckaroo whimpered.

"And let's not forget your disgraceful and clearly unlawful public display of a lewd and lascivious message. Are you still 'so horny,' Mr. DePew? I see you squirmin' a bit and holdin' your privates. I suggest you keep yourself under control for the time bein'."

Another whimper. A small leak. And Marshal Sweet still writing:

"Let's not forget your leavin' the scene of an accident; theft of town property – this plywood and placards and such – and just for good measure, actions detrimental to the intestinal fortitude of a public official. In other words, you made Old Edgar shit his pants."

LB was sweating and looking up at the officer from a near fetal position.

"One final charge and I think we can wrap this up," said Joe Jack Sweet. "Public urination."

"Wha...?"

"I reckon you best roll outta that car and pee on the road here, son. You sure as hell ain't gonna piss yourself once you get inside my squad car."

* * *

"Need a hand?" Max asked Pete in the parking lot.

"Got one," Pete said, unflappable as he pulled Penny's suitcase from the trunk of the Parisienne. He set it on the pavement and then lifted his hook in the air. "What makes you think I need another?"

"Oh, sorry, that wasn't what I... Just offering to help is all. Saw you come in and figured you might, well, ya know."

Pete turned and stared at the black man standing beside him with the luggage cart. He nodded. "I thank you for the offer, but I always do it myself. No sense in paying a bellman when I'm perfectly capable on my own."

"Certainly," Max said. "I'm not really a hotel employee, though. Name's Max, just another guest."

"Apologies," Pete said. "Looks like we've both made incorrect assumptions based on our physical attributes." He hoisted one of Pixie's cases from the trunk.

"Yes, well, anyway, hope you enjoy your stay," Max said. He started pushing the cart away.

"I believe I will make use of that rolling rack you've got there," Pete said. "Since you went to the trouble of bringing it out. I'm Pete, by the way. Much obliged."

"Of course. Here you go." Max turned to leave but stopped short when he saw a pick and shovel in the trunk.

"Something I can help *you* with?" Pete asked.

Sweating, Max pointed at the back of the car. "I notice you have Virginia plates. I'm originally from Baltimore, but I live in the DC area now myself," he said. "Arlington, actually."

"That a fact? Arlington man, myself," Pete said. He closed the trunk. "Westover Village area, to be exact." He extended his hand and Max accepted it.

"This is gonna sound crazy," Max said, "but you do look familiar, like I've seen you somewhere recently."

Pete heaved the larger cases onto the cart. "That so?"

"Maybe at J. Edgar's or, I don't know, there's a bar downtown I go to sometimes..."

Pete studied Max. "Now that you mention it..."

Max waved his hand in the air. "Small world, I guess. Anyway, sorry to trouble you. Enjoy your time here. Quite a town. Just arrived, myself. Suppose I'd better start getting my bearings before more of the day gets away from me." He smiled and stepped away.

"You say your name was Mike?"

"Max," said Max.

"Tell you what," Pete said. "Best place to start enjoying any whack-job town like this is at a tavern. I happen to know a place that's out of this world. In fact, that's the name of the joint, 'Zork's Out of This World Pub and Curiosity Shop'." Let me get these bags upstairs for Penny and Pixie to work on, then whaddaya say you and me grab a shot or two?"

"Absolutely," Max said.

"Absolutely," Pete echoed.

* * *

From a rest area pay phone, Jimi called the room at Lakeside Grove. Janis answered.

"Hey, Jiminy, what's the good word? You on your way back?"

"Yes, actually. Be at least another hour or so, though. Glad I caught you in the room."

"Yeah," Janis said. "Taking a break. Sonny's baldish head was getting a bit too much sun. Not to mention that he nearly drowned."

"What?!? What happened?"

"Call it a good plan gone bad. He figured if he fell into the pool, the lounge chair potatoes would rise up and rush to his aid, and I could go on high alert, checking for tattooed tushes."

"And...?"

"Two middle-aged women rushed over and started arguing over the best way to save a drowning man. Meanwhile, a few guys stirred in their chairs, but no heroes emerged. Probably because they weren't wearing their capes and tights."

Jimi rubbed his temples with his free hand. "But is Sonny okay?"

"He's fine. Wounded pride, but it seems no one was terribly concerned over saving a man in the kiddie pool. Turns out most people – even toddlers – can just stand up in 12 inches of water and save themselves."

"Makes sense."

"So, Jiminy, what about you? Any luck?"

"Yes and no," he sighed. "I can go into the details later, but the TANNUTS member rolls were a bust. Found the lady who ran the group. Essie Fernley. Nice woman, really wanted to help..."

"So, did she?"

"Well," Jimi began, "Essie recalled someone matching Jaybird's description. Unfortunately, she couldn't quite remember when or where other than it was here in the south. We studied the membership lists but came up empty. After that, Essie called one place for me to check on a possible lead. Dead end there, too. Best she could do was give me some brochures for some of their old affiliated clubs. I stopped at one on the way back – Nudetopian Springs – but again, no luck. Office manager there was very helpful and seemed to know everyone and their stories. But no butt tattoos, no facial scars, no Jaybird."

"Damn," Janis said. "Okay. I'm gonna make another run around the place here myself. New set of tanners might be out by now, or maybe some of the die-hards will have spun on their rotisseries."

"Sounds good," Jimi said. "Let's stay the night there again and head out early in the morning. We can chat up some folks in the bar tonight but try to hit two or three new clubs tomorrow."

"There you go planning again!"

"It's what I do."

"Fair enough," Janis conceded.

"Speaking of planning, don't let Sonny forget to call Pepper with an update."

"Sure thing," Janis said. "But by the way, I hope you know what a sacrifice I'm making here."

"Sacrifice? What do you mean?"

"Staring at all these man-butts has ruined my appetite."

CHAPTER 19

(In Which Max Gets Hammered, Pepper Gets Nailed, LB's in the Slammer, and Someone Gets Tailed)

Late Afternoon

AT ZORK'S OUT OF THIS WORLD PUB AND CURIOSITY SHOP, PETE AND MAX started out at the bar.

"Two shots of Absolut for me," Max said to Zork. "How about you, Pete?"

"Well, I'll be damned," Pete said. "You are my kinda fella. Same here, Zork. And keep 'em coming. On me."

"Oh, no," Max said. "I can't have you plying me with alcohol like that. I'm not that sorta guy." He maintained a stern look until he could see a moment of terror wash over Pete's face. Max laughed then. "Just messing with you, Pete. I appreciate the gesture."

Pete allowed himself to breathe again. He smiled. "It's no big deal," he said. "Just a combination of thanks for the assist today and a welcome to East Kibosh."

"I can get the next round, then," Max said.

"No use trading back and forth today. But if we do this again tomorrow…"

Zork set four shots of vodka on the bar before them. "Why don't you fellas grab a booth?" he said. "I'll bring a couple more to the table in a few minutes."

"Sounds good," Pete said. He picked up one shot glass and nodded to Max. "Down the hatch." One after another, they tipped back the shots and then headed to a booth in the center of the far wall – a booth beneath an autographed poster of E.T. the Extra-Terrestrial.

"I knew E.T. had long fingers but never guessed he'd have such fine penmanship," Max said.

"Well, it is just two lousy letters. Nonetheless, probably a stunt autograph double," Pete said. "But speaking of E.T., I need to phone home and check in with someone in DC."

"Take your time," said Max. He was tempted to add, "Give Agent Carducci my best," but refrained.

Pete walked back to the bar and borrowed the phone from Zork. Max could see him throw money on the bar for the phone call. While waiting, Max took stock of the Pub. It truly *was* out of this world. Full-on Area-51-meets-Hollywood-meets-Dollywood. Country kitsch with a heapin' helpin' of B movie sci-fi. Posters filled vast expanses of orange-lacquered pine walls, the space broken up by glass-enclosed shelves of toy robots here and there. But the pub's prized display stood in a dead corner by the bar: Zorkie the Alien, a 4-foot little green man, presumably made of resin or fiberglass. Or possibly stuffed, for patrons inclined to believe in alien captures. The creature sported a stringless banjo, and the display was roped off with a single velvet rope sagging from gold-colored posts. Open wall spaces around the bar were filled with instant-camera shots of barflies mugging with Zorkie. Just because.

Zork-the-taller brought four more shots to the table. Max thanked the bartender and studied the shot glasses – recent *Coneheads* movie promos – that seemed perfectly at home here in East Ki. It was essential to earn Pete's trust, but being an infrequent social drinker, Max hoped he could keep pace with the former agent and tolerate the vodka shots – without spilling his guts (literally or figuratively). He and Pete made eye contact and nodded. Max raised a shot glass, and Pete gave a thumbs up.

A couple of minutes later, Pete was still on the phone when Pixie walked in, followed by Penny carrying the diapered Princess Petunia. Pete saw them and rolled his eyes but pointed his hook toward the table where Max sat. The Peebles females approached.

"I see shot glasses," Penny said. "Must be Pete's table, too, right?"

"Absolutely," Max said.

"Of course, you would say that," Penny replied. "Mind if we join you for a few minutes? Just till Pete gets off the phone?"

"Be my guest," Max said. He was unprepared for the force of Pixie sliding in beside him but managed a smile anyway. "I'm Max," he said. "Also staying at the OSH."

"The OSH?" Penny asked. "Oh, at the Ol Swimmin Hole. Yes, I thought you looked familiar. I'm Penny, and this is Pixie." Pixie made eyes at Max. "And this precious little pooch is Princess Petunia." The dog growled. "She's a little standoffish toward males at the moment," Penny said.

"My husband is black like you," Pixie blurted out, staring at Max. Adoringly. "Soon to be ex-husband, that is."

Max giggled nervously. "Paydro is black? I had no idea." *Oops!* He knew it was a mistake as soon as he said it.

"Daddy told you about Paydro?" Pixie asked.

"Strange," Penny added. "You know Pete from somewhere else?"

"Um…"

Pete returned to the table. "Not supposed to have the dog in here," he said, nuzzling the pampered Poodle, nonetheless.

"She's wearing a diaper, Daddy," Pixie said.

Pete ignored her. "Introductions been made here?"

"Yes," Max said. "Names only so far."

"Daddy, have you been telling people about—"

Max knocked a shot glass across the table. The vodka spilled out and raced across the surface. Petunia began lapping it up.

"Clumsy me," Max said. "So sorry."

"Damn shame," Pete said, studying the spill. "Oh well, the dog enjoys her Absolut, too." He motioned for Zork. Held up his hook, but then changed appendages and held up four fingers. "So, what are you female types doing here, anyway?"

"Don't act so happy to see us," Penny deadpanned. "Just stopped in to tell you we were headed out shopping. Most of the shops stay open till 8 or 9 in the summer, so go ahead and do your own thing for dinner."

"Fine."

"Oh, and because they couldn't find the spare key to the room, I left the door unlocked for now. I wasn't sure who would get back first, and Gertilda might not be around to let us in."

"Whatever."

"Wave to Daddy," Penny said in a baby voice more juvenile than her usual tone. She moved the dog's paw. Another growl. Pixie waved, too, but did not growl.

"So pleased to meet you, Max," Penny said.

"Yes, indeed, very pleased," Pixie agreed. She winked and exited the booth. "See you 'round, I hope."

Max smiled uneasily. He was sweating.

* * *

In Poes Point, Tennessee, LilBuckaroo was hot. Outside, the temperature was in the upper 80s, quite pleasant if you were in a moving convertible. But LB wasn't in the convertible, and he wasn't moving; he was marooned in a 6-foot by 10-foot jail cell at the end of a windowless concrete corridor, far from the reaches of Joe Jack Sweet's air-conditioned office and the rhythmic hum of reception area ceiling fans.

He was tired. Frustrated. Depressed.

Indeed, after starting this journey with such high hopes – which was how he began most journeys – things had quickly gone to shit. This, too, was common to his undertakings. Still, he'd been confident this time would be different. After all, he had Pepper on his side, his ghost-dad in his head, and righteousness in his favor as he strived to preserve what was justifiably his: the family fortune. But now what? Now he had been derailed and jailed like a common criminal while Sonny and the twins were out there *somewhere* roaming free in their quest to steal *his* millions!

Holding up his beltless pants, LB stepped away from the cell bars and considered his quarters. At least the cell had a working toilet and a thin mattress that might prove adequate considering how tired he was. He fell onto the bed. Worry gave way to exhaustion, and he drifted off.

Joe Jack Sweet had other ideas. Moments later, he banged a leather-strapped billy club on the bars. "No rest for the weary, son," he mocked.

LB opened his eyes and lifted his head. Joe Jack had a rolling metal cart at his side. Two plates and a water-filled plastic cup rested on top.

"Dinner is a bit early," the Marshal said. "Leftovers from the Founder's Day luncheon. They may be a bit cold, but I wouldn't complain if I were you."

LB stood and stepped closer. He needed sleep more than he needed food, but any measure of kindness at this point was welcome.

"Today is your lucky day," Joe Jack continued. "My wife, the woman whose father you tried to kill during your reckless adventure, has, for some unknown reason, taken a shine to you. Or maybe it's pity. Regardless, she insisted I bring you this large slice of her world-famous peanut butter layer cake."

LB smiled as much as his situation and burned lips would allow.

"But do not get your hopes up, Mr. Scofflaw," Joe Jack said, again rapping the bars. "In an abundance of caution, I have taken the liberty of poking a plethora of holes in said cake with a fork that I cannot otherwise allow you to use – jailhouse rules, ya know. So, I can confirm there is no metal file hidden inside." He shoved the plates under the cell's bottom lateral bar and then handed the cup to LB between two verticals. "Is there anything else I can do to help make your stay more delightful?" Joe Jack asked with exaggerated sarcasm.

LB was wary of saying anything, but… "Thank you for the food. Am I allowed to make a phone call?"

* * *

Pepper was on the phone with Sonny when the cowbell jangled and Todd entered the law office. She blew him a kiss and directed him to a reception chair while she continued to chat with her boss, taking notes as she summarized:

"So, a strike-out at the ASA, no luck so far at Lakeside Grove, Jimi ran into a dead-end at TANNUTS, Pasco No Pants was a bust, and what was the last place? The one Jimi stopped at on the way back from TANNUTS?" She listened and jotted. "Nudetopian Springs. Got it. So, what's next?" She smiled at Todd. Winked at him, her eyes brightening as he adjusted his crotch. Still, she kept writing. "Okay, so three more clubs planned for tomorrow and then as many as you can on the way back? Sure, sounds good. Yes, I'll make calls to the clubs you mentioned in Maryland and Pennsylvania. And I'll check on that Naturist Society bunch in Wisconsin, too."

Pepper nodded and made an obscene gesture to Todd. He stood, walked stiffly to the door, deadbolted it, and turned the *Open* sign so it showed *Closed* from the outside. Pepper tried to hurry Sonny along:

"Okay, listen, since time is growing short, be sure to check in at least a couple times a day. If I find out anything on my end, I'll want you to know about it asap. For now, I'd better go – got business to attend to. Good luck." She hung up.

Todd twisted the window blinds closed and lowered the roller shade on the door.

"So, am I the business you need to attend to?" he asked.

Pepper hurriedly cleared her desktop. "Maybe. If you play your cards right." She took the phone off the hook again. No need for interruptions.

As Todd joined her behind the desk, she tucked into the top drawer a verbatim memo from an earlier voice mail message: *"I know what you've been doing. We need to talk."* Had it been a woman's voice? Bad connection. So hard to tell.

But Pepper's immediate priority was helping Todd unhook her bra. With that accomplished, she removed her top and looked up into his hazel eyes. He took a step back, admired the scenery, but then said, "I don't want to delay the moment or break the mood, but I have to ask… Tan nuts?"

She unbuckled his belt. "Yes, TANNUTS. All capital letters and all strung together. An acronym. I can tell you about it later. Kind of a long story."

"I like long stories," Todd said, dropping his pants.

Pepper dropped to her knees. "And I like long—"

"Don't talk with your mouth full. But please, feel free to keep your mouth full."

* * *

In the Kurls for Gurls salon parking lot next to the law office, a Steel Blue minivan idled. It bore three bumper stickers: *Honor Student On Board,* and *Bought This Fine Retired Vehicle at Before You Go-Go Car Rental,* and the newest one: *Sometimes I Miss My Husband ... Next Time I'll Aim Better.*

Inside the vehicle, a ginger-haired nine-year-old boy sat in the front passenger seat, reading *Action Comics #700* and ignoring his equally ginger-haired mother who sat behind the steering wheel. She barely blinked as she watched the law office's front door.

"I know what you're up to," the woman whispered.

The boy looked up, saw she was muttering only to her angry self, and then returned to the fall of Metropolis.

* * *

"Busy again, both numbers," LilBuckaroo told Joe Jack Sweet as he hung up the receiver. "Machines not picking up either."

"Too bad," the Marshal said. "I have a three-strikes-and-you're-out policy on phone calls. As I see it, you tried each number twice, so you are over your limit. You can try again in the morning. For now, it's back to the cell. Better eat that dinner and Annabel's peanut butter cake before I get hungry again myself and decide to eat it."

"Dinner and then a good night's sleep, I hope," LB said. "I'm beat." He noticed one of his three remaining cans of *dickTat'rs* on the desk, this one tagged as "Evidence."

"Yes, you are, son. You are very much *beat*, and you just keep that in mind."

The phone rang.

"Joe Jack here." The marshal listened and nodded and occasionally spoke. "Yes, dear. Of course, dear. I won't forget, dear. Uh-huh. Uh-huh. Uh-huh." Joe Jack closed his eyes and appeared to concentrate on his breathing. "Yes, I know it's the Founder's Day Boy's Night tonight. I won't be out too late since tomorrow's a workday. Is Pops skipping it again this year?" More nodding. "Uh-huh. Uh-huh. Yes, dear. I'll be home after the evening bed check. Probably be eleven or so. Uh-huh. Bye, dear."

He hung up the phone, sighed, forced a smile, and ushered LB back down the corridor. "Should be a quiet night. Deputy Brutus over there's sleeping off the bender to end all benders." He motioned to the open cell, where a bear-like lump heaved and snorted in slumber.

"When you finish with dinner, just slide the plate under the door again. The rats will appreciate the crumbs." He laughed, locked LB inside the cell again, and walked away. The corridor echoed when a distant door closed and Joe Jack left the building.

LB started eating his dinner.

* * *

A filling dinner at Zork's had failed to adequately protect Max from the impact of seven shots of Absolut. His head reeled and his thoughts struggled to take root. *What had he really experienced during the meal, and what did he merely imagine?* The line between memory and hallucination was a fine one. And surrounded by so many quasi-alien relics and flights of fancy, he was even more unsure.

"Pete, it's been great," he said, "but I think I should go back to the OSH."

"The OSH?"

"The Ollll Shwimminole, of course," he said.

"Ha. You sounded just like Jennings Prokoff," Pete said. As it happened, the anchor was on the screen of the bar's TV at that very moment. "Man, I despise that guy's voice. Never watch him."

"Helluva guy, though," Max said, nodding toward the TV.

"You know Prokoff?"

"Maybe," Max said. "Can't be sure at thish very moment."

"Need me to escort you back to the B&B?"

"No, no, I'll be fine," Max said. "You jusht shtay here and question your people about thish guy you're tryna find."

Max dropped a ten-dollar bill on the table, saluted Pete, and zig-zagged away from the table. He veered over to Zorkie the Alien, stood there and giggled, slouch-shouldered, wondering what tune Zorkie might play if the banjo had strings. But the poker-faced creature gave up no clues. So, Max left the bar.

It was a three-block walk back to the Ol Swimmin Hole. During that time, Max focused on toeing a straight line and trying to separate *real* reality from drunk reality as he recalled his time with Pete.

By the time he'd made it back to the rooming place, he had latched onto three crucial things: First, Pete continued to get nowhere with his aggressive interrogations of townsfolk regarding the elder Finch, the younger Finch, and any lore over buried treasure.

Next, Pete carried with him a folded age-progression artist's rendering of this younger Finch guy, showing it with each interrogation: "Ever see this guy around? Here's my card if you do. Staying at the Ol Swimmin Hole for a few days. After that, call me at the number on the card. Reward? Don't be greedy; doing a good deed is its own reward."

And finally, Pete carried his gun at all times.

Everything else from the time at Zork's seemed a blur.

* * *

Through the small barred window in the jail cell, LB could see the sun dropping on the horizon. He had finished the sandwich and chips – they were nowhere near as tasty as *dickTat'rs*, he assured himself – yawned deeply, and almost decided to sleep instead of eating Annabel's Peanut Butter Layer Cake. But because he wasn't sure if Joe Jack was kidding about the rats, he decided to finish his meal rather than risk the unknown.

He noticed a small note taped to the plate:

> *Peace offering. Dad had a wild ride but the time of his life.*
> *Enjoy the cake. All of it.*
>
> *Mayor Annabel*

Mayor Annabel? Could the Trophy Daughter be more than she seemed?

The cake was delicious; Annabel was a woman of many talents. LB was inclined to savor the dessert slowly, but he heard Brutus stirring in the cell across the hall, so he ate more quickly.

> *Enjoy the cake. All of it.*

And there it was. Beneath the thickest part of the slice of cake, resting on the plate, a key. LB pulled it from beneath the cake and cleaned it with the provided napkin. He stood and walked to the cell door. The jail was quiet, aside from Brutus's bodily discharges. LB looked down the hall but saw no movement. He called out, "Hello!" but not so loud that the drunk Deputy would be alarmed. He waited. Nothing. No footsteps, no response of any kind.

Still, LB hesitated, wondering how many extra years of jail time he would face because of jailbreak or fleeing custody or whatever other charges Joe Jack might concoct. Then again, the key was from *Mayor* Annabel. Wouldn't that count for something?

He put his hand through the bars and placed the key into the lock. "Here goes," he said, and he gave the key a turn. Nothing happened. Until he pushed on the door.

It opened.

LB tiptoed up the corridor and into the reception area. Empty.

In a basket in Joe Jack's unlocked office, he found his wallet and watch and belt and keys amongst other traveling items, including his hardhat, fake mustache, and glue. He gathered them up and started for the door. But then he remembered bed check. Joe Jack would be back later. And what if Deputy Brutus woke up?

LB rummaged through the Marshal's desk and found a set of keys on a large jailer's ring, several of which appeared to be cell keys. He grabbed the set, hurried back down the corridor, and quietly closed and locked Deputy Brutus's cell door. Then he went back inside his own former cell. There, he hung the jailer's ring on the metal bedpost against the far wall and then arranged the pillow and linens into a reasonable facsimile of a man desperately in need of sleep. Finally, he locked the door behind him with Annabel's cake key and tossed it into a far corner inside the cell.

From there, LB walked back up the corridor and out the back door. Ah, freedom!

But even from the doorway, he could see his car was trapped behind a fence, beneath a canopy, and beyond a locked gate. Impounded. *Damn!* He tried to reenter the jail to look for gate keys – probably on the ring he had just locked up – but the door had automatically locked behind him. *Who tries to break into a jail?* he wondered. *Shit! Now he'd have to steal a car.*

Headlights flashed on. A vehicle rolled forward. LilBuckaroo's heart jumped.

"I think you'd better get in," a voice said from the shadowed driver's seat.

LB did as he was told.

CHAPTER 20

(In Which Sonny and The Twins Try to Connect the Dots, While Max Finds Himself in a Jam and LilBuckaroo Goes On The Lam)

Evening

NORMAN, THE LANKY AND HIRSUTE BARTENDER AT LAKESIDE GROVE'S restaurant bar (called The Altogether Now), brought drinks to the table for Sonny, Janis, and Jimi. Then he pulled up a chair and joined them.

"Here are the names of my contacts at three smaller clubs in the southern part of the state," he said, producing a sheet of notepad paper on which he had drawn a crude outline of Florida with three dots. "I think you said you'd be heading the other direction tomorrow, right? Going north?"

"First west over to Pasco County, and then we'll start back to the north," Jimi said. "Not enough time to go all the way south."

"Right. So, calling these folks might help if you aren't going south but you still think your guy might be in Florida and—"

Janis interrupted. "Sonny, tell me again why we're convinced Jaybird's in Florida."

Sonny leaned forward and moved his right hand slowly across the table. He found his drink and cupped the glass in his palm. "Educated guess is all. If he's still around, he's probably a full-time nudist. Southern U.S. is a good place to start the hunt if that's true. And Florida seems logical. But we simply don't have time to check everywhere."

"That's why I thought you might want to make some calls to the smaller clubs instead of detouring south, spending hours on the road, and visiting in person," Norman said. "These are the personal phone numbers of club owners or office workers. If you want to reach out to them, I think it's appropriate for me to make the initial contact and then hand them off to you."

Jimi nodded. "Thanks, Norman. Makes perfect sense. When can we do that, though? We leave in the morning."

Norman stood. "Tell you what, let me take your dinner order and get that to the kitchen. Then I can take one of you in the back and do the calls while your food's being prepped."

"Perfect," Sonny said. "Maybe I should be on the calls since I can answer any questions they might have about way-back-when."

"Fine with me," Janis said. "But if we get any new people in the bar here to quiz, we might need to borrow your butt so we can show them the tattoo."

"Hold on," Norman said. He stepped into the kitchen and quickly returned with an instant camera. "We normally don't allow using cameras at nudist clubs, but if you don't mind a tight shot..."

Sonny stood and flared his hip in the direction of Norman's voice. "I am ready for my close-up, Mr. DeMille," he said.

"Yupp."

"What's that?"

"It's Yupp."

"What's Yupp?"

"I'm Yupp. Norman Yupp. My last name's not DeMille."

Sonny shook his head. "Everyone is so young these days."

"Say cheese," Norman said.

"You're taking a picture of my ass," said Sonny.

"Good point. Just hold still then." Click. Whirr. The photo blank disgorged from the camera.

"How's it look?" Sonny asked. "Need another?"

"It takes a few minutes for the picture to appear, Uncle Sonny," Janis said. So, they waited, sipping their drinks and watching as tattooed hindquarters took shape on the film. "Looks good to me," Janis said. "And I've become quite the connoisseur of man-butts."

"Okay, then," said Sonny. "Norman, let's go make those calls."

* * *

At the Ol Swimmin Hole, dinnertime was winding down. Max steeled himself to walk confidently through the dining room and avoid detection of his inebriation. He almost made it, his right foot just catching the wheel of the busser's cart. It made a racket, but nothing fell to the floor. *Not very graceful for a spy.* He chilled at the thought. He considered himself a "news lead vetter," but on this case, he was very much in spy mode. It excited him but scared the bejesus out of him, too.

Cautiously, Max climbed the three flights of stairs to where his room stood at the end of the hallway. Except he didn't quite make it to the very end. In his confusion, he stopped one door short. Tried his key, but it didn't work. Tried it again, upside down. It nearly jammed. He removed the key and tried the knob. It turned. The door opened. He stepped inside.

"Who the hell redecorated...?," he wondered aloud, the door shutting behind him. "Where's my stuff? And whose *panties* are these?" He scratched his head, spread his feet apart for better balance, and looked around. "Ohhhh, I get it," he said. "Wrong room. Sorry!" he said to no one in particular, and a little too loud. "Shhhhhh..."

And then Max began to get his bearings. The scattered suitcases looked familiar. A ravaged box of bonbons lay askew in a wastebasket. And hanging from the hook on the back of the door: another hook. Of the prosthetic variety. A spare. Max had wandered into the Peebles suite.

He began to panic. *What if they find me here? Pete will shoot first and ask questions later. I'm a dead man just so Jennings Prokoff can boost his ratings!* But then he remembered: Penny and Pixie and Petunia were shopping, probably till 9; Pete was still drinking and eating and questioning potential witnesses.

He had time to explore. To spy!

Carefully, and without touching anything, Max made his way around the room, taking visual inventory. Even in his drunken state, it didn't take long to zero in on the object of his greatest interest: Pete's file case. *If I can focus and work quickly,* he thought, *this is a golden opportunity.*

But thanks to all those vodka shots, focus was hard to come by. So were attention to detail and a sense of order and caution. Nonetheless,

Max pulled out papers, diagrams, drawings, notes, getting a general sense of the case's contents. Then stuffed it all back inside. Front to back? Back to front? Who could remember? Amongst the materials, he recognized original versions of three things Pete had flashed copies of in the bar: the photo of the younger Jay Finch, Jr., perhaps a high-school graduation photo; the age-progression artist's rendering; and the small and crumpled handwritten note:

KIB__OS H__
ROCK

So many papers. So much to make sense of, and so little time to ponder it all.

The camera.

Yes, the instant camera in his room. Perfect for situations like this when he needed to capture images and not wait for photo lab development. "That's a very fine idea," Max whispered, as if the idea had come from outside his own head.

He started into the hallway, but two couples stood there, chatting, discussing dinner choices, and what they planned to see in East Ki for the rest of the week. *Could be a while,* Max thought, but he knew he didn't have time to waste and couldn't risk being seen leaving a room that wasn't his. Then he remembered the adjoining door to his room. When he'd arrived the day before, he had opened the door from his side. But had he left it unlocked? And were there even knobs on the inside of the doors? Max turned the deadbolt and pulled the door open. Indeed, there were interior knobs on both of the adjoining doors, slightly offset, so they didn't collide in the tight common space. He turned the knob on the door to his room. It opened. *Now, if only the Peebles bunch will leave their door unlocked,* he reasoned, *it'll be free and easy access. Another very fine idea!*

* * *

When Sonny returned to the bar, the food was on the table and Janis was nibbling her seasoned French fries. Sonny shook his head. "No luck," he said.

"No luck getting through or no luck once you did get through?" Jimi asked.

"Both," said Sonny. "Or is it neither? Whatever. With Norman's help, I got ahold of two out of the three people, but they knew of no one matching Jaybird's description. Nor did they recall hearing stories or discussions that would be helpful."

"No Woodstock stories at all?" Janis asked, munching a fry. "That's surprising. Kind of."

"One of the club owners knew of two former members who'd been at Woodstock, but both were women."

Janis swallowed. "Probably not our guy, then."

"Sit, Sonny," Jimi said. "Your food's getting cold." Jimi guided him to his chair, which Sonny toweled before sitting.

"Any luck with the photo while I was gone?" he asked.

"No positive IDs," Janis said, "although one older woman now thinks we were trying to show her porn. We may be kicked out before the evening's over."

"Then our work here may be done," Sonny said.

"And Jimi's been trying to make me work the whole time you were gone," said Janis.

"I just wanted her to go over the map Essie gave me and help chart our travels for tomorrow."

"All work and no play, Jiminy…"

"All play and no work, Ms. *Crack*…"

"Settle down, you two," Sonny said. "It's like I'm babysitting five-year-olds."

Mawing a bite of burger, Janis said, "There's something I've been wondering about you, brother dear. Why would someone like you, someone so meticulous, so precise, and so, well, so … *anal* be let go from an accounting company."

"Financial advisory firm," Jimi corrected her. "And if you must know, I was mostly very good at my job."

"Mostly?"

"There was that one little problem."

"Spill it, bro."

"Certainly," Jimi said. "I have nothing to be ashamed of." He crossed his legs. "Ever hear of decimal dyslexia?"

"D'what, d'who?"

"Decimal dyslexia. Very uncommon. I'm quite special, you see."

"That much we knew," Sonny said. "So, is this thing an actual medical condition?"

"Sort of," Jimi said. "Similar to dyslexia, where a person sees letters or words as if they're mixed up or out of order."

"Seeing *numbers* out of order would definitely be a problem for an accountant, I imagine," Sonny said.

"Financial Advisor. And I don't really mix up the numbers. People who have that issue are afflicted with *dyscalculia*, a disorder that keeps them from understanding simple math and number concepts."

"But, that's not what you have?"

"For me, it's just a problem with decimals."

Janis looked skeptical. "Decimals?"

"Decimal points. Like periods, but for numbers."

"Thanks. I know what decimal points are, but what's your problem with them?"

"My problem is very specific to the placement and interpretation of decimal points in numeric groups."

"Which means…?"

"Well, in numerical sequences, I tend to visually and mentally rearrange decimals. In other words, I can't always recognize or interpret their correct placement. Sometimes they seem to float or move on the page."

"Never understood floating decimals either," Janis said, "but then again, I didn't choose to be an accountant." Before Jimi could protest, Janis held up her hand and added, "I know, you're a Financial Advisor. Or at least were."

"Go on, Jimi," Sonny said.

"Yes, well, you see, sometimes I think the decimal is in the right place, but… Okay, I may have mistakenly ordered the purchase of $30,000 of a certain stock when the client only wanted $300."

Janis scratched her white coif. "How in the world…?"

"Easy mistake. For me, anyway," Jimi said. "I thought I had put the decimal in the right place. Ya know, three-zero-zero-*dot*-zero-zero. As in three hundred dollars, right? Turns out, however, that what I saw was not what I actually entered. The decimal in the middle was really just a period at the end. Three-zero-zero-zero-zero-*dot*."

"And the three-hundred-dollar order became thirty grand," Sonny said. "I take it the stock lost money?"

"Only two-thirds of its value overnight."

"Man, I'll bet you totally suck at playing dot-to-dot," Janis laughed. "Tell ya what, if we let Sonny drive next time, you and me can play a few rounds."

"Very funny," Jimi said. "Enough about me. Let's plan our day tomorrow. Now, as I see it, we should have time to visit three clubs, first heading west from here and then northeast. By my calculations, we can cover, now where did I write that down…? Oh, here it is. With an early start, we can cover roughly 27,500 miles by dinner time. Although that does seem like a lot, now that I think about it."

"Move the decimal two places to the left," Sonny said. "Let's shoot for 275 miles."

* * *

Photographing case file contents with the instant camera was tedious. Noisy, too. The dreadful quiet was violated again and again as the camera clanked and whirred and spewed out picture after developing picture from each film pack.

And then there was the mess. With adrenaline overcoming his drunken haze, Max somehow knew he must be ready to grab everything and disappear back into his room as quickly as possible. So, he'd been lucid enough to bring his wastebasket into the room, and throughout the process funneled developing photos and used-up film packs and flash bars into the container.

He worked quickly, loading film and flash attachments, focusing and photographing on-the-fly, pulling each photo from the camera, and then taking the next picture. He had six film packs, ten pictures each, and was midway through the last pack when he heard a dog barking in the hallway. Max spun toward the door and froze except for accidentally pushing the camera button once more. Then, frantically, he dropped the camera into the wastebasket, stuffed documents haphazardly back into the file case, and rushed to the adjoining room doors. He passed through to his room, dropped the wastebasket to the floor, and shut both doors behind him. Seconds later, he heard someone enter the room he'd just escaped.

Max lowered himself to the floor, his back against the door, listening over his rapid breaths. It was quiet on the other side, until…

"Hmmm, that's odd." A whispering voice, very close to the adjoining door. "How in the world…?"

Silence then. A half-minute of dead quiet.

And then a soft knock on the adjoining door.

Sweating, Max hesitated but then rose to his feet. He exhaled heavily, turned the knob, and opened the door.

"I think maybe you dropped this." It was Pixie, standing there with Princess Petunia under one arm and a still-developing photo in her opposite hand. She held the picture up for Max to see. Even half-developed, he could already see that his last accidental shot had captured a perfectly focused photo of a pair of panties lying on the bed. A *prodigious* pair of pastel pink panties. Pixie winked, tilted her head coyly, pushed out her chest, and stepped into Max's room.

* * *

"Get in," repeated the voice in the car outside the Poes Point jail.

LilBuckaroo stepped toward the vehicle, shielding his eyes from the glare of its quad headlights. As he drew closer, it struck him that the car's vertical grille looked like a giant chrome vagina ready to swallow him up. *What a way to go*, he thought.

Annabel – *Mayor* Annabel – stuck her head out the driver's window. "Well, come on. The clock's a tickin'!"

A minute later, LB was inside the car, and the car was moving away from the jail.

"My turn to give you a ride, but buckle up, mister," the Mayor said. "You know the rules."

LB's head spun with questions. All he could manage was, "What the hell kind of car is this?"

"Edsel," came a voice from the back seat. It was Old Edgar. "Fittyate Citation. Loadedup."

"Dad had the first Edsel dealership in the area," said the old man's trophy daughter. "Unfortunately, the heavily promoted Edsel brand was dead soon after."

"Fine autobeeldough," Edgar babbled.

"Why'd you get me out of jail? Won't the Marshal be pissed and come looking for me? Oh, man, he's gonna throw the book at me for sure," LB whined.

"He might come looking, but he won't throw the book at you because I won't let him. I'm the mayor of this town, and Joe Jack ain't nothin' without me or without Dad's money. He'll do as I say."

"But why'd you want to spring me from the slammer?" As he said it, LB thought the words sounded downright sexy in a B-movie sort of way.

"Mydea," Edgar said. "Hadda tyma malife indaparade. Alls I want is onelasfooldaventcha."

"Excuse me?"

"He wants one last adventure," Annabel said. "One last *fool* adventure, as he calls it. Ya know, the kind where rules…" she sighed "…are set aside and caution is thrown to the wind and the chips fall where they may. Speaking of which, I got the last two cans of your chips from your car. In that bag by your feet. And your suitcase is in the trunk."

"I must be dreaming," LB said. "I'm so tired, I'm delirious."

"No dream. Just one last fool adventure."

"But I can't just go joyriding," LilBuckaroo said. "I'm on my own journey. The clock is ticking, dammit. I have someplace to be – as soon as I find out where that is."

"Boyohboy, amistreedestination," Edgar said from the back seat.

"Good, it's official then," Mayor Annabel Poes Sweet decreed. As soon as we make a couple of stops for dad's part of the adventure, we can continue with yours. Maybe by then you'll know where the hell you're headed."

Five stoplights later, they disappeared into the night.

Friday, August 12, 1994
(One Day Before the Woodstock Reunion)

CHAPTER 21
(In Which the Jailbreak is Discovered, Max is Uncovered,
Pepper Flips Her Wig, and Radiance Readies for a Vengeful Gig)

Morning

AT STRAIGHT-UP EIGHT O'CLOCK FRIDAY MORNING, THE BRONCO AND ITS crew had already been on the road an hour, heading west on I-4 from Kissimmee toward Pasco County, home to the largest concentration of nudist clubs in North America. Janis took a turn at the wheel, with Sonny riding shotgun and Jimi centered in the back seat, flanked by the urn and the gnome, and studying maps, the *North American Guide to Nude Recreation*, and the brochures Essie had given him.

"Can you move a little to the left or to the right?" Janis asked. "I've got a mirror full of Jiminy. Did you know your head is abnormally large? Freakishly so?"

"Has to be to accommodate my abnormally large brain."

"Modesty," Janis said. "Good trait to have."

"We're nudists in training," said Sonny. "No need for modesty where we're headed. Physical modesty, anyway."

"Speaking of which," Jimi said, "take the next exit. We're getting close to Sun-Ray Acres. Coupon for a free day visit in the brochure, by the way. Limit one."

"I'll take it!" Janis cried.

"Oops," said Jimi. "Expired in 1987. Okay, it's yours."

"Little more to the left, if you please, or crouch down, or maybe just trim that licorice cotton candy you call hair," Janis said. Jimi did not comment but stuck out his tongue. "I saw that!" Janis said, adding, "Better behave yourself. We've got another police cruiser following us. This Bronco is a cop magnet."

* * *

Meanwhile, in Poes Point, Tennessee, roughly 550 crow-fly miles northwest of the Bronco bunch, Marshal Joe Jack Sweet woke up late after a long night at the Founder's Day Boy's Night – basically a sanctioned stag party without the stag; just poker and cigars and bourbon and bullshit. This annual event was a treasured tradition because it allowed Poes Pointers – men only, of course – to let their collective hair down for one night. Otherwise, Poes Point was a "dry" town in a "moist" Tennessee county, which meant bourbon or any other devil's brews had to be purchased elsewhere. Luckily, Kentucky, the "bourbon capital of the world," was a half-hour north with the nearest bourbon outlet not far inside the state line – roughly five feet or so.

Knowing he was down a deputy (with Brutus having gotten a ten-hour head start on the bourbon), Joe Jack had imbibed just enough to be polite, smoked a third cigar to be sociable, and turned a blind eye to the poker in order to secure votes come the next election. He had, however, engaged freely in the sharing of bullshit, most of which centered on LilBuckaroo, who had quickly become known as the *des-parade-o*. Joe Jack won sympathy from the boys for his quick action in bringing the reprobate to justice. Reveling in the praise, the Marshal had stayed out later than planned.

Now, a little past eight in the morning, Joe Jack slipped into his marshaling shoes and then waxed his mustache. He did not check on Annabel in her separate bedroom, figuring she was already in her official downtown office working an unofficial crossword puzzle. However, despite running more than an hour behind, he went through the motions of family duty to stay in Annabel's good graces (and in Old Edgar's will) by checking on his father-in-law. He quietly opened the old man's bedroom door and peered inside the room, saw nothing of importance in the drawn-shade darkness, but didn't smell death there either. So, Joe Jack left the house.

Reaching the jail, he heard yelling inside. And there he found Deputy Brutus, partially sobered up but also fully imprisoned.

"Why the fuckya lock me in this time? Tryna teach me another damn lesson?" Brutus yelled, mad as a bear.

"Hush up, Brute," Joe Jack said. "I did nothing of the sort. Don't know how you got locked in. Let me go get the damn key." A full minute later, he returned from his office. "Got a problem," he said. And then, tuning out Brutus's profane protests, he stepped across the corridor to LilBuckaroo's cell. He picked up the empty food plate and purposely dropped it to the floor. The noise should have awakened the dead, but the lump in the bunk did not move.

"Got a big fuckin' problem," Joe Jack said.

* * *

Meanwhile, roughly 150 crow-fly miles north of Joe Jack Sweet's big fuckin' jailhouse problem, Todd was in Pepper's shower, singing a medley of Elvis tunes while Pepper turned on her curling iron. She then let Effyu out to do his business. She watched as the dog dropped a load in the center of the sidewalk and then waddled, snarling, toward a Steel Blue minivan. A ginger-haired, sunglassed woman sat in the driver's seat, seemingly oblivious to the barking dog.

The phone rang. Pepper answered.

"Finally!" LilBuckaroo screamed. "Where the hell have you been? I've been tryin' to reach you for months!"

"I saw you two days ago, LB."

"Whatever. I'm goin' crazy out here. You wouldn't believe what I've been through."

"I probably *would* believe it, but try me."

"It all started at Burger in the First Degree when—"

"They still have those around?" Pepper asked. "I love the Triple Hamicide."

"Yes, they are delicious, but that's beside the point."

"So, get to the point, LB. I need to get to the office."

"Well, there was the transvestite in the bar, the coffee burn, the Heimlich molestation—"

"I think you mean 'maneuver'."

"Not really. Then the graffiti punks ruining my car – with poor grammar, I might add – and the hooker at the Knaughty Pine and the parade fiasco where I nearly killed a 103-year-old man for which I got thrown in jail…" He took a breath.

"Let me guess," Pepper said, unfazed by LB's adventures, "this is your one call from the hoosegow?"

"No, goddammit! I tried to do that last night, but you didn't answer your fucking phone! Phones, actually. I tried both places. More than once!"

Pepper sighed. Outside, Effyu had finally harassed the woman in the minivan sufficiently that she vacated the parking lot. "Okay, LB, settle down. You reached me now. Are you still in jail? Exactly where are you?"

"Not in jail anymore. The mayor broke me out. The mayor and her dad, the 103-year-old."

"Okay, this is weird, even for you, LB. Let me see if I have this right… You nearly kill an old man in a parade, get thrown in jail, and then the lady mayor and the old guy break you out?"

"Yes. Simple as that."

"Oh, boy," Pepper said. She opened the door and let Effyu back inside, then went back to the bathroom to grab her curling iron. Todd stepped from the shower and sashayed nakedly around her, avoiding the hot hair appliance.

"Again, I ask," Pepper said into the phone, "where are you now?" She could tell LB was covering the mouthpiece of the phone: "Where are we?" he asked someone. From another voice, also muffled: "LantaJawja. Hittindaroad soon's I change m'diaper."

"Atlanta area. I think. Stayed in a decent motel last night. No hookers. I finally got some sleep. We'll be hittin' the road as soon after the mayor helps Edgar with his diaper."

"Hitting the road to where?" Pepper asked.

"You tell *me* where we need to go, Peps! Have Sonny and the twins reported in? Have they found Jaybird?"

Todd came into the living room, zipping his pants and singing Jailhouse Rock.

"Very funny, Peps! Tell your new gigolo it's no laughing matter that I've been in the slammer!"

"Yeah, yeah, settle down, LB," Pepper said, contorting her body as Todd felt her up. "He doesn't know your – *ooh, Baby!* – your situation; it's nothing personal." Todd nibbled on her neck, slightly offsetting her wig. She didn't mind. Nor did Todd get flustered when Effyu began humping his left calf. Still nuzzling Pepper's neck, he merely lifted his leg so she could peel away the dog.

"Ooh, Baby? Ooh, Baby! What the hell?" LB whined. "I repeat, did Sonny and the twins find Jaybird yet?"

Todd finished nuzzling. He adjusted Pepper's wig, put on his shirt, tugged the dog's tail without incident, winked at them both, and left.

"Well...?"

"No, LB, they haven't found him yet. They've visited one club, called several others, checked in with one active nudist organization and one inactive one. Nothing yet. They'll start heading back from Florida soon, hitting what clubs they can. So far, it's been a wild goose chase."

Pepper set the dog down, pulled back the curtains, and looked out the window as a neighbor left his apartment and stepped directly in dog shit without noticing.

"Then what's my best move at this point? Intercept them in Florida? Where are they now?"

Pepper released the curtains and headed for the bathroom.

"No. If you go to Florida, you'll be chasing them back north whether or not they find Jaybird. I'm pretty sure they'll keep stopping in at clubs all the way back north just in case. Your best bet is to head east from Atlanta and then start toward Woodstock." She started curling her wig as if it were her real hair.

"Maybe you can intercept them near their destination. Of course, at this point, that's not even necessary unless they find Jaybird. And time is running out on that. My guess is you have nothing to worry about. Nothing to worry about at all."

From someone in the room with LB, Pepper heard, "Okay, got Dad all diapered. Let's load up the Edsel and head to the frozen cadaver lab."

Pepper held out the receiver and stared at it as the curling iron scorched her wig.

* * *

Meanwhile, roughly 450 crow-fly miles southeast of Pepper's sizzling hair, a man's scream – followed by a woman's scream, followed by a dog's bark – rattled the morning quiet at the Ol Swimmin Hole in East Kibosh, South Carolina. Penny Peebles sat bolt upright in bed. The barking was in bed next to her, Princess Petunia on irritable high alert. The screams had sounded like bloody murder not far away. Penny nudged Pete, but he merely grumbled and rolled over in bed.

She threw back the covers, padded toward the door and flipped the light switch. When her eyes recovered from the burst of brightness, she saw that Pixie was missing. Penny hurried to the bathroom, grabbed her robe, stumbled into her slippers, grabbed Petunia, and rushed into the hall. The screams had come from the room next door: Max's room.

Penny knocked on the door but got no answer. Fearing something dire, she ignored the 'Do Not Disturb' sign, grabbed the knob and turned it. The door was unlocked, so she entered, carrying the whimpering dog and taking cautious half-steps.

And there stood Pixie in her sheer pink nightgown. Max was backed up against the far wall, clutching the bedsheet in front of him. He appeared to be nude otherwise.

"Oh, hi, Mommy," Pixie said calmly. "Nothing to worry about here. I was in the hallway walking off a leg cramp when I heard Max scream. It must have triggered a scream-reflex in me, too. A sympathy scream, I guess." She giggled and shrugged. "Anyway, then I ran in to see what was wrong. Just like you did. Out of concern. For poor Max."

Penny stared at her negligeed daughter and then at Max: A black man. Wearing a white sheet. In the south.

Penny's head hurt.

"Just had a bad dream. That's all," Max finally managed.

Petunia then wriggled free of Penny and rooted under the bed, finally wrestling a pair of pink panties from beneath the bed ruffle.

"A real nightmare..." Max added, his eyes glazing and his voice trailing off.

Pixie giggled again.

* * *

Meanwhile, roughly 450 crow-fly miles northwest of Max's nightmare, the phone rang again in Pepper's apartment. Her hair still smoldering, she snatched up the receiver.

"Look, LB, I've told you all I know. Believe me, I want you to get what's coming to *you* so I can get what's coming to me and—"

It wasn't LB. Pepper listened. She started sweating.

Finally, her voice trembling, she said, "So, it was you who called the other day? Said you knew what I was up to? Okay, so tell me what you want me to do."

As the caller gave her the details, Pepper slouched, pulled the smoking wig from her head, and dropped it into the toilet.

* * *

Meanwhile, roughly two crow-fly miles east of Pepper's extinguished bouffant, Indy wiretapper Mike Smyth placed a call that traversed roughly 440 crow-fly miles of phone line to Washington, DC. Junior Agent Junior Carducci, Jr., answered and took notes about the previous day's phone conversations on Pepper Duckenfield's phone lines.

Carducci noted three big takeaways: First, per the update to Pepper from Sonny Muckle, he and the twins had not yet been able to locate Jay Finch, Jr. (known only to Sonny as "Jaybird"). Second, there had been no contact yet from LilBuckaroo Muckle DePew, who might or might not be involved in the hunt. And third, an unknown caller – poor connection, indeterminate gender, Smyth said – had left a mysterious message, presumably for Pepper: "*I know what you've been doing. We need to talk.*"

"Little to go on, but at least we've got confirmation of the hunt for Finch," Carducci said. He paused for a moment and chewed a gnarled pencil. Then, "Here's what I need you to do, Smyth. Check the wiretap recordings again today just after five o'clock and then again at ten this evening. If there's anything of interest to report at all, call me here or at home immediately." He gave Smyth his home number. "I know that's asking a lot, but I think this operation is at the point where we can't afford an overnight delay if we get a solid lead about Finch's whereabouts."

* * *

Meanwhile, roughly 480 crow-fly miles south-southwest of where the Junior Agent had upped the ante with Smyth, Radiance Reynolds's phone rang. At her desk between bouts of morning sickness, she looked through the glass walls of the cubicle farm toward the receptionist, whose thumbs up told Radiance, "Yes, you should take this call."

"Reynolds."

"Radiance Reynolds?"

"Yes, Radiance Reynolds here."

"Good morning, Ms. Reynolds, I'm Leo Wilder, one of the producers here at the Nightly News with Jennings Prokoff. How are you today?"

Reynolds's mind raced and her gut churned. *How dare Prokoff get back with her through a flunkie!* She held her tongue. "What can I do for you, Mr. Wilder?"

"Yes, well, you may be aware that, here at the network, we like to occasionally feature feel-good stories from local affiliates. It creates a sense of community across our smaller-market friends and family while also providing stations the opportunity to play on the big stage and promote their exposure locally."

"I've seen those reports before," Reynolds said. "Again, what can I do for you?" *Fucking Prokoff!*

"Yes, I can tell you're quite busy, Ms. Reynolds, but as I understand it, you've been following a Good Samaritan-type story for some time. Nothing more feel-good than a Good Samaritan, eh?"

"I suppose."

"Yes, well, we have a 90-second slot for a remote live feed this evening, and we wondered if you'd like to share an update on your developing story. Sorry for the short notice, but we had a planned report fall through – about a Diamond Jubilee celebration for a small town in Tennessee, but it seems things went awry during the parade, and now we can't seem to reach the mayor or her 103-year-old father who founded the town. Too much uncertainty there to air that report this evening. Can we count on you to step in?"

Radiance was seething, about to bite the head off the producer even if she had to crawl through the phone lines to do it. "You tell Jennings Prokoff to do three things. First, he can kiss my ass. Second, he can call me himself. And third, he can clear his calendar for the birth of his illegitimate child!" At least that's what she *wanted* to say, but before she could say anything of the sort, she had a better idea…

"Why certainly, Mr. Wilder. I'd be delighted to step in and provide a feel-good update." She fought back an urge to hurl.

"Great," Wilder said. "We can start promoting it right away, you know, just a voice-over during the later segments of the morning shows. Something like, "'Watch for a special 'Feel Good, America!' report from north Florida as Radiance Reynolds brings us an update on an anonymous Good Samaritan who has been making lives brighter in her area for many years.' How does that sound, Ms. Reynolds? We can start airing that promo within the hour and work with your team to do the live feed at 6:50 p.m."

"Why, that sounds perfect, Mr. Wilder. Nothing like live TV to get Mr. Prokoff the kind of attention he deserves, right?"

* * *

And *an hour later* and roughly 30 very-exhausted-crow-fly miles west of Radiance Reynolds's newsroom cubicle, Robin Paloma was in the Moon-Your-Mama Grill, clearing a late breakfast table when he glanced up at the corner TV. A network promo caught his eye: for a live update to air that evening from reporter Radiance Reynolds – *his* Radiance Reynolds – about a Good Samaritan who had so far remained anonymous. And then, piggybacking on the network promo, a local one:

"*Watch WTFU's Radiance Reynolds tonight on the Nightly News with Jennings Prokoff as she reports live from Crosstown Mall at the local Sam Goody record store with an update on the still-unidentified Good Samaritan.*"

Robin left the table unbussed, walked to the kitchen, and stared through the pass-thru and into the Moon-Your-Mama Bar. The bar looked empty to Robin except for the memory of the night before, with Jaybird saying, "We need to talk." And talk they had, complete with

Jaybird's formal presentation of the classic "it's not you, it's me" and "I never got over my one true love" breakup lines.

Hours later, and operating on little sleep, Robin wasn't sure which emotion was stronger – hurt or anger. But one thing he knew for sure – the cure for both was the same: revenge. And though revenge was a dish best served cold, the opportunity before him was red hot. He walked to the cork message board near the pie station, removed the note that read *R. Reynolds* and bore the WTFU hotline number. He tried that number again, got through to the receptionist, but got the brush-off once more.

"Well, Radiance Reynolds," he said, softly but bitterly as he hung up the phone, "since you won't call me back regarding our Good Samaritan, it looks like we'll just have to chat at the Sam Goody. And I know just what to show you that will make you take me seriously."

Robin climbed onto the counter in the kitchen, squeezed halfway through the pass-thru to the bar, and from a shelf just beside the opening, removed Jaybird's framed "Meet Your Bar Manager" photo as well as a small mooning gnome figurine. *By the time Jaybird misses these, all of America will know the identity of Mr. Good Fucking Samaritan,* Robin thought.

And yet…

With the venom of vengeance came doubt. Could he really do this? Should he? Or was the breakup his fault after all – pushing too hard too fast? Not everyone loved as quickly and deeply as he did. Robin felt like crying it all away, a burrowing sadness taking root settling in with the anger.

But within seconds, the rage proved stronger. Robin cleared his throat and steeled his nerve. Pulled himself back into the diner's kitchen. Stared at the tiny gnome and whispered to it, "Okay, little fella, what *does* one wear when exposing a nudist on a live national TV broadcast?"

CHAPTER 22
(In Which Max Gets an Unexpected Invitation, Penny Finds an Unexpected Clue, and Pepper Expects the Unexpected)

Midmorning

PENNY AND PIXIE SAT IN THE DINING ROOM AT THE OL SWIMMIN HOLE, awaiting breakfast. Leashed around a chair leg, between them, Petunia stood watch at the picture window for any male dogs who might storm the fortress. Being a bitch in heat demanded constant vigilance. To wit:

"Oh, look, there's Max," Pixie whispered to her mother. Indeed, the object of her *Paydro-who?* obsession stood at the pastry counter, his back to the Peebles women.

"Now, Pixie," Penny began, "let me remind you it was very lucky your daddy was sleeping off a few too many shots of vodka this morning and didn't find you with Max the way I did. So, not a word about any of it. *Capiche?* After all, your daddy's on a mission. He simply doesn't have time to kill Max this morning."

Awaiting a cinnamon croissant, Max couldn't help overhearing of his imminent demise. He turned.

"Oh, good morning, Max," Penny said, waving him over. "Care to join us?"

Max waved his hand, trying to beg off. "No, thank you, Mrs. Peebles. Ma'am. I'm just here for a roll."

Hearing that, Pixie opened her legs. Petunia growled. Max began to sweat.

"Is Pete up and about?" he asked, looking side to side.

"He should be down soon," Penny said. "But I was just telling Pixie that I think the less we say to Pete about the events of this morning, the better. He's got a lot on his mind. No need to, well, ya know…"

"Please join us, Maxie," Pixie said sweetly. "Let us treat you to breakfast. I feel awfully bad about the, um, the mix-up this morning." She pushed a chair out from the table with a pink-sneakered foot. "Sit!"

Max obeyed. So did Petunia.

"Ah, Max, ol' buddy!" said a stealthy Pete, slapping him on the back. Max felt lightheaded. He peed a little, but managed to eke out, "Ha… Look at that, Pete's here. And so quick and quiet."

"I'm light on my feet, like a ballet dancer in a linebacker's body," Pete said, puffing out his chest. "Good combination for someone in my line of work."

"Former line of work," Penny reminded him.

Pete took the last of the four chairs at the table, looked over his shoulder, and then furtively produced a flask and held it out for Max. "Hair of the dog?" (At this, Petunia whimpered.)

"Already hit my limit," Max said, "for this year, at least."

"Nonsense. It'll put hair on your chest."

"I like a hairy chest," Pixie said. She scooted her chair an inch closer to Max. He scooted his two inches away.

"Coffee!" Pete barked to no one in particular. Then he turned to look Max in the eye. "You remember my mission here, right Max? The one I was questioning people about at Zork's?"

Max picked up a cloth napkin and dabbed his forehead. "Yes, I remember. A little. You're looking for some Finch guy. Or at least some embezzled money."

"That's right. And *you*, my dark and sweaty friend—"

Pixie licked her lips.

"—are looking for a human-interest story in this oddball place. Right? See where I'm going with this?"

Gertilda scurried over with the croissant for Max and a cup of coffee for Pete. "Cream or sugar?" she asked.

"No, I like it black."

Again. Pixie. Lips.

Pete leaned in and lowered his voice. "So, here's what happened: Late last night, just about to close down Zork's, the cleaning guy comes in, see… So, I show him the pictures and ask him if he's seen this younger Finch guy. Turns out, the cleaning guy also does grounds maintenance during the day. Guess where."

Max shrugged.

"The town cemetery, that's where. And get this… He says he's seen our guy more than once over the years, down near the Finch graves. He also says he's seen him wandering around the cemetery, acting all strange, like he's itching to be left alone so he can get away with something."

"Sounds like a solid lead," Max said. He sensed he was on the verge of being invited into the inner sanctum, the very heart of the story. It was a dream come true. He was terrified.

"Could be," Pete agreed. "So, here's where you come in. Whaddaya say you come spend the day with me. At the cemetery. Might need you to help me do a little digging." He held up his hook. "Could use an extra hand after all." He slapped Max on the back again.

And Max peed a little more.

* * *

After Pete and Max left for the cemetery (*another bad idea*, Penny thought, but who was she to tell Pete how to find his salvation?), Pixie and Petunia went for a walk, leaving Penny to a morning of romance novels. But the eerie quiet in the room was distracting, and she found herself staring at the file case on the dresser. It was calling her back in for another look. She closed *From Wench We Came* and stepped over to the case.

She had just started to sort through the papers – clearly, they had been ransacked (no doubt Pixie searching for a missing bonbon) – when the phone rang.

"Peebles room," Penny said.

"Hello," said a vaguely familiar voice. "Is Pete available?"

"No, he's out right now, no telling how long. Who is this?"

"Oh, hello, Petunia, is that you?"

Penny cleared her throat. "It's Penny. Remember?"

"Ah, yes. So sorry," Junior Carducci said. "Innocent mistake."

"Really? Are agents like you ever truly innocent?" Penny asked coquettishly. For some reason, she liked messing with the Junior

Agent. But it suddenly occurred to her that maybe her flirtatious streak had spawned a similar demon in Pixie. "Oh, forgive me, Agent… Carducci, was it?"

"Yes, Junior Carducci."

"Forgive me for being silly. I read too many romance novels, and my mind does take flights of fancy. Do you have a message for Pete? Need a call-back?"

"Well, I don't know if I should leave a message or not…"

"Oh, I'm sure it's fine. I probably know more about this Finch business than you do, Junior. Now that Pete's retired and this case has been officially closed for so long, I don't see the harm in you letting me know what to pass along to Pete."

"I suppose you're right," Junior said. "Very well. I'm afraid I really don't have much to report anyway. At least not yet." He went on to tell her that based on the previous day's phone tap clandestinery, it was clear the Indy attorney and his niece and nephew were still hunting for Finch, Jr., though they did not know his real name. Junior also told Penny that the twins' half-sibling had not been heard from as of the day before, so his role in the hunt was unclear. And he informed her that a mysterious caller had left a cryptic message for the attorney's receptionist, Pepper, raising the possibility that Pepper was more deeply involved than previously believed.

Penny jotted it all down verbatim on an OSH note pad, took Junior's call-back number, and promised to share the intel with Pete when he returned. "It might be evening before he comes back, though," she said. (She did not mention to Junior that Pete now had a confidant named Max or that they might be out digging up bones in the graveyard).

After the call ended, she set Carducci's message aside and went back to the contents of the file case, trying to sort them back into order. A few minutes into the exercise, she pulled out the note the elder Finch had attempted to give his son from his deathbed. It was the original note, crumpled but legible:

KIB<u>OS</u>H
ROCK

She set it aside. And a couple of minutes after that, she noticed something else. On a transcript of a phone-tapped conversation between the elder Finch and his son, this exchange:

> *Jay Finch, Sr.: "Whatever I might have done, son, I never meant for anyone to get hurt. These were bad men who made that money in bad ways. I'm no hero, but if stealing from the crooked rich and giving back to the swindled poor is a crime, I guess I'm guilty as hell."*
>
> *Jay Finch, Jr.: "I know, Dad. I believe you. What you did was noble in the long run."*
>
> *Jay Finch, Sr.: "Oh, Jaybird, it just all got so complicated so fast. All I want is to go back to that time when your mama was alive and we were together, just the three of us. Remember those good days at the old summer house in Goshen? Remember that goofy little gnome I bought for you to give your mama? And how you repainted it in those crazy colors?"*
>
> *Jay Finch, Jr.: "I remember, Dad. We sure had a lot of good times at the OSH..."*

The OSH? Penny looked again at the note pad. OSH: *Ol Swimmin Hole*, in this case. But back then, to the Finch boys, OSH meant something else. It meant *Old Summer House*. She grabbed the note pad and wrote this down, then set the note on the desk. Set it next to the crumpled deathbed note:

$$K I B \underline{O S H}$$
$$R O C K$$

And there it was. The *OSH* in KIBOSH was underlined. Why were only those letters emphasized? Could it really be that simple? Is it possible that Kibosh was never really a destination but instead a deception, merely a word hiding a clue that only the young Finch would understand? Could it be that the money had been at the Old Summer House back then? And if so, was it still there now?

Penny called Junior Carducci right back. He didn't answer. She left a message:

"Yes, hello, Junior, this is Penny Peebles again. I may have discovered something, inadvertently, you understand, but I think it could be important. Could you call me back here as soon as you possibly can? I think we might be able to help Pete get his justice after all."

* * *

After retrieving her scorched wig from the toilet when she had finished with the unsettling phone call, Pepper borrowed some of Effyu's weed. "Need this a little more than you do this morning, pal," she said. Hands still trembling, she rolled up a towel and placed it at the bottom of the front door, then pulled the curtains back a sliver and peeked outside. Another neighbor passed by, stepped in dog shit, and started cursing. Pepper lit the joint and collapsed on the couch next to the sniffing dog.

"Quite the dilemma," she said and then took a deep drag. She held the smoke in her lungs, her chin tucked against her neck. Then, exhaling: "Quite the predicament. Quite the..." She inhaled again and held the smoke for a good twenty seconds. "Quite the shit storm coming."

CHAPTER 23

*(In Which Pete and Max Have a Showdown, LB Gets the
Afterlife Lowdown, Joe Jack Discovers Annabel's Ruse,
and Sonny and the Twins Get Vital New Clues)*

Early Afternoon

CLOUDS BEGAN TO CLUSTER AND DARKEN OVER EAST KIBOSH, WHERE PETE
and Max passed beneath an iron arch of celestial ornateness.

At Kiboshian Memorial Gardens, there were no actual gardens to
speak of. Unless you counted sun-bleached plastic flowers squirming
in the breeze while wedged into concrete pots. Alas, even those hardy
survivors were soon to be culled. According to a sign just inside the
arch, floral displays were to be removed seasonally (sort of) *on or about*
May 15th, August 15th, November 15th, and February 1st. (The latter date
variance from the 15th was presumably so any flowers placed on
Valentine's Day wouldn't be removed the next day. On or about.)

So, no gardens, per se. Nonetheless, on that late morning of
August 12th, three days shy of the next scheduled clearance of clutter,
the place remained festooned with the tattered detritus of Memorial
Day plastic.

Plus all the permanent alien shit.

There was plenty of space kitsch, even here: flying saucers
hanging from shepherds' crooks and extra-terrestrials carved into
granite grave markers, along with such touching epitaphs as, "Now
I really *am* really outta this world," or "They came in peace, now I
rest in peace," or "I told you I saw the little green bastards!" (That
popular gravestone was adorned with quite a galaxy of faux silks and
denuded stems.)

Despite the occasional UFO homage, Kiboshian Memorial Gardens was, for the most part, a peaceful place – except on this day when the air carried sounds of occasional swearing and the dragging and clanking of a shovel and pick.

Pete Peebles and his unpaid hired *hand*, Max Thibodeaux, trudged the gentle rises and falls of the grounds, row by row through the fields of marble and granite and limestone and slate, searching amongst the six hundred plus graves for a single final destination: the burial site of Jay Finch, Sr. and his wife, Lark.

"Third visit to East Ki, and somehow I never made it here," Pete said, pausing and wiping sweat from his upper lip. "Maybe subconsciously I knew I'd have trouble digging even if I did find something of interest, so… well, let's just say I'm glad you're along for the assist, Max."

"I'll help if I can, but I'm not sure what we're looking for, aside from the grave, that is."

"And *that*, sir, is the ever-present dilemma," Pete said. "Finding the hiding spot of this treasure is like judging if something is obscene or not – we'll know it only when we see it."

Fifteen minutes later, with the clouds darker still, they found the Finch grave marker: a simple slab, names and dates alone, no Martian motif. Easy to overlook in the regiments of more grandiose stones.

"Well, here it is," Pete said. "Can you dig it?"

"Excuse me? Did you just flash back to the sixties, Pete?"

"No, goddammit, I mean literally, can you *dig* it – dig the ground around the grave? See if we hit anything beneath the surface."

Suddenly, Max wished he was back at the OSH, even if that meant fending off Pixie.

Not waiting for an answer, Pete removed his shoulder holster and laid his gun on a nearby flat stone. Then he circled the Finch grave and peered out in all directions from this vantage point. He shook his head. "People are absolute idiots," he said. "I find it amazing they would choose to rest in a place like this after they die."

* * *

North of Atlanta, behind a strip mall fronted by a gas station, LilBuckaroo, Annabel, and Old Edgar had arrived at the Freeze and Thank You Cryonics Lab and Cryotherapy Lounge. Edgar smiled at a suspended camera above the door of a mostly windowless building. "Che-e-ese," he said. Apparently, that was the magic word, as the three were buzzed into a small lobby area where they faced another door secured by a keypad. Thirty seconds later, just long enough for Edgar to begin to doze off while on his feet, the door opened, and a man with long bony white fingers held it so they could enter.

"Welcome to Freeze and Thank You," the man said, shaking hands all around. "I'm Jerry Patrick, Executive Director and Chief Operating Officer. I also clean the toilets. And you must be Edgar Albert Poes and Annabel Sweet," Jerry said. "I believe we spoke on the phone." He then studied LB and said, "But I don't think I know the name of this young gentleman... Oh, wait, could you be *Mr.* Sweet? Joe Jack, is it?"

Annabel spoke up. "No, no, my husband, Joe Jack, couldn't make it. This is my son. My son Colby Jack." LB squinted. Annabel took his hand. And Edgar saw another camera. "Che-e-ese!"

"Yes, we have many cameras throughout," Jerry said. He smoothed his facial hair and looked up, then turned his gaze to the thick envelope in Edgar's hand. "Yes, indeed, we take security very seriously here at Freeze and Thank You. Everything from separate entrances for each part of our business to alarms, redundant uninterruptible backup power systems, the works."

Still staring at the envelope, Jerry Patrick licked his lips. "But enough about that. I'm sure you don't want to waste any time. Perhaps we can take care of signing the documents and making your payment in full, Edgar."

"So, what exactly *are* the parts of your business?" LB asked. He couldn't believe he was participating in this. Could there be an additional charge leveled against him for impersonating the son of a police officer?

"Well," Jerry Patrick said, looking slightly annoyed, then forcing a smile, "I'm sure your mother gave you the big-picture view, but here it is in layman's terms: On one side of our operation we offer therapeutic cryotherapy for the living, either for the whole body or focused on specific areas in need of treatment. We apply subzero dry cold for a few minutes, and this helps 'shock' the body into initiating internal chemical reactions for self-repair. Often this can be beneficial to help treat inflammation, manage pain, reduce stress, and perhaps even improve sleep or reduce weight. At least this is what our clients tell us. We make no such claims, you understand."

"Of course not," LB said.

"Of course not, what?" Jerry asked. "Of course not, you don't understand; or of course not, you understand what I'm saying and also understand that we make no such claims?"

"The second one," LB said. "I think." Annabel squeezed his hand and released it.

"Very good. Now, back to business…"

"You said your clients tell you good things," LB pressed. "But do *you* use, what is it, cryotherapy, yourself?"

"Certainly!"

"And you've had positive results?"

"Of course," Jerry said, tersely, but still with a smile. "Nothing but positive results."

"And nothing gets frostbitten? Nothing falls off?"

"Certainly not! We take every precaution, Colby Jack!"

"Che-e-ese!" Edgar smiled toothlessly.

"Very good, Edgar," said the Executive Director. "Now, about that payment…"

But Edgar was wandering toward a large poster on the wall. Annabel and LB followed. Edgar pointed to an illustration. "Gonnaputmeindare," he said.

LB's eyes widened. "That's the biggest thermos I've ever seen."

"Well, we don't call them that here," said Jerry. "Thermos is a trademarked name, of course. Fine company and product, as you surely know. I have some coffee in one right now. But you're right in the sense that our storage dewars *are* also vacuum flasks, just on a much larger scale. We use these advanced systems, technologies, and equipment in the other side of our business – our cryonics lab."

"Which is…?" LB prompted.

"Preservation of the body shortly after physical death," Annabel said. "Dry, frozen preservation for possible future re-animation."

"Gonnaputmeindare," Edgar repeated. "Juslikewaldisney."

"Not gonna happen today, though, Dad," Annabel said. "Long time from now, when your time comes, we'll preserve your body so they can cure whatever took you from us."

"They'll be able to cure old age?" LB asked.

"Well, no one really knows what the future holds, do we?" said the Executive Director. "Now, if we can just get back to … what on Earth is that smell?"

Edgar's face was red. He grinned. "Cutda che-e-ese…"

* * *

"Cut me outta here with a fuckin' acetylene torch if ya have to, dammit!" Deputy Brutus yelled. "Can't believe you lost the goddamn keys. Again!"

"I didn't lose the keys," Joe Jack said. "That des-parade-o scofflaw absconded with them. Don't know how he got out, but he must've made off with the keys when he vamoosed."

"Then call for backup. Get a locksmith. Do something!"

"Now, Brute," Joe Jack said, "just simmer down. Let's think this through. I can't really call for official law enforcement assistance, now, can I? After all, we'd be laughingstocks. The butts of jokes from now till doomsday."

"Locksmith then, dammit! Call Morty Owens."

"Well, now, that could be a problem, too. You'll recall that Morty has threatened to run for Mayor next election. If we call on him to help solve this problem, we create one helluva bigger one. Think big picture, Brute. Big picture."

"Fuck the big picture! Do something!"

Joe Jack exhaled so hard it spawned a belch. "I need to pee," he said, and he walked away.

"Goddammit, Joe Jack, get me the fuck outta here!"

"Be right back."

Joe Jack walked to the restroom in the office area, flipped on the light, closed the door behind him, and used the toilet. He then shook away the dew, zipped up, and shaped his mustache in the mirror. He did not wash his hands.

Reaching for the doorknob, he stopped short. Taped to the back of the door, a note:

> *JJ, I didn't think it was right for you to lock up that poor boy. As Mayor, I'm pardoning him. Had to let him out. Don't be mad and don't look for him. He'll be with Dad and me for a few days on a little road trip to take care of some business. Back soon. Hugs and kisses. A*

"Sonofabitch!"

When Joe Jack reappeared on the cellblock, Brutus said, "What's wrong? Tell me this isn't getting even worse."

"Well...I've got the house to myself for a few days, so that's a good thing, I suppose." The Marshal then approached the escapee's cell. He tried the door. Locked. And then he saw the key on the floor against the far wall.

"Fuck!"

And then Joe Jack noticed the full jailer's ring set of keys looped over the bedpost. So close, yet....

"Double fucking fuck!"

* * *

"Fuck!" Pete said. He was clawing at the ground around the front side of the Finch grave while Max sliced into the topsoil on the back side with the shovel. "Anything back there, Max? Anything at all? How deep ya goin'?"

"Going blade deep. Nothing but dirt."

"Goddammit, we gotta go deeper! Hell, we'll have to go six feet down if necessary. Damn money's probably in the grave with the crummy bastard."

Max stopped digging. "Pete, I can't do that. We can't rob a grave."

"Not robbing a grave, just want to open it up." He clawed at the ground faster, dirt showering the air. "I have no intention of stealing the body."

"Pete," Max said. "Pete. *Pete!*"

"What the hell is it? I'm busy here. I'll be to China before you get to the damn casket. And we gotta work fast. Looking like rain."

"What are we doing?" Max asked. He joined Pete on the front side of the stone. "This is some pretty illegal shit. This can't be worth going to jail for. After all, you don't even know the money's here, do you?"

"I know it's gotta be somewhere." Pete stopped clawing. He wiped his forehead and looked around, his eyes suddenly trained on a nearby stone. "Well, I'll be a sonofabitch," he said.

"What?" asked Max.

"Looka the name on that marker over there." He pointed to a large gray slab with natural-looking irregular edges.

"It says 'Rock'," Max said.

"You know what that means?" Pete stood. Reached into his pocket. Pulled out the copy of the deathbed note, soiling it. "Looka there," he said, showing it to Max:

$$K I B \underline{O S H}$$
$$R O C K$$

"Yeah?"

"Don't ya see what this means? It means we're supposed to dig over there. 'Rock' goddammit. It's not under the Finch stone, it's gotta be under the 'Rock' stone. Genius! The money's not in the obvious place; it's where Finch can keep an eye on it."

"But Finch is dead."

"No matter," Pete growled. "This has gotta be it." He handed the note to Max and began defiling the neighboring gravesite.

* * *

In the heart of town, Pixie Peebles Abercrombie was asked to leave the Martian (Not Mars) Chocolate Shop. After twenty minutes of taste testing samples of nearly every concoction in the place, the tolerant owner finally reached his limit when Pixie tried to get Princess Petunia's opinion on a truffle.

"Chocolate can poison a dog," said the spindly little man with blue-green hair. "If you're gonna kill a dog that shouldn't be in here in the first place, buy something and do it outside."

Pixie huffed, grabbed another toffee bite, and said, "Fine. But for your information, your chocolate is *not* exactly out of this world, Martian or not!" She nibbled and swallowed, trying not to savor. "Besides, Petunia and I are going to the graveyard to check on my new boyfriend."

"Graveyard, huh?" the owner muttered under his breath. "Did ya poison him, too?"

Pixie stepped out the door. It started to rain.

* * *

In her room at the Ol Swimmin Hole, Penny Peebles paced between the window and the phone and the wall clock. It was already midafternoon, more than three hours since she had spoken with Junior Agent Junior Carducci, Jr., and she was still awaiting his call-back. She was hoping, *praying* at times, he would get back with her while Pixie was out shopping, and while Pete and Max were doing God-knows-what at the cemetery.

And then it was raining. That could only mean they would all be back soon. If only…

The phone rang.

* * *

In the light rain, Pete clawed feverishly, attacking the ground at the base of the Rock family's grave marker. "Get over here and help!" he commanded Max, but Max just stood and watched. What he'd once envisioned as a story of redemption and the pursuit of justice was unraveling before his eyes into a tale of obsession, of a descent into madness. Still a good story, he supposed, maybe even a better one, but not exactly what he had pitched to Jennings Prokoff.

"Pete…" Max began as he cautiously approached. "Stop for a minute, will you?"

"Can't stop. It's raining. I know the money is here. Gotta be. Gotta be!"

"How many hunches have you followed so far on this money trail? And how many of them have worked out?"

Pete stood. He pointed his hook at Max. "Thanks to my hunches, I've had more goddamned successes in a year than you'll have your entire life, so I'll thank you to shut the fuck up!"

Max started to walk away, from Pete, from the cemetery, from the story. But he couldn't let it go. He turned back.

"Why didn't you just look for the man first and then get to the money through him? I mean, it makes no sense to me. Here you've had an entire federal agency at your disposal, and you continue to go off on scavenger hunts instead of getting to the money through the perpetrator's son. What about the wiretaps in Indy? Why'd you even start those? Do they even matter anymore? I mean, what the hell, Pete? Why in the name of—"

Pete bounded toward him, "You wanna know why I want to find the money before anyone finds Finch, Jr.? I'll tell you why. Back when this case was hot and before the idiots at the agency closed the file, I worked that angle for a long damn time. Find the man to find the money. But eventually, I figured something out. I figured out that even if I found the guy and brought him in and he talked, well, the money would be lost. It would all get hung up in official bullshit procedures, and a few years down the road, that money would go into some reparations fund. That is unless an entry-level flunkie found a way to siphon and divert. And by God, that's *my* money now. Whether it exists now or not, it's mine! You hear me, Max. It's my goddamn money. No one else has worked like a dog to get it. It's got to be *mine!*"

Max shook his head. "But you don't know it's here," he said softly. "You're basing everything off this one note, and it says nothing really. *Kibosh Rock.* What the hell does that mean? It could mean anything." He held the note out in the rain. "And why is the OSH underlined and nothing else? Hell, that could mean the money's at the Ol Swimmin Hole for all we know."

Max walked away and made it nearly to the archway at the entry before he heard the footsteps behind him. He turned and faced Pete. And Pete's gun.

"How did you know about the wiretaps?" Pete asked calmly.

"What do you mean?"

"You asked about the taps in Indy. We never talked about that."

"Sure, we did, Pete. You must've mentioned it. At Zork's, maybe, when we were drinking."

"And I'm sure we didn't," Pete said. "I'll tell you what I think. I think Carducci sent you to keep an eye on me. I think that little ratfink is using me to do the dirty work and plans to swoop in and nab the money for himself."

Max held his hands up in front of his chest. "That's crazy, Pete. I'm not an agency guy. I don't even know Junior Carducci."

Pete advanced another step. "And yet somehow you know his first name is Junior, don't you?" He pointed the gun.

"Daddy!" yelled Pixie from just outside the arch.

* * *

For Janis and Jimi, the search for their father continued.

But after spending too much time earlier in the day at a Pasco County club called Sun-Ray Acres, and with nothing to show for it but redder flesh and aching feet, the twins and Sonny arrived at their second stop of the day: Solar Bares.

Their time in the Bronco had been mostly quiet. Despite Essie Fernley's mention of once seeing someone matching Jaybird's description, each subsequent dead-end was taking its toll, hope fading with each passing mile and each lost minute. At least two hours behind schedule, they hoped to make this club visit a quick one so they could make the turn and head northeast.

In the Solar Bares office, owner Joanie Varker stood at a counter flanked by essential nudist supplies: sunscreen, bug repellent, sunglasses, flip flops, and beach towels. Ironically, the office-slash-mercantile also sold T-shirts and cover-ups.

Varker welcomed the three visitors but deflected their questions about whether a man with a Jaybird tattoo might be a member or frequent guest. "You're more than welcome to check out the club and enjoy what we have to offer during a day visit, but I certainly can't divulge information about our members to outsiders," she said, wagging a finger in the air at Sonny (thus wasting the gesture). "All I ask during your visit is that you respect those around you. Polite questions are fine, but no interrogations and no gawking, gazing, glaring or staring!"

"Sheesh!" Janis said, back outdoors and out of earshot of Joanie Varker. "She's as protective of members as an iron codpiece!"

Jimi rolled his eyes, but then the visual of his sister's quip breached his reserve. He chuckled. Then laughed. Then snorted and guffawed his way into a persistent giggling fit. Janis looked at him, astonished. Sonny, too, was quietly amazed but said nothing until Jimi's fit subsided, at which point he said, "Okay, kids, let's get nekkid." Again, Jimi went off the rails, doubling over and gasping between howls. Janis merely shrugged, led Sonny to the Bronco, and retrieved their towels.

Moments later, there they stood, Janis and Sonny nude, Jimi trying to compose himself, when two matching gold electric golf carts skidded to a gravelly stop before them.

"Mornin' folks," a portly sixty-ish man said. "Welcome to Solar Bares." He set the brake, hopped sprightly from his cart, and extended his hand to an unseeing, and thus unwitting, Sonny, who maintained a smiling mannequin pose. This, again, set Jimi off.

Janis stepped forward. "Good morning," she said. "Forgive my men here. I'm Janis. Stevie Wonder there is my uncle Sonny, and the hyena is my brother Jimi."

"No worries at all," the man said. He shook Janis's hand and then Jimi's. "Presley's the name. Fred Presley. And this is my missus, Edna." His wife stepped up beside him. Physically, they were a matched set, their bronzed beachball bellies looking for all the world like late-middle-aged pregnancies, the stuff of medical miracles, especially for Fred.

"Yes sir, Presley's the name, but no relation to that singer fella."

"God rest his soul," Edna added.

"I understand you folks are first-time visitors to our little piece of heaven. Well, we're glad you're here. We'd like to give y'all a quick tour of the facilities, if'n you don't mind." Fred addressed Jimi: "Might as well get comfortable like your sister and uncle here. Gonna be a warm one."

Jimi cleared his throat, nodded, and stepped over to the Bronco. He disrobed and grabbed his towel from beneath Essie Fernley's mooning garden gnome. The gnome took a tumble, but Jimi caught it before it hit the floorboard. As he placed it back on the seat, however, he noticed an inscription inked on the bottom of its plaster base, the dedication faded but still faintly legible.

Jimi carried the gnome and a brochure back with him.

Janis spoke first. "Jimi, Edna just told us something you'll be interested to hear." She turned to their tour guide. "Edna, would you please repeat what you mentioned?"

"Surely," Edna said. "Well, I noticed the tattoo on Sonny's, um, *area* there…"

"His butt cheek," Fred clarified.

"Yes, that. Anyway, I simply mentioned that it looked very much like one another fella had. A man at our former club when we lived in northern Florida."

Jimi again studied the inscription on the gnome's base and then handed the brochure to Janis. "Was your former club by any chance called the Grin and Bare It?" he asked.

"Why, yes, how'd you know that?" Fred wondered.

Janis looked up from the Grin and Bare It brochure's picture of their on-site bar. She managed a faint smile, a smile of cautious hope. "I think we need to get on the road again right away, don't we, brother?"

"Most certainly," Jimi said. "But first, Fred, Edna – Fredna – do you recall the name of this guy with the butt tattoo?"

"Of course," Edna said. "His name is Jayson Stockwood."

"Stockwood?" Sonny asked.

"Yes," Fred said. "But most people called him Jaybird. He's usually at the bar there and—"

"Stockwood," said Janis.

"Jaybird," said Sonny.

"Moon your mama," said Jimi, staring at the gnome.

Fredna watched in amazement as the trio scrambled to dress.

"That's my shirt, Sonny," Janis said. "Here's yours."

"And those are *my* pants," Jimi yelled at his sister.

"Oops, sorry!" she said. "First time I try to get into a man's pants, and they're my brother's. Ewww!"

A minute later, they were on the road, leaving Fred and Edna Presley waving and coughing in a cloud of gravel dust.

CHAPTER 24

*(In Which Joe Jack Calls in an "Expert," LilBuckaroo Feels Like
a Son Again, Max Comes Clean, and Sonny and the Twins
Devise a Contingency Plan)*

Midafternoon

POES POINT TOWN MARSHAL JOE JACK SWEET HAD SPENT THE BETTER PART
of two hours trying to dislodge and retrieve the keys from the locked
jail cell formerly occupied by LilBuckaroo. For a while, Deputy Brutus,
who was locked in the cell across the corridor, had been a cheerleader
for Joe Jack's efforts to get the key that would free him. Alas, such
positivity did not come naturally to the caged Brute, so he quickly
reverted to ridiculing and haranguing his boss – damn the
consequences of that later.

Upon his prior evening escape, LB had mockingly left the jailer's
keyring dangling from the front post of the bunk. The other key, the
one Annabel had tucked beneath the cake, lay flat on the floor against
the far wall where LB had flung it after locking the cell from the
outside. It had landed in the worst possible spot. Or so Joe Jack had
thought. Only after trying to force that key away from the wall with a
blast from the garden hose did the Marshal discover there was a far
worse place: under the bunk.

When the hose had failed (and for what it's worth, keys don't float
in flooded cells), Joe Jack had tried lobbing things at the bedpost to
shake loose the jailer's ring. Soon, the cell was littered with a future
police auction's haul of items from the evidence room: 13 guns (bullets
removed after the first lobbed .45 missed its target, somewhat noisily),
17 shoes, 31 dildoes (a veritable Baskin Robbinsesque variety to suit
any peccadillo), assorted beer cans and wine bottles, three baby rattles,

forceps, three yard darts, seven bocce balls, and eight books (including, reluctantly, Joe Jack's personal favorite: *The Joy of Mex: Women Not Afraid to Go South of Your Border*).

And finally, the confiscated can of *dickTat'r* chips.

When all those items lay in a pool of water and broken glass that resembled the aftermath of a kinky prison orgy, Deputy Brutus cleared his throat and said this to Joe Jack: "If we can't call a locksmith or other legitimate professional, at least call Larry Lou."

Joe Jack turned slowly, scowled, and flipped him off. Then he sighed. "Larry Lou, huh? Not a bad idea, actually. But because you waited till *now* to come up with that little nugget, you get to clean up this mess later."

* * *

By the time LilBuckaroo, Annabel, and Old Edgar had finished the tour and left the Freeze and Thank You Cryonics Lab (and Cryotherapy Lounge), Jerry Patrick had his money. LB could have sworn he heard a cork pop just before the door closed. Edgar, also content with the arrangement, soon fell asleep in the back seat, snuffling and snoring, perhaps dreaming of the afterlife – as a cadaver with a future.

Annabel seemed less at peace with the transaction. From the driver's seat of the Edsel, LB noticed that Edgar's trophy daughter did not watch the road ahead; rather, she looked out the passenger side window, mile after mile, watching the landscape pass. He heard sniffles from her, too, complementing the noises from her dad. Sniffles, snuffles, and snores. *Good name for a law firm*, LB thought, entertaining himself in the quiet void. Even his ghost-dad had gone radio silent. And that was okay. Denny DePew wasn't exactly the most supportive and reliable ghost-dad a boy could have anyway.

Finally, the quiet was too much.

"May I make an observation?" LB asked.

Annabel turned to face him, her eyes red. She nodded.

"When we first met, you were kinda hateful to me, cussin' like a sailor, but now…"

Annabel reached out and touched LB's shoulder. "I know," she said softly. "And I'm sorry about that. That damn parade is my least favorite thing in the world. So much preparation, so much stress, so much attention. *Ghoulish* attention, too, if I'm being honest. Most of the people come out only to see if dad's still alive. A morbid curiosity, I guess."

"Why do you do it then?"

Annabel lowered her hand from his shoulder. "Well, I do it for dad. He enjoys it. And I know that each parade could be his last."

"I suppose so," LB said. "You've probably felt that way for years now, though, right?"

"To some degree, yes, but never quite like this. The feeling and the stress have never been this strong."

LB wasn't sure what to say. He drove another mile in silence.

"Can I confess something to you?" Annabel asked. "Something that might creep you out a little bit?"

An image of transvestite Twaletta Tinkle flashed before LilBuckaroo's eyes. As did an image of the dollar-tuckers at the Holes In The Wall Pub. As did an image of Pepper's new man, *Tahhhd*, standing naked behind her in her apartment.

"I've been creeped out a lot lately," LB said. "Pretty sure I'm up for just about anything. What is it?"

"You remind me of my son," Annabel said. "Same build, same hair color. He didn't have that burned upper lip of yours, but aside from that..."

"Didn't know you had a son. I figured that was just a little white lie you were telling at the freezy place. Colby Jack, was it?"

"The same."

"Does he live in Poes Point?"

Annabel looked out the window again for a moment. "I'm afraid he doesn't live anywhere anymore," she said. "Good Lord took him three years ago. Hit and run. He was crossing the street in front of my office in town, and a car just barreled on through. Only had one stoplight back then. It wasn't enough."

"I'm sorry," was all LB could say.

"The worst thing," Annabel continued, but in a whisper, "was that I eventually questioned God and kept asking why, why, *why*... And then I found myself haunted by not only the unbearable grief but guilt, too."

"Guilt? Why guilt?"

"Because I started wishing it could have been Dad and not Colby. After the fact, I was in denial and started bargaining with God, using my father's life. 'Take Dad,' I said, 'and bring back my son.' Crazy, I know, but I couldn't comprehend what kind of God takes such a young man and lets someone else live a century. It made no sense to me. Probably never will."

"So, with me reminding you of your son and driving you and your dad in the parade, what ... did that just hit you extra hard?"

"I suppose so, but only subconsciously at first. It was only after the parade ended that I put it all together and realized what I'd been imagining – that Colby had come back from the dead to take Dad on one last ride."

LB stared straight ahead, the highway north stretching before the Edsel. "Is that why you sprung me from jail? Because you think I'm your son?"

Annabel laughed so hard she snorted. "Oh, good heavens. I know you're not my son. No one else could ever be my Colby. No, I sprung you because ... well, because Dad loved this year's parade more than any of the others; so I think Joe Jack made a mistake harassing you and locking you up. You just got caught in the middle of it all. So, I'm just trying to make things right, that's all."

LB nodded, grateful. He looked in the mirror, at Edgar napping, then at the dashboard clock; like Edgar, it was still ticking after all these years. Tomorrow, they would be at the Woodstock reunion at Saugerties, New York, ready to intercept Sonny and the twins – and Jaybird, perhaps – if they showed up in the Bronco. But today... Today, LB thought they might have time for an excursion or two. One last fool adventure.

"And besides, numbnuts," Annabel said, "don't look a gift horse in the mouth. Just shut the fuck up and drive. And don't speed! Rules are rules, mister, ya got that?"

LB smiled. The trophy daughter was back.

But suddenly, a rush of emotion rose in him, too; because the profane Annabel reminded him of his mother, Winnie – a strong, potty-mouthed tough cookie. And all he had really wanted when she was alive was to be a specialty-chip-off-the-old-block and make her proud.

* * *

Nearly 175 miles lay between Solar Bares in Pasco County and the Grin and Bare It Family Nudist Campground near the town of Tranquility in northeastern Florida. Which meant that Sonny, Janis, and Jimi might be 175 miles from finding their needle in a haystack. But because that possibility, discovered at the center of a maze of dead ends, seemed too good to be true, none of the three dared jinx it by talking about it. For the first 40 minutes after their hasty retreat from Solar Bares, they said nothing, merely driving in silence until a gas and pee break near the intersection of I-75 and SR 98 in Hernando County.

But when they got back in the Bronco, with Jimi driving again, Janis broke the ice: "So, let's say we find our father. What happens if he denies everything or slams the door on us? What happens if he wants nothing to do with us? It's going to be a shock for him, right? What if he has a family, a gaggle of kids and grandkids? Is he just going to accept us and run off with us? I mean, what are the odds of us convincing him to go to Woodstock right away?"

"Whoa, sis," Jimi said. "So many questions. You been sitting on those for a while?"

"Frankly, yes, haven't you, Mr. Practical?"

"Well, yes, I guess I have. Just afraid to say them out loud."

Sonny said, "All good questions, Janis. Unfortunately, we won't have the answers until we actually *have* them. You're right to be concerned—"

"I'm more than concerned," Janis said. "I'm scared shitless!"

"We all are," Sonny said. "It's entirely possible even if we find him – and that's still a big 'if' at this point – that he'll deny or decline. Odds are he'll need time to absorb everything, and with the reunion weekend already on top of us, that's time we simply don't have. I'd say it's a longshot we'll succeed, so just be prepared for that disappointment."

Jimi found himself accelerating, the stress of the conversation causing his right foot to grow heavy on the pedal. At 80 miles per hour, he slowed again, concentrated on his breathing, and then said, "As I see it, if we find Jaybird and lay things out for him, he's going to feel overwhelmed, maybe even ambushed. We're about to rock his world, and since he's obviously using an alias – Stockwood? I mean, c'mon – he's probably been in hiding for twenty-five years, hiding from that hook-handed dude from Woodstock, right?"

"Right," Sonny and Janis said together.

"So," Jimi continued, "the question is, how can we lower his level of *overwhelmingness*?"

"Love it when you use those forty-dollar words," Janis said.

"Well," said Sonny, "on the shock scale, the biggest might be that he's got two kids he didn't know about."

"Right," Jimi said, "but the good news is that that's one shock we can keep a lid on for a while, don't you think?"

"You mean I can't run up and throw my dyke arms around him and cry, 'Daddy!'?"

"Probably wise to hold back on that," said Jimi. "And as an aside, why do you have to have 'dyke arms'? Why can't you just have regular arms like the rest of us?"

"Nothing regular about me, bro."

"Agreed," said Sonny. "But for now, I think Jimi's right. Let's just lead with the fact that I'm long-lost Sonny from Woodstock, and you're my niece and nephew, helping your poor ol' blind uncle fulfill the dying wish of his sister."

"Okay, so what's next on the shock scale?" Janis asked.

"Two things, I think," Jimi said. "First, seeing Sonny again after all this time. That'll likely be the first surprise."

"Hopefully, a happy one," Sonny said. "I admit I'm nervous as a cat about that one."

"Relax, then," said Janis. "Cats have a bad reputation for being nervous. Mostly they're pretty chill and don't give a damn."

"Okay," said Jimi, "so the Big Kahuna of surprises – that Jaybird's got adult children – we hold up on that one for now; and the second surprise will probably be a happy one."

"So, Jiminy Cricket, what's the next surprise to prepare for?"

Jimi exhaled sharply. "Well, if he's been purposely in hiding all this time and suddenly he's been found... Well, how bad does that spook him? Does he take off? With his cover blown, does he vanish again? And if he's that nervous about it, does he even dare risk helping us out?"

"Again," Sonny said, "good questions. Tough questions. All we can do is keep our fingers crossed and hope he doesn't run."

* * *

Dripping wet from the rain, Pixie burst into the room at the Ol Swimmin Hole. "Mama! Did daddy come back here?" she yelled, out of breath. Max, also soaked, came up beside her, breathing hard, too. The only one not panting was Princess Petunia, now scented with Eau de Wet Dog.

"No, I haven't seen your father since he left this morning," Penny said. "Why, what's wrong? Max, you were with him then… What's going on?"

"He pulled a gun on my Maxie!" Pixie screamed. Petunia jumped from her arms and onto the bed. Pixie collapsed there, too, narrowly missing the dog. She sobbed (Pixie, that is) for a dramatic ten seconds and then lifted her head to see Penny and Max staring at her. Petunia looked away. "I need chocolate!" Pixie screamed. She looked at Max and licked her lips. He took a step back.

"Will someone tell me what's going on?" Penny demanded. And Max did, sharing his story of Pete going off the rails, the tale punctuated by occasional outbursts from Pixie. "The cab driver left me there!" she screamed. "I told him to wait, but he peeled out as soon as I got out of the car. What is *wrong* with people?!?"

"Yeah, we had to hurry back from the cemetery on foot because Pete took the car," Max said.

Calmly, Penny said, "Just relax for a moment. Your father's probably just blowing off steam. I'm sure he'll be back soon. Tell me, Max, what's the last thing he said?"

Max looked at the floor. It was time to confess.

"Well, for starters, he asked how I knew about the wiretaps."

"The wiretaps? The ones in Indy? At the attorney's office?"

"The same."

Penny's eyes narrowed. "I'm confused. How did – or how *do* – you know about the taps?"

Sighing, Max said, "The same way I know about Agent Carducci and the whole Finch story. By eavesdropping on Pete in DC. Spying, you might say."

Pixie perked up. She rose from the bed. "Did you say you're a spy, Maxie? Really? Daddy is sort of a spy, too… But if you're a spy spying on a spy, well, that's just so… *hawwwttt!*"

"Oh, good Lord, Pixie, let the man finish," Penny chided. "I'm sure it's not that complicated. A spy… A spy spying on a spy… A spy spying on a spy … who has a hook?" In her mind, Penny saw the cover of a new pirate romance novel, *By Hook or by Crook or by Nookie*. "Oh, boy, I believe it *is* a bit hot in here."

Max took two steps back. Penny stood between him and the adjoining room door. Pixie stood between him and the hallway. Petunia growled. Three females in heat and a hook-handed former agent on the loose. With a gun.

Max passed out cold.

* * *

Larry Lou Deeney was in his Poes Point bungalow, in his bathtub, covered with ice and holding his breath, when the phone rang. Shortly after a brief but exciting conversation with Joe Jack Sweet, he had haphazardly applied theatrical eye makeup, donned a cape, and positioned his finest black top hat over his equally black mullet wig. He then walked the three blocks to Joe Jack's jail – the site of his greatest escape and most glorious claim to fame. (Except that virtually no one knew about it.)

"I have returned!" he announced with a flourish of the cape as he appeared in the cell block.

"I'm overjoyed," Joe Jack said.

"You should be. Hark, do not discount the fact that I came whence beckoned – yea, though I was deep into perfecting my latest feat of derring-do just daring to be done. Enlighten me, Constable… What matter of urgency has compelled you to summon The Amazing Larry

Lou Deeney? May I assume that my assistance is required *toot sweet*, Marshal Sweet?"

"You could say that."

Larry Lou stepped closer to the cell where Deputy Brutus was entrapped. He shook the locked door. "I gather this situation lies at the root of your dilemma."

"Again, you could say that," Joe Jack said. To his credit, Brutus remained quiet.

"And prithee, what have we here?" Larry Lou said, crossing the corridor to the opposite cell. His eyes darted from dildo to dildo. "Founders' Day Boy's Night get out of hand?"

Joe Jack groaned.

"Fear not, Marshal, your secret is safe with me, but please tell me there's not a defiled miniature donkey under that lumpish bed cover."

"You're the only jackass in here right now, Larry Lou!" Brutus yelled. The outburst had been merely a matter of time. "Get me out of here or I'll defile *your* donkey!"

"Promises, promises," Larry Lou teased. "But I am confused, Deputy. If I *don't* get you out, you claim you'll kick my derriere. Astounding trick. You must teach it to me sometime."

"Okay, okay, enough sniping," Joe Jack said. "I've got another urgent matter to deal with. Name your price. What'll it take for you to work your magic and get the keys out of the, um, the party cell, so we can free the deputy?"

Larry Lou stroked his imaginary goatee. (In his haste, he'd forgotten to paint it on for this performance). "I shall require that the prior charges against me be expunged."

"We dropped those charges months ago so you'd keep your trap shut about escaping our little hotel here."

"Ah, 'tis true, but alas, though the charges were indeed dropped, they were not formally expunged from my, shall we say, colorful record of exploits."

"Fine. Your most recent colorful exploits will be expunged. I'll see to it personally. In exchange for your assistance and your *silence* regarding this little setback we're dealing with right now."

"Excellent!" Larry Lou cried. "And with said charges expunged, including the one where I was wrongfully accused of contributing to the delinquency of a bunny rabbit, I shall require the return of said rabbit post haste."

"Can't have your damn rabbit back," Brutus said. "But he sure made a fine stew."

"Hand to heart!" Larry Lou cried out. "Lump to throat. Tears to eyes!"

"Settle down," Joe Jack said. "He's kidding. We donated Rabbit Downey, Jr. to the daycare center."

"Then, I shall require his return. He is my assistant, my confrère, my cuddle bunny."

"Kids, Larry Lou. The kids love the rabbit."

"As do I."

Silence. Ten seconds worth.

"It appears we are at an impasse," Larry Lou said. "Marshal, deputy, have a glorious day."

"Fine, you'll get your rabbit back."

"Excellent. I'm sure the children will understand. Just tell them that rabbits have been known to simply disappear. They'll believe it if you place a top hat near the empty cage."

With Brutus turned away and Joe Jack making himself scarce, Larry Lou went to work. Two minutes later, he tumbled the tumblers, a personal best time. "Ta-da!" he exclaimed, and then tucked the lock picking set back under his hat and left the cell block. Fully expunged, he disappeared.

Six minutes after that, with Brutus emancipated and cleaning the cluttered cell, Joe Jack's phone rang. It was the eagerly anticipated callback from the Executive Director at the Freeze and Thank You Cryonics Lab and whatever-the-hell-else-it-was-called. For the better part of a year, Joe Jack had steadfastly refused to accompany Annabel and Edgar there, but he had guessed – correctly – they had finally gone ahead without him.

"Hello, Mr. Sweet. Sorry I missed your earlier call. Indeed, your wife, her father, and your son have come and gone."

"My son?"

"Yes, nice young man, quite inquisitive. Nasty looking burn to his upper lip, though."

Ah, the scofflaw! The des-parade-o is with them, after all.

"And how long ago did they leave?"

"Hard to say," Jerry Patrick improvised. "Long enough for me to get the cash deposited in our account. It's all set. Your father-in-law will rest in cold comfort when the time comes."

"Yeah, yeah, thanks. Cold comfort, indeed. In the meantime, did they say where they were headed? I'm afraid dear old Dad forgot some of his medicine."

"Oh my, let me see… Now that I think about it, I believe your son said something like, 'Woodstock, here we come.' Does that mean anything to you?"

Click.

* * *

Soon after Joe Jack hastily packed for a scramble toward New York in his black-and-white…

And soon after Pixie and Penny had revived Max and proceeded to wheedle from him the full scoop about his attempts to get, well, the full scoop (about Pete, that is)…

And soon after LilBuckaroo had delighted Old Edgar and Annabel with surprise stops at two roadside attractions: The *Peelings, Nothing More Than Peelings Museum* (tour highlight: North America's third-longest unbroken peel from a scalped apple), and the *Ground Beef Sanctuary for Legless Cattle* (heartwarming humanitarian work for bovine amputees – and tasty burgers in the on-site diner, too)…

… at quarter till 6, Sonny and the twins slid to a gravelly stop in front of the Moon-Your-Mama Grill on the outskirts of Tranquility, Florida, a town which itself existed on the outskirts of *the outskirts* of the suburbs of Jacksonville.

"I thought it was called the Moon-Your-Mama *Bar*," Janis said.

"Bar *and* Grill, according to the brochure," said Jimi. But this has to be it, doesn't it?"

Just then, a man inside snuffed out the flashing neon "Yummm On In, We're Open!" sign and turned the suctioned plastic Open sign in the window to its reverse: *Closed.*

"No, no, no!" Janis yelled, frantically tumbling out of the Bronco. She rushed the few steps to the entrance and pushed against the door just as the man was attempting to deadbolt it. She wedged in a flip flop but managed to pull her toes to safety.

Jimi hurried to her side. "Excuse me! Excuse me! Sir…"

The man inside waved them off. "Sorry, closing early tonight. I have an, um, an appointment. A TV spot in J-ville. Live with Jennings Prokoff." He seemed to do a double-take on the white Bronco and the shadowed man still seated in the front passenger seat with the windows down.

"Sorry to bother you," Jimi said, "Won't take a minute. We've driven a very long way, from Indiana into the south and all over Florida, looking for someone. We were told he might be at the Moon-Your-Mama Bar & Grill."

"This is the grill side only," the man said. His name tag revealed him to be *Robin, Manager.*

"Okay, so, where's the bar side?" Janis asked. She wanted to retrieve her flip flop, but at least it was keeping the door open enough to have a strained conversation.

"Bar side is behind the grill. But you can't get there from here. You have to enter through the Grin and Bare It."

"Fine," Jimi said. "We'll do that. Where's the entrance?"

Robin nodded to the southwest. "The gate's about a hundred feet that way."

"Thanks," Janis said. "We'll get in there."

"One thing you should know, though," Robin said. "It's a nudist camp. Bar's only open to day visitors, overnighters, and full members."

"We know it's a nudist camp," Jimi said. "Not a problem for us."

"Well, it might be," said Robin. "Day visitors have to be inside the gate by five o'clock."

"We'll get a room, then," said Jimi. "Thank you, Robin. Thanks for the help."

"Rooms are full up. Big weekend at the camp. It's the annual Testicle Festival."

"Well, of course, it is," Janis said, dryly, as she finally tugged her flip flop loose from the door. "Not sure I want to know anything more."

But then she couldn't resist: "Okay, yes, I do. Soooo ... what *is* the Testicle Festival?"

"It's a pitch-in dinner. Two-night event this year. Deep-fried turkey testicles and all the fixins. Very popular. Look, I really have to get going," Robin said. He bolted the door and walked away.

Janis looked at Jimi. "Testicle Festival," she said, her eyes suddenly growing wide.

Jimi started back to the Bronco.

"Gotta be *nuts* to eat turkey testicles," Janis said. "But hey, maybe they're so good you want to grab 'em by the *sac*. Ya think take-out's available for eunuchs? Okay, sorry, that was scrotally inappropriate."

Jimi stopped, turned, and stared at her.

"What?"

"For a lesbian, you sure have a lot to say about the male anatomy."

"Sad, isn't it? Sorry. I just get all *punny* when I'm nervous. Maybe I'm just feeling a little..."

"Testy?" asked Jimi. "Ya know, when this is all over, I'm gonna need medical confirmation that we're related."

Beside the building, a car engine started, Robin readying to leave. But as Jimi reached the driver's side of the Bronco, the door handle moved backward. Confused, he stepped and reached for it again, but once more it moved, just out of reach. And then the door was gone, the Bronco backing up fast, stopping, and then moving forward, accelerating until ... a shriek of brakes, the braying of metal against metal, and... "Sonofabitch, I did it again!"

Robin flung his car door open and rushed past Jimi and Janis to the door of the Bronco. "What the fuck, man?!? I don't have time for this!" he screamed at the driver. But Sonny merely shifted into park, turned to Robin, and said, "Just one more thing my niece and nephew didn't mention. They didn't tell you *who* we're looking for. A man who goes by the name of Jaybird. You know him?"

CHAPTER 25

(In Which Barriers are Breached and Limits are Reached)

Early Evening

THE ELECTRIC EYE DID NOT TRIGGER THE FRONT GATE AT GRIN AND BARE IT. A sign on the keypad/call button box read, "Office closed. Club member event in session. Please visit again soon!"

"We are literally within a hundred feet of where we need to be, but we can't get in!" Janis yelled. She got out of the car, tried to open the gate manually, but couldn't budge it. "Look at this thing! Fort Knox should be so secure!" She walked back to the Bronco and reached inside the driver's window, where Jimi had supplanted Sonny at the wheel. She honked the horn. Over and over.

Jimi pushed her hand away. "Okay, let's just think this through."

His calmness pissed her off even more. "If we were gonna think this through," she said, "maybe we should've done that earlier and called ahead!"

"Couldn't tip our hand like that," Sonny said. "Hate to say we need the element of surprise, but we kinda do. At the very least, we need to have our initial contact with Jaybird in person. This is not the kind of thing you talk about over the phone."

"So, Mr. Logical," Janis said to Jimi, "what are our options?"

Jimi sat in the car and pondered that for a moment. "Well, as I see it, we could just wait here for a while and hope someone shows up."

"Good plan," Janis said. "Do nothing and hope. Next!"

"Or, we could walk along the fence where it disappears into the trees and hope it ends at some point and then just enter … wherever."

"Wander into the woods. And hope. Again. Next!"

"Or we can back the Bronco up to the fence and use it to help us scale the barrier."

"Now you're talkin'," Janis said. "Deviously practical and practically devious. Proud of you, brother."

"You two go first," Sonny said. "I'll stand watch."

"Very funny," said Janis. "We saw what happened the last time we left you alone in the car."

"Minor fender bender. The cars are still drivable. Information exchanged. Robin What's-his-name was in too big a hurry to call the cops, so… No harm, no foul, I'd say."

"Tell that to the rental guy when you return the Bronco to Before You Go-Go."

While Janis was still talking, Jimi began backing up. He pulled the Bronco twenty feet off the main drive and carefully backed it into tree canopy shadows within inches of the fence. "Janis, you first," he said as he opened the door and stepped out. Once you get on the other side, you can help Sonny to a safe landing."

"But what if the fence is electrified?" she asked.

"Wooden fences aren't usually wired like that," he said. "Fire hazard, I imagine. But even if it is electrified, that's a chance I'm willing to take. Willing for *you* to take, that is."

"Love you, too," Janis said, and then she was gone, quickly climbing onto the top of the Bronco and lowering herself over the opposite side of the dog-eared fence. "That was easy," she said, but then added, "Aw, man!"

"Aw, man, what?"

"Oh, nothing, just gonna need to wash off my flip flops as soon as possible."

"First things first," Jimi said. He helped Sonny onto the top of the Bronco and then over the fence. Janis eased him down.

"Your turn, Jiminy. It's time to make like The Price is Right and 'c'mon down.'"

"Gonna need these," Jimi said. He slung three beach towels over the fence. "We'll attract a lot less attention if we're nude."

Seconds after Jimi landed inside the fence, the gate opened and a car drove through, no doubt a club member armed with the key code and a craving for deep-fried turkey balls.

* * *

"By 6:52 this evening, I'm gonna have Jennings Prokoff's balls in such a knot he'll have to cut his baby-makers just to unpucker his asshole," WTFU's Radiance Reynolds raged at the bathroom mirror in Crosstown Mall. "There, that should do it," she said as she pulled down the tail of her loose-fitting top and threw a felt-tip marker into the trash. Behind her, a toilet flushed and a stall door opened. A woman with sun-stained skin the color of a woodchuck covered her eyes and rushed from the room, in case Radiance decided to practice on *her* baby-makers.

"You're gonna want my autograph after tonight!" Radiance yelled after the woman.

The reporter then checked her watch. It was probably time to get things set up with the cameraman and field producer (Mr. Soda, as she called him because of his ever-present cup of cola, fizzy or flat), as well as the manager of the Sam Goody record store. The location was hastily chosen simply because it kinda sorta matched the Good Samaritan theme of the report. But the logistics of doing a live report in a public place – a *busy* public place on a Friday night – could be problematic. At a minimum, they would need to work out how to manage troublesome mall lighting and sound. The bigger problem with such reports was to keep idiotic mallrat teenagers at bay – those hooligans who liked to dive into the shot and make goofy faces, obscene gestures, or finger-bunny ears behind her head.

"I hate people," she said aloud. "Especially young people. And here I go bringing another one into the world." She looked in the mirror. Pimples. Two new ones since lunch. *Fucking hormones!*

Another woman entered the restroom, smiled, and did a double-take. "Excuse me, aren't you…?"

Radiance nodded, gritted her teeth, and said, "Once upon a time." Suddenly, it occurred to her she'd be saying that very line many times in the coming few years. God, she hated nursery rhymes, too. And happy endings. And Jennings Prokoff. And Jennings Prokoff's fucking *fertile* happy ending that got her into this mess in the first place.

* * *

In his dressing room in New York, Jennings Prokoff was getting his nails clipped by his personal assistant, the third new lackey in a week. "Still not sure why your *toenails* have to be trimmed before your broadcast, Mr. Prokoff," said the assistant. But Prokoff was lost in thought, wondering about the status of the grand *scoop* Max Thibodeaux had promised. He'd heard nothing since Max's voice mail. But time was running out and the Woodstock reunion was close at hand.

Still, in case the scoop had a chance of coming to fruition during Woodstock '94 weekend, Prokoff had, per Max's wishes, put the network's primary news chopper on alert. He had also arranged for a helicopter to be ready in South Carolina should he suddenly need to transport his justice-seeking former Agent north in a hurry.

But then ... nothing. Silence. Max had gone *incommunicado*. (Prokoff liked that word. No troublesome letters.)

"Five minutes, Mr. Prokoff." Another assistant – but not a personal toe-clipping one – had popped his head into the dressing room and then back out just as quickly.

Prokoff nodded and then addressed the newbie at his feet: "Thatsh fine, ashishtant, um..."

"Susie."

"Yesh, ashishtant Shushie, the toesh are done. Can you get me my pre-broadcasht Hot Toddy now?"

"Already have it right here," Susie said. She lifted the steaming cup from the floor beside her and handed it to the anchor. Then she started gathering up a surprisingly small number of toenail clippings. "Now, where in the world could all of those—"

"Ah, nothing like a fresh shteaming Hot Toddy to coat your throat," Prokoff said.

* * *

At that moment in Indianapolis, Todd clenched his fists during climax. And once again, when Pepper disengaged, her wig came off, the scorched mop clutched in mid-air between Todd's fingers. When he'd finally caught his breath, he asked, "Didn't this hair use to be longer? And less ashy?"

"Mmm-hmm," Pepper said, rising from her knees and inserting herself back into her security blanket of hair. "Once upon a time it did."

The phone rang. Pepper wiped her mouth and stared at it.

"Aren't you gonna get that," Todd asked, pulling up his pants.

"Ummm…" More rings.

"Could be important," he said. "Urgent, even. What if it's Sonny?"

Pepper grimaced and picked up the phone as if it were covered in Effyu's slobbers, which, frankly, was a distinct possibility.

"Hel-l-lo?" she said weakly. The voice on the other end caused her to relax. A little. "No news yet, LB," she said. "Probably nothing new coming anytime soon, but call me back here in an hour or two. I can't really talk now. What? No, I don't have my mouth full." *Anymore*, she thought. "Get your mind out of the gutter, LB. Listen, I gotta go; it's almost time for Prokoff."

* * *

In Penny and Pixie's room, Max lay on the bed and looked at the nightstand alarm clock. He had intended to call Prokoff earlier and provide an update – especially important since there had been an actual development with Pete. But somehow (what with the sudden unconsciousness and all), he had lost track of time. Now Prokoff would be taking to the air very soon, so Max would have to bide his time and call later. Maybe by then, he'd know more anyway.

Pixie still held a cold compress on his forehead, but Max finally resisted and pulled himself up into a seated position. "I'm fine, Pixie," he said, smiling. "Really, I am. I've never fainted before, but I'm feeling steady now. Thank you for your concern."

"I just want you to be all better, Maxie," she said. "Isn't there anything else I can do for you? Anything?" Her voice deepened, almost demonically: "Anything at all?"

Max flashed a quick and nervous smile. "Uh, two things, if you don't mind," he said. Pixie leaned in, eyes wide with hope. A drop of drool glistened in the corner of her mouth. Max continued: "Um, could you *please* turn the air conditioning off and then turn on the TV?"

Across the room, Penny hung up the phone." Still can't get ahold of Junior Carducci," she said. "I left a message warning him that trouble might be heading his way." She sighed and sat on the bed. "I just wish Pete would come back here or call and let us know this is all a big misunderstanding."

"Is that what it is, though, Penny?" Max asked. "Or has this whole thing been brewing for a long time with Pete and just now reached the boiling point?"

"Are you asking out of genuine concern, Max, or are you fishing for details for your story?"

"At this point, I hope there is no story," he said. "But I'm afraid it might end up being a far different story than we imagined."

CHAPTER 26
(In Which a Reunion Happens at Long Last,
and a Secret is Revealed ... Too Fast)

Early Evening

"Sit anywhere," a voice called out from shadows behind the bar. "I'll be right with ya."

The twins stepped around their uncle and led him to a table with four chairs near the center of the room. Jimi draped his towel over an ice-cream parlor-style chair and sat. Sonny and Janis did the same.

"I don't really like being, um, exposed like this," Jimi said, eyeing the bright light over their table.

"For cripes' sake, Jiminy, you should be getting used to this whole 'naked thing' by now," Janis said. "How many nudist colonies have we visited so far this trip?"

Jimi shushed her. "First off," he whispered, "stop calling me *Jiminy*. Sheesh! Most important, don't call this place a 'colony' or you'll get us kicked out of here. Have you learned nothing this trip? Don't you at least remember the sign?"

"What sign?" asked Sonny.

"By the door of the restroom building," Jimi said. "It read something like, 'We're nudists. We're not ants. We're not lepers. Please DO NOT call this a colony!'"

"Okay, okay," Janis said. "We're in another freakin' resort, then. Family-friendly with an on-site nudie bar. I guess already being naked eliminates a lot of the mystery when coupling up at last call."

Jimi shushed her again. "Just behave yourself for once. We've come too far to get kicked out now."

Sonny cleared his throat. "I know we're all nervous being this close to our goal, but please stop bickering. Be my eyes. Tell me what you see."

Jimi leaned closer to Sonny. "Nothing fancy. Looks pretty spartan actually—"

"Wow, looka that moon shot!" Janis shouted, pointing to a giant framed black-and-white poster hanging behind the bar. It featured a retro lunar image, complete with a man-in-the-moon face whose right eye has been penetrated by a giant rocket. "That's gotta hurt," she said.

"I believe that's the iconic image from the classic silent film, *Le Voyage Dans La Lune*," Jimi informed her. "That means 'A Trip to the Moon'."

"Hey, I wasn't born yesterday, mister know-it-all," Janis said. "If I can talk to cats, I can figure out your fuzzy Italian."

"French."

"Whatever."

Again, Sonny cleared his throat.

"Yes, so, as I was saying," Jimi continued, "aside from the Méliès poster and these tabletop framed pictures of a motherly type – presumably the mama we're supposed to moon – it's pretty basic décor in here. Mostly ashtrays and fly strips. Lighting's pretty good, maybe a little too good. Tropical-style white ceiling fans here and there, on low. About ten tables with two or four chairs. The bar has eight stools. Seating is empty so far except for us," he said, "probably because that fried turkey Testicle Festival is going on."

"Everyone but us is out there having a ball," Janis said. "Or two." She crossed her arms over her chest, a smug gesture of triumph for landing the definitive Testicle Festival pun.

Sonny leaned forward, unbunched his towel, and then leaned back again. "So, no sign of our target, then?"

Before either twin could answer, the bartender approached their table. He, too, was naked, except for the de rigueur flip flops and an apron tied at his waist. He had ponytailed white hair, wore round glasses, and bore a scar extending from the corner of his mouth halfway down his chin.

"Welcome, gents," he said, not quite discerning that Janis was no gentleman. His voice was soft and carried an accent – vaguely of New

York but perhaps diluted by many years in the south. "Must be visitors," he said. "Glad you could join us tonight. Grill side is closed this evening, but I'll be glad to bring you some drinks."

"That voice," said Sonny.

"That scar," said Jimi.

"That moon shot," said Janis, pointing not to the framed poster but to the bartender's butt and the bird tattoo just visible beyond his apron.

In unison, they whispered, "Jaybird."

The bartender studied them, leaned in for a better look in the light. "Forgive me for not... Do I know you all? I usually have a good memory for faces, but..."

"Well, it's been a long time, Jaybird," Sonny said, his voice soft and tentative. He seemed to begin sniffling, but then said, "Excuse me, but what is that smell?"

"Crap!" said Janis.

"What?" Sonny asked.

"Literally, crap. I forgot to clean off my flip flop after we scaled the fence and made a run into that outdoor restroom."

Jaybird stared at the white-haired girl – yes, he was certain now she was female. "You scaled the fence? Why would you —"

"Be right back," Janis said. "Don't start without me." She rushed to the door, opened it, kicked her flip flops out the door, and hurried back to the table. "Whew, record time. Didn't want to miss a thing."

"Miss what?" Jaybird asked. "Are you looking for the Testicle Festival? It's out in the campground area, near the pavilion. Should just be getting started if you want to —"

"We're here for you!" Jimi yelled. "I mean, we're here so our uncle could see you." Jaybird looked at the older man's sunglasses and cane and the ribbon of toilet paper stuck to his flip flop.

"Well, not to *see* you exactly," Jimi said. "Bad choice of words. Uncle Sonny, maybe you should explain."

The door opened then, and a beer-bellied naked man with a long red beard stepped inside. "Heya, JB, can I get a coupla brewskis to go? Forgot ours at the trailer and don't wanna traipse all the way back. You know our usual, don'tcha?"

"Sure thing."

As Jaybird stepped behind the bar, the man said, "Craziest thing, fellas. Someone left a pair of women's flip flops out in the yard. They look new. Think I'll grab 'em for the missus on the way out. She says I never bring her any presents. Ha!"

Jaybird returned. "Here ya go, Leslie."

"Thanks, pal. On my tab, of course. Left my wallet in the *other* pants I choose not to wear." Chuckles all around, and then red-beard was gone.

"He did *not* look like a Leslie," Jimi said. "Or sound like one. I thought all Leslie's were British."

"Well, he did have bad teeth," Janis said. "The good news is I don't have to clean my flip flops now."

"So, where were we?" Jaybird asked. He sat again. "Oh, yes, you two brought your uncle to see, er, to visit with me; and Sonny, you were just about to—"

Again, the door. Again, bad-teeth-red-beard-not-British Leslie. "Dropped one of the cans, JB. It exploded just as I was picking up those flip flops. Damn things are covered in beer now. That's not the worst of it, though. One of them shoes was covered in dog shit. Pretty sure Adelaide would take offense at shitty beer-covered flip flops as a present."

Jaybird retrieved a replacement can of beer. "Here you go, Les. Be careful this time."

"You're a good man, Bird," Leslie said. Swinging open the door, he yelled, "Testicles, here I come!"

Janis raised her hand. "Excuse me. I'm no expert, but is it *ever* proper protocol for a man to yell 'Testicles, here I come'?"

Stares and silence.

"Well," Jimi said (beneath the table, he kicked his sister), "back to—"

"Woodstock!" Sonny yelled. He stood then and pointed to the tattoo on his hip.

Jaybird's mouth dropped open. He stroked his chin scar and compared Sonny's tattoo to his. "Sonny? From Woodstock? Back in '69? That Woodstock? That *Sonny?*"

The door opened. Leslie took a step inside. "NO!" they all yelled at once. The intruder backed out the door.

"Sonny?" Jaybird repeated. "*My* Sonny? I'll be a motherfucker…"

"I'd say you've already been one, *dad*," Janis said. Then she smiled uneasily. "Oops."

Jimi kicked her again.

CHAPTER 27
(In Which Sonny, Pepper, Radiance, and Robin Share Their Secrets)

Early Evening

JENNINGS PROKOFF APPEARED ON THE TV OVER THE BAR IN THE MOON-Your-Mama. The sound was muted, but the closed captioning subtitles attempted to interpret the anchor. It came pretty close, minus the slurring, of course. (For anyone not prone to *shwooning* over Prokoff's delivery, muting the sound and reading the closed captioning was a prudent choice). If Sonny, Jaybird and the twins had been reading along, they would have seen this:

"Good evening, I'm Jennings Prokoff, and here are a few of our top stories tonight: First up, major league baseball is officially on strike, leaving no joy in Mudville or anywhere else. In Washington, the Supreme Court has a new jurist as Stephen Breyer is sworn in. And later, our Feel Good America feature from Jacksonville, Florida, where Radiance Reynolds reports on a Good Samaritan still playing hide and seek." (Okay, so the captioning read "Shoe preen Court," and "hide a sheik," but otherwise, it was an admirable try.)

Yes, the immutable Prokoff was muted in the bar, and for several tense moments, the conversation between Sonny, the twins, and Jaybird had gone silent, too. Sonny and Jimi could hardly believe Janis divulged the "Dad" secret prematurely. For his part, Jaybird looked as anyone might in that situation: stunned, confused, dazed. It seemed as if he had turned to stone, devoid of outward human function, not breathing or blinking or moving because all his processing abilities had been redirected inward.

"I'm really sorry," Janis said finally. "I didn't mean to blurt that out. Jimi and I have had a few days to get used to the idea, but —"

"Are you saying I'm Jimi's father, too? How is that possible? How can I have *two* children I didn't know about. What the hell is this nonsense? Who are you people? What the fuck do you want from me?"

And there it was. Jaybird's shock was feeding disbelief, and his disbelief would almost surely soon feed denial.

"Janis and I are twins," Jimi said. "Fraternal twins. We're practically nothing alike, but still…"

"No, no, no… This has to be impossible," Jaybird said. "Hell, I haven't even been with a woman since —"

"Woodstock?" Sonny said. "When you were with my sister Winnie twenty-five years ago? Jimi, Janis, how old are you?"

"Turned twenty-four in May," Janis said.

"Me, too," Jimi said. "Obviously."

"Counting nine months of pregnancy…"

"Okay, okay, I get it," said Jaybird. He was breathing heavily, not quite hyperventilating, but a bit labored. His eyes darted from Jimi to Janis and then back to Sonny. A tear welled in the corner of his eye, but he cleared his throat and said, "Okay, let's say for a moment this is possible. Mathematically, anyway. But if you *really are* Sonny, tell me something that happened at Woodstock when we were together."

"Fair enough," Sonny said. "Well, we ran from the storm after Joe Cocker's set and ended up in your van."

"What kind of van?"

"A VW bus, '63, I think you said. Panel-type van, not one of those with all the windows. And not very colorful. Grayish-blue. Pretty rusty, as I recall."

"That's right. So far."

"We smoked some joints while we waited out the rain," Sonny added.

"Yeah, well, so did a few hundred thousand others at Woodstock," Jaybird countered.

"That Sunday night, we slept in your van. It was then you made love to Winnie, and the twins were conceived."

"Okay. But this could still all be hearsay, some kind of scheme. So, what else? Tell me one thing that only me and the real Sonny could possibly know." Jaybird leaned in, almost challenging the blind man before him.

Sonny smiled. "Only you and I could know this: You made love to me, too."

* * *

At Crosstown Mall, in a sea of shoppers and gawkers and employees and managers and WTFU types, Radiance Reynolds was adrift in thoughts about when she had made love – oh, hell, it had been nothing more than a drunken dalliance – with Jennings Prokoff after that affiliates' party. Sure, she bore some responsibility; she *had* to have known she was drunk when Prokoff started making sense and she could understand every word he had said. Responsible or not, though, what continued to fuel her ever-rising rage was the fact Prokoff would not return her calls.

"Let's see if he can ignore me after tonight," she said under her breath.

"Five minutes to air, Ms. Reynolds," her field guy said. Radiance smiled, gave her belly a quick pat, and puffed out some air. She was nervous, unusual at this point in her career, but determined, too. *She would be heard!*

* * *

Pepper paced nervously, only half interested in her beloved Jennings Prokoff while her *other* beloved, Todd, watched her walk back and forth between the TV and the phone and the window.

"What's wrong with you tonight?" Todd asked. "You're as nervous as a cat." Effyu growled at the word but snuggled up tighter against Todd on the sofa.

Pepper stared at the TV for a moment, the Prokoff broadcast in a commercial: *"Have you been injured, wronged, taken advantage of? Are you losing money, losing sleep, losing hope?"*

"Yes," she said.

"What?"

"Huh?"

"I asked what is wrong with you," Todd repeated. "You're pacing. Something's clearly eating at you. Did I do something?"

A tear came to her eye as Pepper looked out the window again. "Oh, Todd, no… It's just that, well, I just wish Sonny would call."

Todd stood. "Be right back, little guy," he said to Effyu. He joined Pepper at the window. "Is that really all it is? Seems like maybe there's something else."

Pepper leaned her head and her now-shorter wig against his chest. "Yes, there is something else."

"Tell me."

"I feel like I'm being watched."

"Well," Todd said. "That's certainly true. I can't take my eyes off you." The dog perked up. "I said *'off you,'*" Todd clarified. "Not Effyu."

"You're sweet," Pepper said. "To me, and to the dog. But what I mean is that I feel like I'm being watched by someone else." She raised her head and looked out the window again. "Not at this very moment, but I'm certain someone is watching me. Watching *us*."

* * *

Radiance Reynolds could feel the eyes on her, just the mall rats for now, but soon a nationwide audience of eyes that would become *worldwide* once she revealed the message on her belly and exposed Jennings Prokoff for the weasel he was. For the time being, though, it was just the small gathering semi-circled around her in front of the Sam Goody. She smiled and waved at the onlookers, and they all waved back. Except for one man. A man holding tight to a small garden gnome.

* * *

"My gnome is missing," Jaybird said. He had gone behind the bar, taking a break to fix drinks for everyone after the flurry of dizzying revelations. (They all needed liquid reinforcement at that point, along with a chance to breathe and gather their thoughts.) "That's very strange. It's always right here, on the shelf. He's kind of my patron saint for the place."

Janis approached the bar. "I'm getting the strangest vibe right now," she said. "Like there's something missing but also something soon to be found…"

Anthony Purrkins jumped up onto the counter. "Well, look who's here," Jaybird said. He picked up the Burmese. "About time you got sociable. The one night I bring you with me to the bar, and you sleep through the excitement."

Janis smiled. She held out her arms. "May I?"

Jaybird handed her the cat. "This is Anthony Purrkins."

"Yes, I know. He already introduced himself," Janis said, her communication with the animal being a kind of *mental* closed captioning. She petted the cat and closed her eyes. "He says we should watch the TV."

* * *

Max sat on the front edge of the bed, Pixie still at his side, uncomfortably close, watching Prokoff:

"Ash we reported earlier thish week, a 25th annivershary shelebration of Woodshtock ish happening again. Originally shet to begin tomorrow ash a two-day event, the feshtival inshtead began today on Winshton Farm jusht wesht of Shaugertiesh, New York with hundredsh of thoushandsh to attend. We hope to be able to bring you a shpecial live report from the venue tomorrow, sho shtay tuned."

"I think Pete may be headed to Woodstock after all," Max said. He looked to Penny for support. "It seems like a last resort, but, as I see it, even though Pete starts with the black and white of things, the absolutes, he's become increasingly dependent on – even *desperately* dependent on – his gut. And with each dead end on finding the Finch money, he's been, more and more, grasping at straws. I saw that in the graveyard. First, he was digging around the Finch grave, which was a desperate act, but at least logical. And then, working from the 'Kibosh Rock' note, he decided we should dig around the Rock family gravesite. He's shifting with the winds now. What else is left but Woodstock? Would you agree with that, Penny?"

Tentatively, Penny nodded. She was being very quiet. Tight-lipped and not yet revealing what Carducci had told her when he had called back before Pixie and Max returned.

"Still, I can't help but feel like we're missing something," Max continued. "Like *Pete* is missing something. Maybe the answer's in the case file, though I didn't have much chance to study the pictures I took." Penny was watching him. "Sorry about that, by the way," Max said. "No excuse for doing that except I was pretty drunk. Way too much Absolut. I certainly stepped over the line by taking those pictures just for the sake of a story. Really inexcusable to violate your space like that."

"Violate," whispered Pixie. She reached for his hand. For some reason, Max let her take it.

They were quiet then, the three of them, inwardly musing over where Pete might be and what he might do next.

Prokoff came back from the commercial break:

"And now, here with tonight'sh Feel Good America report, we go live to Jackshonville, Florida and reporter Radianch Reynoldsh. Radianch, good to shee you again. I undershtand you've been following an anonymoush local Good Shamaritan. Tell ush what we need to know."

* * *

At the Moon-Your-Mama Bar, Sonny and Jimi joined Janis, Jaybird, and Anthony Purrkins in front of the TV. Jaybird had turned up the sound. Local reporter Radiance Reynolds was on the screen.

"Good evening, Jennings. Yes, several things to share with you tonight. Not much time, so I'll be brief. First, we've been tracking the Good Samaritan in our area for many weeks now, but still no solid leads. We know this much: Our hero is generous, leaving money for the needy in their hours of greatest need but doing so without a trace. And we know that he has long white hair, round glasses, a scar on his chin, and leaves a small garden gnome behind as his calling card…"

Jaybird looked at the empty shelf just as his missing gnome suddenly appeared on screen, very close to the camera at first, but then growing smaller as the man holding it appeared in frame.

"Sounds just like you," Janis said, speaking to Jaybird, and then she recognized the man on the TV screen: "Hey, isn't that the guy from the grill?"

Sure is, Anthony Purrkins confirmed. (Telepathically.) *Take my advice. Don't trust that guy.*

Jaybird took a step toward the TV. "Robin? What's he doing?"

"What are you doing?" Radiance Reynolds asked. *"Get out of here! This is a live report! As I was saying, Jennings —"*

"No solid leads, you say?" Robin yelled, looking back and forth between the camera and the reporter. *"I have your leads, but you never fucking return my calls."*

Radiance pushed him aside. *"And speaking of fucking and not returning calls, Jennings, I have more news for you."*

She lifted her shirt right as field producer Mr. Soda tried to shove the gnome-man out of the picture. Robin deflected the attempt, and the producer's soft drink set sail.

The camera erratically pivoted, panned and zoomed, finally finding the reporter's exposed skin and the PROKOFF DADDY message. It appeared intact for no more than a second before it started dissolving in carbonated rivulets.

"What did that say?" Janis asked.

"Looked like *Fuckoff And Die* maybe," Jimi said.

"Moon your mama! Moon your mama!" Robin screamed, stepping in front of the camera again. He dropped the gnome and held a picture of Jaybird close to the lens. The photo appeared there only a few seconds before Mr. Soda again pushed him aside. In the vacated camera shot, two teenage boys came into focus in the background, facing away. They dropped trou. "Moon your mama! Moon your mama!" they echoed, their act of civil disobedience being the kind that inspires copycats and sparks a fad. (For a split second, Jimi thought about the nuns on the bus.)

And then the live feed went dark, shifting the broadcast back to New York, catching Jennings Prokoff as he sipped from an airline bottle of scotch.

In the bar, silence hung heavy in the air until Jaybird said, "I'm gonna need to get outta town for a while."

Janis looked at Jimi.

Jimi looked at Sonny.

Sonny petted Anthony Purrkins and said, "Funny you should say that…"

CHAPTER 28
(In Which Answers Emerge and Destinies Begin to Converge)

Evening

"WE FOUND JAYBIRD," SONNY TOLD PEPPER OVER THE PHONE.

"What? Where? How?"

"We got a couple of leads as we made the rounds," Sonny explained. "We learned that a man with the Jaybird tattoo was likely to be at the Moon-Your-Mama Bar—"

"Moon-Your-Mama?"

"Yes, long story, but the pieces all began to come together at the last minute. We drove to northeast Florida, found the bar, had a little trouble getting in, but there he was."

Pepper shifted nervously on her feet. "Northeast Florida? Are you by any chance near Jacksonville?"

"Yes, how'd you know that?"

"Well, I was watching Prokoff, and they had a—"

"Yes," Sonny said. "We saw the same report. I assume you saw the picture that flashed on the TV during that ruckus at the Sam Goody."

"I did," Pepper confirmed. "The guy in that picture looked like he could match your Jaybird. Long white hair, round glasses, scar. And the guy holding the picture was yelling 'Moon your mama, moon your mama!'"

"It's true," Sonny said. "The guy in the picture *is* Jaybird. He's been pretty much in hiding ever since Woodstock in '69, and his cover just got blown by a former ... well, by a disgruntled associate."

"Wow," Pepper said. She was quiet then, trying to process what had happened, what was *happening*. But all she could really focus on was what was still to come. "Is Jaybird with you now? If his cover's blown, is he going with you and the twins to scatter the ashes?"

"In a word, yes," said Sonny "And yes again. Okay, that's two words, but both the same word. Yes, he's with us now; and yes, he's going with us. It's all been quite a shock to his system, of course, but he agrees it's a good idea to get out of town for now. I'm calling from his home at the Grin and Bare It Family Nudist Campground. He's gathering up some things for the trip. Meanwhile, to stay out of the way, Janis is talking with his cat and Jimi's watching the Woodstock video. We should be leaving soon."

"Where exactly are you going?" Pepper asked. "There's more than one Woodstock these days." Todd came up behind her and kissed her neck as she listened to Sonny explain their next moves. She squirmed, told Sonny to be careful, and that she hoped to hear all about the adventure next week in the office – or whenever they could get back together. She hung up and stood there, limp but unmoving despite the nuzzling.

Todd disengaged and looked her in the eye. "Was that Sonny?"

"It was."

"And…? Did they find who they were looking for?"

The phone rang again. Pepper figured it was Sonny once more with some detail he forgot to mention. She answered. It was LilBuckaroo. She asked where he was and then shared with him the news that Jaybird had been found. "He's with Sonny and the twins," she said. "And he'll be going with them, leaving tonight." Todd watched her as she nodded silently. She listened and then sighed. "Okay, LB, just hold on. The best thing is for you to meet me at the destination and we can handle this thing together. You might need my help."

She told LB where to meet, reminded him of the 3:00 Saturday deadline, and then hung up the phone.

"So, we're heading to New York…" Todd said. "Long trip. We'll need to leave tonight and take turns driving if we're to make it in plenty of time. I've got one of the rentals outside. We can drive that."

Pepper stared at him. "You're going with me?"

"Of course," Todd said. "Someone has to entertain the dog."

* * *

"So, why is Woodstock so important?" Annabel asked LilBuckaroo after he returned to the table. "And why do you have to be there tomorrow by three?"

She and Edgar sat across from LB in a Mexican restaurant called El Grande Casa. If LB had understood a lick of Spanish, he might not have so quickly agreed to dine in *The Big House*, given his recent incarceration. But being clueless – and absent a Burger In The First Degree nearby, he had gone along.

He quickly became enamored of the Delicioso Margarita. LB wasn't ordinarily much of a drinker. It wasn't that he didn't enjoy an occasional cocktail; it was more that he didn't like to drink *alone*. That left him on the alcohol sidelines, isolated, "socially awkward," as his mother had labeled him. But now, halfway through his Delicioso Margarita, Annabel had finally asked the big questions: *Why Woodstock? Why now?*

LB wanted to lie. He wanted to make up something that would make his motives sound less selfish, but when he looked at Annabel's face, with its beguiling smirk and puffy wrinkles making her look like a Cabbage Patch Grandma, he was reduced to the truth.

"I'm set to inherit a sizeable chunk of money," he confessed. "But that sizeability will drop like a rock if I don't stop something from happening at Woodstock."

"Stop something from happening? That sounds odd," Annabel said. "What kind of inheritance would —"

LB waved her off. Fueled by the margarita, he launched into the backstory. "Out of the blue, just before she died, my Mom dropped a bombshell: she had given birth to two other kids. Boy and girl. They were twins – the kind that don't look alike – and she had gotten pregnant with them at Woodstock. She gave them up for adoption under pressure from my grandpa, Big Buck Muckle."

"Hadda big belt buckle maself once," Old Edgar chimed in.

"Yes, you did, Dad," Annabel said, patting his hand. "You used to wear it all the time until you got so skinny its weight shifted your center of gravity and made you fall down too much. Speaking of which, eat some chips."

"Lefmateeth in dacar," Edgar said.

"Oh, my, you might need those," Annabel said. "Be right back. You can continue your story in a bit, but I think I'll try to phone Joe Jack again. Don't you boys run off now."

For a minute or so, LB and Edgar sat staring and half-smiling at one another. Without his teeth, Edgar looked as if his lower jaw was trying to swallow the top of his head. Which, LB noticed, remained hairless.

"Not wearing your toupee?" he asked.

"Sure, I'm willin' to pay," Edgar said.

"Did you leave your hearing aids in the car, too, Edgar?" LB practically screamed.

"Nope, leftem indacar," he answered. "Don't needem, can hearjusfine." He nodded for a good thirty seconds, and then added, "Your upper lip looks like a baboonsass."

LB smiled. Painfully. "Bad batch of glue and a coffee burn."

"Hemorrhoid cream'll fixyarideup. Lefminetahome. Just Getyasome Mother Pucker's Sphincter Tincture." Somehow, sans teeth, Edgar rattled off that tongue twister perfectly.

"So, Edgar," LB began, desperate to not discuss using ass cream on his face, "I've been curious… Why do you call Annabel your 'Trophy Daughter'?"

Edgar's eyes acknowledged the question. Normally yellow-glassy, they suddenly grew misty, too. "Day she was born," he said, softly and deliberately, "I knew she was dagreatesprize I could ever have. Her mama dint make it through dabirth, but she left me with dasweetest lilgift." A tear rolled into the mottled furrows of his face. LilBuckaroo had nothing to say to that, but Edgar wasn't finished. "Another thing," he said. "Another reason. When Annabel wasjus ninerso, she'd done chores all summer for daneighborsandme. Earned good money. Jusbefore school started that fall, she comes home with a trophy. She hadn't won it but bought it. For me. Said 'World's Greatesdad'." He shrugged. "So, she's matrophydaughter. Got the trophy and the daughter to prove it." He leaned forward and motioned LilBuckaroo closer. "Lemmetellya," he continued. "It's allsabout *fambly*. Rich or poor, that's where dafortune is. Worth more than alldamoney in daworld."

Misty himself, LB looked away as Annabel scurried back to the table. "Open wide, Dad," she said. Edgar did as he was told and she popped his choppers back in place. "Whew, I hurried as best I could," she said, out of breath. "Now, where were we? Oh, yeah, I think you were about to tell me about this inheritance of yours. Something about fraternal twin siblings and how you'll lose a lot of the money unless you stop something from happening at Woodstock?"

LB smiled warmly. "Long story," he said. "Best for another time. So, did you reach Joe Jack?"

"No luck," she said. "Hope he's not doing something dumb like coming after us. He couldn't possibly have overlooked that note I left."

* * *

Joe Jack Sweet had a long drive ahead of him. But at least he knew where he was headed. Or did he? While stopped in middle Kentucky to refuel Annabel's Crown Victoria (he knew his F-250 pickup wouldn't be good for transporting Edgar back home), he called an old Tennessee trooper pal now with the New York State Police.

Carl Capler, now going by "Captain Carl," was working late at the station. After the obligatory long-time-no-see-whatcha-been-up-to briefing, Joe Jack said, "Got a problem, Carl."

"Figured that, ya old fool; what kinda problem?"

"Missing persons. Possible kidnapping. My wife and her dad."

"No shit," Captain Carl said without inflection. "Didn't you once tell me the old guy's like a hundred and seventeen or somethin'?"

"Hundred and three now."

"Well, still a fossil... No offense."

"None taken," Joe Jack said.

"Is this for real? Give me the particulars."

So, Joe Jack did, including the jailbreak and the fact that Annabel had left a note that seemingly quashed any notion of a real kidnapping. "I think she was forced to write that note. Under duress at least, and possibly out of fear for her physical safety and that of the old man." Joe Jack was lying – he didn't honestly suspect duress – but Carl didn't need to know that.

"So," said the Captain, "the jailbreak notwithstanding, you need to keep this on the down-low because it's been less than 24 hours, and the only evidence refutes that a crime has been committed. Am I right?"

"Something like that," Joe Jack replied.

"And they're headed this way, to Woodstock, you say... And that's all you know?"

"That's it."

"Problem is," said Carl, "there's more than one Woodstock. There's the *town* of Woodstock, not far from the station here. Then there's that big-ass 25th-anniversary festival going on this weekend in Saugerties. I'm hearing there could be close to half a million weirdos there; got most of my troops dealing with that crap now. Would prob'ly be out there myself if I wasn't so old and holding down the fort here. And then there's the original '69 Woodstock site in Bethel. Might be some folks gathering there this weekend, too, even though the official anniversary celebration there got shit-canned a week or so ago." Captain Carl said something over the radio to an officer in the field before coming back to Marshal Sweet's call. "So, Joe Jack," he said, "which fuckin' Woodstock are you talkin' about?"

By the time the call was done and Joe Jack was back on the road, he had a plan. Carl had agreed to put out a watch for the Edsel at the Saugerties event. Joe Jack would ignore the town of Woodstock as it wasn't the likely destination, at least not on this anniversary weekend. That meant he could focus on the Bethel location, even though the official festivities there had been canceled. With a far smaller crowd, it would be easier to spot the Edsel, and hopefully, Annabel and Edgar.

Hell, even if he didn't find them and they came home safe and sound in a few days, he figured his earnest effort to track them should keep him in Annabel's good graces – and the old boy's Last Will and Testament.

* * *

Flushed out and uncertain when he might see his home again, Jaybird took one last look and then closed the trailer door. He carried Anthony

Purrkins to the Bronco, handed him to Janis, and said, "You got the litter box, right?"

"Yep," said Janis. "Also got his food and a dish for water and some cat treats. Got the collar and leash, too, even though Mr. Purrkins here assured me he was not the type to run off and join the circus."

Jaybird smiled. "He's a loyal sidekick. I emphasize *loyal* in hopes he won't tell you all of my secrets."

"Too late," Janis said. "These little mental discussions with your cat will bring me up to speed on all your foibles. That's a good word, don'tcha think – foibles?"

"Are you asking me or the cat?"

"I don't have to ask Anthony Purrkins anything out loud. We can communicate without the spoken word."

"That's what worries me," Jaybird said.

"It's more troubling when Janis actually speaks," Jimi said. "Anyway, we should get going."

Jaybird started to step into the Bronco but looked over his shoulder. "I'm sure I'm forgetting something important..."

"Aside from towels, what could a nudist need?" Sonny asked.

"Towels!" Jaybird cried. He dashed back to the trailer and disappeared inside. A minute later, he was back at the Bronco, carrying two towels and a cookie jar. "Almost forgot my stash, too," he said.

"Stash of ... cookies?" Janis asked.

"No comment," Jaybird deflected as he scooted onto the back seat next to Sonny. "Okay, better hit the road. If Robin's involved now, that reporter could show up here any minute."

Jimi started the engine and put the vehicle in gear. But he held the brake.

"Well?" Janis asked.

"Seems like I'm forgetting something, too," Jimi said.

Janis thumped him on the side of the head. "Everything of yours is in the car. The clock is ticking. Let's get outta here."

* * *

"Okay, we'll get outta here tonight," Max said. He was on the phone with Prokoff and had just learned that a network news chopper from

Atlanta was waiting at the Columbia airport, ready to leave in the morning and take him and Penny and Pixie and Petunia to New York.

Although they couldn't account for Pete's whereabouts at the moment, they were going back to square one: Pete's earlier proclamation that he was certain Finch would return to Woodstock. Without a real plan now for finding the money first, Pete would have no alternative but to track the fugitive once again.

But even if Pete wasn't at Woodstock (or couldn't be found in the masses), a story could still be spun, as Prokoff ad-libbed for Max: *"Shomewhere in thish crowd, a man shtill sheeks jushtish after twenty-five yearsh. But where could he be? And what about hish prey? Ish the wanted man alsho shomewhere in thish mashive crowd? For now, Agent Pete Peeblesh ish mishing in action, and hish family ish deshperate to find him."*

* * *

"I'm looking for my husband – ex-husband, that is," said the steely-eyed red-haired woman standing at Pepper's door when she opened it to leave for Woodstock. Startled, Pepper yelped – shades of Effyu. The woman standing before her was the one from the Steel Blue minivan, the woman who'd been watching her apartment, sometimes for hours on end, but usually when Todd wasn't around.

This time, however, Todd *was* around, and he rushed to Pepper's side. "What is it? What's wrong?"

Pepper stiffened and found her voice: "Maybe you should ask your wife," she said. "Your *ex*-wife, I mean." She stepped aside so the woman and Todd could confront one another.

Todd shook his head. "That's not my ex."

* * *

"Your Good Samaritan is my ex," Robin had told Radiance Reynolds while still at the Sam Goody. And then, after the hubbub had died down at Crosstown Mall (although Reynolds remained apoplectic about Robin hijacking her report), he got her to look at Jaybird's photo. She had to admit it looked like the human form of the stick-figure man four-year-old Vinny Vedere had drawn for her just days earlier. Robin's gnome connection made sense, too.

So, after hastily breaking down their equipment, Reynolds, Robin, Mr. Soda, and the camera operator hustled from Jacksonville toward Tranquility. On the way, sitting in the windowless rear cargo area of the news van with Radiance as she took notes, Robin gave up Jaybird's name – "Jayson B. Stockwood, an alias, no doubt" – and described their relationship. He told her about the nudist club and the bar and theorized about a possible connection to Woodstock – though Jaybird had always been quite secretive about that.

Robin even told her about Jaybird's *psycho* cat, Anthony Purrkins.

What he *hadn't* yet told Reynolds, however, was that three other people had come looking for Jaybird earlier – two young adults and an older blind man. Nor had he told her that the blind man had crashed into his car while at the wheel of an O.J. Simpson-like white Ford Bronco. It was *that* piece of not-yet-shared information the field producer and cameraman – seated in the front of the van – would have found useful as they passed a white Bronco leaving the campground as they approached the gate.

* * *

In Arlington, Virginia, Junior Agent Junior Carducci, Jr. drove his black Oldsmobile Achieva into his gated apartment complex. From a mini-cassette player in his shirt pocket, he was listening through corded earphones to case file updates. Because the Friday group update on the cassette included a week-in-review report, he was still listening as he reached the second cross street. Still listening as he reached the third building on the righthand side. Still listening as he inserted his key card at the building door and headed up the stairs. And still listening as he then inserted his key and opened his apartment door.

Inside, he stepped out of his shoes and looked toward the long table behind the sofa. He noticed the answering machine's blinking light. Five blinks, pause, five blinks, pause. He had five messages.

What Junior had *not* noticed, however, thanks to the noise from the mini-cassette player (which he finally turned off), was that the main building door hadn't completely closed behind him. Neither had his apartment door.

Carducci removed his shoulder holster and hung it on the knob of the bedroom door. Then he removed the earphones, unloaded his pockets onto the sofa table and pushed play on the answering machine.

First call: dial tone only. Second call: another tone. Third call: the same.

The fourth call was a staticky message from Mike Smyth, the Indianapolis wiretapper: "Smyth here. Finally have something for you. The attorney called his assistant, this Pepper woman. They found their guy, this fella they call... *[a couple of seconds of static]* ...and Bare It Family Nudist Campground and he's going with them to Woodstock. Sounds like everything is set for them to be at... *[more static]* ...three p.m. Finally, a break, eh? This is the info I think your former partner is looking for. Another thing, though. Sounds like Pepper is... *[static again]* ...this LB character, same time. Done here since everyone is on the move. The check's in the mail, right?"

Fifth call: "Junior, it's Penny Peebles. I've tried to reach you several times since we spoke earlier. Thanks for the info about the old Finch place. I'd love to share that with Pete, but I'm afraid he's gone missing. Junior, we're really concerned about his state of mind right now. I hate to tell you this over the machine, but somehow, he got it into his head that you've betrayed him and that you plan to steal the Finch money from him. I'll call again if I can, but we're leaving the bed and breakfast this evening for another hotel in Columbia. May have to call from an airport tomorrow. Be careful, Junior."

End of messages.

Carducci shook his head. "Well, Pete," he said out loud, "I hope that betrayal shit is much ado about nothing, but if you're MIA, it looks like you'll have to call me if you want to hear the latest."

It was then he noticed his front door was open. He closed it and made a quick visual search of the room: no intruders, gun still in the holster on the bedroom doorknob. *Gotta be more careful,* he thought. He turned the deadbolt and then stepped into his bathroom, took care of business, and went into his bedroom to change into sweats and a t-shirt. When Junior returned to the front room, the door was still closed.

He did not notice that the deadbolt was now unlocked. Or that his car key was missing from the key ring.

CHAPTER 29

(In Which Pepper Gets a Surprise and Radiance Tries to Pull One)

Evening

"IF YOU'RE NOT TODD'S EX-WIFE, THEN WHO ARE YOU?" PEPPER ASKED THE woman at the door.

"Sorry," the woman said. "Looks like I made a mistake." She started to walk away.

"Oh, no, you don't," Todd said. "You've made my fiancée here very nervous and upset. You owe her an explanation."

The woman's shoulders dropped. "It's just that... well, I've followed my ex to this apartment complex a few times. And also to a law office on Academy Avenue. I guess I put two and two together and got twenty-two. Not the first time I've done that. Sorry to have upset you..."

"Wait a minute," Pepper said. "You say your husband, your *ex*-husband has been here and at my office? I haven't seen anyone but you. What could he possibly...?" She turned to Todd. "Do you know anything about this?"

"I'm as confused as you are," Todd said. "There's got to be something you're not saying," Todd said to the woman. "Why would your ex...? Has he done this before?"

"Well, yes. I'm beginning to wonder if he's not some sort of a Peeping Tom. Always seems to be out at night, creeping around, doing some kind of surveillance or something."

"Sounds like that runs in the family," Pepper said. She gave a half-wave and shut the door. Turning to Todd, she squinted and said, "Your fiancée?"

And this time it was Todd who dropped to his knees. He opened a small box. "Will you?"

* * *

"I'd really like to know more about this Will of Winnie's you mentioned," Jaybird said to Sonny. "Her dying wish seems to be driving this whole mission of yours. I've got hundreds of questions, but let's start with these. What was Winnie's motive? Why the urgency? Why Woodstock? What exactly *is* the mission? Oh, and just so I get the full picture, let's eventually get around to what's in it for me."

"Fair enough," Sonny said. "Luckily, we've got a long drive ahead of us and plenty of time to answer your questions and get reacquainted."

"And acquainted for the first time," Janis said.

"Well, you're up there downloading information from my stool-pigeon cat," Jaybird said, "so I imagine you'll know more about me than I know myself."

"Rather hear it all from you," Janis said. "Anthony Purrkins is napping. Plus, he keeps wanting to know why I don't like boys."

Jaybird laughed. "Hard for me to imagine that, too. Which, by the way… No one seemed at all fazed by the revelation that Sonny and I, um, hooked up in the van at Woodstock. I would have expected *some* kind of reaction."

"Honestly, it's no big deal," Jimi said. "So far this week, I've learned I was adopted, that my biological mother died, that I have a blind uncle, a lesbian sister, and a nudist dad. The fact that you're gay is hardly registering on my surprise-o-meter."

"And maybe that's a good part of the answer to your last question," Sonny said to Jaybird. "You asked what's in it for you… For starters, you get ten grand just for going with us. I find it reassuring that you joined us before you learned that. But more importantly, you get the chance to know these incredible human beings you helped create. Good kids, even if they bicker too much."

* * *

Radiance Reynolds's stomach was churning. Morning sickness at night? She knew it happened, but more than likely it was that she did not feel in control. Of anything. All her plans for the live report, for the gut punch to Prokoff, for her *life*, were unraveling. And now, here she was, stuck in the back of a van driving up a twisting gravel road toward the home of a gnome-wielding do-gooder nudist all because some gay maniac wants revenge on his ex and is using her piss-ant fluff piece of a story to get it. Sickening.

"Up here on the right," Robin told the field producer, Mr. Soda. "The place with all the little gnomes around it."

"This is the home of our Good Samaritan?" Radiance asked. "These are the digs of a guy who doles out cash to poor people? I was expecting something more than a ratty old trailer with a trashed-up yard."

"He lives a simple life," Robin said. "Complicated man with a secret past, but a simple life nonetheless."

"Stop the van," said the reporter. "There's a light on inside and a car in the drive. That his ride?"

"Yep, a VW Beetle. Like I said, a simple life."

"So, it looks like he's home then."

"Well, yeah," Robin said. "The bar was dark when we passed it. He's either inside the trailer or down at the Testicle Festival."

Radiance shook her head. "Why do I think that would be the better story? All right, get the equipment ready." She looked at the cameraman. "You put tape in the camera, right?

"All set."

"Okay, let's go, but be quiet and keep the light off until he opens the door. The element of surprise might make this a good story yet."

* * *

Now an integral part of the developing Pete Peebles story, Max drove toward Columbia Metropolitan Airport. Pixie sat beside him, a little too close; Penny and Petunia rode in the back. They had packed lightly, just enough for the night, as they planned to return to East Kibosh once the Woodstock excursion was over. Max's cache of unused surveillance gadgets shared the car trunk with their luggage.

They had left a note for Pete in the room at the Ol Swimmin Hole, saying only that Penny and Pixie would be back soon. Penny planned to call the room later in the evening. If Pete answered, the trip to Woodstock would be aborted and they would return to the B & B within an hour. If he didn't answer, their absence wouldn't matter anyway.

Penny sighed woefully in the back seat. "Maybe you should've stayed behind, Pixie," she said. "Just in case your dad comes back. Or maybe I should have. I just don't know what to think anymore."

"I think we're doing the right thing," Max said. "Wherever Pete is, he'll need you by his side when we find him. By going along now, you can be close enough to come back to Kibosh tonight or be ready to wing it to Woodstock tomorrow morning." Max looked at her in the rearview mirror. "Ya know, Pete is famous for trusting his gut to get his man. But I have a feeling that you have a pretty strong sense of intuition, too. What does your gut tell you, Penny?"

"Well, it's telling me you're right. That we're covering the bases as best we can. But still, maybe Pixie should —"

"Oh, no," Pixie said. "I'm not leaving Maxie's side. I stopped Daddy from hurting him once. Might have to again. I'm his guardian angel. Isn't that right, Maxie?"

* * *

For the longest time, LilBuckaroo had thought his dad, Denny DePew, was his guardian angel. But now, his belly full and the darkness taking hold as Annabel drove into Virginia and toward New York, LB realized that ever since he'd been with her and Edgar, his ghost-dad had gone silent. He no longer whispered ideas or planted notions that seemed foolhardy in the light of day. Maybe Denny DePew had been nothing more than his imaginary friend, LB thought, or perhaps he was one of those little conscience-devils that perch on shoulders like an evil parrot.

For the time being, though, the vocal ghost of Denny DePew was silent, and a welcome sense of calm blanketed LilBuckaroo. Come what may on Saturday, on this night, he felt at peace.

* * *

In the dead calm of the back residential section of the Grin and Bare It, Radiance Reynolds changed her mind. "Before we approach the trailer, let's step behind the van, use dimmer lighting, and tape the intro." The crew, and Robin, did as she directed.

"Okay, roll tape. On my count," she said, "Three, two, one... Good evening. Radiance Reynolds here again, still on the trail of the Good Samaritan in our area. During a live Feel Good America segment on the Evening News with Jennings Prokoff earlier tonight, we learned of the possible identity and whereabouts of our mystery man. And now, here we are, at, of all places, the Grin and Bare It Nudist Colony —"

"Family nudist campground," Robin interjected.

"Cut! Goddammit, who the fuck cares what it's called?"

"Well, the nudists do, for one," Robin said. "It's a family place. Very wholesome."

"With a bar?"

"Well, they don't let kids in the bar, of course."

"Hmmm," Radiance said, "no kids, eh? Might be my kind of place after all. All right, all right, family nudist..."

"Campground."

"Okay, again, roll tape. Three, two, one... Good evening. Radiance Reynolds here again, still on the trail of the Good Samaritan. During our *interrupted* live segment on the Evening News with Jennings Prokoff tonight, we learned of his possible identity and whereabouts. And now, we're here in Tranquility, Florida at the Grin and Bare It ... Family Nudist ... *Campground* about to confront our mystery man. A-a-and cut."

The reporter glared at Robin. He melted in the heat of her animus. "Ya know, I'm kinda having second thoughts about this," he said. "I mean, no matter what Jaybird did to me, he's being exposed like a criminal for doing what ... helping people? Suddenly, that doesn't seem fair."

Radiance was in his face in a heartbeat, assailing him with the most emphatic whisper he'd ever heard: "Look, you, you, you crackpot! What's not fair is you crashing my shining moment on a national broadcast. What's not fair is me not getting to nail Mr. Jennings Fucking Prokoff on live TV for knocking me up. What's not fair is me being out here in the middle of Bumfuck, Egypt at a goddamned nudist colony-campground-whatever about to disturb a naked old hippie do-gooder who probably just wants to be left the fuck alone. But ya know what, buster? Tough shit, that's what! Ya know why? Because this is the goddamned news, that's why. Love it or hate it, it's my fuckin' job, and I'm here to do it because you – yes you! – blew the lid off this thing in such a way that I have no other choice. So, step aside and shut the fuck up and let me get this over with!"

Seconds later, Reynolds stood at Jaybird's door, her hair perfect, the sweat dabbed away, a smile on her face. She knocked. Waited. Knocked again. Waited some more. A third time. Nothing. "And now the sonofabitch isn't even home!" She grabbed the door handle. The door swung open.

* * *

Pepper opened her door and looked left and right. No sign of the weird woman in the minivan. Todd followed her out, carrying a large suitcase. Suddenly, the trip ahead of them wasn't just a Woodstock meetup with LilBuckaroo; if they could get the necessary license in New York, they would go from Saugerties – site of the official Woodstock 25th anniversary event – to Niagara Falls and take the plunge. So to speak. (By the way, Pepper said yes. Actually, she said, "Yes, yes, yes!" and then, during a post-proposal quickie, she said, "Yes, yes, yes Baby, yes!").

So, out the door they went.

* * *

So, in the door they went, the camera light at full tilt, with Robin leading (technically, he wasn't a complete breaker-and-enterer since he had a few belongings to retrieve).

"He's not here," Robin said. Radiance stared at him, hand on hip. "Kill the light," she said.

The crew, including Robin, looked around. "The TV's still on," said the camera operator.

"Anything else strange about what's here right now?" the reporter asked Robin.

He turned a slow 360, squinting, focusing, thinking.

"Well?"

"What's strange isn't what's here," Robin said. "It's what's *not* here. The litter box is gone. The cat's food bowl is missing, too." He took another slow spin. "The cookie jar is gone, too."

"The cookie jar?"

"Well, he never kept cookies in it, of course." Then Robin frowned. "Yeah, the cat being gone and the stash, er, the cookie jar being gone… well, that tells me that Jaybird is gone, too."

"But his car's here," said Mr. Soda.

"True, but…"

"But?"

"Well, it's just that I'm wondering about that blind guy and the younger man and woman who came looking for him earlier." He pulled from his pocket the piece of paper with the Bronco's license plate and Sonny's information written on it. "I wonder if he went somewhere with them in their white Bronco."

"A white Bronco?" Mr. Soda asked. "We passed one of those on the way in."

"Shit!" Radiance exclaimed. "You mean we were that close to getting this guy? Why didn't you mention the Bronco earlier?" She snatched the paper from Robin's hand and read it.

"I didn't think it was important at the time," Robin said. "And what do you mean 'getting this guy'? Is that what this is about? Getting someone? Making someone pay? For what?"

"You tell me," Radiance said. "You're the whistleblower here. What kind of revenge are you out for?"

"Hey, looka this," Mr. Soda said. He pointed at the coffee table. A small gnome, half painted, lay atop a newspaper, along with paints and brushes.

"Yeah," Robin said, "he usually bought unfinished gnome castings and painted them how he wanted."

Radiance stuffed Robin's note into her pocket and studied the makeshift studio. "Well, what have we here?" She slid the protective newspaper from beneath the gnome. It was the *Weekly Sun* from the week before. A news item had been circled with a felt tip pen: *Local Woman Robbed of Rent Money*. It was the story of Agnes Schwartz, the subject of Reynolds's most recent Samaritan report – notwithstanding the Prokoff debacle. "Definitely our guy, I'd say. This little clue ties him to that gift-and-run exploit the other day."

"Told you it was him," Robin said.

"Okay, okay, but then tell me this. If you're so certain he's gone, maybe with your Bronco people, why is the TV still on?"

Robin stared at the screen. An image was freeze-framed there. Paused. "It's a video," he said. "The Woodstock video. That's the famous peace-sign nun. You don't suppose he could be headed to Woodstock for the 25th anniversary, do you?"

* * *

"I know what I forgot," Jimi said.

"What?" Jaybird asked from the back seat.

"I'm pretty sure I left the TV on. I had paused the Woodstock tape to carry something to the Bronco and then just left it like that. Sorry."

"Hey, not a big deal. I can call someone from the camp to go in and shut it off later. I always leave the door unlocked. Most of the residents do. In the meantime, I'm curious – any idea how long before we get to our destination? How many miles is it?"

"Actually, yes, I know that," Jimi said. "According to my calculations from the road atlas, it's just shy of 10,000 miles."

"What?!?"

Sonny laughed. "Something you should know about your son is that he has Decimal Dyslexia."

"Okay, a thousand miles, then," Jimi admitted. "Either way, got a long night ahead of us."

* * *

"All right, it's been a long night," Radiance Reynolds said. After finding the trailer empty, she had taped an impromptu report hyping the Good Samaritan as now being a missing person, stopping just short of calling him a hippie do-gooder on the lam. To Robin, she said, "Look, we need to get the tape back to the station if we're gonna get the report on the eleven. Thanks for your help, even if you did ruin my fucking national report."

"My pleasure," Robin said, not specifying which part he took pleasure in, the helping or the ruining.

Radiance's pager buzzed, then, and an alphanumeric message appeared from a Prokoff lackey. "Well, it looks like I got your attention, after all, you sonofabitch!"

Saturday, August 13, 1994
(Reunion Day)

CHAPTER 30
(In Which Jaybird Gets Grilled)

Early, Early Morning

AS FRIDAY NIGHT CEDED TO SATURDAY MORNING, THE BRONCO MADE ITS way north-northeast on I-95. Janis, Jimi, and Jaybird took turns at the wheel, making good time and stopping only for the usual necessities: restrooms, gas, snacks, and clearing the car of the litter box smell when Anthony Purrkins made his presence known in the dark.

Before midnight, the dialogue had tended toward explaining everything – the mission, the money, and the method used to locate Jaybird after all these years. But afterward, as everyone took turns napping, the conversations ran a predictably unpredictable gamut:

Jimi and Jaybird:
> Jimi: *I know this whole thing's a shock. It was for us, too. I think we may need therapy at some point.*
> Jaybird: *Who? You or me?*
> Jimi: *I'm thinking Janis goes first; then it's a toss-up.*
> Jaybird: *Probably right.*
> Jimi: *Speaking of kids...*
> Jaybird: *Were we?*
> Jimi: *Well, Janis is pretty childish, so... Anyway, did you ever really want kids?*
> Jaybird: *Never seemed in the cards because, well, ya know, the mechanics of it all. Up till now, I've just had Anthony Purrkins and a few of his predecessors to care for. But yeah, I guess I would've liked kids along the way.*

Jimi: *And now that you have some… What's the biggest surprise of having kids now?*

Jaybird: *I guess I thought you'd be smaller.*

Janis, Jimi, and Jaybird:

Jimi: *Should we call you 'Dad'?*

Janis: *Good question. Grand Exalted Sperm Donor doesn't seem quite right.*

Jaybird: *Well, I think you have to earn the right to be called Dad. Speaking of which, I'll want to hear about your adoptive parents when the time's right. I owe them a debt of gratitude for raising you.*

Jimi: *That'll come in time. But, for now, we need to be able to call you … something. And it feels wrong somehow to just call you Jaybird.*

Jaybird: *Okay, well … how about Pops, then? Or maybe Grand Exalted Pops…*

Janis: *Well, Pops seems a bit grandpa-ish, but I suppose you'll grow into it; and you do rock the white hair – like I do.*

Janis and Jaybird:

Janis: *Why nudism? Why is that your thing?*

Jaybird: *Well, it just feels good. Being naked is very freeing, don'tcha think?*

Janis: *Actually, yes, it is. Okay, I'll give you the naked thing, but why the garden gnomes?*

Jaybird: *They make people smile. And I'm a sucker for a little guy with a stiff, pointy hat.*

Janis: *Paging Dr. Freud…*

Jaybird and Sonny:

Jaybird: *Can you tell me about your eyesight? When and how did you lose that?*

Sonny: *I lost it at Woodstock when that lawman guy went crazy. He attacked you, and I had to do something to stop him. I grabbed hold of him, and he struck back at me. I fell hard against a rock – it wasn't very big, but I hit it just right.*

Anyway, I was in a coma for nearly a week, woke up blind and with some memory loss. Got back most of the memories, but never my vision.

Jaybird: *So, it was my fault, then.*

Sonny: *I never thought that, not even for a minute. Blame the lawman if you must. But I've just always been grateful that your face was the last one I remember seeing. Of course, your face was covered in mud at the time.*

Everyone:

Jimi: *Pops, can you tell me about the whole lawman-with-the-hook thing? What was that all about?*

Janis: *Like to know that myself.*

Sonny: *Me, too. We didn't really get an explanation at Woodstock. Everything happened so fast and I was in a coma when he came to the hospital later to question Winnie.*

Anthony Purrkins: *Lawman? Hook? More secrets, Daddy Jayson?*

Jaybird: *Long story, as such things tend to be, but here goes: My dad was a financial guy —*

Janis: *Hey, it runs in the family, Jiminy!*

Jimi: *Not anymore.*

Jaybird: *Anyway, my dad was a good man, but he worked for some bad people who made their money in crooked ways. To ease his guilt over being involved with them, he came up with a way to divert their ill-gotten wealth into other accounts. From those accounts, the money could still grow, but he could take what he needed and do something good with it.*

Janis: *So, your dad was a Good Samaritan, too, then?*

Jaybird: *Well, the men he worked for called him a thief. By the time the shit all rained down, I'd gone off to Canada to avoid the draft – being homosexual and a conscientious objector didn't count for much with the draft board when powerful men had a score to settle with your dad – and then he got sick: a heart attack and two strokes after.*

Jimi: *Wow. That's tough all the way around.*

Jaybird: *Yeah, it was. I kept tabs on my dad, though, and when the end came near, I returned to New York, playing hide and seek from the law. That's when I first heard about Woodstock. The Aquarian Exposition. It sounded like a ray of sunshine in a world that had turned hopelessly dark. Nothing was gonna keep me from being there. But in the meantime, I had to stay outta sight, never knowing who might rat me out or arrest me. I took a chance, late one night near the end of July, and sneaked into the hospital to say goodbye to my dad. He was so weak. He also knew the room was bugged, so he spoke carefully and passed me a scribbled note.*

Sonny: *What did the note say?*

Jaybird: *It said Kibosh Rock. But it wasn't so much about what he had written but more about* how *he had written it. Again, kind of a code. And then the hook-handed agent guy rushed in, and a scuffle ensued. It was all I could do to get out without being apprehended. I had tried to stuff the note in my pocket but must've dropped it as I scrambled to get out of there. It was the last thing I had from my dad, and I lost it. A few weeks later, Captain Hook, as I affectionately call him, well, he showed up at Woodstock. Somehow, that bulldog sonofabitch found me, covered with mud, in that sea of people.*

Jimi: *And the money? Is that what you've been using for your Good Samaritan deeds?*

Jaybird: *Deeds? More like "exploits" if you believe that reporter, Radiance Reynolds. But to answer your question: yes and no. When he learned how sick he was, my dad withdrew the money from those secret accounts – and we're talking a couple hundred thousand – and then hid the cash.*

Janis: *Hid the money at the place the note said – in code. Right?*

Jaybird: *Right. So, after he died, I took what I needed for a while. Just enough to establish a new identity and make a fresh start, first in Canada and then back home in the U.S. But then I took some more money to buy the bar. Once that was all set up, I started giving back, doing good with the money that had come from the bad guys.*

Sonny: *You're both a Good Samaritan and Robin Hood.*

Jaybird: *Nothing so noble, really. Just a chip off the old block doing what seems right. I still do what I can, although it's not as much as it once was.*

Jimi: *So, the money's pretty much gone now?*

Jaybird: *Mostly, but it did a lot of good over the years. Atonement, I guess.*

Sonny: *Sins of the fathers…*

Jaybird: *Yes, that.*

Janis and Jaybird:

Janis: *Okay, Pops… Important shit now: Gilligan's Island… Ginger or Mary Ann?*

Jaybird: *Ginger or Mary Ann? You know I'm gay, right?*

Janis: *Pretend you're not. Ginger or Mary Ann?*

Jaybird: *I think I'd choose the Professor regardless. Something about him would turn me gay even if I weren't already. But what about you? Ginger or Mary Ann?*

Janis: *Definitely, Mrs. Howell.*

Jaybird: *Lovey? Why her?*

Janis: *At her age, I think she'd be the most grateful for some bedroom action. Plus, I'm a sucker for a feather boa.*

Jaybird: *Not sure even Dr. Freud would touch that one.*

Jimi and Jaybird:

Jimi: *I can see that Janis is a lot like you.*

Jaybird: *The gay thing?*

Jimi: *I was thinking the hair and the – don't tell her I said this – the quick wit. But sure, the gay thing, too.*

Jaybird: *True, true, and true.*

Jimi: *But I haven't quite figured out how I'm like you. For Janis, I imagine it's like she's found answers, found a piece of herself maybe, by finding you. I know she never quite fit in at home, so now she probably feels a little less … odd.*

Jaybird: *Are you her official spokesperson now?*

Jimi: *Seems like it, doesn't it?*

Jaybird: *I think Janis can come up with lots of words on her own.*

Jimi: *You're on to her already. Not surprising. You two are, well, again, you're a lot alike.*

Jaybird: *Which brings us back to your question. How are you and I alike? Right? Well, Jiminy – sorry, channeling Janis there – from what I've witnessed so far, I think you and I are alike because we can be the calm in the storm. We have caring hearts but are also rock steady. Time will tell, but I'm pretty intuitive about such things ... son.*

Sonny and Jaybird:

Sonny: *After Woodstock, did you ever look for Winnie and me?*

Jaybird: *No, but yes.*

Sonny: *That pretty well covers the bases. Covers your ass, maybe.*

Jaybird: *Ah, but remember, I'm a nudist. Covering my ass is not usually a priority.*

Sonny: *Good point, but did you look for us or not?*

Jaybird: *Well, if you remember, when we were in the van, I suggested a place to meet afterward in case we got separated. Someplace after the weekend was over.*

Sonny: *I remember.*

Jaybird: *I made my way there after Captain Hook attacked; had to find some clothes and then hitchhike because I couldn't risk going back to the festival site for my van. I ended up staying at the meet-up place two full days, even though I should've been on the run again. You and Winnie never showed up.*

Sonny: *But you know why we couldn't get there, right?*

Jaybird: *Now I do, and I understand. I was kind of heartbroken at the time, but I couldn't indulge that emotion for long, not with Captain Hook on my tail. Pete Peebles was his name, by the way, according to my dad.*

Sonny: *So, did Peebles know about the meet-up place? Did he track you there?*

Jaybird: *He knew about it because of targeting my dad, and he did show up there eventually. But I knew the land better than he did and was able to get away. To this day, I find it amusing that Peebles was so close to the money then that it could've bitten him.*

Sonny: *I wonder whatever happened to that guy?*

Janis and Anthony Purrkins:

Janis (silently nuzzling the cat): *C'mon, Anthony Purrkins, one secret about Jaybird. Just one.*

Anthony Purrkins (telepathically spilling his guts like yesterday's hairball): *I call him Daddy Jayson, but ... hmmm... Well, here's one: whenever he breaks up with a guy, he tells me it's because he never got over his one true love.*

Janis (looking into the back seat where Jaybird and Sonny napped): *One true love.*

Anthony Purrkins: *Aside from me, of course.*

Janis and Jaybird and Anthony Purrkins:

Janis: *As a lesbian, I am bound by a strict code of orientational boundaries and restrictions to never touch a testicle – even from a non-human species.*

Jaybird: *Understandable.*

Janis: *Still, I'm curious... What do turkey testicles taste like?*

Jaybird: *Chicken, of course.*

Anthony Purrkins: *Actually, more like chicken livers. Tasty enough, but not my favorite.*

Janis: *So, what is your favorite, Anthony Purrkins?*

Anthony Purrkins: *My all-time favorite pitch-in leftovers were from Sam and Ella's Salmon Saturday pitch-in. Too bad about that food poisoning, though. I miss Sam and Ella.*

CHAPTER 31
(In Which the Circle Tightens)

Morning

RADIANCE REYNOLDS CLIMBED ONTO THE CHOCKED HELICOPTER DOLLY, pulled open the port side passenger compartment door of the Bell 206L LongRanger, and started to step in. Eager to make the trip to New York and finally confront Jennings Prokoff in person, she had done as he'd instructed by alpha pager message: *Meet ATL netwk heli at Columbia SC airpt 9 am. Fly 2 Teterboro NY 2 meet Prokoff.* Interpretation: she was to board the network's regional helicopter, normally hangared in Atlanta, at 9 a.m. at the Columbia, South Carolina airport for a flight to Teterboro Airport. Teterboro was near Saddle River, New Jersey (where Prokoff had an estate). From there, she assumed a car would pick her up and she'd be taken somewhere for a one-on-one with the father of her child. *No doubt, he'll offer me hush money or a prime network gig, or both,* she thought. Either way, it was worth her trouble driving several hours through the dead of night from Jacksonville to Columbia.

So, there she was at 8:56 a.m. on a Saturday morning, exhausted and toting a large carryall whose most essential items were a mini-cassette tape recorder and a barf bag. She often got queasy on helicopters; morning sickness would almost certainly seal the deal for blowing chunks.

Worse yet, there were other passengers.

"Who the hell are you people?" Radiance demanded. But after a quick round of introductions, she still knew nothing about why Max, Penny, and Pixie were on *her* chopper. (Not to mention the dog in the diaper – literally a pampered pet.) But there they were, facing her, squirming and squeaking in their leather seats. *God, I'm tired of people staring at me,* Radiance thought. It was quite an epiphany for a TV reporter.

At 8:59, the turbine engine wound up into a high-pitched whine, and the rotors began spinning overhead. A couple of minutes later, the blades' smooth whirring escalated into a lawnmower-like sound. Finally, at 9:03, the LongRanger lifted off, its landing skids relaxing and drooping slightly as they rose from the dolly. The chopper turned 90 degrees, its nose dipping as it accelerated and lifted skyward, destination New York.

* * *

Meanwhile, on terra firma, the visitor population of the Catskills region of New York state was due to grow in a matter of hours.

Heading northeast on I-81, Joe Jack Sweet had stopped (ironically) in Woodstock, Virginia, for a double dose of donuts and a canned soft drink. While stopped, he called Deputy Brutus and asked him to swing by his house. Although certain Annabel and Edgar would not have returned yet, Joe Jack had to make sure he was not on a fool's errand chasing fools.

After an early morning start, LilBuckaroo, Annabel, and Edgar were making another detour: passing through Philadelphia on I-95, Edgar wanted to stop at the Edgar Allan Poe National Historic site, which featured a home Poe had once rented during his five years in Philly. "Plennyatime," Edgar had said, upon which Annabel had puppy-dog-eyed LB into making the stop.

The Bronco, meanwhile, was, at that very moment, also on I-95 and passing within 2 miles of Edgar Allan Poe's Amity Street house in *Baltimore*. They did not stop, but Jimi, at the wheel, whispered, "Ride, boldly ride, if you seek for Eldorado." Janis looked at him as if he were possessed.

And in the second hard-to-rent Bronco, a match for the one Pepper had reserved for Sonny and the twins, she and Todd were heading east-northeast on I-80 in Pennsylvania. Near the town of Eagleville, they passed Bald Eagle State Park. Pepper adjusted her wig and lay her head on Todd's shoulder as he drove. Effyu snorted and farted. All was right with the world.

Which brings us back to the LongRanger chopper, where Princess Petunia barked uncontrollably as Radiance Reynolds *barfed* into her airsick bag, a delight that went on for nearly two full minutes before subsiding, at which point Penny asked, "First time in a helicopter?"

Radiance stared at her and her cohorts. She sighed and searched for a mint in her oversized bag. "First time in a helicopter while pregnant," she said. "And now that I've told you that little secret, maybe you can tell me again who you all are and why you're on this flight."

"Congratulations on the baby!" Penny said, her delicate voice up an octave. Radiance forced a smile.

"Yes, congrats," said Max. "To answer your question – we're on our way to New York to meet up with Jennings Prokoff in pursuit of a story."

"Small world," Radiance said. "What kind of story? You don't look like reporters to me."

"We're not," Max replied. "But we're involved in the story. And it appears you're involved in part of it, too, actually."

And so began the filling in of many blanks and the connecting of many dots. Skeptical at first as the tale began to unfold, Radiance soon extracted her cassette recorder and her notebook. *Maybe this story – of the nudist Good Samaritan, now on the run, being hunted by a former federal agent – could be extra leverage in her bargaining with Prokoff for a network gig,* she thought. After the baby, that is. And with that, she threw up again.

CHAPTER 32

(In Which LilBuckaroo Wins a Prize He Doesn't Want,
and Pixie Wants a Prize She Can't Quite Get)

Late Morning

EDGAR WAS OUT OF LEAK-RESISTANT UNDERGARMENTS.

"Sorry, Dad," Annabel said. "I thought we had one more in the glovebox. Looks like we'll have to make a stop."

LilBuckaroo was driving the Edsel on the Garden State Parkway in New Jersey, making good time, but not good enough to feel comfortable about reaching Woodstock '94 at Saugerties by 3:00 if they stopped. After all, there was bound to be heavy traffic closer to the venue. And then there was the matter of finding where Pepper had said to meet up.

"Isn't the diaper he's wearing good enough for now?"

"Maybe good enough for number one," Annabel said, facing her dad and reading the growing distress on his face.

"But not nummer poo," Edgar offered.

So, they took the next exit and continued east a few blocks.

"Drugstore over there," Annabel said, pointing to the north side of the street. "We can all go in, use the restroom, and I'll get Dad his undergarments. Won't take but a few minutes, and we'll be back on the road."

LB turned at the next light and doubled back.

"Get ya some Mother Pucker's for yer baboonassmouth while yeraddit," Edgar said.

After parking the Edsel, LB said, "Why don't I just go on in and get the diapers while you two are getting ... unsituated."

"Andda Mother Pucker's!" Edgar managed.

"Got it, Edgar."

"Not yet yadon't."

Golden Olden Days Pharmacy & More occupied the first floor of a three-story rusty-brown brick building. Everything about the place looked true to the Olden part of its name; and through the windows, LB could see that the inside space seemed a bit dark. Just before he opened the front door, he noticed a cornerstone block: *Est. 1894.*

As he stepped inside, a raucous shout of "Surprise!" greeted him. Overhead lights popped on, flashbulbs flashed, noisemakers noised, confetti confetted, and a one-man band struck himself up. LilBuckaroo's head jerked side to side as he tried to take it all in. Much like the Tournament of Poeses Parade, he found himself the center of attention in a spectacle, a hullabaloo, a celebration of some kind.

A man stepped forward. He sported thick black-framed glasses and greasy salt-and-pepper hair slicked back from a Shar Pei forehead. He extended a meaty hand. "Congratulations, young fella, your timing is perfect!"

"Wha—?"

"You, my friend, are the 100th customer on the 100th day of our 100th year. I'm Elmore Golden, owner of the Golden Olden Days. My great-great-grandpa built this Golden establishment. On behalf of myself and the entire Golden family, as well as local dignitaries, members of the press (more flashbulbs) and our staff, present and past..." (he made a sweeping motion with his hand toward the impressive assemblage) "...we thank you for your patronage and welcome you as our special Golden guest."

LB's eyes darted person to person, face to face. He spit confetti and tried to speak to the expectant crowd. All he could manage was, "You've already had a hundred customers today?"

"Oh, good heavens, no. Merely ninety-nine. *You* are the hundredth. Hence the extravagant welcome. We counted ourselves, of course, thirty-five of us, as I recall, not to mention the regular morning shoppers and the busload of nuns heading north to Woodstock."

"Look, I just came in here for some—"

"Healing lip balm, may I assume?" Elmore said. "Golden aisle 3, but for a rash like yours, I highly recommend Mother Pucker's Sphincter Tincture. Golden aisle 7. What else can we help you find?"

"Depends."

"Depends on what?"

"Depends on what an old man might wear to, ya know, take a leak without actually leaking."

"Ah, that would also be Golden aisle 7. We keep all the nether region apparel, ointments, and lubricants over there. Even have bathing supplies there in the Golden shower section."

"Thanks."

"Oh, but you might want to stock up, because you, sir, are the recipient of a $100 shopping spree! Just shop to your heart's content for up to 10 minutes, pose for pictures, and sign a brief three-page waiver, of course."

"Look, I really don't have time for this. Seriously. In a big hurry. Thanks for the, um, the effort, but —"

"Oh, but you *must* be our honoree, sir. You're the one-hundredth. We've had this planned for months. All year, in fact. We can't reset everything. We can't *uncount* you!"

"Sure you can," LB said. "Look, I'll just leave, and you can celebrate with the next person."

"Oh, very well," Elmore Golden said. "Sorry, everyone. Looks like it'll have to be a do-over. Scoop up the confetti. But young man, as you leave, please back your way out the door. That'll make it more like a true reversal, you see."

LilBuckaroo shook his head but did as asked. Still facing the celebrants, he stepped backward out the exit door, only at the last second catching a peripheral glimpse of Edgar walking in. "Surprise!" yelled the resilient throng. The one-man band started an encore. Flashbulbs flashed, noisemakers noised, and...

"Aw, shit," LB muttered. He followed Edgar and Annabel back inside the store.

* * *

Radiance Reynolds emerged from the restroom at the helicopter hangar in Richmond, Virginia – a gas-and-go stop. She was feeling somewhat better but knew she needed something in her stomach. A small spiral coil vending machine sat on a countertop in front of the hangar office. Pixie stood in front of the vending machine.

Radiance stepped beside her and cleared her throat. Pixie turned, smiled, giggled, and went back to the business at hand: freeing a third Kit Kat bar from the machine. The first two had spiraled to freedom from the rack (on the way to their ultimate Pixied demise), but the third was merely dangling, taunting, keeping the chocoholic in literal suspense. Pixie started shaking the vending machine; it hardly budged as it was bracketed in place on the countertop.

Radiance backed away and walked closer to where Max and Penny were in discussion.

"I got ahold of Junior Carducci," Penny was saying. "He said he'd neither heard nor seen anything of Pete since early this week in DC. But then something happened…"

"What do you mean, something happened? While you were on the phone with him?"

"Well, yes, but not really. When I was on the phone with him, he discovered that his car key was missing, and when he looked out his window at where he had parked it, the car was gone."

"You don't think Pete could've —"

"I think it's possible," Penny said, a tear forming in the corner of her eye. "Junior said he always shuts his apartment door behind him, but he found it still open last night just after entering. And then he was certain he had shut the door and turned the deadbolt, but he later found it unlocked again."

"As if someone was in the apartment with him and then left but couldn't lock the door from the other side?" Max asked.

"Exactly."

Radiance came closer. In full reporter mode, she said, "So, you think this Pete fellow – your husband, right? – stole this Junior guy's car? I don't suppose you found out the make of the—"

The pilot whistled into the cavernous hangar. "Whirlybird's fueled and ready to go, folks."

"Maxie! Mama!" Pixie's shrill cry echoed through the hangar. Her arm was caught in the small machine.

* * *

Back inside the Golden Olden Days Pharmacy & More, Edgar had gloried in the revelry, chatted up the other revelers, and was now on his shopping spree – ten minutes of reckless consumer abandon at a quarter mile an hour behind a wobbly-wheeled-and-finely-festooned Golden cart. LilBuckaroo helped the cause by piling in a few packages of undergarments and a tube of Mother Pucker's.

Meanwhile, as one hundred dollars in merchandise was being gathered, LB's millions lay in peril, more so with each passing minute. He looked for Annabel. She stood amongst the town dignitaries, chatting and glad-handing and glowing as she watched her dad collect his prize. Her eyes connected with LB for a moment. She was beaming.

LB smiled.

You're turning soft. It was the voice of Denny DePew, his ghost-dad, back in his head to turn the screws. "Shut the fuck up, Dad," LB said quietly. And then he noticed a small plastic "You're Priceless!" trophy and picked it from the shelf. Indeed, it bore no price sticker, but it had Annabel's name written all over it. Figuratively, at least.

Elmore Golden then yelled, "Time's up." And for LB's fortune, maybe it was.

* * *

A desperate few minutes later at the Richmond hangar, Pixie was finally free from the small countertop vending machine. Well, almost. Her oversized arm was still wedged in the undersized product-receptacle-flap-thingy in the door. But Max and the hangar manager had been able to unlock the unit and remove the door, thus extricating Pixie. Max then paid a substantial sum to the hangar operator to cover the cost of a replacement door.

"Grab some snacks!" Pixie yelled as she was led away, wearing the vending machine door with Max helping support its weight. Radiance and Penny both grabbed some of the exposed products and ran toward the refueled helicopter. Its engine was already fired up and the rotors were churning.

CHAPTER 33
*(In Which a Helicopter Follows a White Bronco
to a Place Where Suspicions Rise)*

Afternoon

JENNINGS PROKOFF MET THE HELICOPTER AT TETERBORO AIRPORT. Although the anchor had a helipad at his Saddle River estate, the pilot had radioed ahead and strongly recommended at least a partial refueling, which would not have been possible at Prokoff's home. A cameraman met them there, too, and the journalists boarded while the chopper was being hot-fueled, rotors spinning. The cameraman took a seat up front next to the pilot; Prokoff chose a rear-facing seat with the center padded console to his right. He figured he could rest his drinking arm there. He tapped the large flask in his jacket pocket, reassuring himself he was all set for the trip.

Penny, Pixie, Petunia, Max, and Radiance had all de-coptered as quickly as possible to use the restroom but had returned and were again filing in. Max helped everyone in first and then took his position. Radiance sat next to Jennings Prokoff, the armrest between them. It was as close to him as she'd been since the night of the affiliates' party. He looked smaller than she remembered. Grayer. He was also not naked.

Radiance smiled as genuinely as she could muster. Deprived of her opportunity to privately confront him after the failure of her *public* confrontation, she took the high road and opened her bag. "Snack?"

As Prokoff peered inside the bag, Pixie got excited. "Ooh, ooh, ooh!" she cried, wiggling her fingers, her face beaming and breath fogging the vending machine door glass she sported like a shield. "Got a Fifth Avenue?"

"Nope," Radiance said. "Just some nacho chips."

"Darn," Pixie said. Nonetheless, she gestured for a bag. Radiance tossed it, but it banked off Pixie's glass front. She appeared crestfallen, more so when Princess Petunia retrieved the bag from the floor and ripped it open.

"Hello, Maxsh," Prokoff said. "Long time no shee. You, too, Radiansh. Care to introduche me to our other gueshtsh?

"The one on the floor is Petunia," Radiance said. "Princess Petunia to be perfectly precise. That's her person, Penny Peebles. You know Max. And behind door number three is Pinkie Peebles."

"Pixie, not Pinkie," said Pixie.

"Precisely. Pardon my faux pas. *Pixie* Peebles."

"I'm guesshing there'sh a shtory about the apparatush you appear to be shtuck in."

Pixie nodded. "Kind of a long story—"

Prokoff raised a hand. "Shorry, no time for long shtories. Nothing more than ninety shecondsh on the evening newsh. Pretty mush my pershonal limit, too."

Everyone buckled in, and the LongRanger lifted off. It mostly followed SR 17 northward. Max quickly updated Prokoff. Radiance, still playing nice, added what she knew about this Jaybird person believed to also be the object of Pete Peebles's obsession.

"I have reason to believe," she said, "that he's headed toward Woodstock with a blind man named Sonny Muckle and two younger people."

"Those would be Muckle's niece and nephew," Penny added.

Radiance pulled Robin's note from her bag. "They should be in a white Ford Bronco, Indiana plate," she said. "Headed out from north Florida last night. Assuming they drove all night, they should be on or near the New York State Thruway soon."

* * *

"New York State Thruway's closed, man," said Todd, some ten minutes later, in his best Arlo-Guthrie-at-Woodstock-'69 voice. He and Pepper and Effyu had just merged onto I-87 from I-287 at Hillburn just inside the New York state line from New Jersey. "Except it wasn't really closed then," he added. "Just a couple of exits shut down. Major traffic jams, though."

"I hope we don't run into anything like that this time," Pepper said.

"Probably nothing to that degree. We are getting rain, though." He turned on the wipers. "Looks like that's a Woodstock tradition."

"How do you know so much about Woodstock, anyway?" Pepper asked. "You're too young to have been there in '69."

"Well, as you've discovered, I know a lot about sixty-nine." He turned toward her and winked. "But seriously, I have a lot of downtime at Before You Go-Go. Since the 25th anniversary of Woodstock was coming up, I went to the library and read up. I've also seen the documentary about the festival on video."

A minute later, they encountered their first rest area inside the state, an elaborate travel plaza at Sloatsburg, complete with covered parking garage and amenities far surpassing the typical roadside stops in Indiana. Then again, this was New York, and the Sloatsburg plaza was just over 30 linear miles from Central Park.

"Potty break and time to fill the tank," Todd said. He exited the Thruway and guided *their* Bronco into the parking garage.

* * *

One minute behind Pepper, Todd, and Effyu, the other Bronco took the same exit and pulled into the same parking garage. After finding a spot on a center row of the garage, Sonny, the twins, and Jaybird stepped out of the vehicle and stretched.

"This is all new since I was through here last," Jaybird said. "Impressive, isn't it?" He yawned, having just awakened from a short nap, and then leaned in to put a collar and leash on Anthony Purrkins. He picked up the cat and turned away from the car. As they stood there, Anthony Purrkins nuzzled his cheek, applying furry pressure that held Jaybird's face in place. It was then that Jaybird saw something in the near distance. "Sonny," he said, "I wish you could see what I see."

"Tell me," Sonny said.

"Blast from the past. Come with me."

Jimi and Janis watched the three of them – Jaybird holding Sonny's hand, Sonny tapping with his cane, and Anthony Purrkins on the ground, straining at his leash and avoiding the swings of the cane's red tip. They walked across the aisle and ten cars down, stopping before a rusting hippie-style VW van covered in hundreds of colorful peace signs. It looked like it had just emerged from a huge Woodstock '69 time capsule. From the distance, the twins could tell Jaybird was describing it for Sonny.

"Gotta pee," Janis said.

"Let's find a restroom, then," Jimi said. They made it twenty-five feet before Jimi grabbed her arm and pulled her beside a pickup truck.

"What the hell, Jiminy?" He shushed her and pointed. She followed his finger to a woman and a man walking a dog and disappearing into a shadow. "Was that ... *Pepper?*" Janis cried.

Again, Jimi shushed her. "That's certainly what I thought."

"What is *she* doing here?"

"I don't know," Jimi said. "But I have to think that if she was supposed to be here, Sonny would've told us."

"Should we tell Sonny she's here? Or maybe just chase her down and ask her?"

"I have a bad feeling about this," Jimi said. "I have a bad feeling about Pepper."

"You think she's been following us?"

"I don't know. It's possible, I suppose. I wasn't really on lookout. Except that..."

"Except what?"

Jimi's eyes tightened; his face tensed. "Did you by any chance notice that—"

"Helicopter?" Janis said, finishing his thought.

"So, you did see it."

"Kinda hard to miss it. It seemed to swoop down close and then stay on us until we turned in here."

Jimi nodded, but Janis could tell there was more he wasn't yet telling her. "What is it?" she asked. "Don't hold back on me now, bro."

"Okay, I'm just adding everything up here."

"Are decimals involved?"

"I don't think so."

"That's a relief."

"Here's the thing..." Jimi said. "First, Pepper gets us an O.J. Simpson-like Bronco after Sonny instructs her to get something ordinary." He held up his index finger. "Also, Sonny couldn't reach her several times when he tried to call." Another finger. "Then, there's the matter of her not providing any solid information during the trip – we basically had to bring it all together on our own." Finger number three. "And now this helicopter follows us from north of Paramus on 17 all the way to here." A fourth finger.

"And then there's the matter of that man she was with just now," Janis added, holding up her own index finger. "Did you get a good look at him? Could that have been ... LilBuckaroo?"

"I didn't get a good look," Jimi said. "He went into the shadows as soon as I saw him." He relaxed his hand and stopped counting. "Could be LilBuckaroo, I suppose. But then again, this all happened so fast we never got to see a picture of him, did we? Seems like Pepper should have provided that to us somehow."

"And one more thing," Janis said. "Sonny told her we found Jaybird and where we were heading. Do you think she's here – with LilBuckaroo – to make sure we don't fulfill our mission?"

"Well, it is possible, isn't it? And if that *is* LilBuckaroo with her, then they're in cahoots."

"Devious," Janis said. "And as an aside, I love the word 'cahoots'."

* * *

Shortly after briefing Prokoff, everyone with a window in the helicopter had been on watch for a white Ford Bronco. They spotted it near Ho-Ho-Kus, New Jersey. The copter had then swooped down, confirmed an Indiana license plate, and followed from a low altitude all the way to the Sloatsburg Plaza, where the Bronco had disappeared into the parking garage.

After hovering over the plaza for just over ten minutes, the pilot cleared his throat. "Mr. Prokoff, I have to tell you that we need to be careful with our hover time. We did little more than a splash-and-go hot refuel at Teterboro. And since we tailed the Bronco at highway speeds and are now stationary, well, I just don't want to cut our range too close."

"We'll be fine," Prokoff said. He turned to face Radiance Reynolds. "While we wait, maybe you can tell me what happened during your live report."

She looked at him with disbelief, like she had just spotted Bigfoot. Two thoughts assailed her: First, he wanted to talk about that *now* – with people around? And second, he had just uttered an entire sentence without an 's'."

Penny saved her. "There it is!" she yelled. "The Bronco! It's leaving the garage!"

The cameraman pointed the camera and zoomed in on the vehicle.

"Headed north?" Radiance asked.

"Yep."

"Then let'sh follow. Keep the camera on that Bronco. Are you recording thish?"

"Yessir."

"Good. But shave lotsh of tape for me. We'll need it when we get on the schene.

"Um, Mr. Prokoff, sir?"

"What ish it?"

"There's another Bronco down there now," said the camera operator. "Maybe a dozen car lengths back. Also Indiana plates."

CHAPTER 34

*(In Which LilBuckaroo Changes Course, Prokoff Goes Live,
and Things Fall into Place – Literally)*

Afternoon

JUST MISSING THE BRONCOS AT THE SLOATSBURG TRAVEL PLAZA, LilBuckaroo gassed up the thirsty Edsel, got back in the car, and announced he had made a decision. "I don't think we should go to Woodstock '94 after all," he told Annabel.

"Oh, but we're so close," she said, "and it's important to you. Here, you missed a spot..." She dabbed some extra Mother Pucker's onto his upper lip.

"Thanks. Yes, it was important, but maybe for the wrong reasons. I'll still have a nice inheritance, even if I have to share. And we're behind schedule anyway. The whole trip has been that way. I don't know. Just doesn't seem like things are falling into place the way I thought they would." He looked at the sleeping old man in the back seat. "Annabel, when you left the table for a few minutes at the Mexican restaurant, Edgar made me think... Ya know, when I started this trip, I wanted two things. First, I wanted to make some stops to try to drum up business for my chips."

"They really are delicious," Annabel said, "even if they do look like penises."

"Yeah, there's that. But I also wanted to make sure that the only family I have left didn't take part of *my* money. And ever since I made that decision, I've had nothing but trouble. I've seen my dream girl drift away; I've had my car vandalized and impounded; I've been injured and arrested, and now I'm an escapee driving a stolen car."

"Now, wait just a minute, buster," Annabel said. "Technically, you did not escape. I let you out. And this is not a stolen car. I simply asked you to chauffeur us on a trip with my dad."

LB shrugged.

"And nothing bad has happened since you started out *with us* on this fool adventure, has it? I mean, haven't we all enjoyed this little excursion, taking it one day at a time, one *mile* at a time?"

LB recalled the look on Edgar's face as the old man had been on his low-speed shopping spree, and Annabel's face as she had watched her dad in his glory.

"So why not just continue on to Woodstock?" Annabel asked. "We've come this far, haven't we? Oh, I'm sorry if we slowed you down. I know it's been all about Dad's adventure so far. But enough of that; it's time to reach *your* destination."

"That's just it," LB said. "I think it's the wrong destination now. But I do have a better one in mind." He started the car, pushed the Teletouch 'D' in the center of the steering column, and pulled away from the gas pump. But before pulling onto the New York State Thruway, he stopped and once more put the car in 'Park.' From the glove box, LB retrieved the small plastic trophy. He handed it to Annabel. "Almost forgot to give you this," he said. On the bottom of the trophy, he had written, "To my favorite co-pilot." Annabel grinned, and off they went.

* * *

North of Sloatsburg, a light rain had begun to fall on the helicopter. Radiance was now riding co-pilot after the chopper had landed long enough for the camera operator to climb into the rear passenger compartment; that's where Prokoff was planning his live report.

"Tell me when we get the Broncosh in view again," Prokoff yelled to Radiance. And then to the camera operator, he said, "We can do a live newshbreak intro from inshide the chopper. Are you in touch with the shatellite truck and the shtudio?"

"Yessir, Mr. Prokoff." Unbuckled, the cameraman edged closer to Prokoff, setting his focus.

"Good. Tell me when the uplink and downlink are eshtablished. And pilot, let me know when we get near Shaugertiesh."

* * *

The Woodstock '94 event at Saugerties was initially planned to be "2 More Days of Peace & Music." However, the Saturday and Sunday festival soon grew to include a third day. The added day was tacked on *before* the original opening day, so the festival kicked off Friday, August 12. It was hot and dry that day, so the crowds came early. By Saturday midafternoon, when the rains settled in, a couple hundred thousand people were already ensconced at Winston Farm and into their second day of music and merriment.

The New York State Thruway was not closed, but traffic was predictably heavy and backed up at the northbound Exit 20 Saugerties toll plaza. It was shortly before 2:30 in the afternoon as the two white Ford Broncos crept toward the exit ramp. Overhead, the network news helicopter hovered. With satellite communications established, Jennings Prokoff began his report, breaking in live and interrupting a broadcast of the movie "Heidi." Viewers were outraged. But they watched anyway. Though not everyone tuned *into* a Prokoff newscast on purpose, few people could bring themselves to look away once he came on air.

The pilot interrupted Prokoff's interruption of the movie: "Mr. Prokoff, we're going to have to set down very soon. Dangerously low on fuel. Too much low-speed flight and time in the air. Not safe to continue hovering."

"Nonshenshe," Prokoff said, still on camera. (The cameraman, sensing something more eventful than Prokoff's prosaic outro, kept the live feed *live* despite the anchorman's "cut" gesture.)

The pilot did not argue but quietly moved the helicopter from where it had hovered over the highway to where it now hung over a parking lot densely packed with empty cars on SR 212 near the top of Exit 20, which was closed. There the copter began to sway in a subtle pendulum motion as the pilot made small adjustments in its vertical position. Then, hovering at less than 300 feet, the sound of the chopper changed. The whine of the engine had ceased even as the blades continued to rotate. The helicopter's freewheeling unit automatically disengaged so the rotors could spin without resistance from the stalled engine. On the ground, a handful of people ran from inside a merchandise tent.

"Hold tight!" the pilot yelled. "Hard landing!"

And so it was.

During the impact, the camera had bounced off Pixie's unbreakable vending machine window, swung back, caromed off of Prokoff's head, and then nearly knocked the cameraman unconscious. The camera dropped to the floor, intact and still broadcasting while its former operator moaned and held his skull. Prokoff felt his forehead, too, a welt already rising from the sharp, quick blow. He sweated and stammered, shook away the sudden mental cobwebs, but otherwise showed no physical effects from the crash. Penny caught her breath, unbuckled, and gently scooped up Petunia, both also unscathed. Pixie's eyes darted wildly. Her delayed scream started as a guttural growl and pitched ever higher to operatic proportions. Max reached out and took her hand. She leaned her head into his shoulder and came down an octave. In the cockpit, Radiance said, "Goddammit! Made me wet my pants!" She popped open the door and took a tentative step out into the rain, which began to dampen the rest of her.

The pilot had dropped the chopper onto the now flattened merchandise tent. Strewn about were the shredded remnants of the canopy, strung from the stalled rotor blades like a toilet-papered tree; and on the ground lay its former merchandise: T-shirts and bandanas mostly, now a messy sea of tie-dye. "Free T-shirts!" Radiance heard someone yell, and the crowd that had retreated during the copter drop rushed forward and began looting the detritus.

Penny tended to the cameraman. He claimed to be fine but was obviously woozy. Prokoff also looked dazed and struggled to catch his breath. He shook his head again to gather his faculties, felt for his flask in his jacket pocket, and then picked up the camera and handed it to Max. "Here," he said. "You'll have to do this. I'm sure there's an on-off button somewhere. Let's get out of this stupid bird." For the moment, no one had yet noticed that Prokoff's slurring lisp – his trademark – had miraculously vanished with the blow to his head.

Max exited the copter and lay the camera on the ground. He helped the others out. Prokoff grabbed the camera and handed it back to him. "Let's get this done," he said, clear as a bell. He stepped into a strategic position near the rear of the helicopter so Max could frame the shot, including the chopper, the looting throng, and of course, him.

"In three, two, one…"

Max pushed a button. The camera didn't start smoking or anything, so he took that as a good sign.

"Jennings Prokoff on the scene here at Woodstock '94 at Saugerties after a somewhat dramatic entrance as our helicopter just made an emergency landing." He motioned to the goings-on all around him. "It appears everyone on board escaped without serious injury, although we are all perhaps a bit shaken up by the ordeal. Nonetheless, we came here with a job to do, a report to file, and so we are on the scene, prepared to bring you that report."

He started moving. Max followed with the camera.

"As you can see, our entrance here just off Exit 20 has caused a bit of a stir, with the crowd in a near frenzy and merchandise literally flying off the rack. But we are here not solely to report on this massive festival, but also on a developing situation involving *these* people…" He stepped over next to Penny and Petunia and Pixie, who tried unsuccessfully to hide behind her vending window. "We're also here trying to locate their husband and father, a man named Pete Peebles, a recently retired Federal agent."

Max gave him a thumbs up. Prokoff seemed remarkably lucid and on-point.

"It is believed that former agent Peebles may now be in in the midst of this massive Woodstock '94 crowd in an attempt to finally bring a former fugitive to justice." Prokoff motioned Max to follow him with the camera. With the ongoing T-shirt frenzy in frame behind him, Prokoff now stood beside Radiance Reynolds.

"Joining me here now is north Florida station WTFU reporter Radiance Reynolds. It is strongly suspected that the anonymous Good Samaritan Radiance has been following in her area is the same man Pete Peebles has been trying to locate since the original Woodstock festival in 1969. Radiance, what new information can you share with us?"

Reynolds, the front of her mauve pant-suit pants now wet, saw her opportunity at last. "What new information can I share, Jennings? What new information? How's this for new information... I'm preg—" But at that moment she noticed that the camera's red tally light wasn't on. She went ballistic, growled, and lunged at Max. "You idiot, the goddamned camera isn't even transmitting!" She swung her large carry-all bag, hitting Max him in the head. He dropped the camera, which landed on its side at his feet.

But there were other cameras on the scene, from festival-goers and two rival networks, quickly reacting to the helicopter crash. The network cameras fed live reports of the entire affair, including Pixie coming to Max's rescue, using her vending machine door as a shield against the rampaging Radiance Reynolds.

* * *

"Wonder where that helicopter went?" Jaybird asked. "No matter." He took Sonny's hand and squeezed it. "It's been a long time since we've been at Woodstock, hasn't it, Sonny?"

"Long time no see," Sonny said. He chuckled nervously, and added, "But we came here to fulfill a mission, to carry out Winnie's wishes. Let's get to it."

* * *

As Penny had helped Max to his feet after being clobbered by the pregnant reporter, she saw that the Bronco had worked its way onto the closed exit ramp anyway, bypassing security personnel who had left their posts in the hubbub of the chopper crash. Penny saw people stepping out of the vehicle. "Come with me," she said. Carrying Petunia, she and Max rushed off to investigate while Pixie continued taunting Radiance with her shield.

* * *

The rain was light as Sonny, Jaybird, and the twins stepped out of their vehicle. Sonny held out his arms and spun slowly. He stuck out his tongue to catch the rain. It didn't just feel like rain. It felt like home.

"Oops, can't forget this little guy," Janis said. She reached in and picked up Anthony Purrkins. *Rain; yippee!* said the cat in a sarcastic transmission to Janis. *Gonna need a towel soon.*

* * *

As Penny and Max neared the Bronco, a woman reached inside and brought forth an animal. It was a dog. And that dog immediately saw Princess Petunia and bolted for the diapered pooch who struggled free of Penny and raced off, back toward the helicopter, losing her diaper in mid-stride. Effyu gave chase. Penny and Pepper hurried after their pets. Max stared at Todd. Todd shrugged and rushed off, too.

Max then noticed the second Bronco, stopped near the base of the ramp, where a man tilted his head skyward, letting the rain patter against his face. Max ran to the man. "Are you...? Naw, you couldn't be." Short, dark-haired, and bearded, the man looked nothing like Pete Peebles's prey. Max looked around. "Where is everyone? Aren't you traveling with...? Who the hell are you? Where did you get this vehicle? *Where is Jay Finch, Jr.?*"

CHAPTER 35
(In Which Secrets are Revealed, Truths are Exposed,
a Disastrous Miracle Happens, and a Surprising Couple Couples)

Midafternoon

ROUGHLY 53 STRAIGHT-LINE MILES AWAY, WHERE THE GROUP HAD STOPPED near Filippini Pond at the site of the original Woodstock festival in Bethel, New York, Janis handed Anthony Purrkins to Jaybird. She then walked with Jimi and Sonny toward the crest of the small rise where the ceremony would take place. Sonny carried the urn.

As he cradled the cat in the light rain, Jaybird watched his adult children ascend to the place where they were conceived. He then leaned against the rusty peace sign-covered van they had bargained for in the Sloatsburg travel plaza parking garage. ("Three grand and a dozen joints? It's yours, man, as long as I can use *your* ride for a few days. Gotta get to Saugerties for the festival.") Now, Jaybird stroked the cat and whispered, "This is the place, Anthony Purrkins. All those hours you spent by my side watching that video; well, this is where it happened. Woodstock. This is where I met my one true love – aside from you, of course."

The cat stared at him blankly.

"And here we are again. Sonny and me, together after all this time. And now with Janis and Jimi. And with you. And the rain. It seemed perfect before, all those years ago. And now, little guy... Well, it seems perfect again. Just a different kind of perfect, I guess." Jaybird hugged the cat a little tighter. "I don't know where we go from here, but right now, here we are. And that's enough, don't ya think? Maybe that's all there can ever be."

Janis hurried back down the hill. "What are you telling this poor cat? He was sending me messages he needed to be rescued. Something about sentimental bullshit?" Jaybird laughed and handed her Anthony Purrkins. He started to follow them up the hill, but then stopped and turned a slow circle, looking over the grounds. Squinting, he could almost imagine the scene the way it was twenty-five years earlier: the multitudes and the music makers and the mud. His own rusty old van. And Sonny.

And Winnie.

The rain picked up. Jaybird joined the others.

Perfect.

* * *

Meanwhile, at Saugerties, careers were going up in smoke. Jennings Prokoff had lost his slurring lisp; the trademark linguistic malfunction had been jolted into submission with the fall of the chopper and the blow to his head. And Radiance Reynolds found herself going from the self-anointed persona of *wronged woman* to that of shameful slut, courtesy of this exchange which was captured by competing network cameras:

Reynolds: *You knocked me up, you sonofabitch!*

Prokoff: *I did nothing of the sort. How could I have done that? We've had only one brief conversation at a single network event in a room with hundreds of people.*

Reynolds: *Bullshit, motherfucker! It was at the party after the affiliates' meeting. You came on to me, and I'd had just enough alcohol to believe your load of crap.*

Prokoff: *I didn't even attend the after-party. I made my speech, thanked the stations for their support, and then went straight home. I had an early flight the next morning for Mississippi and—*

Reynolds: *Wait a minute, what did you say?*

Prokoff: *I said I had an early flight to Mississippi and—*

Reynolds: *What the hell? You said* Mississippi *perfectly.*

Prokoff: *I'll be damned. You're right. My mouth works! Sally sells seashells by the—*

Reynolds: *Yeah, well, your dick sure worked, too. Don't lie to me, shithead. I know who I'm banging. Most of the time, anyway.*
Prokoff: *Well, so do I. I haven't had sex with anyone but my wife since the last Woodstock. And besides, I got a vasectomy in 1985!*
Reynolds: *Really?*
Prokoff: *Sincerely.*
Reynolds: *Oh, shit... Mary, mother of God... Sweet jumpin' Jesus...*
Prokoff: *What?*
Reynolds: *Um, was there an entertainer at the affiliates' meeting?*
Prokoff: *As I recall, yes. That impersonator fella, the one that does a spot-on impression of me – or of me when I used to sound like me.*
Reynolds: *Sonofabitch... I got knocked up by Dickie Smalls!*

During all of this, the camera on the ground – the one that had been rocked from Max's hand – was also transmitting; it had clicked on again when it landed on the pavement. Laying sideways, it picked up the entire conversation with accompanying waist-down shots of the anchor and the wet-pantsed reporter getting wetter in the rain. And then, when Prokoff and Reynolds parted company, the camera refocused on two dogs – Effyu and Princess Petunia – going at it like oversexed newshounds.

Pepper and Penny arrived on the scene just as the dogs finished. They separated the cavorting canines and smiled at one another in embarrassment. In the distance, music played. Hordes milled about in the rain. But there were no signs of LilBuckaroo or Pete. As both women scanned the scene, they said, in unison, "I wonder where..."

But then Pepper's thoughts were taken elsewhere. She finally noticed her darling Prokoff, standing a few yards away. Her heart trapezed skyward and her face flushed. The rest of the world fell into soft focus around the edges as her eyes trained on the anchor. Since Todd had entered her life, Pepper had spent few moments fantasizing over her beloved newsman, but now here he was, tantalizingly close. With Effyu in her arms and Todd nearby assisting Max, who was attending to the injured cameraman just inside the helicopter door, she felt herself gliding through the rain toward the anchor.

Prokoff was leaning against the chopper. He looked around, stole a sip from his flask, and tested his new verbal acuity: "One Mississippi, two Mississippi, three Mississippi. Saskatchewan, Susquehanna, San Francisco treat… From Saugerties, our top story, story, story, story…"

"Excuse me, Mr. Prokoff…? *Jennings*…" And with that, Pepper swooned and passed out. Todd saw her drop. He abandoned the wounded cameraman. Rushed to his beloved. Lifted her head. Dislodged her wig. Prokoff took another drink. "Senseless," he said. The network cameras took it all in.

That is until Penny stepped into frame. She held up a picture of Pete. "I'm looking for this man, my husband," she said. "He may be driving a black Olds Achieva, or he may be on the grounds here at Woodstock. If you see him, don't approach, but please, *please* tell a police officer or a security official. And Pete, if you're out there watching – and since this isn't on Prokoff's network, you just might be – just come home before it's too late. I have news, too, sweetheart." She patted Princess Petunia's belly. "I have a feeling you might soon be a grandpa."

"How did you know I'm late for my period, Mama?" It was Pixie. She patted her own belly through the glass, and then grinned and giggled as if she had just licked a smudge of chocolate from her lips.

CHAPTER 36
(In Which the Reunion Happens)

Midafternoon

AT BETHEL, BLANKETED BY A DARKENING SKY AND COOLED BY GUSTING winds, they had gathered in a small circle on the rise near Filippini Pond. There, Jimi, Janis, and Jaybird had taken turns gently spreading the ashes from the full and heavy urn. They made small dustings, tiny circles close to the ground as the rain fell. Large drops of rain now, heavy and determined. Drops with singular substance. The kind that explode when they land.

Earth, wind, fire, water. All present. All fleeting, yet eternal.

And with each thoughtful release of ashes from the urn, they spoke of loss and gratitude. Of moments shared and moments missed and moments to come that would be emptier without Winnie there.

In the distance, a small stage was being built and a sea of tents blew uneasily in the wind, their fabric undulating like the rise and fall of swelling waves. Few people were inside the tents, though; the visitors were scattered all over the hallowed grounds, smaller in number than in 1969 – tens of thousands instead of hundreds of thousands – but reverent and pure in spirit. Pure in their longings, too, for peace and love and equality and unity.

Above, another helicopter hung watchfully.

And on the road below this ceremonial rise, a white-over-turquoise Edsel rolled to a stop. Janis wondered if it was someone arriving to verify that they had met the deadline and fulfilled their mission. But she dismissed that notion when a woman emerged and helped an elderly man from the back seat. A much younger man, the driver, followed. *Nasty looking upper lip on that one,* Janis thought. The younger man helped the others up the hill, holding an umbrella over them as they slowly climbed the gentle slope.

Jimi stepped away from the circle to meet them. "Hello," he said. "I don't mean to be rude, but we're having a private family ceremony here."

"Then you must be ... my brother," LilBuckaroo said. He handed the umbrella to Annabel and extended his right hand, which Jimi accepted. The handshake became a hug, and the hug produced tears.

When they separated, Jimi said, "So, I guess that wasn't you that we saw with Pepper in the... No matter. Come join us." He led LB into the circle of family. Annabel and Edgar kept their distance.

"Sonny," Jimi said, "LilBuckaroo is here." He guided Sonny's hands to meet LB's.

"Hello, uncle Sonny. Before you say anything... I'm not here to interrupt or stop what you're doing," LB said. "That was my plan at first, but not anymore." He hugged his uncle and then stepped over to Janis. She handed Anthony Purrkins to Jaybird, and then LB took her hands in his. "I'm your brother," he said. "You're my family. All of you. I'm here because... Well, because you're all I've got left." He looked back at Edgar. "And I'm slowly learning that family is all I really need."

Jaybird set the cat on the ground, and then put his right arm around LB's shoulder. "Then I'm sure you're welcome here. All of you are." He motioned for Annabel and Edgar to come into the circle. "Sonny was about to take his turn spreading the ashes, but maybe you should go next, LilBuckaroo, and say something if you'd like. We've been spreading small circles."

LB stared at the urn at Sonny's feet. When he opened his mouth to take a deep breath, he was engulfed with grief. Annabel hugged him fiercely, but for LilBuckaroo, it felt like the hug he had long needed from his mother. Once he settled himself, LB spoke softly. "I loved you, Mom," he said. "We weren't good at expressing that, but then again, maybe we just had a different language for it. More than love, I respected the hell out of you, too. You dealt with... You dealt with *loss*. And you dealt with me. You raised me without giving in to the urge to kill me even though I'm sure I gave you good reasons to. You *made* something of your life, Mom. You made things that will go on and on.

You made a difference in the world. Hell, you even made a difference to those damn rescued poodles in Morocco." He laughed. So did the others. "Most of all…" He paused and looked around. "Most of all, you made a family. And we're here. With you. *Because* of you."

Under the thickening rain, LB took the urn and sowed ashes in a small circle as the others had done. Then he handed the vessel to his uncle.

Sonny worked to swallow his emotion, and in time found his voice: "Winnie, I love you more than you could have ever known. You were my best friend. I was older, but I followed your lead. I wanted to be more like you. Even though I wanted to *be you* when I grew up, I knew that was a silly notion, because the most important thing you taught me was to never, ever really grow up at all. So, now, here we are. You brought us together. You're here with us, and you always will be." He paused, tilted his face to the rain, and held tight to the urn. "You always said that a fortune saved is a fortune earned. Well, because of how you've brought us together here, you've surely earned your fortune in a fine and wonderful place that seems so far from here … but maybe it's not that far at all."

Sonny bent down, tipped the urn, and spilled out more ashes.

After a minute of silent reflection, Janis said, "Everyone, wait here." She ran down the rain-slickened hill to the van, and then returned with the gnome and handed it to Jaybird. "Would you mind if we left this here, in this place, for our mama?"

Jaybird took Sonny's hand and placed it on the gnome. "What do you say, Sonny? Personally, I think Winnie might just kinda love this."

Sonny nodded. "I think so," he said, and together they placed it among the circles of ash. "Just one more thing, though…" Sonny turned, dropped his pants, and bent slightly, mimicking the gnome and laughing like a child. "C'mon kids, enough tears… Moon your mama!" And they did, all of them, finding joy beneath their grief.

Still holding the umbrella over her dad, Annabel looked over to find Edgar's suspenders undone, too, his pants on the ground, undergarments and all. He was grinning uncontrollably. "Aw, hell," Annabel said as she tossed away the umbrella. "Might as well join this rite of *assage*."

On the road below, a school bus loaded with nuns slowed and stopped, the sisters watching and pointing. For Jimi, his now-or-never juvenile fantasy moment was finally at hand. He waved at the holy passengers, pointed to his bare bottom, and then flashed the hand sign for peace. One nun laughed and returned the peace sign. Another gestured the sign of the cross. The rest merely smiled uneasily as the bus pulled slowly away.

Janis high-fived her brother. "Well, Jiminy, ya did it. And ya know what nuns always say at a time like this…"

"So many possibilities," Jimi said, "But why don't you just tell me what they say?"

Janis cocked her head. "Asses to asses, in God we trust."

"Ya know, I never really feel safe standing next to you," Jimi said. "It's raining, there could be lightning, and you're tempting fate – especially since Catholics don't really go for cremation."

"Well, you started it by mooning the nuns."

"Nuh-uh."

"Yeah-huh!"

"Kids!" Jaybird yelled. "This is a ceremony. Of sorts. Quit showing your asses – behaviorally, I mean."

Janis looked at Jimi and laughed. "Seems like our new Pops is a natural at this parenting thing."

And the skies opened up. A deluge.

Annabel helped Edgar pull up his pants, and then LilBuckaroo led them cautiously down the hill to the Edsel. Janis took Anthony Purrkins, and she, Jimi, and the cat made a run for the van.

Jaybird stayed put. Sonny stayed with him and held his hand. "Twenty-five years, Sonny," Jaybird said over the rain. I can almost hear the music and hear the laughter. And smell the marijuana."

"And feel the love," Sonny said.

Jaybird hugged him. "Our clothes are getting soaked."

"So they are," Sonny said. He stripped and laid his clothes on the grass. Jaybird did the same. And they stood there, feeling the wind and the blessed rain on their skin. And they knew for certain Winnie was with them, too.

Finally, Jaybird picked up the urn and tipped it to empty the last of the ashes. But it remained heavy, and Jaybird felt something shift inside the chamber. He turned the container upside down.

"I'll be damned," he said.

"What? What's wrong? Sonny asked.

Jaybird picked up the bundles of cash from the ground. "A fortune saved is a fortune *urned*," he said, and he handed a bundle to Sonny.

"So, we had our trip bonuses with us the entire time, eh? That sneaky bitch," Sonny said. "God, I miss her."

Jaybird bent down to pick up the lid to the urn. It lay on the ground, upside down and collecting water. And there, taped inside it, in the pool of rain, another surprise.

CHAPTER 37
(In Which All Hell Breaks Loose)

Late Afternoon

JOE JACK SWEET HAD STOPPED AND GASSED UP IN MECHANICSTOWN, NEW York, and was finally on the road again, heading northwest on SR 17 toward Bethel. The closer he got to his destination, the faster he drove, propelled by the prospect of finding and surprising Annabel and Edgar, of being the hero, the knight in shining armor.

The sight of a hippie van coming toward him made him smirk. "Sorry I may have to crash your party, you peaceniks," he said aloud, "but I'm on a mission."

And then he saw the Edsel.

It was another half mile before he could make a U-turn in front of a "No U-Turn" sign and head back southeast. He gunned the engine and gave chase. But so did a local trooper. Speed trap. Joe Jack pulled over.

In his side mirror, he watched the gray-haired officer stride forward. "My, oh my, what *is* the hurry?" the officer declared. His mirrored aviators reflected Joe Jack's mirrored aviators, which reflected back again.

"Afternoon, officer, um..."

"Officer Moon. Sergeant Franklin Delano Moon, at your service. I'll let you gather your license and registration. Wait here while I run the plates." Before Joe Jack could protest or explain that he, too, was a peace officer, Sergeant Moon was out of earshot. So, he waited, his frustration mounting as the Edsel got away. But by God, he was on a mission! A mission unraveling with each passing second, with each passing Lumina and Festiva and Sonata and Achieva.

He had to go. He had to go right now. So, he did.

* * *

More than an hour after leaving the site of the ceremony, Jaybird knocked on a familiar door. As he waited for a response, he studied the rusty key that had been taped inside the lid of the urn. He knocked again and looked the place over: the clapboard cabin was in disrepair outside, its blue-gray siding shedding its painted skin, thickets of brush advancing over the windows, gutters sagging. "Haven't been to the old summer house in quite some time," Jaybird said. "Looks deserted." He knocked once more. The group waited in silence.

"We're probably trespassing now, and I doubt the key will work..." But it did. The door unlocked. "Is it breaking and entering if you have a key?" he asked. The others shrugged. They followed him in.

Inside, it was like a time capsule from the 1960s, its mid-century modern motif out of place in this wooded locale. The front room was musty, but also held the scent of the woods.

"All right," Jimi said, "we drove 53.3 miles – give or take – to get here from Bethel, and you wouldn't say a word about where we were going. So, what gives, Pops? What is this place? Why are we here?"

But Jaybird was stepping away, toward the back of the room, where a cart with a TV and a video player stood, their cords disappearing beyond an open bedroom door. There was a sign taped to the cart: *PLAY ME.* Jaybird turned on the TV. Turned on the VCR. Pushed *Play.*

Winnie appeared on screen, in closeup: "Well, if you're watching this tape, you must be with Jaybird because only he would recognize the key he gave us back at Woodstock in '69, and only he would know where to come. So, thanks for completing the mission and bringing us back together. If only I could be there with you..."

The TV screen went dark. A woman appeared in the bedroom doorway, holding the unplugged TV cord. "Surprise!" she said.

Sonny's knees nearly buckled at the sound of her voice. "Winnie?!?"

"Hey, kiddo," Winnie said, dropping the cord. She took tentative steps at first and then longer strides until she reached her brother and pulled him into a long and hard embrace. "I know it's only been a few weeks since I saw you, but it seems like forever." She looked around the room. "I hardly know who to hug next," she said, and motioned them all toward her. Janis lowered Anthony Purrkins to the floor. She and Jimi and Jaybird came forward. "My children and their dad," she said. "Never thought I'd see the day." She pulled them in and held them there. "Never thought I'd see the day," she repeated, her voice breaking.

Releasing them, Winnie then saw LilBuckaroo, Annabel, and Edgar. "LB, I didn't think you'd be here."

"I can certainly say the same thing," he replied, his voice quavering in that zone where disbelief, anger, and joy fused uneasily.

"I can explain that," she said, "and I will. What I can't explain is how you ended up here when I made a deal with Pepper over the phone to make sure you ended up at Saugerties and didn't interfere here."

"Well, I'm not sure what kind of deal you made with her, but she did tell me to meet her there," LB said. He shook his head. "She said to meet there because that's where Sonny and everyone would be, and if I could get there in time, I could keep them from taking part of my inheritance."

"Yes, that's what I instructed her to say. I knew you'd try to disrupt things."

"Yes, I was planning to."

"But you didn't?" Winnie asked. "Why not?"

"*Fambly*," Edgar said. "That's why."

Annabel jumped in. "LB was with us, and we were headed to the other Woodstock. But in the end, he felt it was more important to find the place that meant so much to you." Then she added, "I'm Annabel Sweet, by the way, and this is my dad, Edgar Albert Poes. We've grown very fond of your son."

"And we madedamnsure he put Mother Pucker's on that baboonsass lipahis."

"Well, I'm grateful," Winnie said. "Pretty goddamned surprised, too, but happily so."

"I think we're all surprised," Sonny said. "Probably even the cat." Anthony Purrkins was rubbing up against his leg. "Goddammit, Win, it's time for some answers. For starters, how the hell are you still *alive*? And whose ashes did we just spread at Woodstock?"

Winnie started coughing. Not a diseased coughing fit, but a gentle cough provoked by sudden laughter. "Well, let's just say that Auntie Gen finally got to use those Woodstock tickets." ,

"But *why*, Winnie?" Sonny took Jaybird's hand in his. "Why do this? Why put us all *through* this?"

Winnie scanned the room. "This is why," she said. "Bringing you all together in a way that helped you not only find one another but also gave you someone to depend on."

"Depends on? Sure are," Edgar said, his face relaxing in tandem with a happy release from his bladder.

Winnie stepped before Sonny and Jaybird and joined her hands with theirs. "And this... *This* is why, Sonny. I knew that if I ever just flat out prodded you to go find your lost love, you'd resist and deny ever being smitten with Jaybird in the first place. But I knew the truth even if you couldn't face it or say it out loud. I knew how you felt – and how you *were* – before we ever left Woodstock. I knew that this man who gave me these children wasn't really meant to be mine or even mine to search for. This was *your* quest, Sonny. But you never would've accepted it without a little nudge, without a little deception. And I couldn't let you live your life that way."

Winnie released their hands. She turned then and addressed everyone. "Aw, who am I kidding? I'm just a manipulative bitch, I suppose, but I knew it was the best way for you all to find your family – and maybe even find a piece of yourselves – with or without me. Kinda like me pushing everyone out of the nest to make sure you knew how to use your wings, I guess." She laughed. "That shit sounds pretty fuckin' profound, doesn't it?"

Sonny reached for her, found her face, caressed it for a moment – and then thumped her on the side of the head. "Seems like being terminally ill sure made you a softy."

"Oh, fer Chrissake, Sonny, what I had was just a bad and lingering case of bronchitis. But I also had that plan to get you unstuck and start living the life you were destined for. Hell, do you know how easy it is to reserve a hospital room whether you *medically* need it or not? All it takes is a generous donation and a few guys willing to play doctor."

"Oh, mom, that's gross," LilBuckaroo said.

"Actors, LilBuck. I'm talkin' about the actors I hired to play medical personnel. Sheesh! Anyway, since Sonny is blind, it was pretty easy to pull off."

"But *I'm* not blind," LilBuckaroo said. "I saw you in the hospital. Pretty convincing in a devious way, I'd say."

"None so blind as those who will not see, Kiddo. And I'd say the apple doesn't fall far from the tree on the devious part. You got that gene from me and your grandpa, Big Buck Muckle."

"Had a big belt buckle maself once." Edgar mused again. "Did we already talkaboutdis?"

Jimi cleared his throat. "Forgive me for being insensitive in this lovely and unexpected family moment, but even though we're grateful for the discovery of our heritage, part of the reason Janis and I took the leap of faith to go on this mission was because of the money."

"Yeah," Janis said. "If you're not dead – and so far, I'm glad you're not – then that means there's no inheritance."

"Yes, you're right about that," Winnie said. "There's no inheritance, at least not yet, but there is a nice little fortune to be split in the here and now. You'll be well taken care of, beyond the money you probably discovered in the urn."

"You mean *this* money?" said a voice at the front door. Pete Peebles stepped inside the room and closed the door behind him. He brandished his gun and a strapped bundle of cash. "Found this and more like it in that hippie van outside. Imagine that." He pocketed the money and hurried to Jaybird. Pointed the gun at his head. "Long time, Finch, Jr."

"Not long enough," Jaybird said.

"You're in no position to be a wise guy right now," Pete said. "Quite the gathering here at the OSH. If my wife hadn't done her homework and connived with my former partner, I might've missed the party myself."

"Well, this is the second party of ours you've crashed," Winnie said. "Maybe next time you should wait for an invitation, asshole."

Pete fired his gun upward. Asbestos-laden debris rained down from a drop ceiling tile. "This is all the invitation I need," he said. "But I take it this little get-together isn't just a family reunion, but also a housewarming, right. Funny thing… I missed that little detail the first time around, but there it was in the last update to my files. An update from about a year ago. Guess what that detail was, Finch?" He nudged Jaybird with the gun.

"No clue, Captain Hook."

"Oh, you really aren't being smart right now, Finch. Insulting a man who's got a gun to your head?"

"So, what was the update?" Jimi interjected, hoping to defuse the situation.

"Coming to daddy's rescue, eh? Johansen, isn't it? Jimi Johansen?"

"Jimi Finch, now."

"Noble," Pete said. "Foolish, but noble, and nobility deserves an answer. That particular file update noted that this long-abandoned property got a new owner about a year ago – one W.M. DePew. Didn't register with me at the time."

"Well, now that you know you're in *my* house," Winnie said, "surely you saw the 'No Trespassing' sign at the end of the lane."

"Absolutely, I saw it. And I also absolutely don't give a fuck." Pete motioned Edgar and Annabel and LilBuckaroo deeper into the room and pulled Jaybird toward the front door. "Now, here's what's gonna happen. First, Finch here is finally gonna tell me where the rest of the goddamn money is, and if he doesn't, or if what he says is unsatisfactory in any way, he gets a bullet. Maybe more than one. I get to choose the body parts to wound, big or small, essential or not so much."

"And second?" Sonny asked.

"What'd you say, blind man?"

"You told us what comes first. So, what comes second?"

"We'll play that one by ear," Pete said. "But I'm hoping we don't get to number two."

"Already got there," Edgar said.

"Can I take him to the bathroom?" Annabel asked nervously. "*Is* there a bathroom?"

"Just the outside shithouse by the big rock," Jaybird said. "Probably grown over by now. No tellin' what's inside there either."

Pete pushed Jaybird against the door frame, gun to his neck. "Outside shithouse by the big rock? Is that what you said?"

Jaybird nodded.

"Outside shithouse… as in the OSH? As in the *rock* by the OSH? So, that's where your old man hid the fuckin' cash, Finch? Is there any left there now? C'mon, cough it up. Answers or bullets!"

Anthony Purrkins was circling toward the door.

Don't do it, Janis communicated to the cat.

Got to, he said. *He might hurt Daddy Jayson.*

Too many people here, Janis said. *The gun might go off.* But Anthony Purrkins was already in the air, bounding from the floor at Jaybird's feet and up against the gun-toting arm of the mean man.

And the gun *did* fire as Jaybird struggled with Pete, their bodies locked together, Pete's hook slashing wildly, the gun pointing skyward and then at the floor and all around the room. Annabel ducked and pulled her dad to the floor. LilBuckaroo tackled Winnie and Sonny. Jimi stepped in front of Janis.

Another shot then before Jaybird managed to bring Pete's elbow hard against the door frame.

From outside, someone kicked open the door. Joe Jack Sweet.

As Pete and Jaybird fell together in a heap on the floor, the gun flew from Pete's grip and skated across the floor. Old Edgar reached for it.

"Nevermore," he said. And two more bodies fell.

One Year Later:
Saturday, August 12, 1995

EPILOGUE
(In Which … Oh, Just Read the Damn Thing!)

Midafternoon

SONNY WALKED OUT OF THE MOON-YOUR-MAMA BAR, HIS WHITE CANE arcing and tapping before him, and holding Jaybird's hand. Winnie escorted them. All were nude, except for their flip flops, Sonny's sunglasses, and the blindfold Jaybird wore.

Winnie led them past the outdoor restroom building to a spot some fifty yards inside the front gate. In the humid 90-degree heat and beneath cloudy skies, she positioned the men facing a four-foot-by-eight-foot welcome sign. "Okay, here it is," Winnie said. "Jaybird, you can take off your blindfold."

He slipped the knotted bandana from his eyes and stared in silence at the sign.

"Don't just stand there," Sonny said. "What's the surprise? Be my eyes. Tell me what you're seeing."

Jaybird swallowed, cleared his throat, and said, "Well, for starters, there's a giant mooning gnome statue, fiberglass, I imagine, and maybe five feet high, pointing to a sign. A new sign. Big, but not too big. Colorful, too. Reminds me of the famous Woodstock '69 poster."

"A sign, huh? What's it say?"

"May I?" Winnie asked.

"Of course."

"It says, *'Welcome to **Noodstock**™, a Peaceful Place for Nudists of All Stripes. Home of the Moon-Your-Mama Bar & Grill™.'* In smaller letters below, it says, *'A Finch, Muckle & DePew Family Nudist Campground'.*"

"It sounds perfect," Sonny said. "Are the letters raised?"

"Yes, they are," Winnie said. She and Jaybird led Sonny to the sign. He traced each embossed letter with his fingers and wiped a tear from beneath his sunglasses. Then he ran his hands over the gnome. "Yep, he's mooning, all right!"

"I guess this makes it official, doesn't it?" Jaybird said.

"Well, it's been *legally* official for months now, but yeah, this kind of declares to the world that we own the joint," Winnie said. "The Grin and Bare It is a lovely memory. *Noodstock* is ready for an exciting future."

Behind them, the main gate opened and a car entered. A small car. Pink-over-white 1959 AMC Metropolitan, with fiberglass cat ears on its hardtop roof and bouncy whiskers on the grille. Magnetic door signs revealed that *Janis Finch, Cat Psychic,* had arrived. She cranked down the passenger window. "Look what the cat dragged in," she said, pointing first to Anthony Purrkins in the cat carrier on the passenger seat, and then to the car behind her – a white Volvo wagon with a *For Sale* sign in the window. Jimi eased forward, his car again full of his belongings. "Got my stuff," he yelled through the open passenger window, "All set to move in. And just in time for the second night of the Testicle Festival. Sorry I missed the official ball drop last night. Hey, great looking sign. And that's an impressive gnome, too."

"Guess this means we're in gnome-man's land, huh Jiminy?" Janis yelled back. She pulled the Catropolitan off the main drive, exited the vehicle, and then carried Anthony Purrkins to Daddy Jaybird (*Daddy Jayson* just didn't seem appropriate now). "Clean bill of health at the vet," Janis said. "Although he's down a little in the weight department."

"Understandable," Jaybird said. "Considering..."

* * *

Meanwhile, in Poes Point, Tennessee, LilBuckaroo was at Annabel's side at the graveyard. "Still hard to believe he's gone," she said. "All that way, all those miles, all those *years* and then... Damned old fool."

"Well, if anyone can eventually cure what killed him, Jerry Patrick at Freeze and Thank You will make it possible," LB said.

Annabel laid a single rose against the granite slab. It was not really a gravestone, for there was no grave beneath it. Rather, it was merely a marker, etched to document a life that had been lived ... and lived out:

> *Joe Jack Sweet*
> *1932 - 1994*
> *Devoted Husband, Father, and Public Servant.*
> *Lived Bravely, Died Heroically.*

Behind them, a horn blared. Joe Jack's killer (accidental killer, of course) pushed his cane against the horn ring on the Edsel's steering wheel. "Not gettinanyounger," Edgar called out.

"I think he wants some leftover birthday cake," Annabel said.

"It'll ruin his appetite for dinner," LB said.

"No worse than those *lickTat'rs* you've got him hooked on."

"Hey, it's the chip that licks ya back," LB said. "New and improved. Which reminds me... Got my first test batch of the new line almost ready."

"*SpecTat'rs?* So soon?"

"What can I say? I work quick."

"Ooh, I can't wait to see the packaging," Annabel said. "You used my tagline, right?"

"Yep ... *These Tat'rs Only Have Eyes for You!* Brilliant, Madam Mayor. Very, um, appealing."

"Flatterer."

"Oh, and I'm gonna have to work this evening at Burger In The First," LB added.

"Again? You've had nothing but trouble since you opened that place. I thought you hired a night manager."

"I did, but you were right about Larry Lou Deeney. He disappeared."

* * *

Meanwhile, in Indianapolis, Indiana, Pepper stepped through the door at Before You Go-Go. Her husband, Todd, was on the phone, sitting tilted back in his chair, his long legs across his desk, and his heels out of his loafers. Actually, Todd wasn't *really* on the phone. He had seen his wife coming and picked up the receiver, pretending to be trapped in an endless conversation. He gave Pepper the just-a-minute gesture of an upraised index finger. This he did every few seconds, and every time he did, Pepper stepped halfway closer to his well-worn soles. In less than a minute, Pepper had reached the front of the desk, knocked the shoes from his feet, and then cleared away all the desktop paraphernalia in a single sweeping motion.

"The windows," Todd said. "Someone might see in."

"Let 'em watch," Pepper replied.

"The door, then. We don't want someone coming inside."

"Well, I do," Pepper said, squaring up her new strawberry blonde wig. "As long as that someone is you."

* * *

Meanwhile, in Atlanta, Georgia, Pepper's former crush, Jennings Prokoff, sat in a post-premiere meeting for his new Saturday late-morning children's show, *Kids Say the Most F*cked Up Things*. Actually, the title was *Kids Say the Most F*cked Up Things, with Jennings Prokoff and Radiance Reynolds*.

Radiance was at the large conference table, too, breastfeeding the illegitimate son of Dickie Smalls, the impressionist who had assumed the anchor role at Prokoff's old nightly newscast. Radiance looked at the child in her arms. Lovingly. Her life no longer seemed quite so *F*cked Up*.

For Prokoff, however, his fall from grace was complete, courtesy of the falling helicopter. He could now speak like a normal human being. It had ruined his life.

* * *

Meanwhile, in Arlington, Virginia, Junior Carducci, Jr.'s life was also in tatters. He had been fired by "The Agency" for "negligent security protocols and improper use of federal equipment."

Nonetheless, he *was* an agent again. Agent-in-training, actually. Ensconced in his cubicle at a DC-area Before You Go-Go, he crammed for his exam, highlighting text in *Now You're an Agent: The Art and Science of Renting Vehicles to People Who Probably Don't Really Need Them.*

Penny Peebles still called Junior from time to time. He suspected she wanted to … hook up.

* * *

Meanwhile, with Pete still missing after the skirmish at Finch's old summer house (from where he escaped, flush with cash), Penny sequestered herself in their Westover Village home. Surrounded by ShitPoo puppies – the spawn of Effyu, the Shih Tzu and Princess Petunia, the Poodle – she was penning the final words of her novel-in-progress, *Baby, Baby, Don't Get Hooked On Me.*

She missed Pete. A little. But she was getting by, thanks to a sudden addiction to chocolate, frequent conversations with Junior Carducci, and her rechargeable Happy Hookster MyteeMax.

* * *

Meanwhile, Max Thibodeaux was working as a freelance videographer, at that moment covering a burglarized New York City Origami shop where events had just unfolded. Between listening to his police scanner and eavesdropping at area bars, Max was frequently first-on-scene and could then sell exclusive footage to local and national affiliates. After the Saugerties helicopter debacle, he had mastered how to turn on the camera, load it, and make sure it was recording. He had also learned to stay away from men with hooks, vending machines, and chocolate shops.

* * *

Meanwhile, back in Arlington, Pixie Peebles Abercrombie screamed, "Maxie!" and sat up in bed, jolted from her exhaustion-induced afternoon nap/coma. Seconds later, her husband, Paydro Abercrombie, stood in the doorway, holding Max, their six-month-old son. Paydro was indeed the child's father, but because Pixie had frequently called out for *Maxie* throughout her pregnancy, the name stuck.

Paydro tossed Pixie a mini-chocolate bar (as a trainer might toss a dolphin a fish) and left the room, still none the wiser.

* * *

And Pete...?

In the grill side of the Moon-Your-Mama, Manager Robin Paloma approached a table.

"Afternoon," he said to the bearded man in the corner booth. "Don't think I've seen you in here before. Good day to be inside, though, isn't it? Hot, muggy, cloudy... Not the best Florida has to offer. So, what can I get for you today?"

"Less chitchat for starters," the man said. "Aside from that, a burger, all the fixins. Fries, crispy. Whatever full-strength soda ya got."

"Got it," Robin said. "Anything else?"

The man raised his prosthetic hook from his lap to the tabletop and pushed the menu aside. "Not unless you can get me a bottle of Absolut."

Sweat suddenly rising, Robin backed away.

* * *

Meanwhile, on the other side of the wall separating the grill from the bar, Janis was helping Jimi make his way to the table where the others had gathered. Jaybird had already delivered drinks. "Seems like you're getting around better these days," he said to his son.

"Yep," Jimi said, "three surgeries later. Amazing how much damage one little bullet can do."

Tell me about it, Anthony Purrkins mused to Janis as he rubbed against her leg. She picked up the cat, pulled over a chair, and sat at the table with Jimi, Sonny, Jaybird, and Winnie.

"Coulda been worse," Sonny said.

Not much!

"At least you made it through," Winnie said. "We all did. Rough goddamn year, but here we are, all together again." She raised her glass. The others did the same.

All together again? Ha!

Janis stood and carried Anthony Purrkins to the bar. She nuzzled him. *All right, little guy, it's just you and me... What's bothering you? Hairball on the horizon?*

Funny, the cat communicated. *No. It's, well, I miss my tail.*

Ah, I see. Well, I, for one, really like your new shorter tail. It gives you even more character. And what other cat can say they got their tail shot off while saving their human? You've got quite a story to tell, Mr. Purrkins.

The cat fidgeted and looked Janis in the eye. *Speaking of telling a story... Will you do me a favor?*

If I can, sure, Janis agreed. *Name it.*

Well, since you have those workable thumbs, would you help me write a new soap opera?

Hmmm, that's interesting, a cat who wants to write a soap opera.

Yes, well, it seems that, lately, my favorite, Like Dust in a Whirlwind, So Are the Days of Our Bold and Restless Lives, *has gone stale. And it's got nothing to top the story we've been living.*

Probably right, Janis said. *So ... what would you call your new soap?*

Maybe... "Naked as a Jaybird at the Moon-Your-Mama Bar & Grill?"

Janis closed her eyes and mulled that over. *Hmmm...*

Anthony Purrkins twitched his bobtail. *Nah, never mind. Who'd believe it anyway?*

THE END. (OR IS IT?)

BEFORE YOU *GO-GO...*

Thank you for taking this adventure.

If you enjoyed *Naked as a Jaybird at the Moon-Your-Mama Bar & Grill*, please tell a friend, share your love for the book on social media, leave a generous rating or review online, or buy a copy as a gift for someone who needs to laugh. Better yet, do all the above! (This is the shameless self-promotion part of the book.)

To learn more about this book, future books, and other stories of full-frontal absurdity, visit NakedNovel.com

Till next time...

Peace | Love | Equality | Unity

ACKNOWLEDGMENTS

I'm forever grateful to some pretty wonderful (and wonderfully pretty) people for their assistance with this book:

The talented members of the venerable Indiana Writers' Workshop. Special thanks to the active members whose critiques, encouragement, and inspiration influenced this book: Teri Barnett, John Clair, June McCarty Clair, Ramona Henderson, Sylvia Hyde, Mark A. Lee, Tony Perona, Cheryl Shore, Jeff Stanger, and Steve Wynalda.

Carolyn Hawkins of the American Association for Nude Recreation, for her answers, influence, friendship, and overall delightfulness.

Animal Communicator Annie Sever-Dimitri, for her amazing spirit and for enlightening me regarding her unique gift and professional practice.

Amy Rollins, for her keen legal-eagle wisdom and support.

Master Cheese Maker Bill Hanson, who had the answers I needed (yes, about cheese) when others came up short.

The countless anonymous experts who contributed essential online information via commentary, descriptions, specifications, videos, etc.

Thank you all!

AUTHOR'S NOTE

In 2019, after decades of writing a bazillion words for others, I decided it was time to put *my* name on a book cover. Oh, sure, I had toyed with writing a novel before. Quite seriously, in fact. And that was the problem: my fiction work had always been *too* serious. I had wanted to write "The Great American Novel (a term to be said aloud, with gravitas – and an echo). But I'm a slow learner, so it took me years to figure out it was more important to write "A Really Good American Novel" (less gravitas, kill the echo). Plus, I wanted to have fun.

Thus, I foist (good word, *foist*) this twisted tale upon you, dear readers.

Notus Interruptus...

As I write this, my husband has just left the room carrying a bottle of liquor and a hot dog costume. It's not what you think. He's a good man. A great man. Outstanding husband, dad, and grandpa. It appears I have ruined him.

But I digress...

I was far too young to attend the original Woodstock event in 1969, but I've been forever there in spirit. Maybe that's why I bear a tattoo symbolizing peace, love, equality, and unity. And perhaps that's why I admire those who heed the free-spirited call of nudism – in particular, the brand of wholesome, family-friendly, social nudism promoted by the American Association for Nude Recreation (AANR). This organization, founded in 1931, was known as the ASA (American Sunbathing Association) during the primary story period of this book. The name changed soon after. Good group, AANR. Check them out.

Lastly, and turning serious (sorry)... I conceived and wrote this book during a difficult period: civil rights under assault, rampant social unrest, global pandemic. Loss of my dad. Writing *Naked as a Jaybird at the Moon-Your-Mama Bar & Grill* made me laugh and helped me cope. I hope it does the same for you.

Be kind to one another.

Bob Chenoweth

ABOUT THE AUTHOR

Bob Chenoweth was born naked, and often returns to the state of undress (near his home in the state of Indiana.) After ghostwriting several books for other people, he finally chose *this* book to put his name on. Strange man. Ask anyone.